False Start

False Start

rebel farris

THE
FALLING SMALL
DUET, PART ONE

FALSE START

Published by Mad Lane Books
Austin, Texas, USA

ISBN: 978-0-9997849-0-7

Cover Illustration by Javier Chavarria of MaeIDesign.com
Cover Design by Regina Wamba of MaeIDesign.com
Interior Graphics from Depositphoto.com
Edited by Traci Finlay
Proofread by Sandra Depukat of OneLoveEditing.com
Formatted by Erik Gevers

For my Seoul Sisters.

Without your love, support, and boundless inspiration—I never would have been able to imagine such strong, unique characters from such varied backgrounds capable of absolute love and steadfast loyalty.

.

Chapter One

I'm a living, breathing contradiction. It has taken years of soul-searching and even some therapy to come to terms with that. I'm okay with it. Yet, I'm not exactly at peace. Baby steps. One foot in front of the other and I'll find my happy place, right?

"Can't believe you're finally doin' this, Mads," Holly says from the passenger seat of my car. She radiates excitement as her head snaps in my direction. Her glossy strawberry-blonde ponytail swings with the movement, catching the fading sunlight.

I turn in to the parking lot of the strip mall, pulling my car into the nearest empty space. I cut the engine and let out a long breath. "Sure am." I give a reassuring smile because my voice came out hoarser than I expected.

I clear my throat and try to gather my courage, leaning back against the headrest. I turn to Holly. Her pale blue eyes are filled with questions.

"Stop looking at me like that. I'm not backing out."

"You don't have to do this today…"

I don't know what I'm thinking. They say you shouldn't make life-altering changes under duress. It's been four years, and honestly, I should be well enough away from "duress." If I'm fully into the acceptance stage of grief, then this is indeed a rational decision.

"Nope. I'm doing this. Positive thoughts are the only shit allowed near me today."

Holly breaks into a huge grin. "I'm so fuckin' excited! You're gonna love it." She clasps my cheeks in her hands. "Your ideas are awesome. You're awesome." She plants a kiss on my forehead, then releases me. "I don't even think I was this excited *my* first time."

"Probably because you were nervous. No, wait—*that* would be the reaction of a sane person." I bark out a laugh. "What did Matt say this guy's name was again?"

She pauses and purses her lips. "Dexter McClellan." She narrows her eyes, raising a perfectly groomed eyebrow. "You're stallin', bitch. Get outta the damn car, and get your ass in there."

"Let's do this," I say and fling the car door open, hopping out of the seat.

Glancing around the parking lot, I don't notice anything out of the ordinary. *Stop being paranoid, Maddie. It's just nerves.* I shake off the nagging inner voice and face the darkly tinted glass storefront. *Inhale, summoning strength and courage to move forward. Exhale, releasing my fears and reservations.*

The little five-storefront strip mall has that cute vintage vibe that looks like it was built in the fifties. It fits in with the trendy SoCo neighborhood of South Austin, Texas. It's just past sunset, but the sky is still light, making it impossible to see anything aside from my reflection in the windows.

"Come on," Holly grumbles. She stands at the front of my car with her hands on her slim hips. Her head's cocked to the side, lips pressed together fighting a grin, toe tapping her exaggerated impatience.

I step forward hesitantly, shaking my head at her and biting my lower lip to hide a grin of my own. We reach the door, and a wave of cool air greets us as an electronic chime announces our presence over the hum of tattoo guns and background music.

I halt in the doorway. Directly behind the counter is a

man. A black tattoo trails down the right side of his neck. It disappears under a black V-neck that stretches over broad shoulders and defined arms, one of which is covered in a half-sleeve collection of smaller black and gray tattoos. The chime causes him to look up, and I lock gazes with the most unique shade of aqua-colored eyes.

I'm quickly snapped out of this trance as the door smacks into my butt, causing me to stumble forward. My flushed cheeks burn as I drop my eyes to the floor to avoid confirmation that anyone noticed. It's already embarrassing enough without proof that there were witnesses.

"What's up?" he asks, his deep voice causing me to glance up.

My teeth clamp down on my lower lip to keep from gaping. My hand goes to the rubber band I keep around my left wrist. I pull it and let it snap against my skin.

My mind goes blank, and I frantically try to remember why in hell I'm standing in front of this man. The longer I stand here, the more horrible this situation feels and the harder it becomes to think.

His full lips tip up in a knowing smile, revealing two perfect, adorable dimples.

Oh, fuck me. My cheeks heat up—again. *What is wrong with me?* I haven't blushed since… well, I can't remember ever blushing. I never thought people actually had bouts of chronic blushing. Not to mention that I don't get flustered over men. I'm almost twenty-seven years old, not a fucking starry-eyed teenager.

"She's here for an appointment with Dexter McClellan. Is he here?" Holly interjects. My eyes shift to her, and she's smirking at me. She's going to give me so much shit for this.

Please ground, swallow me up, now.

"You can call me Dex. You must be… Maddie?"

I look back to find him staring at me with his hand extended. I nod my confirmation.

I need to get my shit together. *Shit. Think.* I can't understand what it is about this guy that's setting my anxiety off. I haven't been like this in over a year. I look down to his hand and will mine to move forward to connect with his. I don't want to be rude.

His grip is firm. Not quite what I was expecting. It's more professional, and I relax a tiny bit.

"What can I do for you today?" he asks, looking at me. His eyes are intense, penetrating, but have a world-wary look I recognize all too well.

I close my eyes briefly and pull my hand away, shifting my weight to the other foot as I silently curse myself for wearing my ratty Led Zeppelin tee and overlarge sweatpants that have to be cinched up at the waist to keep from falling. This shirt has more holes than a cheese grater. When they told me to wear shitty clothes that I wouldn't care if I got ink on them, I may have gone too far. I tug down the end of it to cover the exposed flesh of my stomach. I'm not going to survive this, but I can't leave now without looking like a fool.

"Actually—" My voice breaks on the word, and I swallow hard and try again. "Actually, I want to get two pieces done. One right here, on my wrist. It's pretty simple. I drew it myself." I pull my drawing from my purse and hand it to him. "Also, I wanted to see if you could sketch another larger piece for me to come back later to get."

He breaks into a full-blown smile. *Those fucking dimples.* It's mesmerizing. I have to look away.

"Right. I think I can help with this. Come back to my station."

He towers over me as he places his hand on my lower back and leads me into the shop. My shirt has ridden up again back there, so when his warm hand meets my bare skin, I nearly jump from the shock.

Baby steps, Maddie. You'll be alone for the rest of your life if you freak out every time a man touches you. That's me, though, the walking contradiction. If I could get my body and my brain to actually agree on something, I probably wouldn't be single.

Twelve Years Ago

"Maddie, can you hurry up? Brad's gonna be here any second," my best friend Lisa Lombardi urged.

I stood in front of the full-length mirror and stared at my reflection, tugging at the bottom of the summer dress. It was shorter than I felt comfortable wearing, but we didn't have the money to replace clothes often enough to keep up with my growth rate. We weren't rich by any definition of the word. My mom was just a clerk at the local library. So, I didn't have a lot of clothing options for the first party of my senior year since the week before I was approved to graduate early.

"You look fine," Lisa said, barely looking up, more interested in the *Teen* magazine she was flipping through than our conversation. "You've been with Brad for almost two years now and never put out. I think that means he's into you. You have no one to impress. Stop stressin'."

"I wish I could wear your clothes. You've got a way better selection than me."

"No, you don't," she said in a snarky tone.

Lisa was over six feet tall, but she was slender and lithe. She was just a tad tetchy about her height since she towered over most boys at our school. I wasn't a munchkin at five feet eight inches, but I couldn't wear her clothes.

I sighed, not knowing what to say. I could've told Lisa how I thought she was beautiful and that she had a model's body, but it's not like I hadn't done it a million times before.

"Maddie, Brad's here," my mom called. A few seconds later, the door to my room popped open and my mom's head appeared. "You should get going."

"I'm ready," I said, tugging my dark auburn hair into a messy bun. I kissed her cheek, then grabbed my purse, checking to ensure my phone and keys were in it. "Love you, Mom."

"I love you, too. Be safe." She pulled me into a warm hug, and the familiar scents of vanilla and lavender enveloped me.

5

"Have I told you that you're the best mom ever?"

"Yeah, you're pretty awesome, Miss Cat," Lisa added.

"I don't know what you two are up to, but I already said you could go to the party. Now get," my mom said with a chuckle, waving us out with a shooing motion.

Lisa and I linked arms as we dashed out the door and down the rickety wooden steps of my trailer to the road where Brad waited by his convertible, smoking a cigarette. He started after he quit the tennis team at the end of last season. I rolled my eyes at him, opened the door to the car, and got in. I wasn't thrilled with his new habit.

Lisa jumped into the back seat. Brad got in the car and leaned over to kiss me, but I was repelled by the ashtray scent of his breath and turned away from him. He made a frustrated sound and mumbled, "Whatever," as he started the car and pulled away.

The ride to the party was quick. No one talked due to the noise of the wind rushing through the convertible and the blaring country music on Brad's radio. When we pulled up to the party at Nic Gallo's house, Brad killed the engine. I could hear the loud music thumping from somewhere inside.

Nic Gallo was one of my best friends. He had lived in the same trailer park as Evan—my other bestie—and me, while his parents saved money to build this dream house—a beautiful Southern farmhouse off the lake with a full wrap-around porch.

I'd be lying if I said I wasn't envious. My mother and I lived in a mobile home out of necessity. Nic was just a tourist that got to escape.

Brad and Lisa went off in opposite directions as soon as we passed the front door, but that was standard operating procedure for us. We'd meet back up later. I went off in search of Evan and Nic. It took a while to make my way through the house since it seemed like everyone at the party wanted to talk to me about something. Most of it questions about my summer, or stories about theirs. I had no idea why people felt the need to share what happened in their lives.

Maybe it was just because I listened to them? My mom had raised me to be a good listener.

I located Evan in the kitchen, talking to the new kid. Once he looked up and made eye contact with me, I launched myself into his arms. He spun me around once and set me down next to him, kissing my cheek.

Evan had been in my life since the day I was born. Our fathers had been friends since grade school. Our friendship cemented in third grade—his fifth grade year—when I bloodied his nose for making fun of a girl with glasses. Evan was a good-looking guy, with his unique hazel eyes, but there was just something about knowing what a person looked like with a saggy diaper that killed any chance of sexual attraction.

"Where've you been?" I asked, still clinging to his shoulders to find my balance. "I've missed you."

"We started football practice this week. You know that," Evan said with a smirk.

"Yeah, well, still missed you."

"Happy Birthday," he said, his features softening.

"Thanks. You know it was yesterday, right?" I asked, scrunching up my face.

"I did," he nodded and tilted his head toward the refrigerator. "Nic and I got you a cake. It's in the fridge."

"You guys didn't have to do that." I hated when people made a fuss over me. I didn't have a lot of birthday parties growing up. We never had the money, and if I were honest, I knew a lot of people, but only three people truly knew me.

"The hell we didn't," he said with a huge shit-eating grin. "We want cake."

I shook my head at him. "We should work on the Charger this weekend for a little quality time. You think Gary would be down for that?"

"Of course he would. When I left, Dad was grumbling about why his favorite girl hadn't been by all week." He tucked me into his side and turned his attention back to the new kid, who was so quiet I had forgotten he was standing there. "Jared, you haven't met my little sister yet, have you?"

I lightly punched Evan in the stomach.

"This's Maddie. Maddie, say hello to Jared Wilson."

I looked up into icy-blue eyes. My breath caught. The new kid was tall with a lean, muscular frame, and built in all the right places. Golden tanned skin, a mess of black, wavy hair, and those eyes. I realized then that I was just staring at him.

"Nice to meet you, Gerald."

Evan doubled over with laughter, and the new kid's eyes widened before he smiled.

"It's Jared," he corrected.

"That's awesome, Mads," Evan said, still laughing. "Way to make the new starting quarterback feel welcome."

"I think I need a drink," I mumbled, trying to look anywhere but at Jared.

"Allow me," Jared said as he guided me toward the keg in the backyard with a gentle hand between my shoulders.

As we moved through the house to the back door, his hand fell away. "I hope this isn't too forward. I'm pretty used to being the new kid. I tend to push boundaries often."

"Why's that?" I asked, looking to him, my brows furrowed.

His cheeks were slightly pink; I wondered if that was the remnants of blushing. The thought made me smile.

"Military brat." He shrugged. "My dad just retired, moved us out here."

"Really? What did he do?"

"He was a three-star general, high-level stuff. I don't know much about it other than the formalities."

"Sounds cool. I bet you've been all over."

He nodded. We got to the keg, and he handed me his cup. He pulled a new one from the package on the ground and filled it up.

"Yeah, I haven't lived in the States very long. He was mostly assigned to command overseas posts."

When he was done pouring my beer, he traded me for his cup.

"Want to go sit over there?" he asked, pointing to two

Adirondack chairs away from the house, near the edge of the lake.

"I interrupted your conversation with Evan. Weren't you two talkin'?"

"Nothing important, just football stuff. Looking to mix it up. I'm hoping you're not a rabid football fan."

"Hardly," I said, scrunching my face up. "I don't mind watching Evan and Nic play, but it's not life consuming for me the way some people are about it around here."

Jared was easy to talk to and interesting. I'd never met anyone like him in my small town of Canyon Lake, Texas, for sure. *There are benefits to being a good listener.* We made our way over to the chairs to continue the conversation.

"What grade are you in?" he asked.

"I'm a senior."

He raised an eyebrow at me.

"I'm serious. I'm graduating two years ahead of schedule. I busted my ass in summer school and took tests over the last three years to skip classes."

"How old are you?" he asked, his brows drawing together.

"I'm fifteen."

His eyes widened. "Your parents are okay with you going off to college?"

"I wouldn't say Mom's happy about it. But I got a full scholarship to St. Edwards. It's a Catholic university over in Austin, so it's close enough I could drive there every day if I had to. Though, that would be a shitty commute. How old're you?"

"Seventeen."

I nodded and stayed silent for a moment. I wondered if our age difference bothered him.

"Can I tell you a secret?" he asked.

"Sure." I eyed him warily. I wasn't certain that we were at the secret-sharing stage yet.

He held his hand next to his mouth and said in an exaggerated whisper, "I'm drinking apple juice."

I laughed. "No way." I grabbed his cup and sniffed it. Sure

enough, it was apple juice. I studied him as I handed his cup back to him. "You normally raid the fridge for apple juice at parties?" I eyed him over my cup as I sipped my beer.

"I'm no thief." He smiled deviously as he pulled a flask from his back pocket.

I burst out laughing. I had tears in my eyes. "Oh, Lord! I've never met anyone who snuck nonalcoholic beverages into a party. In a flask, no less."

He shrugged, a gentle smile still in place. "I'm not a big drinker, and I most definitely never drink and drive. I don't know anyone here that well. I wanted to swing by and meet more than just guys from the team."

"From what I've seen so far, you absolutely suck at mingling." I scrunched up my nose.

"My goal wasn't to meet everyone from school, just the interesting ones, and I think I've excelled at that." He took my hand, brushing his thumb over my knuckles.

My heart skipped a beat. Jared pulled me toward him, and my mind went blank, my eyes drifting shut. His fruity breath rolled over my lips, the fingers of his free hand skimming over my cheek before diving into my hair and grasping the back of my neck. Tingles traveled through my body at his touch, and I may have whimpered. Then reality came crashing back.

My eyes popped open. "Stop—I have a boyfriend."

He dropped back in his seat, muttering something that sounded a lot like, "Lucky bastard."

"I'm sorry. I think I should find him. I didn't realize we'd been out here so long." I skittered out of my chair and backed toward the door of the house. I tried to give him a smile, but it was weak. If I was honest with myself, I didn't want to leave him and wanted him to kiss me more than anything I could remember. "I guess I'll see you around. It was nice meetin' you, Gerald." I winked, turned on my heel, and walked back into the house.

# Chapter Two

Now

I'm sitting in a reclining chair at Dex's station, trying to ignore the heat and sensations of his body pressed against my arm and his elbow pressed against my ribs as he works on the new tattoo on my left wrist. The vibrations of the needles penetrating my skin aren't distracting enough. At least we're both facing the same direction in this position, and I don't have to avoid his eyes. I just stare at the industrial ceiling tiles above, watching the texture blur and distort as my eyes unfocus. The hum of Dex's tattoo gun joins the hum of others nearby, filling the silence.

The shop is, for the most part, an open space with six stations separated by half-wall partitions, and a door centered on the back wall to what looks to be a hallway. Each of the artists has their unique style decorating their little sections, but Dex's is surprisingly bare. There are two other artists currently with clients, but I can only see the one across from me, now that I'm sitting.

Through the smudges of black ink, I can see the bar of music, done in my own handwriting. The lines aren't straight or perfect, but it's me and what's very close to my heart—music.

"What song is this?" Dex asks.

Dex has been silent since we decided on the size and placement. I'm not normally one for small talk. *Shit!* I already forgot what he just asked me. I stare at the side of his head. Shaggy waves of dark brown hair curl up behind his ear. If I had to guess, I'd say he's about my age. A year or two older at the most.

"You okay? Still with me?" He stops and turns his head toward me, his brows drawn together. His face is no more than six inches from mine. I can feel his breath on my cheek. I meet his eyes with a sharp inhale. His gaze drops to my lips and back up.

"I'm good. I've a high pain tolerance."

Overshare much? That stupid flush creeps over my cheeks, and I bite down on my lower lip. Now, Dex is smiling.

"Is it from your favorite song?" he asks.

"Oh, well… umm, sort of… It's, uh… 'The End of What I Knew' by Stateside." I know why I don't want to talk about it, but do I have to sound stupid in the process?

He nods but remains silent.

"It has a special meaning for me," I add.

"I don't really know their stuff. But I remember them from the news a while back when that guy was murdered," Dex says.

That guy. It's hard to believe that people can be that removed from it. Hell, the only reason the media let it go was because that kidnapped girl escaped after being held for ten years. She gave them something else to feast on.

"Wasn't the guitar chick from that band a local?" the tattoo artist in the next station chimes in, leaning over the half wall that separates us. "What was her name?"

"No clue," Dex shrugs.

"Ugh, it's on the tip of my tongue," he says, frowning. "Whatever, I'll remember it."

"Hey," Dex says. "Since you're here. Is that your sketch?" Dex points to a piece of paper resting on the half wall.

The tattoo artist picks it up and studies it. I can see through the paper with the overhead light shining through—

it's a sketch of a hummingbird.

His face scrunches in confusion. "Nope, not mine."

"It was sitting on my chair when I got in earlier," Dex explains.

The artist shrugs, looking over his shoulder. "I can ask the other guys."

"Cool," Dex says with a nod.

I hold my breath for a few more beats, but he doesn't go back to the previous topic or look at me again. The tattoo artist leaves to talk to the other artists. I exhale slowly. I feel like I'm melting into a puddle as all the tension drains from my system.

"What kind of music do you listen to?" I ask. I'm not all that interested, but I feel like I have to divert attention from going back *there*.

"Lots of stuff." From the side of his face, I can see his nose scrunch up like he is deep in thought. It's cute. He stops working and turns to face me. "There's not much new stuff that I'm into these days, but right now I've been listening to a CD my brother gave me from an old band of his. I guess my mood has been more in the punk realm lately."

My breath catches, the tension returning with a vengeance. The punk music scene in Austin is small—it was even smaller back then. Chances are good, he knows. He has to know who I am, or this is the world's most freaky coincidence.

My mind whirls. "Have you ever see any live shows?"

"I wish. I'm usually too busy to go to any concerts. You listen to punk music, too?"

I nod.

Holly rushes into the room like she's running from the law and plants a smoothie in my free hand. She pauses, studying Dex with a keen interest before leaning over me to inspect the progress.

"Looks good," she says with a smile before retreating to the long counter against the back wall and hopping up. The door chime sounds again, and I can hear voices by the front desk.

I smile back. Holly jerks her chin toward Dex and waggles her eyebrows suggestively. I shake my head. She rolls her eyes at me.

Looking to deter Holly, I say, "Matt said you were good at photorealism—"

"Shit. I forgot. I was gonna give you this," he says as he sets down his tattoo gun and rolls toward the counter. Removing his gloves, he retrieves a binder and places it in my lap. "Matt?" he asks, tipping his chin down.

"Matt Durham. He's a bouncer at the club where I work," Holly interjects.

Dex stops and looks at her, eyebrows raised. He has a scar that cuts through his left eyebrow. It transforms his pretty-boy face into something more masculine and rough around the edges. Obviously, he knows the place. I'm used to this reaction by now. It comes with having a best friend who's a stripper. She garners certain looks, and I've developed a protective instinct the size of a mama polar bear over the years.

"Hey, Pretty Boy, back to the tattoo," I say with mild annoyance. It's just a job; she's not a degenerate.

His eyes snap to me for a moment, a crooked smile gracing his face before he grabs new gloves and rolls over to my arm.

Placing my smoothie between my knees and opening the binder, I suck in a gasp at the sight of the first drawing. Dex looks at me curiously. I run my fingers over the sweeping lines and turn the page.

"These… they're amazing," I whisper, staring at the book.

"That's my portfolio. It may help you in deciding exactly what you want to do next time."

I think I murmur, "Okay," as I study his sketches. The amount of detail is awe-inspiring. Some are dark and moody, some are cheerful and happy, but all are so realistic they almost look like photos. One of those rare photos, like Dorothea Lange's *Migrant Mother*, where the emotion slaps you in the face and stays with you long after you stop looking.

A couple of the pages have pictures of finished work on actual body parts. They look like someone took a picture and somehow injected it into skin. It's amazing.

"Wow, you're good. The detail..." I point to a picture of a tattoo covering someone's rib cage that's roughly the size I'm looking to get done. "How long did it take you to do that one?"

He pauses and leans over the binder to get a better look at the picture. His arm presses further into my ribs, and the back of his shoulder brushes the bottom of my breast. The tips tingle and tighten in response. An involuntary gasp escapes my lips. His body stiffens slightly, but he doesn't move or look at me. Mortified doesn't even begin to describe how I feel. I feel like I'm sexually assaulting him with my whacked-out hormones.

He shifts on his stool and moves to work on my wrist, brushing past me again, and I suck in my lips and bite down to keep from reacting.

"If I remember correctly, that one took about eight hours."

My gaze fixes on Holly. Her lips smash together, and her shoulders are heaving in silent laughter. I send her my best die-bitch death glare, which only makes her worse, and she tries to cover her audible laughter with a cough. I close my eyes to try and shut out this whole—everything.

Collecting myself, I continue with my questions.

"Really? That seems fast. Do you do it all at once? I can't imagine sitting here being stabbed with tiny needles like this for that long."

"Nah, I believe we broke that one up into three sessions, but it just depends on what you feel comfortable with." He shrugs. "If we break it up, you'll have to wait three weeks between each session. It's up to you."

"I'll have to look at my schedule," I choke out. I can't imagine how I'd survive sitting through this three more times over a month and a half. And that's got nothing to do with the tattoo, and everything to do with him.

He gives me a searching look and goes back to his work. I look at Holly, and she knows what I'm thinking. I know she knows because we've been friends long enough that we share that quasi-telepathy thing. She starts making immature kissy faces, feeling up an imaginary lover like kids in elementary do to make fun of their friends. It's stupid, but I happen to love her brand of stupidity. I fight to suppress my laughter with an overly serious scowl until we can't contain ourselves anymore. Both of us burst into a fit of laughter. We really are a pair of overgrown children.

He turns to look at me, and I cock an eyebrow at him. I press my lips together to keep from laughing in his face, but my shoulders are still shaking with silent laughter. His demeanor changes.

"Believe me, I'll take my time," he says in a voice low enough that only I can hear. "You get the best I have to offer."

His tone releases a flood in my nether regions. *Is that a suggestive tone?* I'm momentarily confused, my brain trying to catch up. *Is he still talking about the tattoo?*

"And since you're charged by the hour, I'll make sure to drag it out," he says with a wink, a small smile playing on his lips.

"I wasn't—" I start, then stop. Fuck, my brain is officially fried. What the fuck do I say to that? What is wrong with me?

A skinny dude with dark hair pulled into a low ponytail, and more piercings in his head than I can count, unintentionally comes to my rescue when he walks up to Dex's station. He leans over to see my tattoo in progress. His eyes wander over my body before he notices me watching, and he looks away.

"Hey, man, you got a call in the back office."

Dex leans back and sets his gun down, wipes a wet paper towel over my arm, and pulls off his gloves with a snap. "Well, I suppose it's good that I'm done here." He rolls to the trash can to deposit his gloves and turns toward me. "You have time to hang out so I can take this call before we finish up? I still need to wrap it and give you aftercare instructions."

"Yeah, sure," I reply as I study my first tattoo. My skin is red, and the lines of ink are raised. The surrounding area is still smeared with some black ink, but I can already tell that I love it. It's so fucking cool. The first of many, I hope. I can't stop the smile that spreads on my face.

He leaves the room, and Mr. Ponytail walks to the front counter. The second Dex is out of sight, I feel a tension ebb from my body that I hadn't realized was there. Like the room cleared and there is more air. I'm not sure why I'm reacting to him this way. Sure, he's attractive, but I know a lot of attractive guys. None of them turned me into a bumbling idiot. Holly hops down from the counter as I stand to stretch my legs. Her hand snakes out and yanks my arm closer for inspection.

"I love it," she says, smiling at me.

"Me, too," I agree. "Why were you running when you came back from the smoothie shop?"

"You're jokin', right? I couldn't miss the show. Seriously, I haven't seen you give more than a passin' glance at a guy since *he who shall not be named*. And you're not disappointin'. This's quite the spectacle."

"Whatever, it's not like that at all."

"Ummm hmmm," she murmurs. We stand there for a minute before Holly places her head on my shoulder. "I'm bored."

Strains of "House of the Rising Sun" play over the shop's low-volume speaker system.

I turn to Mr. Ponytail. "Hey, can you turn the music up?"

He looks at me curiously and shrugs, then turns up the radio. I look around to survey my audience. There are four artists, two customers, Mr. Ponytail, and two young girls flipping through binders of flash art in the waiting area. I hook Holly's waist with my arm and pull her to me. Our hands clasp together, careful with my new tattoo.

"Dance with me," I command in a low, manly voice.

She's used to this. Random dancing is a specialty of mine.

I lead her through a horrible version of a waltz I learned long ago in a dance lesson. She keeps up, occasionally tripping or stumbling against me. Toes are stepped on twice, but her head is thrown back and laughing. I try to keep a serious face and chastise her when she messes up in a mock version of the voice that old Mrs. Turner used during those long-ago lessons. When she's laughing so hard she can't keep up, I dip her and grind my lips hard into her cheek. I stand her up and realize that everyone has stopped what they're doing and are watching us.

I play along and pull the sides of my sweatpants out and drop into a curtsy. There are some laughs and claps, and one of the guys starts catcalling.

I blow kisses and drop a few more curtsies.

"Thank you, thank you. I'll try *not* to be here all night." I turn to head to Dex's station and halt in my tracks.

Dex is leaning against the door frame, arms crossed over his chest, looking sexy as hell. He has a sly half smile, revealing one adorable dimple, and he's staring directly at me. My face heats at the realization that he's been watching my little performance. I'm not sure why it bothers me. One would think I hadn't spent time performing in front of tens of thousands of people in a stadium. Even if it was only a brief stint in the spotlight. I drop my gaze to the floor and hurry back to the chair. He follows me, grabbing gloves, ointment, and plastic wrap and sets to bandaging my wrist without a word.

"Tell me about this other work you want done," he says when he's finished, rolling to the counter to put away his tools.

He nods attentively as I describe the other tattoo and explain where I want it and what size. He listens, makes some suggestions, and overall, I feel like he understands what I want. We make arrangements to meet up later in the week to go over his initial sketches. I search the calendar on my phone for an available time this week. *I'm too busy for my own good.* We finally settle on a time we're both available.

"That's it? I guess I'll see you Thursday afternoon?" I ask.

He nods in confirmation and smiles. "I'm looking forward to it."

"Laine," the artist from the next station shouts.

I freeze. A cold chill seeping into my bones. I turn to face him; we all do.

"That was her name," he adds with a wide grin. "The chick from the band on your tattoo."

I nod in reply.

"Yeah, something like that," Dex replies. He turns back to face me.

I school my features to hide my panic.

"What're you doing Friday night?" Holly asks.

I stomp on her foot.

"Ouch, bitch!"

"Don't mind her. She has a mild form of Tourette's." I plaster on a smile. "See you later," I say as I grab Holly's arm and shove her toward the door. She cackles wildly.

When we make it to the car, Holly lets loose.

"I don't get you one bit, woman. You should've invited him to your birthday party. What would it hurt? It was obvious that that guy had your panties drenched, and I haven't seen you look at anyone like that in a reeeeeeeeeally long time." She shakes her head at me.

"Because, Holly, I'm not even remotely interested in starting any kind of relationship, even something casual. You know that perfectly well. He just makes me... uncomfortable." I glance back to the tattoo shop but only see the reflection of my car in the windows.

"Does he make you uncomfortable? Or does he get you all hot and bothered, dreamin' about when you're like *Oh God, Dex. That's it right there. Faster. Harder. Ooooooh*," she says in a mimicking voice while humping the air in front of her and rubbing her hands over her breasts.

"Oh my God, I'm cutting you off from caffeine for the rest of the day," I say, covering half my face with my hand.

A guy walking by catches sight of her and almost face-plants into the sidewalk, tripping over the curb.

I bite down on my lip to hold back my laughter because I want to be mad at her, but I just can't. I burst out laughing as the almost-face-planter adjusts himself before going into the tattoo shop. I put the car in reverse to leave when Holly throws her hand toward my chest.

"Fuck! I forgot my phone. Be right back." She's out of the car and in the shop before I can fully process what she just said. She comes out looking at her phone and typing something into it. She climbs in. "Let's hit it, bitch, or we're gonna be late for practice." I scan the parking lot again, and still there's nothing. See, it was just nerves.

Then

I was looking at the ground, mentally cursing myself when I ran smack into Nic in the doorway. His arm swept around my waist, crushing me to him.

"There you are. I've been looking all over for you," Nic whispered to me, his full lips brushing against my ear.

Whoa.

The thing about Nic was that he was a harmless flirt. Well, with me anyway. Gorgeous as he was, with his stylishly messy hair and moss-green eyes, he was a bit of a man-whore. I was pretty sure he'd slept with nearly every girl at our school and some from neighboring towns. Leaving a trail of angry deflowered girls in his wake, he was the likely cause of Lisa being my only girlfriend. He faithfully reminded me that I was the only one of the *Three Amigos* with boobs through shameless flirting, though he was never serious about it.

"I think maybe you've had a few too many, Lucky." I grasped his dark brown mop of hair and pulled so I could see his face.

"Neddie," he said, giving me his signature, panty-melting half smirk. "I was looking for you. You want to go out tomorrow night?"

"Yeah? Where are we going?"

"I don't know, dinner… a movie. I didn't think that far into it." He shrugged. "Whatever you consider the perfect date."

I froze. "Date? What on earth are you talking about? For one, you don't date. Two, I'm—"

He grinned at me shamelessly. "You're right. I just figured since you and that dicknugget broke up, you might need a good distraction."

I stepped out of his embrace. "Broke up? What are you talking about?"

"Yeah, Lisa told me when I saw them going in—" He stopped abruptly, biting his lower lip. He stiffened as his green eyes widened and darted around.

"Going in where?" Anger started boiling in my veins. I knew I wasn't going to like the answer. "Going in where, Nic?" I said again through clenched teeth.

"Shit," he said, running his fingers through his hair.

I pushed past him and stormed through the house searching for either Lisa or Brad. After clearing the first floor, I stomped halfway up the stairs until Evan wrapped an arm around my waist, hauling me back against him. I looked over his shoulder and saw Nic behind him.

"Don't, Maddie," Evan warned.

"No, Evan. I want to see. I don't want to leave them room for excuses or lies. Either of them."

My face was heated, and my hands curled into fists. I pushed Evan's arm from me and stormed down the hall. It had to be one of the bedrooms.

I opened the door, and there was my best friend with her ass in the air, her face smashed into a pillow moaning, while my boyfriend pounded away at her from behind.

Wow!

I vaguely registered the "Oh, shit" coming from Nic.

As I stared at the train wreck that was my life, I felt oddly numb. I thought maybe I loved Brad, but I didn't feel jealousy. No, what made my stomach twist into knots and the ache build in my chest was Lisa. Uncontrollable, hysterical laughter bubbled up in my throat.

Brad's head whipped to the side, and his eyes widened in shock. He jumped back like he was touching a hot frying pan and covered himself while frantically searching for his jeans.

"Baby, it's not—" I hated that he called me baby. It was gross and so unoriginal.

"It's not what?" I said bitterly. "What it looks like?"

Lisa flipped over and pulled the blanket over herself.

"How could yo—?" I said to Lisa, my voice catching on a sob in my throat.

"Oh please, you're only with him because you're selfish. You just want to keep him away from anyone who actually wants him. Don't get all high-and-mighty about it."

"I'm not... Lisa. It doesn't hurt that *he* did this." Tears welled in my eyes.

Evan hauled me back against him and turned us toward the stairs. I could hear Nic yelling something, and Evan was talking to me, but none of it was registering. I just couldn't do it anymore. I couldn't breathe. It felt like someone had put my heart in a vice. Ten years of friendship, thrown away for a cheap fuck at a party. *Oh, my God.* I pulled away from Evan and bolted down the stairs. I had to get out. I couldn't face anyone after this. I wasn't going to let them see me cry because they'd assume it was over Brad *fucking* Boyd.

I lost my footing on the last few steps, my vision going blurry from the tears building in my eyes. I would've fallen flat on my face if not for a strong arm that caught me. I couldn't see who it was and didn't stick around to find out. I turned and bolted out the front door, running down the street, around the corner to the end of the parked cars. I landed in the grass on my knees as the dam broke and tears poured down my face.

After I'd calmed down enough to speak clearly, I called my mom.

"Of course I'll come get you. Just let me put my shoes on. I'll be right there."

"Thanks, Mom. Love you." I disconnected the call and sat down in the grass to wait for her, alone.

Chapter Three

Now

I'm sitting at a stoplight. It feels like all traffic lights have declared war on me and are determined to stop me every chance they get. I tap my fingers on the steering wheel and look at the time. My appointment with Dex to go over the sketches was five minutes ago. *Dammit! I hate being late.* I slam the heel of my hand into the wheel and shout at the light to hurry the fuck up already.

I pull into the parking lot of the coffee shop ten minutes late. By the grace of God, there's a parking spot up front, next to a matte-black Harley with chrome trim. I almost knock the bike over backing out of my car because my stiletto heel got caught in a crack in the pavement.

I'm a mess. A literal freaking mess. Maybe I need to get laid. Four years is a long time... No, not a good line of thinking when heading in to face Dex.

Just imagining his face if I pulled out that stupid contract my personal assistant, Chloe, forced into my hand this morning makes me laugh. Holly had given Chloe and Bridget, the head of legal at my company, the lowdown on the tattoo artist, and now I have a legal contract to start a relationship. He'd probably run away at breakneck speed, screaming. The mental image makes me laugh. What kind of woman makes you sign a nondisclosure agreement to sleep with her? I'd assume one that's nothing but trouble, that's what.

I smooth down my pencil skirt before opening the door. It's a business-wear day, thanks to several high-level meetings, and my hair is up in a neatly coiffed french twist. I've got my power suit on, and I'm hoping I didn't just scratch the heel of my Louboutin. Yes, in business I wear my money. I worked hard to create a successful record label and want to project the hard-earned respect when I enter a room.

Fortunately, it's not often that I have to dress like this. I try to lump meetings on the same day. Not that this kind of clothing is uncomfortable, but I've always been a jeans and T-shirt girl. The only real treat to business days is the lingerie. Lace, garter belts, and stockings have a magical effect on a girl's confidence. Well, at least mine. I can pretend to be a sex kitten, even if I'm more the schoolmarm type these days.

Before I can even reach for the door, it swings open and a young guy wearing a T-shirt from my nearby alma mater holds it for me. He whistles low as I pass. I shake my head, purposefully striding past him to the counter to order my tea. I hate coffee—never understood how people could consume that crap, but I do envy their ability to borrow copious amounts of energy from a drink.

I order a black tea with honey from the girl behind the counter and search my purse for my wallet, then remember it fell out of my purse when I slammed on my brakes after being cut off on the way over here. Mess confirmed again. I pinch the bridge of my nose.

"I'm sorry, I just have to run out to my car and get my wallet real quick. Can you go ahead and make it, though? I'm supposed to meet someone here, and I'm already late."

The poor girl looks apologetic. "I'm sorry, ma'am—"

"It's okay. I got it," says a deep voice over my shoulder. "Coffee, black."

The hairs on my arms stand on end. I know that voice, but I'm afraid to turn around; he sounds like he's standing close behind me. He tosses cash on the counter and waves a hand at the girl when she asks if he wants his change.

"Meeting someone?" he asks. "Wouldn't by chance happen to be a boyfriend? Or someone you're considering getting to know a little better?"

Oh God, Dex hasn't recognized me, and he's hitting on me?

Awesome.

"Umm... no. And I'm not interested in having a boyfriend or getting to know anyone better."

"That's too bad. You should give the poor guy a chance."

I spin around to face him, forgetting just how close he is. "Why do you—" I lose my balance and start to tip over, and he grabs my hips, pulling my body against his to steady me. When I look into his eyes, he has a half smirk, half pout on his face, which is adorable and dangerous. He knew it was me and was flirting with me. I already forgot what I was asking. *How does he scramble my brain like that?* My body flares with heat as I become aware of his body pressed against mine.

This is not the right time. This is not the right person. I need to get my shit together.

I step away from him so he can no longer touch me.

Dex grabs our drinks from the counter. "After you," he drawls and motions to the tables.

After removing my blazer and hanging it from the back of a chair, I drop into the seat as he sits across from me. He looks me over, focusing on the gold cuff bracelet that covers my first tattoo.

"Are you sure you want to do this? Ink isn't for everybody, and this's a big piece."

"Don't assume that you know the first thing about me," I snap. I dig the rubber band out from underneath the bracelet and snap it. I can actually feel it as it hits the days-old tattoo. I take a deep breath, "I'm sorry. I'm taking my frustration over something else out on you. Rough day and all that."

His eyes widen briefly, and some unreadable emotion passes through them.

"I'd like to. Get to know you," Dex says, and a half smile

grows on his face, revealing one of his adorable dimples.

I laugh at myself. A*dorable*—the guy is about six and a half feet, built like some type of fighter, and covered in most visible places with tats. I'm sure that screams *adorable* to most sane people.

When I finally snap to, I realize I'm leaning toward him over the table. I'm not sure how that happened. He's like a magnet, and I'm a pile of metal filings. Parts of me tremble before letting go and succumbing to the attraction. If I get too close for too long, I'll be all over him. I shake my head as I lean back.

"That's not a good idea."

"I'm beginning to like bad ideas," he says, leaning across the table to recapture the distance. His smile grows to full-blown, and I have to close my eyes.

"Do you have the sketch?" I ask. I need a distraction, now.

I peek open one eye to find him pulling a sketch pad out of a leather bag on the floor next to his chair. With his eyes off me, I feel like I can breathe easier. It doesn't last long. He opens his sketch pad and places it in front of me. He rises and pulls his chair next to mine and sits so close our arms press together.

Doesn't he realize what this does to me and that it has to stop?

"I did two. One in black and gray, and another in full color. I forgot to ask which you'd prefer… We can change the colors if you don't like them."

He almost sounds nervous. I turn to him, and he's gnawing on his full lower lip. Color me fucking surprised. He *is* nervous. One corner of my mouth twitches up into a tiny smile at the thought.

I flip back and forth between the two images. They steal my breath. The tattoo is three calla lilies wrapped up in an intricate knotwork of thorny vines. Each thorn has blood dripping from it, and the blood drops transform into music notes that spin around the flowers and vines in random patterns. The way he drew it, you can almost see the movement of the notes. One would think that the color would be more beautiful simply because it was colorful, but the depth and beauty of the detailed shading in the black and gray is equally amazing. He took my simple ideas and made them a work of art. It's beautiful, though beautiful isn't an adequate word here. It's perfect. I feel a lump forming in my throat and squeeze my eyes shut before I make a fool of myself.

Dex clears his throat. "If you don't like it, I can come up with something else."

My lids fly open, and I try to see through watery eyes. Here I am, moved to tears, and he's taking my silence as a rejection. Something about that gets to me. I blink several times to clear my vision.

"No—no, I love it," I try to say, but my voice is gravelly with emotion. His shoulders visibly relax. I clear my throat. "I know what it feels like to put your heart on display to the public through your work, so thank you. It's perfect." I'm not sure why I just said that.

Dex stares at me without blinking, his eyes roaming over my face. Silent. I should've just kept my big mouth shut.

I turn my attention back to the drawings and ask, "Can we do the black-and-gray one, because I like all these areas of shading and the lines here, but make the center calla lily and maybe the blood drops red like you have in the color?"

"That's what I pictured in my head when I drew this up. I just went with showing you the two opposing views to give you options. I think it'll look great."

"Awesome." I close the sketchbook and move to stand. "Well, I won't waste any more of your time. I'm sure you have plenty of clients that need their consultations or work done, too."

He places his hand gently on my arm, halting my movement. "It's pretty rare that someone puts this much of themselves into a tattoo. I don't usually meet with anyone outside the shop. You're an exception to the rule. Can I ask you a question?"

"Yeah, shoot," I reply without hesitation.

"Why the calla lily? You know in most cultures it's called the *death flower*, right?"

"You can't ask that one. I'll have my assistant call and schedule the appointment. I'll see you then." This time when I stand, he doesn't move to stop me. Instead, he stands, too.

"Wait, can I see you again?" he asks.

I start to respond that I'll see him when we do the tattoo, but he raises a hand.

"Not just when you come in for your appointment."

He's biting his lower lip again, but he's looking straight at me. He's nervous but still not intimidated. I like that. I just can't imagine asking him to sign the contracts, and Bridget's right that I need them since any idiot could pull my family and me back into the spotlight with a juicy bit to the paparazzi. Not to mention jeopardizing all that I've built at Mad Lane Records.

"I already told you that's not a good idea," I say as I turn and start walking toward the door.

He matches my pace and holds the door open for me, leaning in to whisper as I pass him. "It's an excellent idea."

I can't help but grin at his persistence. "I'm sorry, Dex. You seem like a nice enough guy, but I don't date. And I don't mix stuff… like business and pleasure, so whatever you're looking for, it's not me."

He turns to a couple around our age walking toward us from the parking lot.

"She says I'm *a nice enough guy*," he directs to the guy.

"Ouch," the guy responds. "That's rough, bro."

Dex turns back to me with a dimpled smile. He leans in close to my ear as we keep walking toward my car. "That's definitely a first for me."

I arch a brow at him in question.

"I've never gotten the *nice guy* blow off."

"Well there's a first time for everything," I reply and smirk at him.

"Yep," he says with a roguish grin. "Even a first time for *mixing stuff?*" He arches one brow back at me.

I want to slap my own forehead for walking into that one. I've got to admit, though, I'm enjoying his playful banter. I shake my head in response and fight the grin struggling to break free on my face.

As we approach my car, I see him eyeing it with interest. He touches a fingertip to it as if testing that it's real. He whistles low and mumbles, "Sweet ride," under his breath.

"Thank you," I say. "She's my baby. Well… one of them."

He turns back to me, an expression of shock on his face. "This is yours?"

"Yeah, I've had to rebuild her more times than I care to admit, but she's worth it." I smile because my car isn't just a car to me, she's family. She's a 1966 Shelby Cobra s/c Roadster, candy-apple red with an off-center racing stripe. I bought her about three years ago as something to calm my mind during panic attacks, but I'm not going to tell him that.

He makes a curious sound, and I look up to find him staring at me like someone would look at art in a museum. I begin to feel uncomfortable under his gaze that seems to see straight through me. I move to the door and get in.

I notice him attaching that leather bag to the tail of the motorcycle next to my car and grabbing the helmet left on the handlebars. *Such a bad idea. Tattooed guys that ride motorcycles are never a good idea.*

"Bye, Dex. See you round."

"Yeah… you will," he says to me with a twinkle in his eyes. The mischievous smile on his face sets off warning bells in my head. He slides his helmet on and starts the bike with that unique sound that only a Harley can make.

I fasten my seat belt and watch him disappear in my rearview mirror as I pull out of the parking lot.

As I lean into the curve, my wheels slip a little and I readjust. Bonnie shouts at me as I pass her, though I can't hear her over the rush of wind and the sound of my heart pounding in my ears. She turns in a slow circle, holding her stopwatch and watching me make round after round on the track. My muscles burn and my mouth is dry from breathing so hard, but I can't give up. This is my last chance to improve my skate time and get my jammer status back.

Last season was my big return to roller derby after more than three years out of the game. When I came back last year, I didn't expect that I would've fallen so far behind.

As I round the track for the last lap, I push myself as hard as I can. I push past the pain until I feel that perfect euphoria that comes with adrenaline. When I round the last curve before the finish line, my wheels lose their grip on the track and fly out from under me. I hit the track with an *oof* and pull my knees and arms to my chest so I can fall small. I skid across the concrete floor before coming to a stop at the track's outline. I lie motionless, trying to fight back the tears. My hip is scarlet with rink rash, and I'll have a monster bruise in a couple of hours. *Fuck.* I was so close, but isn't this just perfectly in line with my life right now? No matter how hard I try, things just won't go back to the way they used to be. I'm stuck.

I skate down to the center of the track and stop in front of Coach Bonnie.

"I'm sorry, baby girl," she says. "You'll still skate, but I can't give you back jammer yet." She holds out her arms for a hug. I gladly roll into them. Inside I'm crying, but on the outside, I just rest my head on her shoulder. I'm spent.

"Go, get your gear off," she orders with a smack on the butt. "We've got somewhere to be tonight, and the first shot's on me, birthday girl."

I attempt a grin as I move to join the other girls on the benches.

Everyone is chatting noisily, pumped for the after-practice

celebration tonight.

"Did you make it?" Holly asks.

I flop down on the bench. "No…" I groan through a rush of air. "You didn't see that spill six fucking feet from the finish line?"

Holly's shoulders droop. I fucking hate this because I feel like I let her down. I let them all down. The other girls follow with their words of support and encouragement. We all do this for the love of the sport and friendship, so no one is going to hold it against me.

"I feel like I need to hump something," Holly says and latches on to my leg. I pick her up by her thighs, and we both go crashing to the ground in a pile of giggles and mock punches. She knows how to distract me from my shit mood.

"All right, bitches, settle down," Bridget yells. "Save the humping for the bar."

Catcalls follow this. Ruby tries to tickle me, and I pull her down. Soon, practically the whole team is in a pile, laughing and wrestling.

This is why I skate. This is my home, my family. I fucking love these girls with all my heart.

Now

We arrive at Ruby's, a little bar in South Austin's SoLa district. I met Ruby, the namesake, when I joined the team years ago. Her family has owned this venue since shortly after she was born. These walls, covered in kitschy paraphernalia, hold a lot of my own personal history. It's a dive bar, but it's our dive bar.

The whole team's here tonight to celebrate. Even some people from the rest of the league have joined us. There's a sea of women in funky tights, knee-high socks, and *Hellcat* team shirts. Holly stops me just after I walk in the door.

"Here, shit, I almost forgot." She digs in her purse and pulls out a tiara, complete with tulle and magenta fur.

It matches our team colors, and the rhinestones on the front spell out *Birthday Bitch*. She places it on my reluctant head. I frown at her.

"Don't give me that look. It's tradition."

I grumble a protest, but I'm swept toward the bar for a shot with Bonnie.

After a while, we move to the tables the girls have pushed together, right next to the giant taxidermy jackalope. There's a birthday cake in the middle of the table, and I take the seat nearest to it. Holly comes to the tables with a stack of shot glasses and a bottle of Smirnoff Whipped Cream vodka. I laugh and shake my head at her.

It's karaoke night, which they only do once a month, so she has to yell over a startling rendition of "Sweet Child O' Mine." "It's tradition, bitch!"

Holly passes out shots to everyone in our group. I accept hugs and birthday wishes from everyone. I know I should be happy that my friends care enough to go to all the trouble, but I've never been a birthday person. It's such a self-centered thing to celebrate, and it's never been my cup of tea, because my birthday, in particular, is shrouded in shit memories. I always just end up drunk trying to enjoy the effort my friends put into it because I know it comes from a good place.

I study the collection of hubcaps on the wall, chatting with Bridget and her flavor of the week when I feel muscular arms wrap around my waist from behind and a kiss planted on my cheek.

A low voice whispers in my ear, "Happy Birthday, Mads."

I try to look at who it is, but the hug lasts a little longer than necessary, and I wiggle to turn. Asher.

"Hey, you. You're just in time." I motion to the bottle and shot glasses, and he moves to pour his shot. He's been to enough of these to know the drill.

When the song is over, Holly grabs the mic. She climbs on the stage followed by Chloe and Bridget. Asher returns to my side and wraps his free arm around my back. I lean into his shoulder.

"How's it goin, my people?" Holly shouts into the microphone.

Ruby is back at the bar ringing the cowbell that hangs off the wall. People shout and yell and clap and slap tables. It's a deafening roar of a response.

"Well, most of you know why I'm up here, but for those who don't, tonight's my best bitch's birthday."

This is greeted by more raucous noise.

"You see that sexy thing over there in the awesome

headgear? That's our Maddie. Asher, get your hands off her."

Everyone who knows us laughs. Not Asher, though. If looks could kill, Holly would be long gone. I straighten myself, and Asher's hand falls away.

"Well, she's single and horny and is looking for the best birthday fuck ever, so don't be afraid to try your luck, guys."

The whole bar erupts in catcalls and laughter. Shouts of "Pick me" or "I got yours right here" rise up from the chaos of noise. It's embarrassing, so I flip her off.

"Now, baby, don't be that way. You know I love you. Seriously, though, not many can pack a bar with people who love them. And we all love you because you're the shit. Happy Birthday. Everybody join me in singing Happy Birthday to our Maddie."

Bridget, Holly, and Chloe lead the song, and everybody in the bar joins in. I stand there feeling incredibly awkward, but still thankful that I have such great friends.

When they're finished, Chloe's pink bob swishes around her face as she grabs the mic. "Now that we've entertained her, I think it's time she entertains us. How many of ya want to hear her sing something?"

Oh, no.

The bar erupts again, and people start chanting my name. *Maa-dee Maa-dee Maa-dee.*

Nope. That is a hard limit for me. They know I can't get on a stage again. *How could I? It just doesn't seem fair that I get to when* he *can't.* I turn toward the front door, and Asher grabs my hand.

"I'll go up there with you. It won't be that bad. Just like old times, right?" he says.

I stiffen at that, and he squeezes my hand. It's somewhat reassuring. But I can't fully set aside the guilt that has settled into my stomach like a lead weight.

He drags me to the DJ, and after a brief conversation, the DJ nods and gives him another microphone. Chloe meets me at the stairs to the stage. I'm two steps below her, but that puts us eye to eye.

"I'm going to make you pay for this later, you know," I grind out through clenched teeth, forcing a smile on my face.

She smiles at me, but I think I see fear in her eyes. Well, one can hope. I haven't been on a stage for a little over four years for a damn good reason, and I haven't been on this stage, in particular, in what feels like forever.

I stand on the stage, holding the microphone and focusing on the monitor in front of us. When the song starts and "Love Shack" pops up on screen, I can't help but laugh.

The story never gets old with Asher, but I don't remember it at all. The first time I got drunk in front of him, he says I sang this song on repeat like a broken record. Or, really just the chorus. I swear he's making it up, but the fact that he chose this song instantly relaxes me.

I start singing, and the world falls away. I go into the zone. It's almost like I haven't left the stage behind, and soon I have the whole bar clapping and singing along with me. I miss this, but I wouldn't admit that to anyone. It feels like coming home.

Asher does the male vocals with a comedic edge. He's never been much of a singer, and it says a lot that he's up here with me now.

When the song's over, I take a bow and blow kisses, then rush off the stage like the devil's on my heels, my eyes trained on the ground. I run smack into a wall of muscle in my hasty escape and stumble back, about to fall on my ass when he catches me. I know who it is before I even look up. Goose bumps spread across my entire body, because I know those tattooed arms.

"Those were some impressive karaoke skills. Can I buy a drink for the birthday girl?" Dex says, and the vibrations of his voice tickle my ear.

A shiver dances over my skin. I've had enough to drink at this point that my defenses are down, and I make no move to back away from him.

"What're you doing here?"

"A little birdie gave me an invite." His lips twitch on one

corner, tipping up. That damn dimple reappears. *Dammit, Holly.* "Drink?" he asks again.

I look up into his unusually striking blue-green eyes and nod. Maybe I just stare. Neither of us moves for a good bit like we're hypnotizing each other, until someone bumps into me. I'm smashed up against him. His arms wrap around me, and our bodies press together. A wave of desire rushes through me, making me feel faint for a second. I need space. I turn away and, out of some subconscious masochistic place within me that's clearly begging for trouble, I grab his hand, leading him to the bar.

Then

A final tear tracked down my face and clung to my chin, refusing to let go. The murmur of voices from the party behind me was far enough away that the crickets in the field next to me were louder. It was dark out, the houses about a quarter mile apart, no streetlights, and just the glow of a full moon keeping me company.

The ache still lingered in my chest as images of Lisa and Brad ran through my head on repeat. I couldn't help but wonder how long it had been going on, how deep the betrayal ran. I couldn't shake the feeling I'd wake up and realize this was a bad dream. It had to be a nightmare because I couldn't process a world where my best friend, the girl I'd known forever, would be so callous. *What had I ever done to her?*

A throat cleared behind me. I jumped at the sound and turned to see Jared.

"Hey, you leaving?" I asked. I cringed as my voice, raspy from crying, grated in my ears. I brushed the tear away from my chin.

"I was," he stated, walking to the truck in front of me.

It was a 1957 Ford F-100 Pickup in cherry condition. I'd been checking it out for some time as a distraction while waiting for my mom. The truck was a rich dark color that looked shiny and black, but I wasn't sure that it was black since it was too dark to tell. I watched him as he unlocked the door, folded back the seat, and pulled something out. It wasn't until he came closer that I could see it was a guitar.

"Nice truck," I said, sniffling and wiping away the last evidence of my tears.

He grinned. "Yeah, Sara's my baby."

"Sara?" I asked.

"Hey, at least I didn't name her Christine." He grinned.

I chuckled. "Well, as long as you're not secretly Randall Flagg, we're cool."

"No, I don't look good in cowboy boots or denim jackets."

He's a car guy and a horror fan. Interesting.

"I don't know. You could probably rock the boots. You're in Texas now, son." I laughed when he made a face like he sucked on a lemon. "What made you pick a '57 F-100?" I asked as he sat down next to me. I plucked a blade of grass from beneath me and twirled it between my fingers.

Jared seemed like a cool guy, though, it came as a bit of a shock that he was so good at distracting me. It helped that we seemed to have a lot in common.

His jaw dropped. "You're into cars?"

I nodded. "Why shouldn't I be? That's like me asking you why did you pick a classic and not some sporty rich-kid car?"

He laughed and shrugged. "I don't know. I like trucks— the best body styles were in the fifties. I got a sweet deal on this from a friend of my dad's in Arkansas. It was his father's, who'd passed away. It wasn't running. Had a bit of rust on the wheel wells, but the frame was solid. The engine needed cleaning and fluids. My dad gave me the paint job as a present for my birthday this year."

"When was your birthday?"

"Last month," he replied.

"Well, happy belated birthday."

"Thanks," he said with a smile. "Yours was yesterday, right?"

"Yeah," I answered as I peered past him, my mind drifting

back to Lisa and Brad, finding it strange that neither had come looking for me.

"How long were you guys together?" He motioned back to the house.

I looked at him, confused. What would make him ask about that?

"I'm sorry about what happened." His lips pursed into a frown. "I overheard someone talking about it back at the party."

I cringed at the proof of my worst nightmare. "Longer than I care to admit."

"You want to talk about it?"

"Not really."

An awkward silence stretched between us.

"Do you know how to play that thing?" I gestured to the guitar. "Or do you just carry it around to impress the ladies?"

"Are you impressed?" he asked, one corner of his mouth twitching upward.

I snorted. "It depends on if you can actually play it."

"Well, let's see." He scrunched up his face as if he were thinking. "I know."

A look of utter concentration broke out on his face as he adjusted his guitar. Then he started playing "Mary Had a Little Lamb."

I burst out laughing, my thoughts about Lisa's betrayal fading into the background. I was expecting him to play something serious. Maybe even something popular to impress me.

"I take it you're thoroughly impressed?" he asked.

I threw my head back, holding myself up on my elbows and shaking out my hair. "Oh, God, yes. Take me now, Guitar Man," I said, trying my best Southern belle impression. My head fell back further as a laugh burst out of me.

He drew in an audible breath. I looked up to find him facing me, his eyes shadowed. I forgot to breathe. The way the moonlight highlighted his features made him look like a stone statue. He was beautiful.

He strummed a few notes, breaking the silence and the moment. I sat up, looking at my feet as if they were the most interesting things in the world.

"Name a song you know the words to," he finally said.

"Ummm… like what? What can you play?"

"Lots of stuff," he said.

"Play what you like." I shrugged. "I'm a captive audience… until my mom gets here anyway."

He looked thoughtful for a few moments and then played a song that sounded familiar, though I couldn't quite place it. Then he started to sing.

He had the voice of an angel, if angels sang "Wish You Were Here" by Pink Floyd with a deep, raspy voice. His voice sent shivers down my spine. My lower belly clenched. I closed my eyes and absorbed it. I may have been reading too much into it, but I felt like the notes, the lyrics, were speaking to my soul. Something inside me was coming alive that had been asleep my whole life.

When he finished, we sat in silence, letting the last chords echo in our minds.

"Thank you," I said, glancing at him. He nodded and smiled softly, but the concern in his eyes still caused his brow to crease a little.

"Do you know the words to 'Hotel California'?" he asked.

"Uh, yeah," I replied. "Who doesn't?"

"Then sing it. I'll play it for you."

"I don't sing in front of people."

"Now is a good time to start. Come on."

"I don't even know if I'm any good."

"You have the sexiest voice I've ever heard. Your singing voice must be amazing."

My stomach fluttered. How could I say no to that?

"Fine," I mumbled, looking down at my lap.

His fingers flew over the strings, bringing to life the intricate sounds of the Spanish-influenced guitar. I was in awe. He was good. He knocked twice on his guitar, signaling my cue to start singing. I started, and my voice immediately cracked. After a few more notes, I found my stride. I sang the song the best I could, putting my heart and soul into those lyrics, trying to find the haunting emotions that lay behind the words. When the song was over, he sat his guitar in the grass and leaned over me, grasping the back of my neck.

"You're amazing," he said, sounding as awestruck as I felt. My fingers curled into the front of his shirt. His eyes searched mine. "Can I kiss you?"

Speechless, I nodded, and he leaned in. My breath stalled in my lungs. My eyes fluttered closed as my lips parted. His lips gently brushed over mine as my phone rang. He leaned his forehead to mine.

"You need to get that, huh?" he asked breathlessly.

"Yeah." My voice came out as a hoarse whisper. "It's probably my mom. She should be here by now."

He moved away. I reached for my phone. It was a local phone number, but one I didn't know.

"Hello?"

"Are you Madelaine Dobransky?" a strange male voice spoke over the line.

"Yes," I answered.

"I'm a nurse at Hardin County General. You're listed as your mom's primary emergency contact. I'm afraid there has been an accident. You need to come to the hospital. Do you have a way to get here? I can have a police squad car sent to pick you up."

My chest squeezed. My mind raced as I tried to think of what I needed to do next.

"You still there?"

"Umm... yeah. Sorry. I can get a ride," I said, struggling to draw in a breath. "Is she okay?" Tears welled in my eyes again as thousands of worst-case scenarios played out in my head.

"I don't have a status update on her yet. They just brought her in. I'll try to find out more before you get here."

"Okay, I'm on my way," I said with barely contained hysteria.

I turned to Jared, who was looking at me with concern. It made me want to break apart right there on the spot.

"Do you need a ride somewhere?"

"He said my mom's at the hospital, that she's been in an accident." Unbidden tears spilled onto my cheeks.

"Hold on. I'll be right back." He rushed to his truck, put away his guitar, then came back to help me off the ground. He tucked me to his chest as he murmured soothing words to me. When he started driving, he reached out, threading his fingers with mine. It was a spot of warmth in the numbing cold that had settled over my body.

Now

As I approach the bar, I release Dex's hand, immediately missing the warmth of the contact. I lean over the bar and yell for Ruby's dad, Frank, to get his attention. When he turns, his smile lights up his face, and he moves toward us. He hugs me, practically pulling me over the bar.

"Do I get a kiss from the birthday girl?" he teases.

"Of course, even if you're late to the party." I plant a kiss on his cheek, and he releases me. I slide back until my feet hit the ground. "Frank, this fine gentleman right here would like to buy me a drink." I motion to Dex.

Frank eyes him suspiciously, his smile faltering a little. I chuckle to myself because Dex doesn't seem to be at all bothered by the scrutiny. He holds Frank's gaze as if communicating something back to him. Frank's a big guy with a ZZ Top-like beard and a round belly. He's an old-school biker with tats, leather vest, and steel-toed boots. He can be intimidating. His eyes effectively convey that he's experienced in causing serious damage and will do so if he decides he doesn't like you.

"You know if you hurt her it'll be the last thing you do?" Frank says, breaking the epic stare down.

"Furthest thing from my intentions, sir," Dex says

45

reaching out his hand. Frank takes his hand in a firm shake. "Dexter McClellan, nice to meet you."

Frank smiles his approval, and just like that, the tension is gone.

"Frank Winchester. What can I get for you, son?"

"Beer, whatever's cold. And whatever she wants," Dex replies without hesitation.

Frank's eyes turn to me. "The usual?" he questions, raising one furry eyebrow.

I nod, and he moves down the bar to make the drinks. I turn to find Dex looking at me again. His lips tip up into a sexy smirk as his head tilts like he's trying to piece a puzzle. He leans closer.

"Just when I think I've figured you out." He's still smiling when he shakes his head, looking to the floor. "You're never what I expect. You surprise me." When he looks back up, his gaze pins me to the spot. His eyes are heated, serious. "And people stopped surprising me a long time ago." He reaches out and traces his thumb along my lower lip.

He's standing so close, his warm breath feathers across my cheek. I look down at his hand as it falls away and peek up at him through my lashes. Whatever he's doing to me, I can't describe it. I'm frozen to the spot.

Frank slams our glasses on the bar, jolting me back to the real world. "You two kids be good tonight, you hear?" he says and walks away chortling, fully amused by his antics.

"I need to pay him," Dex mutters, looking confused. I only hear him because the next song hasn't started yet.

"Just leave it in the tip jar. That's what I do." I shrug. "He never takes money from friends and family. Must mean he likes you," I shout with a grin over the now-playing music.

We turn to take our drinks back to the table when a woman steps in Dex's path. I can't hear what she's saying to him, but her hand trailing down his chest gives me a good idea. There is an irrational pang in my chest that I'm trying to overcome when I feel a tap on my shoulder. I set my drink back on the bar and turn to look at the person.

I squeal and leap into Evan's arms. He spins me around in his usual ritual before placing me on my feet and kissing the corner of my mouth.

"Asshole! Why didn't you tell me you were gonna be in town?" I say as I punch his shoulder.

He clutches his shoulder in mock pain and laughs. "Well, I wouldn't be able to surprise my favorite girl for her birthday if I called ahead of time, now would I?"

"Fine. I'm glad you're here. You're staying at my place?"

"Of course. The Charger was unlocked, so I stuck my bags in your back seat. You really should stop doing that, you know."

"Yeah, yeah. Not even back two minutes and already giving me big-brother lectures." I pull him back and hug him again. "God, I missed you."

"Are you driving out tomorrow?" He tips my chin up so I'm forced to look at him. "I want to go with you, you know."

Pulling my chin from his hand, I look down and tug the rubber band. The snap reminds me I'm still alive, kills the numbness that threatens to take over. It wasn't always enough, but this is me doing better. *Yay.*

"Yeah. We made plans. Everyone will be at your parents' place. I'm just driving out to the cemetery at some point. No big, you don't have to come with." Then, in attempt to lighten the mood, I force a smile and say, "I think your dad's grillin'."

I turn back toward the bar as he responds. "I'm going with you."

We're both facing Dex now, who seems to have gotten rid of his female companion and is watching us with interest.

"You're gonna have to tell me what you've been up to," Evan says in my ear. "I've been here long enough to know something's up."

"Is that your way of fishing for an introduction?" I ask. He grins, and I roll my eyes. "Evan, this's Dex," I shout so they can both hear me.

Evan reaches out his hand. "Evan Langford, Maddie's brother."

I jab a sharp elbow in his side, but he doesn't react. They shake hands and size each other up. Males and their testosterone, I'll never understand. Evan's a big guy. He spends a good portion of every day at the gym. He's a trained killer. US Army, Special Forces. It shocks me that they're both around the same size. Dex is maybe an inch or two taller. They both have tattoos, though Evan has fewer due to military regulations.

They still haven't let go of each other's hand.

"All right, enough of that." I grab my drink from the bar. "Are we gonna join the party or sit here for an all-night pissing contest?" I wink at them and head to the table.

"Hey, I'm gonna go see what's up with that cute PA of yours," Evan says with a wink, moving off in the direction of the pool tables.

I grin, sitting down at the table. After a moment, Dex pulls up a chair next to me.

"These all girls from your team?" Dex asks.

"Only the ones wearing team shirts. There're other people here from the league, and some from work."

"What kind of sport do you play?"

"Roller derby."

He leans back in his chair. "I'll have to check that out sometime."

Ruby places a flaming shot glass on the table in front of me. I know I should slow down, but if you only cut loose once a year, you might as well do it right. Especially since this time of year, things invade my mind that I'd rather forget.

I blow out the shot and down it, slamming the glass on the table. Everyone near us cheers. Dex pulls me close to him and whispers, "Happy Birthday," in my ear. Tingles race over my body. I remember that I need to move away from him, but my hazy mind can't remember why, so I just snuggle closer.

Then

As soon as we parked outside the emergency room, Jared was out of the truck, opening my door. I slid from the seat and crossed my arms in front of me to hide the trembling as we walked toward the sliding glass doors. There were two police officers inside talking to each other. I rushed past them to the service desk.

"I'm Madelaine Dobransky. I'm here for my mother, Catherine Dobransky." The man in scrubs behind the desk looked up at me with pity in his eyes, and I knew something horrible had happened. My knees went weak, and Jared supported me, bracing me with a gentle arm.

"Just a second, miss." He looked up, and his eyes flashed toward the two police officers. Any hope I had that this was a broken leg immediately vanished.

"Can you tell me where she is?" I asked. "How's she doing? Can I see her? Please?" My heart raced, and my breath trembled as I exhaled.

Without looking up, he held up a hand to halt my questions. "We spoke with your mother's secondary emergency contacts. They'll be here as soon as they can catch a flight. They authorized us to speak with you, which we needed because you're a minor."

He was talking about Gary and Rachel, Evan's parents. They'd gone to North Carolina for a cousin's wedding.

He tapped on his keyboard, then met my eyes. "Your mother's condition is listed as critical. That's all I can tell you right now. If you have a seat, I'll see if I can find a doctor to give you more details."

I turned to find the two police officers behind me.

"Would you like to sit down?" One of the officers—the shorter one with a receding hairline—gestured toward the chairs in the waiting room. His face was somber, and his eyes radiated concern.

I shook my head, unable to speak. Jared held me against his chest, and I leaned into him.

The taller, younger officer said, "Maddie…"

My face scrunched up in confusion. How does he know what name I go by?

"I'm Officer Webb. Your mother and I are friends." He shifted his weight, looking uncomfortable. "You know the police station and the library are next to each other?"

I nodded, still confused as to why I hadn't known about Officer Webb.

He continued. "We have lunch sometimes. She talks about you a lot. I wanted to be here to tell you about what happened. I'm so sorry." He looked away. When he spoke again, his voice was strained with emotion. "She was hit by a red-light runner crossing the highway. He was speeding. Her car rolled several times, and she was trapped in the wreckage. First responders were able to get her out and bring her here…"

He kept saying stuff, but I could no longer hear him through the rushing sound in my ears. Black spots clouded my vision. Jared was pushing me toward the chairs as he spoke to the officers. He guided me into a chair, and with a gentle hand on the back of my neck, made me lean over.

"Breathe, Maddie," Jared soothed. "Breathe."

My vision started clearing as I listened to his calming voice. I looked around the room and tried to focus on anything that would take my mind off reality. The room was empty other than the neatly lined rows of chairs, a TV softly broadcasting CNN, and an older couple holding on to each other across the room.

I'm not sure how long I sat there staring at them. My mind an utter blank, devoid of any thoughts. Jared sat next to me and wrapped an arm around my shoulders at some point. When the doors leading to the ER opened, my gaze snapped in that direction. A woman wearing scrubs and a surgical cap strode toward me. When I met her eyes, the last piece of hope died.

"Are you Madelaine Dobransky?" she asked.

I couldn't speak. I knew what was coming and I didn't

want to hear it. Hearing it would make it real, and this couldn't be real.

Jared squeezed my shoulders and answered for me. "She is."

"I'm Dr. Hall-Meyers, chief of surgery. I'm sorry..." Her lips kept moving. I heard none of it. I just kept chanting to myself that this was a nightmare.

Jared knelt in front of me, and I could see his lips moving, but I couldn't hear a thing he was saying. I closed my eyes and rested my forehead on his shoulder. He rubbed small circles on my back, but I barely felt it—there was a pervading numbness spreading over me. There were no tears, no nothing, just a soundless void where my life once was. I looked around the room, searching for my mom. This wasn't real. She'd be coming through the doors looking for me, so mad that I left the party when I knew she was on the way.

A boy around my age, maybe a little older, walked out of the ER into the waiting room. He had a bandage on his head, and his arm was in a sling. I was staring at him because he was the only motion in an otherwise motionless room. He walked to the older couple sitting across from me, but his brown eyes were locked on to mine and didn't look away.

"Can't you have her father do that? She's been through enough already," I heard Jared ask.

"He's dead too" were the only words I could force out as I shifted my chin on Jared's shoulder, still looking at the other boy staring back at me.

The boy closed his eyes tightly and turned from me when the woman laid her hand on his uninjured arm.

Jared said something else to the officers and doctor. The next thing I knew, I was floating. Not floating, but being carried. I could hear the steady rhythm of Jared's heart where my ear rested against his chest. He placed me back in the truck and dialed a number on his phone. I still didn't hear any of it. I just stared out the window of his truck, seeing absolutely nothing.

Chapter Six

Now

The party is a success. More karaoke and more alcohol. I'm afraid now I'm a little bit smashed. I'm standing next to the pool table as Dex and Evan finish their game. They seem to have gotten over whatever it was between them by the bar. Now they're acting like they're best buds.

I try to be graceful as I walk to our table, only stumbling once, I think. I snatch up my purse and dig out keys. I turn back toward the pool table, only to be confronted with a face, framed in neon-pink tresses, so close to mine it startles the fuck out of me. I yelp and fall back, crashing into the table. Smooth, Maddie, real smooth.

"Definitely not, lady." Chloe rips the keys from my hand.

"Not what?" I ask. "I was looking for a DD. I'm drunk, not stupid. You can't have them either," I slur, trying to snatch the keys back.

She holds them overhead, and I stumble forward to catch them. It confirms my drunkenness because that stops me from getting them, and Chloe's shorter than I am.

"Yes. I'm the DD tonight. This is sweet tea." She shakes her mostly empty glass, causing the ice to rattle. "I haven't had anything since the shot during your birthday toast. Which was…" She squints at her phone. "Over four hours ago. I'm good to go."

"Awwwww… my baby bitch is taking care of me. I love you." I throw my arms around her neck. Chloe's only twenty-one, which makes her the youngest of our group of friends.

She starts rubbing my back. "Yeah, I think she's ready to call it a night," she says over my shoulder to someone behind me.

I turn to find Asher. "You leaving?" I ask. He nods. I dive into his arms, hugging him. "I love you, too, Ash. I don't know what I'd do without you. You be safe."

He chuckles. I can hear the rumble from where my ear presses into his chest. He squeezes me tighter. "What am I going to do with you, woman?"

"See me on Monday?" I ask, peeking up at him.

A shadow passes over his eyes. "Yeah, Monday." He releases me and steps back. "I'll see you then, Mads." He smiles weakly, grabs the back of my neck, pulling my head toward him and kissing my forehead briefly. "Take care of her," he says to Chloe, then leaves.

Evan puts an arm around both Holly and Chloe, winking at me. "We'll meet you at the car."

I'm now alone with Dex and a few straggling barflies.

"Thanks for coming," I say.

I wave to him and then clasp my hands behind my back to stop myself from doing further weird hand shit. I feel… awkward. *What am I doing?*

My skin twitches; the muscles in my core clench just thinking about his touch. It's been four years since I had sex. That seems a bit ridiculous, even for someone with my hang-ups. I should try to be normal for a night. That's what normal people do, right? They hook up? Yep, decision made. The alcohol might be impairing my judgment, but I'm going to do this. It's making me forget the myriad of reasons why I'm still single and bold enough to do something about it. That's good, right? Why am I asking myself questions? See, I just did it again.

I saunter toward him, trying to be as seductive as possible.

Dex's eyes look wary as he tracks my movement. I reach up, thread my fingers through his hair at the nape of his neck, and pull his head down to me.

"You know, I was thinking…" I whisper in his ear. His body stiffens. I lean back to look into those cerulean eyes. "There's a room in the back. The bands that play here use it as a greenroom."

In the blink of an eye, Dex has thrown me over his shoulder. "Oooo… you're gonna be all caveman about it. I can work with that," I taunt, giggling.

He heads out the front door.

"Hey, you're going the wrong way," I protest.

He doesn't say a word as he carries me out to the parking lot, his thumb tracing small circles on the back of my thigh. It does wicked things to me. My body thrums with excitement. He finally stops and I slide down him, the friction lighting me up. I feel his arousal where we're pressed together. My heart feels like it's going to pound through my chest.

We're alone in the nearly empty parking lot. He doesn't move, so I decide to get things in motion. I run my hand up his chest and over his shoulders, intending to pull his face down to mine. Only he wraps his long fingers around my wrists in a firm grip and moves them behind my back. An audible exhale escapes my lips at my arousal from the gesture. My head drops back in surrender, allowing him better access.

"Maddie." His voice is low and quiet.

I lift my head and look at him. I mean, really look at him. If I'm not mistaken, he looks angry. It's hard to tell because there seem to be two of him.

"You need to go home and sleep it off. You've had too much to drink tonight." He releases me, then steps back.

"Dex?" I whisper, searching my brain for some way I misread his signals. He couldn't possibly be rejecting me. "I thought you—"

"You thought what?" His eyes narrow and his voice is cold. "That this was only going to amount to a cheap fuck in the back room of a dive bar?" He rams his fingers into his hair forcefully. "Go home, Maddie. I expect this from the majority of the female population, but I hoped you were different."

I have to pick my jaw up off the parking lot. My fuzzy brain cannot understand why he's so angry. Embarrassment and anger flood my system.

"Seriously! You're all like, I want to get to know you, Maddie. Go out with me, Maddie. Let me touch and tease you, Maddie," I say in a mocking voice. "And now you're telling me to fuck off? Because you're not getting it when, where, how… and where you wanted?" I take a step forward.

He mirrors me, taking a step back. "That's what you think this is?" he asks, his voice an angry calm.

"Then what the fuck is this?" I throw back.

"Has anyone ever told you no?"

"Of course people tell me no. All. The. Fucking. Time," I seethe. "What? You think I'm just some spoiled princess? Well, I've news for you, buddy! Everything I have, I've worked for." Tears start building in my eyes, and I have to breathe deeply to stop them.

"That's not what I'm saying! Will you just stop?" His voice is loud as he yells over mine. It's so powerful and booming that it completely scrambles my booze-addled mind. I blink. "Will you just listen to yourself? Yes, I want to get to know you. Yes, I want to take you out on a date. That has nothing to do with sex in the back room of a bar."

"I don't have time for this shit. You know what? Fuck you. Fuck you and your fucking tattoo. Consider this my cancellation." I give him the finger and turn away. I'm so angry or drunk—or both—I stumble over my own feet and fall. I quickly right myself and glance around, but the parking lot is still empty, save for Dex and me. Dex probably saw it, but fuck him.

I move around the empty car we're beside to my car and fall into the passenger seat. The conversation between Holly, Evan, and Chloe stops. I squeeze my eyes tight to keep back the tears fighting their way out. Why am I crying? I've no idea. This was a huge mistake. I pull the rubber band on my wrist until it can't go any farther and let it go. I feel nothing. Fuck this numbness.

Then

I didn't remember the ride home. Jared's feet thunked heavily on the hollow floors of my mobile home as he carried me through the front room.

"I got you," Jared whispered softly.

"How did we get here?" I whispered.

"Nic gave me your address. They couldn't get the county CPS to the hospital tonight, and I didn't think you wanted to stay in that waiting room until tomorrow morning. It took some convincing..." He trailed off as he looked around, determining where to take me.

I pointed toward the hall. He followed the direction. The white-paneled walls had a faint glow, the sheer red curtains framing the moonlight spilling into the small dark bedroom. Jared deposited me on my bed and turned as if to leave.

"Stay." The word leaked out of me, the plea almost a whisper. "Stay with me, please."

He got down on his knees until he was eye level with me.

"Of course," he said, running his hands up and down the sides of my arms. "You're cold." He tugged my red comforter up around my shoulders. "Do you want something to drink? Are you hungry?"

"Shower."

"I'll get it started for you." He rose and turned on his heel toward the bathroom.

I stood underneath the stream of hot water with no real recollection of how I got there. The only thing that I could think at that point was, why wasn't I crying? I cried when my father died. I was only five years old, but I remember crying. With this, I had nothing. Nothing, but a dull, aching numbness. A cold that even the steaming hot water couldn't penetrate.

I felt like the world's worst daughter. I'd caused my mother's death and I couldn't even manage to cry about it. I killed her by being a whiny, sniveling little bitch over something as stupid as Lisa fucking Lombardi's dumb-as-fuck betrayal. *Why couldn't I fucking cry!* I stood underneath the stream of water, not moving until I realized the water had turned cold.

Getting out of the shower, I could hear Jared's muffled voice in the living room. I wrapped a towel around me and walked quietly down the hall, shivering as beads of water trailed down my skin. Jared was sitting on the couch with his back to me, his phone pressed to his ear and his free hand running through his hair.

"Yes, sir. I will... no, sir... no, sir. Yeah. First thing in the morning. Okay. Good night, dad."

He disconnected the call, then ran his hand through his hair again. He rubbed his hands over his face, releasing a long sigh. Leaning back on the couch, he stared at the ceiling. He must've caught sight of me because he jumped from the couch and spun around to face me, quicker than my eyes could track.

"Are you okay? Can I get you anything?" he asked as if trying to coax a cornered animal.

I shook my head, gripping the towel around me a little tighter.

"You probably want to be alone, but I don't want to leave until you have someone else here. It's three in the morning. I can stay. On the couch. Do you have any spare blankets or pillows I can use out here? I can get them myself—just point me in the right direction."

I didn't respond, just stared, my mind racing a million miles a second. He moved around the couch to stand in front of me, his fingers lightly touching my chin, urging me to look up at him.

"What can I do?" he asked again.

I tilted my head. I honestly didn't know how to answer that question. I closed my eyes. When I opened them, he was still there. Those icy-blue eyes with the dark blue rim around the irises searched my face for answers I couldn't give. As stunning as those eyes were, I couldn't drag my gaze away from his lips. His tongue darted out a little as he wet his lips. It was distracting, and that was what I needed.

"Make it stop," I said as I reached for the front of his button-down shirt. "Make me feel something other than this…"

He had a woody, earthy scent that filled my nose as I leaned into him. Pulling him to me and stretching up onto my tiptoes, I pressed my lips to his. Maybe I stunned him, because at first, he didn't move. He stood there, still as stone. I pulled at his shirt. My lips moved over his, urging him to react. His tongue slipped into my mouth as his hands came up to grasp the side of my face, his fingers tangled in my wet hair. All thoughts ceased as goose bumps spread across my body. My heart raced and I gasped for breath as his thumb brushed over my cheekbone. Every sensation consumed my mind until my only thought was him. He was so warm. I wanted to be that warm. I desperately wanted to forget everything about the whole damn night.

The muted sound of buttons raining down on the carpet snapped me back into focus. His shirt tore under my hands before I realized what I was doing. My hands ran over his warm, hard flesh. His hands found my thighs and slowly smoothed up to grasp my hips. He pulled me against him. My heart rate increased with nervous excitement. Our bodies sealed together with only space for the threadbare towel separating us. His hands firmly gripped my bare ass, grinding me against him. I moaned into his mouth. I felt his hard length pressed against my belly through his jeans. He pulled back panting, resting his forehead on mine.

"We shouldn't do this. You've been through too much," Jared said between strangled breaths.

"I need you," I begged.

His hands curved up my side to my waist. "Maddie…"

I kissed him again to stop any more protests, but he pulled

back. I thought it was to say something else, but with the pressure between our bodies gone, the towel fell away, leaving me naked before him. His eyes traveled down my body. Before I could blink, his lips crashed back into mine.

There was nothing gentle in his kiss anymore. My mind was overwhelmed. His hands returned to my ass in a firm grasp as he lifted me from the floor. My legs wrapped around his waist. We were moving, but I couldn't tell where. My eyes were closed and my mouth sealed to his. My fingers threaded through the locks of his hair as I held him. My back hit the rough, textured wall. The bumps scratched and pulled at my skin. Pleasure coursed through my veins, setting my body ablaze. I moaned as my grip on his hair tightened. His hips jerked into me, rubbing his jeans into my core.

"Jared…" I gasped.

Shifting my weight to one arm, Jared found my breasts with his free hand. He began trailing kisses from my ear to my collarbone. He pumped his hips again and again. I cried out as his fingers rolled across my nipple. My body jerked, it felt that good. *Was that an orgasm?* We were on the move again. My back hit the covers of my bed.

He started to back up, whether to get away or just to breathe for a second, I wasn't sure. I didn't give him a chance. I couldn't let him go. I needed him. He made the thoughts stop. I sat up on the edge of the bed. I latched my finger through his belt loop, tugging him to me as I used my other hand to undo his belt and pants. As the zipper hit the end, his erection sprang free. His pants dropped to his thighs; curiosity made me bold. I grasped it, and his hips jerked. I loosened my grip, afraid that I'd hurt him.

I wasn't sure what to do. I tentatively stuck out my tongue and touched it to the tip of him. His whole body shook with a tremor. I looked up to meet his eyes. He stared at me intensely. His expression was unreadable. His fingers wrapped around my wrists. He jerked my hands away from him. My heart pounded in my ears. Panic seized my chest. He was going to reject me.

"Please," I pleaded. Fear coursed through me at the thought of losing this connection. "I need you. Just now. I'm not asking for anything else."

The sound of his pants hitting the floor broke the silence of his answer. He nudged me to lie back on the bed as his body moved to cover mine. He grasped both my cheeks in his hands as he rested his weight on his elbows, forcing me to meet his penetrating gaze.

"God, you're the most beautiful thing I've ever laid eyes on. You don't have to ask me for anything. The moment I met you, I was yours."

His fingers fumbled at my core, teasing me as he lined himself up at my entrance. My body tensed as he thrust into me, expecting the pain that I'd heard would be there. It didn't happen. It felt weird—stretched and full—but it wasn't painful, just foreign. I watched his eyes shut tight, his shoulders tense as he pulled back slowly.

"Maddie." He sighed my name as if it were a prayer. I couldn't take my eyes off him. His reactions were fascinating. "I'm not going to—ah—"

He pumped in and out, eliciting sounds from me that I never knew I could make. His eyes flew open and locked on to mine, his mouth dropping open to release a guttural groan as he jerked and shuddered. Collapsing on top of me, he planted a messy kiss on my lips.

"That was..." He started to pull away from me. I wrapped my arms and legs around him, keeping him in place. "Amazing," he continued.

"Thank you," I mumbled, unsure of what else to say.

He pulled back with a gasp, breaking my hold on his shoulders.

"I forgot to use a condom." Panic infused his features.

"I'm a virgin—" I said. His eyes widened fractionally. "Well, I was, but I take birth control. For skin care. So, we're safe—unless... Do you forget a lot?"

He shook his head. "No." He relaxed a little, but he was still tense.

I chuckled at his panic. The laugh made my inner walls clench. He groaned, burying his face in my neck.

"If you keep doing that, I'm going to come again," he warned with a muffled voice.

He lifted his head, looking into my eyes. Searching. "Never mind. I think that just became my favorite sound."

He moved his hips against mine. I moaned from the sensation of the friction.

"That one's a very close second," he whispered, and his lips brushed against my ear.

Shivers chased down my spine. Tears finally spilled as he made love to me again. When we were both spent, he pulled me to his chest, the tears continuing to fall. He held me tightly as sheer exhaustion pulled me into a restless sleep.

Chapter Seven

Now

Holly's the first to break the silence in the car as we pull out of the parking lot at Ruby's. "What the hell was that about?"

"I *really* don't want to talk about it," I grumble and turn the radio on to drown out any more interrogation.

Jared's seductive voice croons over the airwaves. I smash the Off button so hard, I swear the plastic cracks. I let out a frustrated scream through clenched teeth before giving way to the sobs built up in my chest. I'm not even sure why I got so mad. What would've happened if he said yes? I'd do or say something, slip up, and he'd realize the freak that I am. It wouldn't have been a good idea. This crying isn't over Dex; it's just the amalgamation of everything that has me weary to the bone.

Evan undoes my seat belt and pulls me into the back seat between him and Holly. It's a bit clumsy, and I almost kick Chloe in the face in the process. They sandwich me between them, comforting me as my heart pours out. I feel like I've fallen into a well of dull, aching numbness that I've been struggling to climb out of for so long. Every time I get close enough to see the light of day, something pulls me back down. *I'm not meant to move on. I don't even think I deserve to.*

"Oh baby, you do," Holly croons in my ear. *I must've said*

that out loud. "You're one of the strongest people I know. You've such a big heart, and you put everyone else ahead of you. You just need to do you, instead of taking care of all of us."

"Strong," I scoff, releasing a puff of air. "I've been such a chickenshit I haven't set foot in that part of the studio in over four years. That's not strong at all."

"Maddie, that's completely understandable," Chloe argues. "That's why no one schedules ya in the studio. No one expects ya to go back there. Ya know we get it, right? The fact that ya even enter the building is more than most could handle. And it's not like you're sitting around on your ass moping. Between the House, Derby, the girls, your bands, and scouting—I can barely keep up with ya, and I'm only your assistant."

"Yeah, well, it's obviously not working. Everyone's getting restless—and then I try to—I don't know, let loose? Look where that gets me." I motion my hand out the window as if Dex were still standing there.

"You want to tell us what happened?" Evan asks, brushing my hair out of my face.

I sigh, reluctant. They won't stop until they have the story. "I offered him sex, and he acted… I don't know. He got super pissed about it." I cringe and shake my head as some of the alcohol haze clears. "Maybe I just read him wrong… Either way, I'm not doing that again anytime soon. With him or anyone else." My voice grows hoarse on that last bit, and I clear my throat.

"I'm sure that's not it. Ya didn't see the way he looked at ya," Chloe offers, looking back at me through the rearview mirror.

I cringe at the thought. I've learned the hard way that romance isn't in the cards for me. I had my shot. When a relationship is romantic in nature, people have a harder time letting shit go. They hold on to your faults and mistakes like a score card.

Relationships for me have to be purely functional. I've

emotional ones through my family and friends, where I get all the love and support I need. Then there are sexual relationships. Not that I've had any of those, but should the situation arise, I'll just keep the two separate. Life is less messy, less painful when everyone knows their place and what's expected.

Maybe I should've explained it to him. Nope. Scratch that—it's a horrible idea. Talking to people about emotional shit has never been my strong suit.

"God, you're so weird," Chloe protests. "It's not normal for a twenty-seven-year-old woman to give up on romance."

Am I talking out loud again?

"It's not giving up, Chloe. It's realistic. My heart was given away a long time ago. Stringing someone along only hurts everyone in the long run, I've been there before. Just because I can't fall in love doesn't mean I'm heartless and won't care if I hurt someone."

Everyone in the car goes silent. I think that's the most I've ever said to explain my motives to anyone. Even these three, who know me better than anyone.

"Fuck him, then," Holly adds eloquently, breaking the silence. "You're the hottest, most badass bitch I know, and there are plenty of guys out there dyin' to get in your pants."

I laugh. "I don't know," I say, picking at a thread that has come loose from my shorts. "I think I just need to focus on work. Nate's been up my ass to write some new shit. He thinks he can get me to record something now that I started playing again. I don't know. I don't want to be in the spotlight again."

"I still think that a deep dickin' is the answer to your problems," Holly says, smirking. "Maybe Evan can volunteer for that?"

"Ewwwww… gross," Evan and I say in unison and then break out into laughter.

"I can't believe you just suggested incest as the answer to my problems."

"What can I say? It got you to laugh at least." Holly gives

me a sly smile. "Besides, it's not technically incest."

"Close enough!" Evan protests. "The only thing more disgusting would be doing you."

"Can't argue with that," Holly retorts. "Even though the disgustin' part of that scenario is definitely you."

She smashes me down into Evan's lap as she punches his shoulder. He grapples with her, and soon I'm caught in what has to look like an alley-cat brawl. Have I mentioned that I love my family? Well, I do. As dysfunctional as we are, there's nothing but love in this car, and for that I'm thankful.

Then

I tried going back to school two weeks after the accident, but I was dead inside. Life became a series of circumstances where I had to choose one evil or the other, and no matter what I chose, it chipped away a little more until I was just a shell of the girl I once was.

Bury or cremate? Estate sale or donate? Emancipation or foster care?

Rachel and Portia, Evan and Nic's moms, held my hand and walked by my side through all of it, yet the choices were ultimately mine. At the age of fifteen, I'd lost my protective bubble of having a parent, and consequently, lost my ability to enjoy what was left of my childhood.

It pissed me off when kids my age would remark how they envied my newfound independence. I would've traded it all back to feel her comforting hug again. To smell her familiar vanilla-and-lavender scent one more time.

I officially moved in with the Langfords a few days before attempting to go back to school. Gary and Rachel were named guarantors of my life insurance inheritance during the reading of my mom's will. I'd been staying in Evan's room while he slept on a cot in their home office, but we finally moved all that office furniture out and my bedroom stuff in.

I saw Jared at school that day before he noticed me. He was walking down the hall with Nic and Mike from the football team. They were laughing. I felt my heart crush in my chest because he looked happy, and that was the way it was supposed to be. I knew he had bugged Evan about me every day since I last saw him at the funeral, but I told Evan just to tell him that I was all right and to stay away. It would've been the most selfish thing in the world to drag him into my fucked-up reality.

He stopped at his locker to exchange a book when he looked up and caught me staring at him. Sadness instantly transformed his eyes. He grabbed a bouquet of flowers from his locker, said something to the guys, and walked over to me.

I couldn't take my eyes off him. I felt something for him that I'd never felt before, but it didn't alter the reality of my situation.

He stopped in front of me, flowers in hand. It was a bouquet of red calla lilies. How he knew they were my favorite or that I would be there that day was beyond me. I had a suspicion that a certain boy I was living with had something to do with it.

"How are you holding up?" he asked, meeting my eyes.

I shrugged, tired of saying "fine" or "okay" as I had been all day. I tentatively took the proffered flowers from him.

"Evan said those were your favorite. I picked the color, though. Your room was decorated in red. I figured you'd like it."

"They're beautiful, but you really shouldn't have."

"Maddie—" He took a step forward as if to touch me. I flinched, and he halted, dropping his hand to his side. "You don't have to go through this alone."

"I'm not alone, Jared. I have Rachel, Gary, and Evan. They're taking good care of me. You shouldn't waste your time on a girl you barely know. I have to go."

I stepped back, looking around to find the nearest escape route. That's when I noticed everyone in the hallway had stopped and was staring at us. My stomach heaved violently, and I had just enough time to dive to a nearby trash can. I puked my entire lunch and then some. When the spasms in my stomach subsided, I realized that Jared had my hair in one hand and was rubbing soothing circles on my back with the other. *How mortifying.* I pushed him away and ran toward the exit as he called after me.

I burst through the doors, my eyes glued to the ground. My breathing was labored as I sprinted down the hall. I looked up just before I crashed into a solid body so hard that we both fell backward on to the ground. Papers fluttered through the air above my head. My nose burned and ached from the impact. I scrambled to my feet and began gathering up the papers I'd stupidly knocked out of the other person's hands.

"I'm—I'm so sorry," I pleaded, the taste of vomit still on my tongue, making my voice thick.

Blake Johnson looked back at me, readjusting his askew glasses and rubbing a hand over his chest. His chest must've been what damaged my nose.

"It's okay, Maddie," Blake said as he moved to his knees. "I got this."

"No, I need to help. This's my fault." Tears welled up in my eyes.

"Well—" He offered me a warm smile. "If you're going to help, can you try getting them in order? I have to turn this paper in. It was due last week, but I had to make a trip to get it from my car."

I relaxed a little. He wasn't offering condolences or treating me like I was fragile. Blake was a good guy, same age as Evan and Nic. A lot of kids at school thought he was weird. He never really talked to anyone. Spent most of his time hanging out in the computer lab. We had a lot of classes together because we both took the advanced and accelerated courses that most kids our age didn't. He was always friendly and pleasant when I would ask him a question in class.

"Yeah, sorry," I said and began shuffling through the papers, looking for the page numbers. "I'm missing one through three and page six."

"I've got them." He held out his hand, and I placed the

papers in it. He handed me my bouquet of flowers. "How're you doing?"

"Huh?" I looked up to see concern written all over his face. "Oh, not good. Obviously, I'm a mess. I'm sorry—" Tears threatened to burst forth. "I need to go. I'm sorry again for running into you. Hope you do well with that paper."

I started to walk past him. He placed a hand on my elbow, halting me.

"I'm sorry, Maddie—" His eyes pleaded with me.

"It wasn't your fault." I tilted my head. Why was he apologizing for *me* running *into him*? "You were just in the wrong place at the wrong time." I offered him a half-hearted smile.

"Yeah, but—"

"It's okay, really. I gotta go. Take care, Blake." I pulled my arm from his grip and headed to the parking lot.

It was the last week of winter break. It had been four months since I last saw or even spoke to Jared. I transferred to the online public school option the state of Texas provided. I'd finally decided to return to school to finish up the year. In those four months, I hadn't left the apartment. I was hiding, and it made me feel weak. I didn't like considering myself weak. There was just one thing left holding me back. I was determined to leap that hurdle, no matter how painful it would be.

Evan told me frequently that Jared never stopped asking about me. He hadn't dated anyone else. Hadn't so much as looked at another girl. That last bit was probably a lie, but it gave me the warm fuzzies before guilt swept through me. He frequently called for the first month but gave up when I consistently refused to take his calls.

I stared at the clock above the TV. "You sure you told

him to be here at four thirty?" I asked Evan, who was sitting next to me on the couch enthralled in a *Dukes of Hazzard* rerun.

Evan looked at the clock and waved a dismissive hand at me. "Yes, and he still has ten more minutes to be on time. Relax, the guy was practically clicking his heels at the mention of you wanting to see him." He snorted a laugh. "Not that he'll be that excited when he finds out why you asked him to come over."

The only reason guilt hadn't eaten away at what was left of me was because I pushed it down, refusing to face reality. This conversation was seriously long overdue. I'd run out of excuses that seemed even remotely acceptable to continue putting it off any longer. I wrung my hands, staring at the TV but not seeing it.

Several minutes later, Rachel popped out of the kitchen. "Can I get you anything before we go, Maddie?" she asked. A mask of worry marred her beautiful features.

I just shook my head as nerves burrowed even deeper.

"You'll be fine, sweetie. Jared's a sweet boy." She smiled and hugged me, kissing my forehead before grabbing her purse and walking out the door.

Gary, Evan's dad, followed her path silently. Gary was an older, graying version of Evan, but still quite handsome. He gave me a smile that didn't reach his eyes before he kissed my forehead.

"You'll be fine. We won't be more than five minutes away, and Evan's staying here, just in case," he said before he turned to follow Rachel out the door.

At four thirty on the dot, there was a knock at the door. Evan hopped up to get it.

"There's my cue," he said before opening the door, letting Jared in.

My breath caught in my throat. Jared was more beautiful than I remembered. His inky-black hair was slightly longer than before, giving him a shaggy bed-head look. It definitely worked for him. He had on well-worn dark blue jeans, a blue-

and-black flannel shirt over a plain gray tee, and Doc Martens boots. There were dark circles under his eyes. He looked tired, but there was a glimmer in his eyes as they moved to me. We stared at each other without speaking for God knows how long. Evan coughed loudly.

"I'm going to be in my room," Evan said, jamming his thumb in the air over his shoulder. "Holler if you need me." He turned and left us alone.

"Hey," I said timidly, offering a lame wave as greeting. I didn't move from the couch.

"Hi," he responded. He took a step forward. Then his conflicted thoughts were running across his face, plain as day.

I knew I couldn't delay any longer. I took the chickenshit way out, again. I stood up. Jared froze, his eyes widening as they dropped to my middle.

"How far along?" he asked waving his hand toward my slightly protruding belly.

"Four months," I tried to say, but my voice gave out. It rasped as a coarse whisper. He looked to be thinking heavily, so I assumed he heard me.

"Is it mine?" he asked. He wasn't freaking out yet, so I relaxed a little.

"Yes. I'm sorry. I've only ever had sex that one night with you. The doctors say that my birth control just failed. I'm not asking anything from you. I've the life insurance money from my mom. It's enough. I just thought you should hear it from me that they're yours before you hear it from anyone else."

A slow, shaky grin spread across his face. "They?" he asked.

"Yep, twins. Guess you should've thought twice about having sex with the unluckiest girl on the planet."

He stared for a moment and then made a face at me. "This isn't unlucky," he said, his voice stern. "I'm not going to lie. It's scary as shit, but it's not a bad thing." He blew out a breath as he ran his hand through his hair.

"May I?" He held a hand toward my belly.

I nodded my consent. I couldn't breathe, much less talk.

This wasn't how I expected this to go. I was prepared for him to be angry, yell at me, or something.

He fell to his knees and ran his trembling hands over my belly before laying a kiss on my belly button. Then he looked up at me with those breathtaking eyes that were full of tears but looked so incredibly happy.

Tears ran freely down my face. For the first time in a long time, I had hope.

Chapter Eight

Then

It was a quarter 'til midnight, and the ballroom was already clearing out. I was sitting at a table at our senior prom with Evan's girlfriend, Stacey, and Nic's date, Robin. Jared and Evan were laughing, rough-housing as they stumbled over to us.

"Where've you boys been?" I asked.

"Nowhere," Evan answered quickly. He wasn't looking at me when he answered. That meant he was hiding something.

"Is it cold there?"

"Huh?" Evan now looked to me, perplexed, as he pulled Stacey from her chair, sat, and pulled her into his lap.

"I wasn't aware that nowhere was a place." I shrugged. "But since you've been there, you can tell me all about it." I smirked as I placed my elbow on the table, my chin in my hand, pretending to be enraptured by the prospect of his discovery.

"Uh… whatever," Evan said. "Don't forget I can still hold you down and fart in your face."

"Oh, my. How sexy is that?" I deadpanned. "I can see now why you're with him, Stace." Though the thought of the last time he did that sent a wave of nausea over me.

Jared knelt by my chair and smoothed a hand over my

eight-month belly. He grinned up at me, his eyes laughing, before he sat in the seat my bare feet occupied, moving them to his lap. He went to work kneading my swollen appendages. I let my head fall back and moaned from the pleasure of it.

"You guys need to get a room before Preggers, here, has an orgasm from whatever the fuck you're doing to her feet," Nic said as he sauntered to our table.

"You ready to go?" Jared asked softly.

I nodded. Jared placed my shoes back on my feet, then helped peel me out of the chair. He grabbed my hand as I admired the red calla lily on the wrist corsage he'd given me earlier that night.

I looked around one last time, catching sight of a guy standing in a darkened corner. I couldn't discern his features. He wasn't wearing a tux or a suit as most of the guys were, just a button-down and slacks. Even more curious, he seemed to be staring at me. I looked down to my corsage again, feeling uncomfortable as Jared tugged me from the room. I couldn't say I ever got used to the lingering looks people gave me due to my condition.

Evan was following us, but I wasn't sure how he managed that feat since he never once came up for air while sucking face with Stacey.

I looked to Jared in confusion when I realized we weren't heading to the parking lot. He smiled mischievously in reply and pushed me into an open elevator, backing me against the far wall as his lips descended on mine. This wasn't one of our chaste kisses; it had fire. A resulting heat started deep in my belly. I was vaguely aware of Evan in the background, saying something about taking the next one, but he wasn't really the object of my attention.

When the short elevator ride was over, he led me out to the hallway. At the end, a sign posted next to the door read Honeymoon Suite. My eyes widened, but I kept quiet. Part of me was thrilled as much as the rest of me was wary.

It had been a little over four months since I told him about the twins. Four months of chaste kisses and hand holding. Four months of study dates, movie dates, and dinner dates. Jared had wanted to put on the brakes and really slow things down, get to know each other. Properly date me before we took it to the next level, or back to the next level.

I didn't mind it, but I didn't feel it was necessary either. I was all-in with him. He was supportive and sweet. He took care of me, attended all the doctor appointments, and genuinely seemed to be excited about being a teenage dad. It was kind of mind-blowing. I trusted him from the moment he didn't freak out about the babies. He wasn't out to hurt me.

The music wasn't bad either. He played for me and the babies often. That was when he spoke to my soul and made every bit of stress just melt away.

Was he trying to give me the traditional prom night package deal? I kicked that thought to the curb when I realized I didn't care. I was horny as hell and only had eyes for him.

He opened the door. Stepping back, he urged me forward with a hand on the small of my back. A trail of rose petals led down a short hallway into the bedroom. I followed it, expecting it to end at the bed, but instead it curved around the corner. Rose petals were scattered atop the bed, but curiosity had me pursuing the trail.

It stopped at a closed door. I looked back to Jared. He had a small smile playing on his lips.

"Go ahead," he urged. "Open it."

I gasped. There had to be at least a hundred lit candles in all shapes and sizes on every available surface. In the center of a large bathroom sat a huge tub filled with bubbles to the brim. Relaxing blues music played softly from a small radio on the vanity.

Jared came up behind me and wrapped his arms around me, his woody, earthy scent surrounding me. He'd done this for me.

I melted into him and could feel tears welling in my eyes, so I forced myself to breathe. Damn pregnancy hormones had me blubbering like a fool over everything.

"I thought you could use some pampering after being on your feet for so long. Consider it payment for coming with me tonight. I know you didn't want to."

I started to protest, but he stopped me with a finger over my lips.

"And it gives me an excuse to get you naked."

Goose bumps broke out over my skin as his hands retreated. Brushing my hair over my shoulder, he placed a kiss where my neck and shoulder met. Until that moment, I wasn't convinced I believed in romantic love, but I was beginning to believe I was in love with him. Even though I wasn't quite sure what that meant.

He slowly unzipped my dress. It fluttered to the ground at my feet. I shivered in anticipation. My skin tingled under his touch as he turned me to face him. His eyes grazed over my body.

"You're so fucking beautiful. Since I've met you, all I have to do is hear your name, but seeing you like this…" He closed his eyes, breathing deeply. "I'll wait, because this—" He gestured to the bath. "—is for you to relax. But after that, I can't be held responsible for my actions. Every cell in my body is screaming at me to have my way with you."

My breath caught in my throat. "I don't want to wait," I wheezed out.

I didn't have time to think before his mouth was on mine. We were pulling off our remaining clothes. It was clumsy. Teeth clashed as we stumbled and tripped our way to the bed. I'd never wanted anything more in my life. And that made it all the more beautiful.

We broke apart as I tugged his undershirt over his head. "It's only my second time. Third, if you want to get technical. Go easy on me. I might not be able to last that long," he said.

I just stared at him as the realization of what he was saying settled in. I took a deep breath to cut off the tears that threatened. He gathered me to him, pushing my hair away from my face.

"I love you, Maddie," he said, as he brushed his thumb

over my cheek. "I have since the moment I met you."

As he searched my eyes, I searched his. I could see the sincerity there, lying underneath insecurity and hope. I'd made him doubt when I pushed him away. Now he was putting everything on the line, hoping for a chance at what he wanted. I could kick myself for causing him pain. The thought of the time wasted between us. The dam finally broke as the one thing that I hadn't dared to hope for was just made true—someone loved me.

"I love you, too, Jared," I croaked, and I felt the rightness in those words.

My limbs felt like jelly as I stood in the hotel shower. I watched, mesmerized, as my belly distorted with the movement of tiny hands and feet. The doctors told me because they were twins, they'd come early. We left the sex a surprise for the birth, but I just knew they were going to be little boys. I loved them already. They were everything. My family.

I shut the water off and stood there, my hands pressed to my skin, unable to stop the smile that was making my face ache. I had to show Jared. It wasn't the first time they were moving, but they were exceptionally active this morning.

Jared laid some clothes on the counter after collecting the mountain of candles into a huge cardboard box and taking it down to the truck. He also informed me that there was a day-after-prom party at the lake and that we were just going to chill out and have a relaxing day of fun in the sun.

When I got out of the shower, I was floored—Jared had brought my prepregnancy bikini instead of my maternity swimsuit. I put the bikini on and stormed out of the bathroom.

Jared was sitting on the bed watching TV. He looked up

and froze. I placed my hands on my hips and gave him my most pissed-off look.

"What the hell were you thinkin'?" I demanded.

At that, he rolled over on the bed in laughter.

"Oh, my God," he said, words muffled by the pillow. "You should see your face."

He didn't stop laughing. I searched for the nearest thing, which was the TV remote, and threw it at him.

"It's not funny. Please tell me you brought my maternity swimsuit?"

His face scrunched in confusion. "What in the hell is a maternity swimsuit?"

"A swimsuit for pregnant women, dumbass. Pregnant women don't wear bikinis."

His shoulders were still shaking as he peeked up at me. "It looks hot."

At my not-amused expression, he buried his head back in the pillow to laugh some more.

"Whatever," I huffed and went back to retrieve the sundress and flip-flops he also brought.

Once dressed, I stormed out of the room, slamming the door behind me. He could finish packing up our stuff by himself.

Down in the lobby, I found Evan and Stacey. Evan was downing a muffin from the continental breakfast table, but one look at me and he almost choked.

"What's up with you? You look ready to go on a murder spree."

"Nothing. I don't want to talk about it."

"Tell me," Evan said as he started massaging my shoulder nearest him.

"He brought me a bikini to wear," I mumbled.

"He what?"

"He brought me a fucking bikini, okay? If he had told me about any of this, I could've given him my maternity suit..." I turned to Evan.

His face was turning red, and his shoulders heaved up and

down.

"Are you laughing?" I asked.

He folded over in laughter.

I looked to Stacey. "What's with boys laughing about this?"

"It's not that funny." She shrugged. "I've no clue."

"Spill it, Ev. What the fuck are you guys going on about?"

"I can't tell…"

I shot my hand out and twisted his nipple with every bit of strength I had. He grappled to get away, but I wasn't budging.

"Oww, oww… okay, okay, mercy."

I stopped and stared at him. "Out with it, asshole."

"Fine, Nic bet him a hundred dollars that he couldn't get you to wear a bikini today."

"Then you're on my shit list, too, for not stopping him."

"Maddie, is it that big—" He stopped abruptly when I picked up his muffin and threw it smack in the middle of his forehead. Blueberry juices dotted his face, and I wanted to laugh, but I didn't want him to get the wrong idea.

That was the downside to my relationship with these guys. I wasn't just a girlfriend, like Stacey, or a piece of ass, like Robin. I was one of the guys. I just happened to have female parts. They pranked me just like they did each other. I let out an exasperated groan and stood.

"Fucking boys! I'll get y'all back for this. You'll pay. Maybe not today, but you'll pay."

The ride to the lake was mostly silent. After Jared figured out I wasn't speaking to him, he stopped trying to engage me, though at the party, he didn't leave my side much, either. We met up with the other guys from the football team and some of their dates. Jared kept next to me the entire time. I let him because I wasn't that mad, but he still needed to be punished.

I was just biding my time. We were sitting on the tailgate of his truck when Nic arrived with his parents' Jet Ski in tow.

My eyes widened, and I lit up like a kid on Christmas morning. I loved riding the Jet Ski. I started to get up to see if I could ride when Jared tugged me back.

"Where are you going?" he asked softly.

"I wanna ride the Jet Ski," I stated, shrugging him off.

"I don't think that's a good idea. I don't want you to get hurt." His brow furrowed. He motioned to my stomach. "Besides the doctor said you should take it easy."

"I've ridden that Jet Ski lots of times, and I've never gotten hurt. I'll be okay. And the doctor also said that we're past the danger point and the babies'll be fine if they're born now. It's not a big deal."

"Maddie... just don't, please," he said, his frustration becoming apparent on his face. "Besides, you don't have anything to wear in the water anyway."

"What do you mean? I'm wearing a bikini." I narrowed my eyes at him. "You're perfectly aware of that."

"Maddie, I'm sorry. It was a stupid bet. I thought at worst it would be funny. Now that I've seen it, you certainly can't parade around in that. Pregnant women are hot. You're hotter than most. The guys don't need to see that." He tugged me between his legs and kissed my forehead, letting out a breath.

I wanted to melt into him and stay there, but then it clicked. I wasn't comfortable walking around, displaying my pregnant belly in that bikini, but I was stubborn enough to do it just to watch him squirm. I backed away from him, holding his eyes as I slowly pulled my dress up and over my head. I tossed it on the tailgate next to him, then gave him my best mischievous smirk.

His eyes widened. He swallowed heavily. I knew I had him.

I turned around and sauntered to Nic, swaying my hips as much as I still could. Nic had finished unloading the Jet Ski into the water and was walking up the lakeshore when he spotted me. He was frozen in place watching me approach. When I was directly in front of him, I pulled back my arm and delivered a punch to his gut. He folded over.

"That was for thinking up this stupid bet."

"Worth it," he wheezed.

"Fucking idiots, the lot of you," I grumbled. "Where's the life jackets?"

"What?" he asked, still straining to catch his breath.

"Life jacket?"

"You can't ride like that." He motioned to my belly, and I rolled my eyes to the heavens.

"I can and I will."

"You're not gonna listen to reason, are you?" He squinted at me with one eye open.

I shook my head, and he sighed wearily.

"I'm not stupid, Nic. It's not like I'm going out there to do tricks and hop waves. I just want to drive around the lake and be out on the water for a bit. There's nobody else out there right now. The water is calm. The babies'll be fine. I'll be fine."

"Fine. I'm going out with you then."

I shrugged and followed him to his truck.

We had been out on the lake, just coasting around in lazy circles, for about thirty minutes when it hit me like a kick to the gut. All the muscles in my belly clenched up, and pain rolled over me like a tidal wave. I gasped and let up on the throttle.

Nic leaned forward. "You okay?"

I nodded, still unable to speak. We floated there in the middle of the lake, rocking with the gentle sway of the water. I felt a pop that seemed to reverberate through my body, and clear fluid gushed from between my legs.

"Oh, God. My water just broke."

Nic jerked and flew back, falling over the edge of the Jet Ski. The Jet Ski lurched to the side violently, and I clung to it, trying not to fall over myself.

"What are you doing? We need to go to the hospital. Get

back on."

"Fuck, no. I'm not touching your baby juices, that's disgusting."

"Nicoli Lorenzo Gallo, stop being a fucking idiot and get up here now," I said through clenched teeth as another contraction rocked me. I waited until it subsided. "Just splash some water up here and get on."

"Uh, no. You couldn't pay me to touch that thing without it being bleached and scrubbed first."

"That's just stupid. It's not like I just dumped Ebola all over the seat—it's just amniotic fluid. It won't kill you. Now hurry up."

"I'd rather swim."

I looked to the shore. It would take him a good ten minutes to swim that far, but it served him right for being stupid.

"Fine. Have fun with that."

I started the Jet Ski back up and eased it away from him, then headed back slowly to the shore. When I banked the Jet Ski, I breathed through another contraction before climbing off and trying to drag it up the beach farther. Evan saw me from where he sat with Stacey and rushed over to help.

"Is that his payback?" He smirked, nodding his head toward Nic, who was still swimming to shore.

"No. You done with that?" I pointed to the red Solo cup clutched in his hand. He tipped his head back and drained the rest, before handing it to me. I used it to pour lake water over the seat while Evan watched me curiously. When I bent over with my hands on my knees to breathe through the next contraction, his eyes widened.

"It's time?"

"Ready or not," I said with a nervous smile, taking off the life jacket and throwing it on the seat of the Jet Ski.

Evan's face lit up, and he wrapped an arm around my back, walking me up the shore to the truck.

Jared was deep in conversation with some of his teammates, still sitting on the tailgate of his truck.

"Hey, asshole," Evan shouted at him. "It's show time."

He looked up, saw us, and jumped off the truck, knocking over a beer. I saw it almost as if it were in slow motion as he turned and grabbed the nearest piece of cloth to clean it up, which just happened to be my dress.

"Jared, don't—" I started, but it was too late. My blood boiled. I shrugged Evan off and stormed toward him. Jared looked from me to his hand, and I could see the moment it registered what he had done. He started laughing, the bastard.

"I'm gonna rip your balls off and shove them down your throat," I shouted and quickly waddled after him. "You'll never have children again."

He took off, hiding on the other end of his truck, still laughing at me.

When I reached the end of the truck, I stopped and clung to the truck bed as another contraction hit me. Jared stopped laughing and took a step toward me, but at that moment I wanted to kill him, and I'm pretty sure he could see it on my face because he stopped in his tracks.

"You're a dead man, Wilson," I panted out as the ability to breathe came back to me. I took off after him, but he kept to the opposite side of the truck.

"Looks like y'all are both going to end up in the hospital," Mike interjected. Everyone laughed. We probably did look like fools, but I didn't care.

"Shit, this's an awesome start to the birth video." Evan chuckled, and I noticed he had pulled out the video camera that he had on standby for when I went into labor.

"Watch out, Jared. She has a mean right cross," Nic added as we continued to circle the truck. I hadn't noticed him join us, but Jared was doing a good job of keeping my focus.

"Maddie, I'm sorry." Jared tried to placate me. "I wasn't thinking."

"You're damn right. All you do is think with your dick. I can't go to the hospital like this, and I sure as hell can't go in smelling like beer. Stop laughing, fucker."

"Come on, Mads. You gotta admit it's pretty funny," he

said with a wink. "I love you."

I couldn't help the grin fighting for control of my face. That was the thing about Jared—he was always so happy and carefree. He was like standing near the sun; you forgot about all the dark parts of life. Just reveled in the warmth and glow.

"That's not fighting fair." I doubled over again and groaned loudly.

He bolted around the car to my side.

"Nut check!" I shouted as I smacked the back of my hand over his manly parts. I stood up and laughed.

"Who's not fighting fair now?" he asked breathlessly, grabbing himself and falling to his knees.

Everyone was rolling in laughter. I got a few high fives.

"Goddammit, you're fucking awesome, Ned," Nic said as he ruffled my hair. "Sure you won't ditch this tool for me?"

"I'm sure," I said dryly and groaned at the tightening muscles and repressed ability to breathe as a real contraction hit me.

Nic stopped laughing and helped me into the truck while Evan helped Jared off the ground. "We'll be right behind you," he said, and then we were off.

Chapter Nine

Now

As I wake to the quiet hum of my fan, I'm aware of the sunlight streaming through my windows. Just the sight of it makes me cringe. *I shouldn't have drank so much last night.*

It's the day after my birthday, which means today we drive home to visit family—both dead and alive. It's not my favorite day of the year. The only blessing this morning is that it's oddly quiet.

I stumble out of bed and step into the warm steam of the shower. The hot water feels good. I stay there for longer than needed, letting the water cascade over my skin. When I'm done, I grab my robe and sit down to towel-dry my hair because I'm not sure I can take the loud whir of my hair dryer. Then I brush my teeth and head downstairs, where the aroma of bacon permeates the air. My stomach growls fiercely.

Halfway down the stairs, I can hear the strains of laughter and the murmur of happy conversations coming from the kitchen, and it brings a smile to my face. I step through the archway to find Evan and two eleven-year-old identical twin girls, Cora and Cat, manning the stove. Chloe stands at the coffee pot. Holly, sitting at the kitchen table, is corralling runaway Cheerios for her three-year-old daughter, Hope.

"Stop, that's enou— Look what you did," Cat whines as she gouges her skinny elbow into Evan's side. "You're cleaning that up, mister."

He chuckles. "Oh no, I agreed to supervise this venture. I didn't agree to clean jack shit."

"Uh-uh. You poured that shit down the side of the pan. I told you to stop. You did it, you clean it," Cat says, smacking her spatula on the counter and tossing her long, black hair over her shoulder.

Chloe finishes pouring her coffee and turns in my direction, freezing. I hold my index finger to my mouth with a restrained grin. She smirks and turns to sit at the table with Holly. No one else has noticed me, yet.

"That's the law of the land, Uncle Ev. You mess it up, you clean it up," Cora says in defense of her sister. She doesn't turn from the griddle filled with bacon in front of her, but her shoulders are shaking with silent laughter.

"Et tu, Brute?" Evan clutches his chest dramatically and stumbles back a few steps.

"Oh, Lord. The old man's having a heart attack," Cora says. As she turns to face him, I can see the mischievous smirk playing on her lips.

"Maybe it's a stroke. He *is* speaking all garbled," Cat says, stepping to her sister's side. She taps her bottom lip as she looks Evan over. "Doesn't he seem shorter? Isn't that what happens when you get old?"

"Yeah, and they start getting all flabby. I don't suppose you've been skipping gym time, have you, Uncle Ev?" Cora asks. Her wolf-like blue eyes narrow, so much like her father's.

"No—"

Cat gasps. "Oh, poor guy. Is that a gray hair? Time's catching up already? It's okay. We can clean up your mess since you're obviously getting too feeble to do it."

Holly blurts out a laugh. "Looks like your minions are turning on you, Evan."

Evan curses as he grabs the pan off the stove just as

smoke starts curling from a burnt pancake and tosses it in the sink while grumbling "...just like your mother."

Cora returns to her task, removing cooked bacon from the griddle.

Cat walks over to Evan and wraps her skinny arms around his waist. "It's okay, Uncle Ev. We still love you, even if you're old and decrepit."

"I'm not—"

I burst out laughing. I can't hold it in anymore. Everyone turns to face me with mixed expressions of shock, maybe even a little fear. I shake my head in amusement.

"See, we'd be done already," Cat whines. "Now the surprise is ruined. Get your act together, old man." She punches Evan's shoulder.

"Me?" Evan counters in mock outrage, rubbing his shoulder like it hurt. "If you would've just been a good little minion—"

"Children, children, let's stop with the bickering now. Okay?" I interject.

"See! I'm a child. I'm not old." Evan fake pouts.

I look to Holly and Chloe as I walk to the fridge to grab some orange juice. "You two are supposed to be keeping these kids in line." I hook my thumb over my shoulder in the direction of the three stooges.

"Uh-uh. I've got my hands full with this one," Holly defends, chasing another Cheerio little Hope drops. "The twins and the man-child will just have to arm wrestle their differences out. Not my problem."

Just then, I hear a squeal behind me. I turn as Evan hoists Cat over his shoulder and moves to the open area of the kitchen near the archway. He starts spinning while smacking her butt. "Say it," he demands.

Cat is giggling and squirming to get free. "Okay, okay. You're not old."

"And..." he prompts as he smacks her again.

"Owwwww! Okay, fine," she shouts between giggles as he tickles her relentlessly. "Oh, young, handsome lord and master. I've sworn fealty as your minion. I'm sorry for my betrayal," she drones the line she has said many times in her life.

He deposits her back on the ground, pats her head and ruffles her hair, earning a scowl. "See, there's a good li'l minion. Now, run along and finish our feast preparations."

I turn back to Holly and Chloe, who are barely containing their mirth, and join them at the table. A warm pair of hands gently squeeze my shoulder. I look up to find Evan's hazel eyes sparkling. He bends down and kisses the corner of my mouth.

"How's the rejection artist faring this morning?" he whispers in my ear, then flops into the chair next to mine in an arrogant, lazy sprawl.

He doesn't break eye contact. I know what he's doing— he's gauging my reaction, trying to read me and see how much damage my ego took, and how much of a mess he might have to handle.

I bite back the knee-jerk groan and look back at him with my defenses down. They're always down for him, my best and oldest friend on the planet. I thread my fingers with his and give him a reassuring squeeze.

The words *I'm fine* are on the tip of my tongue, but die instantly as I turn back to face the rest of my friends. Behind them, on the sideboard table lies a single blood-red calla lily. It's tied to a rolled-up piece of paper with a short length of black silk ribbon.

"Who did that?" My voice squeaks as the mounting pressure in my chest clamps down.

My eyes dart to everyone in the room. They all look confused, so I wave my hand wildly toward that thing—the flower—in the center of that table. One by one, they all confirm my worst fear—they had nothing to do with it.

"Don't touch it," I rasp out and move to the phone to make a call.

Thirty minutes later, Holly and Chloe have taken the kids to Holly's apartment above my garage. Evan sits in the front room watching me pace the floor like a caged tiger. He hasn't said a word since I got off the phone, and I'm afraid to look at him because I know I'll see anger. I just can't deal with that over the violent storm of emotions raging inside me.

I answer the knock on the door, and Detective Martinez strolls in. He looks around the foyer and whistles under his breath.

"It's been a while since I've been in this house." He draws his focus back to me. "You said on the phone you had something of concern to show me?"

I nod and close my eyes as a wave of forgotten memories flows over me. Detective Martinez isn't much older than I am, maybe five to ten years. He's average height, average build. He has classic Hispanic features: olive-toned skin, dark eyes, dark hair with a hint of gray at the temples. It's been years since we were last in the same room. I motion for him to follow me and lead him to the kitchen where the flower and note still sit untouched.

"Has anyone here handled this?" he asks, his narrowed eyes glued to the flower. When I don't answer, he turns to look at me.

I shake my head because I still can't speak. It took all I had to get what little I could to him over the phone.

He snaps a few pictures with his phone and then pulls blue latex gloves and evidence bags out of his pocket. He puts on the gloves and carefully unties the ribbon. He places the ribbon and flower into separate bags and then unrolls the paper before sliding it into another bag. After he zips it up, he reads the note. His brows draw together as he studies it.

I watch with apprehension. His silence is making this whole situation harder. I hold out my hand, silently asking to read it. He hesitates but hands it over anyway.

```
Nice to hear you sing again. I'm
watching after you.
```

The message is typed in an uneven font that looks like the product of an old-fashioned typewriter. My hand starts to shake so badly I almost drop the note. Evan takes it from my hand to read it, as well. He curses.

Detective Martinez clears his throat. "I'd like to speak with your security team to see if any gaps in their routine would give us a window when this could've been left here. And I'll need to look at your video feed."

"I don't have a security team anymore." My voice croaks; I clear my throat and finish. "I let them go about six months ago. I hadn't had any threats, and the media buzz died down. I didn't think I'd anything to worry—"

Evan cuts me off with a curse. "Maddie, they never found out who was sending the flowers the first time, and like it or not, your name's still out there. People know who you are. You can't just drop your security." He breathes deeply, trying to rein in his anger. "Why didn't you talk to me about this?"

"Because you were in Afghanistan at the time, and I didn't think it was a big deal."

"Well, I'm calling a private security firm, then you're hiring them." He looks at Detective Martinez. "She'll have a team in place this week. Until then, I'll be with her."

Detective Martinez nods. "Can you get the video footage for me?"

"Sure, follow me," Evan says. Before he clears the archway, he turns back to me. "Don't go anywhere. Me and you are gonna have a little chat when I'm done."

My eyes fall to the floor, and I swallow heavily. He's right. Normally, I'd bristle at his bossiness, but not this time.

I'm in my study, going over the latest P&L sheets for the studio and record label when I hear the front door slam. It's Monday, and I didn't go into the office, but that wasn't necessarily my decision alone.

"Mom, we're home. Where are you?" Cat calls out. Her voice echoes in the foyer.

"I'm in the study."

Moments later, two giggling girls stumble into my office. They have their dad's wavy black hair and blue eyes, but the rest is all me. They're, quite simply, the most beautiful things I've ever laid eyes on.

"What're you doing?" Cora asks.

"Nothing that can't be put aside. What's up?"

I shut my laptop and shuffle the papers aside as the girls plop down in the chairs across from me. They look at each other before turning to me. I perk up, knowing they want to talk.

"How was the first day of school?" I ask. I think no matter how much time has passed, I'm always going to worry about how they're adjusting.

They look at each other before Cat answers with a shrug. "The usual."

"Except for Tweedle Dumb."

"And Tweedle Dumber."

"Why do we have guards again?" Cora asks.

I know I can't escape this conversation any longer. "Because the Flower Guy is back again. That's what we found Saturday morning."

Their faces fell instantly.

"Oh…" Cora says as she swallows.

"I'm sorry, Mom. That really sucks."

"It's not your fault—nothing to be sorry about. I'm just sorry you have to go through this again." I close my eyes, wishing things were different for them. I just want them to have a normal childhood. One without stalkers and security details. It's times like these that I feel regret for my choices in life.

"Did you run into Josh?" I ask Cora, looking to lighten the mood.

"Yes, she did," Cat supplies, nudging her sister's knee. Cora blushes scarlet. "It was so funny. We were coming out of the locker room after gym class—you know, where the stairs lead down to the cafeteria? Anyway, she slipped halfway down and slid down the stairs like some cartoon character that stepped on a banana peel."

"My ass's still sore, both literally and figuratively."

"Yeah, and to top it off, she lands directly in front of Josh. His buddies even laughed at her—I think he was, too, but I couldn't see his face when I was coming down the stairs. She was redder than she is now."

Cat folded over in laughter, and I'd a hard time keeping my own in check. It wouldn't do to laugh at my girl.

"So... what did he say?" I ask, trying to move past the embarrassment.

"Nothing really." Cora shrugs. "He did laugh at me. Then he just helped me up. He was turning purple trying not to laugh more because he could tell it was pissing me off."

Cat is my loud-mouthed, brash girl. She's smart and fearless. People are drawn to her like moths to a flame. She can also be a bit ruthless, brutal in her candidness. Cora is the strong, silent type. She always seems a bit shy, except around family, but I know that she's the instigator, the brains behind the operation. She's calculating and can form plans to rival even the best chess master. I pity the fool that ever tries to take my twins on. Together, they're a force to be reckoned with.

"And?" I supply, waiting for the real news.

"He asked if I wanted to go to the movies this weekend. On Saturday. At five to be exact."

"He did!" Cat says. "And you have to let her go, please.

Josh is the hottest guy in school. This places us at the top of the social pyramid this year. It's a coup. Maggie Hausberger thinks that he'd obviously go for her since she's captain of the cheerleaders this year. But that's not happening on my watch. I won't let those fake Barbie blondes take over my school. Plus, it's not like she won't be chaperoned—one of the Tweedles will be with her. Come on, mom."

I smile slyly. "Of course. Did you think I'd say no? Cora, you're a smart girl. I trust you to do the right thing. And if you don't already know what that is, then I've failed you as a parent already."

Some might say I overindulge the girls, but I haven't always been a perfect parent. I had them too young and made a lot of stupid decisions. Their lives haven't been normal by anyone's definition. Growing up on tour buses, traveling the country, homeschooling with private tutors... it's been hard on them.

Cat grins at Cora. "Told you."

Cora's face lights up, and she dashes around my desk and into my arms.

"God, Mom. Have I told you lately that you're the coolest mom ever? Because you are and I love you so much."

"Okay, okay. I already said you could go. No need to butter me up further."

"Actually..."

"There's one more thing..."

"There's this new girl at school, and she's freakin' gorgeous—"

"—and awesome."

"We really like her."

"And we want to ask her to stay the night on Friday."

"You'll love her."

"Please say yes."

I laugh heartily. *Like I said, I pity the fool.* "Okay, but—" I start to say.

"Yes!"

"You won't regret this."

Why do I get the feeling that I will?

"Her name is Audra, and she already said yes."

"And her dad will drive us home from school on Friday so he can meet you when he drops her off," Cat says.

Cora's sitting on the edge of her seat, biting her lower lip. That's when I know I've been played, but I can't begrudge them. I created these monsters.

Chapter Ten

Then

Crying interrupted my reverie as I sat in my room, mulling over the future. Jared was leaving in a few days. He'd already signed a six-year contract with the Army before we'd met, following his father's footsteps to join Special Forces. A fact I only found out shortly after telling him about the twins. I hurried across the hall to the nursery.

It was Catherine Rose making all the fuss. Her swaddle had come loose, and her little arms were thrashing around her tiny red face. She was the little troublemaker of the two. I cradled her and she quieted down, making sucking sounds as she tried to eat her fist. *Hungry.*

Offering her my breast, I made soothing cooing sounds as I wrapped her blankets back around her little arms. I walked to the other crib to check on little Coraline Lily. Tingles ran down my spine as the milk let down. The other little angel was still fast asleep, and I thanked my lucky stars. They usually wanted to feed around the same time, and to try to juggle them both without an extra set of hands was difficult.

I sat down in the rocker as she continued to feed. Motherhood was rough, and I'd only been at it for a little over two months. There were days I wanted to cry. I thanked God when we finally graduated. That the babies were born only two weeks before graduation was a small blessing. Classes were pretty much wrapped up by then, and I only had a few final exams to complete. I'm not sure if I would've finished school if I'd had them earlier.

"I thought I heard someone fussing," Diana said as she breezed into the room. She leaned over the occupied crib.

Diana had been a godsend. I honestly thought Jared's parents would hate me for ruining his future. At the very least, I thought they'd look at me as the white-trash girl from the wrong side of town that was completely irresponsible. They hadn't, though. They hadn't been anything other than supportive, inviting me into their home to help me juggle the twins. I already loved them.

"Cat was hungry," I said. "I expect Cora to wake up any minute."

"She's already awake. Aren't you, Lily Pad?" Diana cooed as she picked up the other precious bundle. She gently rocked the baby, staring down into her little face with such love it made me want to cry. "You ready for the other one, Mama?" Her gaze tracked to me.

I balanced Cat on one arm and shoved the nursing pillow under her little body, adjusting her to make room for Cora at the other breast. I got another wave of relief as little Coraline latched on and began to feed. I leaned my head back on the chair and closed my eyes.

"Do you have any plans for today?" Diana asked in a soft voice.

"Other than this every couple of hours, no," I answered, opening one eye. She smiled, still entranced by the babies.

"You're doing great, you know?"

My eyes met hers. "Huh?"

"You just get this lost look every once in a while," she clarified. "Like you're scared that you're going to do something wrong. But you're doing great. None of us have the answers, and being older doesn't mean that you know any more about what you're doing than anyone else."

"Thank you," was all I could think to say.

"I should be thanking you," Diana said, her eyes getting watery. "I couldn't have asked for anything better than these precious gifts. Anyway, Jared's down in the music room, but I think he was planning something for you guys today. You know since—" She cut herself off, offering me a sad smile.

Cat unlatched with a soft pop as her tiny body went limp with sleep. Diana gathered her up and started patting her back gently until she burped. Cora followed close behind her. We put them back to bed and tiptoed out of the room, careful not to destroy the rare quiet time.

With nothing else to do, I decided to see what Jared was up to. Down the stairs at the front of the house, in what was meant to be a formal living room, was where they kept a baby grand piano. There were various other musical instruments, all of which Jared knew how to play. His level of musical talent amazed me more and more every day.

As I got closer to the archway leading to the room, I could hear the soft melodic sounds of the piano playing a melancholy tune. It was heartbreakingly beautiful. It wasn't any written piece, just notes that Jared's fingers found as he let the music take over. He played for me often.

"When are you going to start writing this stuff down?" I asked. "Seriously, the world needs your music." I sat next to him on the piano bench and rested my head on his shoulder.

He wouldn't answer me just yet. He had to find a stopping point before his mind would process the question. Eventually, the notes slowed and tapered off. He turned and kissed my forehead.

"I don't know. I can't stop long enough to write down the notes. If I do, I lose the melody. I've tried—I've just never been able to write. Not one of my many talents, I suppose." He offered me a soft smile, and my heart skipped a beat. "I've a present for you." He pointed across the piano.

Leaning up against the wall was a black Fender Stratocaster with a gray paisley print. Tied around the neck was a big red satin bow.

I looked at him, confused. "You bought me a guitar?"

He grinned. "Yeah, it's your favorite. Plus, these hands—" He lifted my hand to his mouth and kissed my knuckles, smiling that devastating smile at me. "These long beautiful fingers are perfect for playing guitar. There's more," he said as he jumped up, still holding my hand, and dragged me across the room.

Next to the stunning guitar, on the floor, was a rectangular guitar case full of music tools and paraphernalia.

"I got everything you need to play, plus extra strings and stuff. And you remember that blues album we were listening to the other day that you liked?"

"Uh-huh," I drew out hesitantly, not sure where he was going with this.

"That guitar player's name is Stevie Ray Vaughn." His eyes were wide with excitement. "He lives in Austin. Normally doesn't teach guitar, but he and my dad go way back. I called and got him to agree to give you lessons in the fall. When you go there for school."

"Are you serious?" I flung myself toward him and threw my arms around his neck. "That sounds amazing. Plus, if I learn to play and read music and stuff, when you come home on leave, I can write up the music you make. That would be so awesome."

"I love you." His voice was gentle as his thumb brushed over my cheek.

"I love you, too."

He smiled a huge, bright smile, and I couldn't help myself. My lips crashed into his as I tried to say everything for which I had no words. I never thought it was possible to love someone so much. He and the girls had become my everything. The thought of him leaving was unbearable.

"Dance with me," I urged.

"Now?" His eyebrows drew together. "There's no music."

"You don't need music when you have it in your soul. Sing to me."

I was thrilled when I found out that he had been taught basic ballroom dancing for his dad's many formal military functions. I loved to dance.

He started singing. I rested my head on his shoulder and closed my eyes as he led me around the small space to the melody he sang. A contented smile graced my face. My heart was so full.

Now

It's Friday, and I've been cleaning every square inch of my house since early this morning. I'm restless and agitated. I don't know why I thought this creep's interest in me had waned with the end of the band. I deluded myself.

I was stupid—too stupid—because something could've happened to the girls.

Evan found a security company, and we hired guards for the girls, but it takes time to assign guys willing to move in and become full-time protection detail. Until then I'm pretty much grounded, and Evan's out today following the girls and Audra's mystery dad as an added security measure.

Standing in the kitchen, I throw the sponge into the sink with a strangled scream between clenched teeth. I need to relax. The girls will be home soon with their new friend. I walk to my study and stare at my wall of guitars, contemplating which one I need right now.

My eyes catch the acoustic in the corner of the room, cradled by a stand on the floor. Jared's guitar. The one he carried with him all the time when we first met. He left it for Cat, which is why it doesn't hang on the wall with the rest of my collection.

I grab it with the intention of going to my favorite spot to play—outside on the patio. Watching the water in the pool calms me, centers me.

I open the door. Shrieking, I fall back, clutching my chest. The pool boy is standing there with his fist raised as if to knock on a door that's no longer there. He grins and drops his hand.

"Umm, hi," he says.

Caleb is the neighbors' kid. I think he's a senior in high school this year, but I'm not sure. My girls have a crush on him. They've had one since he moved in next door, three years ago. He's been cleaning neighborhood pools for as long as that.

"Shit, Caleb. You scared me half to death," I say, righting myself. "Did you forget your keys to the pool house again?"

His lips tip up into a smirk as his eyes roam over my body. I realize I'm still wearing booty shorts and the form-fitting tank top that I clean the house in. He slowly shakes his head.

"No," he says, and I swear his voice is deeper, husky even. "It's the fifteenth."

"Oh, sorry. I completely spaced… Hold on. Be right back."

I leave him at the open door, setting down the guitar. I can't believe I forgot that his payment is due today. I only hope I have the cash on hand. I rummage my purse and thankfully produce the needed funds without having to resort to begging him to take a check.

I turn back hastily and nearly slam into his chest. I jerk back and look up at him. His eyes are dilated, and he's too close. I take a step back and then another as he follows me, mirroring my movements with an almost predator-like slowness. Unease settles in my gut. My muscles tense and move to a defensive position of their own accord.

"Caleb, what're you doing?" My voice hitches, as my back hits the counter, and he places his hands on either side of my hips, trapping me in. My fists clench. The skin across my knuckles are already tight from bruising.

"I turned eighteen last month."

I nod. "Happy belated birthday?"

"You know, you and I've a lot in common," he says as he stares at my breasts, unabashed.

"We do?" I ask, forcing a fake smile.

"You haven't had a guy here, aside from your brothers, since I moved in. You must get very lonely, Miss D."

I'm stunned, and despite the fact that he's a good-looking

kid, I'm no Mrs. Robinson. I've no desire to be in the same line for the opposite sex as my daughters.

"You're too funny," I say, trying to deflect the best way I know how.

Pretend this is a joke. I really hope it is.

I don't want to get in trouble for hurting the neighbors kid, but he probably should back up. I shove his shoulder, trying to move him away. He doesn't move, not an inch. He only grasps my hand and pulls it to his lips. He sucks my index finger into his mouth. My thighs clench, and my eyes widen.

I cannot be getting turned on by this. I need to get laid by an actual man, ASAP.

I twist my wrist out of his grasp and use the heel of my hand to strike the center of his chest. Not full force, but enough to let him know I mean business. He finally stumbles back. His mouth hangs open in shock for only a second before he recovers with a look like a cat that just cornered a mouse.

"I know you're lonely. I can see it in your eyes. Every woman needs to be fulfilled. I can be that person for you. No strings."

I groan and aim for my most stern mother voice as I admonish him. "Caleb, that's *so* not appropriate. My *needs* are none of your business. You *need* to leave."

I grab his arm—which is quite solid—and drag him to the front door. His shoulders slump in defeat. Once I have him on the front porch, I shove the wad of cash into his hand, then slam the door and lock it.

I lean back against the door and slide down as hysterical laughter bubbles up my throat. *Fuck, what is my life becoming?* It's sad. The thought of fucking him repulses me. The fact that the pool boy knows about my dry spell, that it's that obvious, is pathetic. I've never felt this amount of sexual frustration, ever. I don't know what's changed, but it feels... I don't have a word for it.

An image of Dex springs to mind. What it would be like

to have his hands all over me. That little bit's enough to tip the scale and have me seeking relief. I pull my shorts to the side and tentatively run my finger over my seam, imagining what it would feel like if Dex touched me there. I push two fingers inside myself. I close my eyes and moan, seeing those beautiful sea-green eyes. I recall his muscular arms covered in tattoos. I stroke myself over and over, thinking of him and the way tingles lingered on my skin in the wake of his touch. My legs convulse, and my core muscles tighten. I press my thumb to my bundle of nerves and send myself over the edge in a short, quick release that only has me wishing for the real thing.

"Dammit, what am I doing?" I mutter.

I quickly right myself and check the peephole to make sure Caleb isn't still around. I breathe a sigh of relief at the sight of an empty porch and take a step back. I need to get to my music. Wishing there was some work to do on my cars instead, I storm toward the back door, grabbing the guitar I'd abandoned. I lift the strap over my head as I pace the patio. Tuning the guitar quickly, I fall on to the edge of a lounger.

I breathe deeply to calm down. The way I'm feeling, all I want to do is smash my hands into the strings and rip out chords, but I've the wrong guitar for that. There's a storm of emotions swirling through me. I can't make sense of any of them. I pluck a few notes, and my heartbeat starts to slow.

I play a song I've been working on for a few weeks. It's new material. I play and sing, putting my loneliness and frustration into every note, every word. The more I sing the words, the more I realize that this song says everything that my soul, heart, body and mind refuse to communicate to one another.

When I finish, I stare at the gently lapping water of the pool. This is why I love music; it's my therapy. I feel calm, more clear about my decisions.

"I didn't know you played." A deep male voice jolts me. I spring from my seat as I spin to see Dex standing between my two girls.

My heart is racing, and I vaguely register my hands trembling. *Why's he here? How does he know where I live?*

"What're you doing here?" My voice is laced with venom.

The twins, standing next to him, look between Dex and me, confusion stamped on their faces.

"I didn't know this was *your* place," he says as his eyes wander around, taking it all in. "It's impressive. Yet another mystery to add to the list of Maddie."

"You're not answering my question."

"This is Audra's dad," Cora interjects. "You two know each other?"

My mind's still reeling. Dex's the father of my girls' new bestie. Great. Fantastic.

"What the hell, Mom?" Cat asks.

"Cat," I say in a warning tone.

"How do you know him?" Cora questions.

I look to Dex, who has his hand on the shoulder of a gorgeous little girl. There's a similarity in their facial features, but her emerald eyes and red hair must come from her mother. *Can't say I saw that coming.*

"He was my tattoo artist."

"Ooooooh—oh, shit!" Cat exclaims.

"Cat! You're really making me reconsider the language policy in this house. Cut it out."

"It's fine. He lets Audra talk how she wants," Cora supplies. "That's how we met. She dropped her books and papers in the middle of the hall at school and let out the most creative string of curses I've ever heard. I knew then that we'd be best friends forever." She has a brilliant smile on her face, but I recognize the evil mastermind gleam in those eyes.

My girls are around Holly and Chloe too much to not pick up on the tension between *the tattoo artist* and me. She's about to pull something. I need to cut her off right quick.

"Why don't you girls go show Audra your rooms? Get her settled?"

"I know what you're—" Cat starts.

"Cat!" I yell to cut her off.

"Yes, Mommy Dearest. We'll even check her bag for wire hangers while we're at it."

"No wire hangers!" Cora gives her best Joan Crawford impersonation.

I hear a deep chuckle and turn my attention to Dex, who's watching us with amusement. It's a stark contrast from his anger last Friday. The girls start whispering to each other and giggling.

Remembering my manners, I add, "It's nice to meet you, Audra."

"It's nice to meet you too, Mrs. Wilson." Audra says.

I suck in a breath and hold it for a beat, then force a smile. "It's Miss Dobransky. But you can call me Maddie."

"Oh, cool." She smiles broadly, exposing dimples just like her dad's. "Well, thanks for letting me stay the night, Miss Maddie."

"Oh, BTW," Cat says. "We invited Caleb to dinner tonight."

"You should've seen his face light up when I asked," Cora says. "I think he might have a thing for Cat."

Oh, God. I rub at my temples, wishing I had a useful superpower that would solve this. Whatever *this* is. I have no words. We have an open policy about dinners around here. We invite people to join us all the time.

"You should stay for dinner too, Mr. McClellan," Cat adds.

"I'm sure he has—" I start to protest.

"Sounds great," he responds.

And that seals it. Tonight's gonna be awkward as fuck.

When they close the door behind them, I drag my gaze back to Dex. He's standing, back straight, feet apart, and arms crossed over his chest. He has a spellbinding ownership of the space, and fuck if it doesn't turn me on. He drags his gaze over me, starting at my toes and slowly working his way up. My nipples tighten in response. He finally makes eye contact and quirks a questioning brow.

"Is this what you always wear to greet the father of your

kids' friends?"

His question knocks me back into reality. I look down and realize that my hardened nipples are putting on a show through the thin white tank. *Oh, God. Why didn't I think to change earlier?* I cross my arms over my chest.

"Uh, no. This's what I usually wear to clean house. And today I had a rare day off, so I've been cleaning all day. Then the pool boy showed up... and I've just had a lot on my mind... I don't know, I just forgot." I'm rambling, and I can't stop. I'm getting flustered when I never get flustered. I'm not ashamed of my body, and I'm most certainly not shy. Not to mention that I've been on stage in front of way more people in less than this. Plus, I've made my decision about him.

I drop my hands and stand up straight, looking him in the eye. Well, I try at least. His gaze is bouncing over my body. It's quite humorous. "You just find out that I've two daughters and that's the first thing you ask?"

His gaze finally lands on mine. "It's that distracting." His dimple appears with the showing of a smirk.

I don't know whether to laugh or moan at the heat in his eyes. I choke back both. *I need to stop this. Right here. Right now.*

"Look, Dex. I understand I've been giving you mixed signals, at best, and I apologize for that. You should know, what I offered you at the bar is all I'll ever be able to offer you." He raises a hand to stop me, but I shake my head and take a step toward him. "No, let me finish. Because the moment you crossed the threshold of this house, that offer was off the table. Actually, the moment you laid eyes on my girls, it was done. What I do to... meet my needs—" I swallow thickly. "—never crosses over to my family life. Never. You get me? I'm not ever going to be one of those moms who parades a string of boyfriends around in front of her kids. Plus, I haven't exactly been honest with you about who I—"

"I already know who you are," he interrupts, his deep, calm voice resonating in my ears. "In fact, I have a whole file on you, Laine."

No. Please don't let it be him. My toes start tingling. Dizziness sweeps through me. The tingling travels up my body, and I'm unable to move. Black spots invade my vision, and I struggle to take a breath. Dex lunges toward me. I feel weightless as my vision goes black.

Chapter Eleven

Then

When I stepped out of the steamy shower, my body felt more relaxed than it had in weeks. After months apart, while Jared was in basic training, we had just spent the night together. It was everything I'd hoped it would be. We had spent every available moment in each other's arms knowing this was only a brief reprieve.

In a few hours, I'd head back to Texas, and he'd be off to advanced training for Intelligence Analyst and then Special Forces training until sometime early the next year.

I wiped the steam from the hotel bathroom mirror, not recognizing myself. The dark circles that plagued my eyes the past month were gone. I looked happy, glowing even. Our relationship had only grown stronger in the last few months as we wrote letter after letter to each other. Before Jared left, I didn't think I could love him more, but I was wrong. I felt as if my heart would crack open from the fullness.

I ran my hands over my breasts. They were achingly full, which meant I was going to need to go to Diana and John's room and feed the babies soon. The girls were probably awake and in full fuss mode. Knowing Diana, she was trying to pacify them to give us time. That's what we lacked—time.

When I opened the bathroom door, Jared was pacing back

and forth, deep in thought. He didn't even notice me.

He looked different from before basic training. His hair was shaved close to his skull. His muscles were larger and more defined. And the uniform. I never thought I'd be one of those girls to go gaga for a uniform until I saw him decked out from head to toe at his graduation ceremony.

I cleared my throat, and he halted midstride. His bag was already packed and sitting on the bed. My heart plummeted. I knew he was leaving soon, but that made it more real.

"You're gonna wear down the carpet there if you keep that up." I offered him a wan grin, and his shoulders relaxed, but his face didn't change from the frown he wore.

He gathered me in his arms and took a deep breath, squeezing me.

"Hey, you okay?" I asked.

He sighed and kissed my forehead before pulling away. The tension returned to his body.

"Yeah, I'm fine. We need to check on the babies soon."

"I know," I replied, moving to my open suitcase to pull out my clothes.

Jared stood motionless, silent, watching me as I dressed. I probably should've been more bothered by his mood, but knowing we were on a deadline to get him back on post, I felt the same. My heart ached with the thought of letting him go again. I knew we'd be fine. We'd survive this. Summer was almost over, and I'd be starting college soon. It would keep me busy enough that I wouldn't sit around, dwelling on the pain of separation. *We'll be fine.*

"We need to talk," he said.

I froze in the middle of pulling my shirt over my head. When my head breached the collar, he was sitting on the edge of the bed. Elbows on his knees, he was staring at his hands as he wrung them together.

"Okay, so talk," I said, hesitantly.

"It's just—" He paused, taking a deep breath. "I know that once I say what I have to say, there's no taking it back. I know it needs to be said, but I don't—" He cut himself off and sat in silence.

"What are you trying to say, Jared? Just spit it out. You're scaring me."

"I'm trying, Maddie. I just—I think you shouldn't wait for me." He stared at the floor.

"What do you mean?" Dread flooded my body, making my fingers and toes feel numb.

"We both know where this goes from here. I'm going Special Forces, which means if I pass the selection course and go to the Q, we won't see each other at all for the next year, and after that, I'll probably deploy."

"You're breaking up with me?" I asked in disbelief.

"I just think it's best, Maddie. You're only sixteen. You haven't had the chance to experience most of what the world has to offer."

I went on the defensive. "You mean you haven't gotten to fuck other girls?" My stomach dropped. I felt like I was going to throw up.

He rose to his feet. "This isn't about me. I'm doing this for you. Can't you see that?" His eyes welled with tears.

"All I see's a coward, running away from his responsibilities," I said, angry and hurt.

"That's not fair. This plan was in place before I knew about the twins. I can't get out of it. Don't you think I would? This is killing me. I feel like I can't breathe fully without you and the girls."

"Then why? Why do this? Why push me away? You know I'd wait for you an entire lifetime if that's what it took. I love you." The tears broke free from my eyes, flowing down my face.

"I'm not going to marry you and have you end up one of those lonely, bitter military wives. Abandoned at a post, while your husband's overseas. Giving up your life to raise the kids," he said, his voice growing louder. "You're better than that, Maddie. You have so much potential. So much ahead of you."

"Don't do this," I pleaded, reaching for him.

He grasped my cheeks, forcing me to look at him.

"You're so fucking smart, and beautiful, and talented. You have the world at your feet, and I won't let you throw it away for me." His eyes pleaded with me.

"You don't mean this." I shook my head from his grasp and turned away.

"You start college in a few weeks. Your scholarship. Your guitar lessons."

"Stop talking about what I have and tell me why you're taking away the only thing that really matters," I yelled, turning back to him.

"I love you, Maddie. I'll always—"

"Where?" I sobbed.

"What?"

"Where's this love?" I threw my hands up, gesturing wildly around the room. "I can't see it. I'm certainly not feeling it. So, show me, Jared, because actions speak louder than words, and all I'm hearing is that you don't want me."

"It's right here. This. One day you'll have everything you ever wanted out of life, and you'll thank me for pushing you toward it instead of keeping you for myself."

My legs gave out, and I collapsed to the ground as sobs took over. I gasped for breath. The walls were closing in, and I couldn't breathe. I couldn't believe it, didn't want to believe it. Though, it felt real as Jared grabbed his bag and walked out the door, leaving me alone in that hotel room.

Now

"What the fuck did you do to her?" Evan asks in an angry whisper-yell.

"I didn't do anything. I told her that I knew who she was. She fainted. I brought her in here," Dex replies.

"Look at you, making chicks swoon and shit. Tell me you're gonna hit that?"

"Shut up, Marcus!" Dex yells. "If he hits me because you're being a douche, I'm gonna kick *your* ass."

Who the fuck is Marcus?

"Mr. Langford, you need to calm down. I know your record of service for our country. I wouldn't want to charge you with assaulting a police officer."

Is that Detective Martinez? What police officer is Evan about to assault? Confused, I blink my eyes open.

I'm lying on the couch in my living room. The throw blanket is pulled up to my chin, leaving my feet hanging out the end, cold. The world spins around me as I sit up. I take in the four men, who've yet to notice I'm awake.

Evan has Dex pinned against the wall with his forearm across Dex's chest.

Detective Martinez stands near them in a drab suit. Next to him is another man I've never met. Marcus, I presume, is wow. He's a very large, very cut black man with close-cropped hair and a square jawline. A black-and-gray tattoo that looks like flames, or something, peeks out the strained left sleeve of his plain white T-shirt. He also has a word tattooed on the left side of his neck in an elaborate script. I can't read it from across the room.

I start to shove the throw aside and rethink the move as I remember what I'm wearing. I wrap it around my shoulders as I stand and catch Dex's eye. He's the only one facing me. He pushes Evan's arm away and crosses the room toward me, raising a hand as if to touch me. I hedge back, and his arm drops.

"Are you okay?" he asks. "I caught you before your head hit the concrete, but the rest of you?"

"Police officer?" Those are the words repeating in my mind and the only thing I could think to say.

"Yeah, I work undercover, the organized crime unit." Dex lets out a breath and runs his fingers through his hair. "The tattoo artist gig is my cover, though I take other clients, like you, by referral to keep up appearances. Martinez, here, asked the chief if I could be pulled in on this case since it might help with the—well, he has some interesting theories, and I'll let him explain, but you've gotta believe me, I had no idea it was you. Or, I mean, that you were Laine Dobransky. You don't look like the cover of Rolling Stone that they have in your file."

My stomach turns at the mention of that damn cover.

"Well, you do, but it's not immediately obvious," Dex continues. "Your hair is shorter, the red a bit brighter and you have on less clothes and makeup—I'm going to shut up now." He swallows thickly.

Marcus bursts out laughing. "Smooth, real smooth, playa."

My gaze lands on him. "Who're you?"

He clears his throat and stands up a little straighter. "Marcus Lions. I'm his partner." He offers his hand to shake. His hand swallows mine with one of those limp shakes from a guy trying to show he can be gentle with a lady. I'm not impressed.

"And you knew about this?" I direct my question to Evan.

"Yeah. They pulled me in at the school today. Detective Martinez figured I'd be watching the girls. But I know about as much as you."

"How long?" I look back to Dex, trying to keep the anger out of my voice. "How long've you known?"

"Chief pulled me in on Monday. I didn't know before that. The fact that we met before this has more to do with Holly, but I can't discuss the details of that case."

I sigh internally. *Fucking great.* I look to Detective Martinez. His eyes are darting back and forth between Dex and me.

"You care to explain how he—" I gesture to Dex. "—is going to help with my case? Why it's become such high priority that you'd pull in two undercover cops to cover it?"

"I've been thinking this for a while now," Martinez replies. "But I couldn't do anything about it because your stalker went silent. I think your stalking case and my murder case are related."

My whole body tenses at the mention of his *murder case.* My finger itches to snap the rubber band on my wrist, but there are too many eyes on me right now to show any weakness. I take a deep breath and force myself to meet his eyes.

"I've been waiting for the stalker to reappear. And listen, Maddie, we've known each other for a long time. You made my career. They promoted me to detective to handle this case and assigned me to the murder case because of you. These are the only cases I haven't solved. I trust McClellan and Lions to keep you safe. I want to catch this guy and see if he matches my evidence."

"You didn't find anything on the letter left on Saturday?" I ask.

"No, it was clean. This guy's very methodical. It's why we haven't caught him in the eight years I've been on this case. I'm willing to bet this guy has some military background, likely intelligence related. He knows his way around computers and security systems. He's never left even a hint of evidence. So, he's smart. It's not an unlikely assumption either, with your connection to the military." He says the last part while casting a glance in Evan's direction.

"So, you want to have Dex go undercover as my private security?"

"Not exactly," he says, now looking nervous.

I tilt my head, curious, and wait for the explanation.

"The chief only signed off on this plan if we keep his current cover intact. Which means, he'd go undercover as your new boyfriend. And Marcus can work with Miss Holmes."

I cock my head. "Holly? Why does Holly need to be involved?"

"Since Miss Holmes lives on your property and her level of access to you, it's possible that she may encounter the suspect."

"I just don't see why he can't be my security guard. I can't go around pretending he's my boyfriend. It'll complicate things," I protest.

"It would put his cover at risk to pose as your security. Not a lot of tattoo artists moonlight as hired muscle. On the other hand, you've been to his place of employment and gotten a tattoo from him. It's entirely believable that you two met and took an interest in each other. Unless… is there a conflict of interest I should know about?"

"No."

"Yes," I say at the same time as Dex. "His daughter and my daughters are friends."

"Yes, I'm aware." Martinez nods. A little grin tugs at the corner of his lips.

Why does it seem that every male in my life enjoys seeing me in discomfort?

"All the more reason for me to work this case," Dex defends. "If he were to attack the girls while Audra is around, she could get hurt, too."

"Well, then how about the fact that the last time I saw you we ended up trading insults?" I throw back. "I'd say we don't work well together."

"Maddie—" Dex sighs, pinching the bridge of his nose. "I apologize for what was said Friday night. We can move past that. I'm a professional. All I need to do is shadow you for a few days. You introduce me to people you know as your boyfriend, and after we catch the perp, you can tell everyone we broke up."

"Won't we have to make it believable, though?"

"You don't think people will believe that I'm dating you?" he asks, his lopsided smirk revealing that damn dimple.

"Not what I meant," I say as I fight an eye roll. "What about Marcus? Why can't he be my new boyfriend?"

"Maddie, Holly most definitely has a type," Evan says. "And Marcus fits perfectly for Holly because of Hope. People might assume he's the father." He runs a hand over his shorn hair. "Just drop it. It's happening. It's for the best."

I glare at Evan, the traitor. Your best friend is supposed to have your back in an argument, not take the opposing side, right?

"I've also made contact with your girl before," Marcus adds. "You know, at her place of business?" He has the grace to look sheepish about that admission.

"So, it's settled?" Dex smiles. "I'm gonna need a copy of your schedule for the coming week."

"You two are welcome to stay for dinner," I announce, looking to Marcus and Detective Martinez.

"I'm down." Marcus grins.

"I've got to get home to the wife and kids, but thank you for the offer. I'll see myself out." The detective nods and turns to leave the room.

"Chloe'll be here in twenty minutes. You can go over my schedule with her," I say to Dex. "I'll be in the kitchen until then."

Chapter Twelve

Then

I pushed the sleeves of my flannel shirt up my arms as I climbed onto the bed, then hung the last poster on the wall. The trinity was complete. I took a step back to look at my handiwork. Stevie Ray Vaughn, Jimi Hendrix, and BB King were the sum of my displayed hero worship.

"It looks great," Diana said as she stepped up beside me.

"Thanks," I replied with a half-hearted grin.

It was a bittersweet moment. I'd been commuting daily my first two years of college. Diana had offered to help with the babies. I hadn't expected any help, and I was infinitely thankful for it, but it was expensive and time-consuming to commute like that. Diana and John insisted that, with my busy schedule heading into my final two years of college and being eighteen, I should move into a dorm and enjoy my college years before they were gone.

The girls were staying with them. I was going to be all alone. It was only a two-hour drive from school, but it felt like I was abandoning the girls and I hated that feeling.

I felt a tug on my shirt and looked down into gorgeous clear-blue eyes framed with black curls. My dad had blue eyes in the pictures I saw of him, but I was still shocked when their eyes lightened from baby gray to Jared's blue. I had my mother's brown eyes. She held her arms open, signaling that she wanted to be picked up.

"Hey, Kitty Cat."

"Dis your new woom, Mommy?"

I nodded, unable to speak without breaking down in tears.

"Is that me an' Coowa's bed?" She pointed to the vacant bed on the other side of the room.

I stifled a sob as I shook my head. I turned to find the General standing behind me holding a sleepy Cora.

"This one's down for the count, and we have a good drive ahead of us. You're all unpacked?"

"Yup," I answered with a watery smile.

"Well, I guess that's our cue. I'm sure you have things to do," Diana said. She looked over at me with watery eyes and continued, "You're going to be fine. The girls are going to be fine. It's only temporary, and they're young enough that they won't remember this. You can come home anytime, but you need to make school your priority."

"I know," I choked out. "Thank you, Diana, John. For everything. I don't think I'd've gotten this far without you."

"Yes, you would. You're a very smart and capable young woman. We love you." She smoothed down my hair and cradled my face in her hands with a smile. She gave me a kiss on the cheek and held her arms out for Cat.

I squeezed my baby tight. "You be good for Nana and Pop Pop, okay? I love you." I gave her sweet cherub cheek a kiss and let her go.

"Lub you, too, Mommy," Cat said, snuggling into Diana's arms.

I crossed over to Cora, who was fully asleep, and kissed her cheek. "I love you, sweet Lily Pad."

"Make us proud, Maddie. And don't forget dinner Saturday."

"I will. And I won't," I said with a grin.

I walked with them outside. Too soon, they were pulling out of the parking lot, and I made my way back upstairs to my dorm. Tears streaked down my face as I shut the door behind me. I sniffled and wiped at the tears, the sound echoing around the room. It was too quiet. I sat on the bare, empty bed reserved for my future roommate and studied the meager assembly of things that were all I had.

Looking to distract myself, I pulled out my guitar, mini amp, and headphones. I sat on my bed and got lost in my music. Ignoring the tears streaking my face, I closed my eyes and let the music carry me away from my depressing thoughts.

I was in my own head space, not realizing that I wasn't alone until a finger tapped my shoulder. I nearly jumped out of my skin as I yelped and yanked off my headphones, looking up into laughing hazel eyes shadowed by a short bob of perfect, dark brown waves.

"I win—I got a music major this year," she said over her shoulder.

I looked behind her to the tall blond guy placing a box on the other side of the room. I blinked, and she was looking back at me.

"I'm Sloane, your new roommate. That's my boyfriend, Max. And you?"

"I'm..." I thought about it for a second. "I'm Laine."

No one had ever called me that, but I'd been going to this college for two years and had made zero friends. I was always referred to as *that girl*. This year was going to be different. I was going to be different. I'd make friends and start a new chapter of my life.

I wasn't going to continue to mope and pine and hope that Jared would come back to me because it was clear that he wasn't. He hadn't come home during leave once in the last two years. He hadn't called or talked to me, and if Diana or the General had spoken to him, they never told me about it.

Evan had disappeared into the military life with Jared, though he called often. Nic had gotten swept up in fraternity life at UT, and we only hung out every couple of weeks or so.

No one here bothered to talk to me because I was *that kid*. The one who was too young and didn't belong in college.

This year I was the same age as the entering freshmen.

"Hey, where'd you go?" Sloane asked, waving her hand in front of my face.

I gave her a small smile. "Sorry. Are you okay with me taking this side of the room? You weren't here, so I just picked, but if you like this side better, I can move."

"Girl, you're all unpacked already, and both sides are identical, so no. I'm not making you move. But I've a feeling I'm gonna like you." She grinned and sat on my bed next to me. She had a little blue gem pierced into her nose. "So, dish, tell me all about you."

"What do you want to know?" I asked nervously. My social skills were a little rusty. If I ever had any. Most everyone I knew had been around my whole life.

"Everything. Here, I'll go first—"

"Hey, I'm gonna go down and get the rest of your stuff," Max said.

"See, like that, I have him trained well." She grinned, and the light winked off her blue nose ring.

"You're a fucking laugh riot, Slo," Max grumbled as he left the room.

"Anyway, where was I?" She tapped her finger on her bottom lip. "Oh, yeah. I'm a fashion design major. Just turned twenty-one. I'm completely straight. You've met my boyfriend, Max. I'm totally cool with it if you're not, hetero that is. I've a twin, but he goes to UT. I hang out with him and our friends there more than people here. My dad's a retired pro boxer, so there's that. Hmm… My favorite food is bacon, I love Dr. Pepper, and candy of choice is Red Hots or anything cinnamon. Oh, and I love to run. Your turn."

Holy God, that was a lot of information. I considered it for a minute. I was normally a private person, but that had gotten me nowhere in college. I did have to live with her, and she seemed nice. I wasn't going to tell her about the twins, though. I'd made the decision years ago when I first started college, it wasn't anyone's business but my own. I'd had enough of the disdain from the people in my hometown; I didn't need to carry that to college. No, I was at college to learn, and I couldn't afford to be distracted by unnecessary drama.

"I'm a music theory and business double major. I'm not gay—I don't think. My dad died when I was five. He was a fireman. My mom died when I was fifteen. She was a library clerk. I've no siblings, biologically, but my godparents, both sets, have sons who're basically my big brothers. One's in the Army, Special Forces, currently deployed in Iraq. The other goes to UT, but I don't get to see him much. Favorite food is bread or pasta of any kind, I'm a Coke drinker myself, and I love cake, specifically chocolate, but any kind will do. Does that cover it?"

"Yeah, wow. I'm sorry about your parents."

I twisted my fingers together nervously and offered an uneasy smile. "Thanks. I shouldn't've said that. It's kinda a downer."

She bit her lower lip and stared across the room. Her eyes suddenly widened. "Have you turned twenty-one yet? We can totally hit up Fifth Street on the reg this year."

"Ummmm, no. I just turned eighteen."

"But this is the junior dorms?" She looked confused.

"Oh, I know. I'm a junior."

"Oh, shit. You're her. You're the kid. I've heard about you." She waved her hand at my widening eyes, dismissing my mortification. "Oh, nothing like that. Small campus, anything noteworthy gets around. People always talk about the genius scholarship kid who kicks everyone's ass on tests and fucks the grading curve. Though I did hear you have one of those fuck-off-and-leave-me-alone attitudes. I, actually, kind of hero worshiped you for a while. You blew off that dick, Jack Sprader, freshman year. You just turned and walked away without saying a word. Stone-cold blow off. That's so fucking cool. Now you're my roommate. We're so gonna be besties, I'm warning you now. And I totally have the hookup for fake IDs, so we'll consider it my housewarming gift to you."

"You don't have to do th—"

"You're eighteen now, so you totally have to go out. I'm under official college roommate oath to ensure that you have the full college experience."

She got up and started opening boxes as Max brought in another.

"Oh, speaking of… we're going out tonight. Some of my friends are in a band. They're not bad, but not great either. The venue they're playing at is eighteen and up, so you can totally come." She turned to face me abruptly. "Do you have a car?"

"Yeah."

"Good, then you can pick up my brother. He plans on drinking tonight and doesn't want to drive, but Max drives a two-seater, and I've nothing. Max's my personal chauffeur." She looked up and grinned with a wink.

My brows drew together in confusion. Why couldn't she ride with me and Max pick up her brother? I wanted to ask, but I didn't know her well enough to know how she'd react. What came out instead was a timid, "Okay?"

"Awesome. Let me unpack this shiz, and I'll give you directions." She looked me up and down for a moment, contemplating something. "What size are you?"

"Uh, medium top. Size eight in jeans."

"I got you on bottom, but I'm going to search your stuff for suitable shirts. We can make do tonight, but I'll take care of you soon enough."

"Okay?"

Boy, was I in trouble. I'd no experience with this girl stuff. All I had was the fear of the unknown.

Now

I've just finished draining the pasta when my phone rings. I rush to the charging station on the far counter to answer it before it switches to voicemail.

"Hey, ho," I greet, having seen that it was Sloane on the

caller ID. "What's up?"

"Nada," she says with a sigh. "Well, that's a lie. Lots of stuff. Do you want me to start with the good, the bad, the ugly, or the devastating news?"

"How about you start with devastating and work backwards?"

"Fine. I got fired."

"What! Why?"

"Nothing except these pretentious fashion douche-knockers can't handle an opinion without it *impeding their vision*." She says that last part in a nasally, snooty voice that makes me stifle a laugh. "Whatever, I think it's time for a career change anyway. I loved working as your stylist. I could see myself doing that for other people, I mean, if you're dead set on never being famous again. You haven't changed your mind, have you?"

"No. No, I haven't. You know how I feel about it. It's not good for the girls."

"Maybe in six years? When they ship off to college?"

"Maybe," I say to appease her. I've no intention of purposely stepping into the spotlight ever again. "That's devastating, what's the ugly?"

"Max is leaving me for another woman."

I can't say I'm entirely shocked. They've been together for twelve years, engaged for the last four. If they really were in love, they would've pulled the trigger already. They seemed to be just clinging to each other out of the comfort of the familiar. We were expecting something like this to happen, sooner or later. I honestly don't know what to say because I think it's for the best, but I know she's not ready to hear that. My strength as a friend has never been about having the right words. I just wish she were here so that I could hug her, then hand her a pint of her favorite ice cream and a bottle of vodka and just listen.

I wait for her to continue, but she doesn't. "Do you want to skip to the bad?"

"Yes," she says with a sob. "Goddammit, I miss you. I

need you here right now. We could do shots and play with that voice-distortion app, and make fun of people on their way to work while hiding in bushes like old times."

I feel a tap on my shoulder and whirl around to face Dex.

"Need any help?" he offers.

"Who's that?" Sloane asks.

"No one, just security."

"I thought you fired them months ago?"

"I did, but I got another flower."

"What? Why didn't you call me immediately? Or even Holly could've called! I can understand you—you're not particularly forthcoming with any information—but Holly should've called. That bitch is hearing from me next."

I hold up my hand to Dex while she rants.

"It just happened Saturday, and things have been rather crazy around here."

"Well, I suppose that brings me to the good news. I'm moving back to Austin."

"Really? That's awesome. Give me the expected timeline. You gonna stay here until you find a place?"

Holly comes in to check on her cupcakes, sees that I'm occupied, and starts finishing up the dinner preparations for me, directing Dex to help her.

"Well, I've some things to wrap up here. And I need to schedule movers and all that stuff. I think I'll be back in time for Thanksgiving. I'm probably going to stay at my dad's for the holiday and then stay with you after. For a little bit. I've the funds to get a place. I just miss you guys. New York sucks without you."

"Okay. I'll let Holly know you're going to call her. And that you're staying with us after Thanksgiving."

Holly perks up at the mention of her name and starts listening in.

"We're fixin' to sit down for dinner. We have guests tonight, so it might be a while. You want me to tell her to call you?"

"Yeah, sounds good."

I watch Holly shove serving bowls into Dex's arms and point him to the dining room. He leaves.

"Okay, love you. See ya soon."

"Love you, too. Bye." I hang up the phone and look at Holly as a thought occurs to me.

"Who's that?" she asks.

"It was Sloane," I say quietly and step closer to her. "She's going to call you. Mainly to bitch you out about not telling her about the stalker. But, you have to swear to me—on all that is holy—that you won't say a word to her about Dex."

She rolls her eyes at me.

"I'm serious. This's serious. He's risking his life for us. And yeah, I could tell her the lie we're feeding everyone else about him and Marcus, but I don't want to lie to her. And they told us no one outside of you, me, and Evan can know."

"Bitch, please. You know I got you."

"You do?" I ask and raise an eyebrow. "Because I sure wouldn't want to have to murder you in your sleep. Remember, I know where you lay your head at night."

"I swear," she says, holding up her right hand and grinning. "You couldn't live without me, though. I seriously think you're just waiting for scientists to figure out a way to turn my eggs into sperm so you can have my babies." She waggles her eyebrows.

I purse my lips. I don't want to laugh, but the idea is so ridiculous I find my shoulders bouncing with silent laughter.

I'm interrupted by the front door slamming and shouts of male voices. I look at Holly, and we both take off to see what the commotion is. I skid to a stop in the living room at the sight of Dex and Marcus pointing guns at someone hidden from view on the other side of the stairs.

Oh my God, where are the girls?

Feet pound the stairs as Evan shouts, "Lower your weapons. He's authorized."

Curious, I take a few more steps until I can see the intruder.

"Lucky!" I shout as I run and wrap my arms around Nic's

neck, completely forgetting about the guns.

His keys clatter to the ground as he drops his raised hands and plants them on my ass with a smirk. "Now there's the greeting I was expecting."

I pull back and smack his shoulder. "Shut up with your suggestive bullshit and unhand my ass."

The girls come racing down the stairs behind Evan as Nic lets go to turn to them.

"Uncle Lucky!" the girls shout as they push past me to hug Nic.

"That's what I'm talking about," Nic says as his gaze moves over my shoulder with a frown. "Your security team certainly has a new look."

"That's not—" I stop. I can't think of what to say. I turn back to Dex and Marcus, both looking awkwardly casual, guns no longer in sight.

"I'm her boyfriend, Dex." Dex approaches with his hand extended to Nic. "You are?"

"Nic Gallo," Lucky supplies as he returns the handshake. His mouth is pinched as he eyes Dex and Marcus. He holds back any commentary, but I know I'll have to answer for it later.

I can tell when the name sparks recognition in Dex's eyes because a look of shock appears before he gets his expression under control. His eyes dart to me with a curious look.

"This one's mine," Holly says, sidling up next to Marcus with a huge grin and wrapping her hands around his muscular arms.

I close my eyes to keep from rolling them as I shake my head. I should've known she'd enjoy this a little too much.

"Marcus Lions," he says, extending his hand to Nic.

"Boyfriend?" Cora asks.

"Whose boyfriend?" Everyone turns to the front door as a purple head of hair peeks around the edge of the door, indicating Chloe's arrival. I only now notice that the door was left half-open in the commotion.

That girl changes her hair color more often than anyone

I've ever seen. I think she's a natural blonde, but I haven't ever seen it because roots never have time to show between color changes. She freezes when she notices all the people in the not-quite-large-enough entry.

"Mom and Dex," Cora supplies.

"Oh, my God, this means we're practically sisters," Cat squeals to Audra.

Cora and Audra join in with squeals of their own.

Oh, Lord. This is gonna be bad.

"That *is* an interesting development," Nic says with raised brows.

"I second that," Chloe mumbles, her brows drawing together.

"Did you bring us anything back from LA?" Cat asks Nic.

"Of course, it's in my bag. Let's go up to my room, and I'll get it for you," Nic says, picking up his bag from the floor. "Dinner?" he asks me.

"Ten minutes," I answer and watch them move up the stairs.

"Did you see the one I got?" Holly says to Chloe, rubbing her hand across Marcus's chest.

Marcus grins down at Holly, not at all minding her attachment to his arm. *Oh, God. What am I going to do with that woman?* He introduces himself to Chloe while my mind drifts back to dinner preparations.

Dex leans in to whisper in my ear. "Should I be worried about my daughter going into a room alone with a porn star?"

"I think *I* should be more worried about the fact that *you* know who he is," I say with an eye roll and turn back to the kitchen.

"You keep interesting company."

I turn back to face him as my protective instincts surge. "Who the fuck are you to judge?"

His hands go up in surrender. "No judgment, just making an observation."

"I've known Lucky—Nic—since the day I was born. And

despite his professional choices, he's a stand-up guy. He's family. So, watch your words, Dex. I protect the ones I love."

"Hey." He stops me with a hand on my shoulder. "I'm not saying anything here. I'm just trying to understand. You're never what I expect. You throw me at every turn."

I shrug my shoulders to dislodge his hand.

"Welcome to the island of misfit toys, Dex." I expand my hands in front of me, gesturing to the room as I walk backward. "The only thing I expect from my friends is loyalty and honesty. What they choose to do apart from that is up to them. I've no room to judge anyone. But here's a tip. You might want to stop tryin' to understand me because you're not going to like what you find. Okay?"

"That right there only makes me want to know more," he says with a smirk, exposing one dimple.

"Whatever." I throw up my hands. "I've to finish getting dinner on the table."

Then

I regretted my new life choices as I pulled up in front of the house in Central Austin, just off the Drag. I insisted on wearing my Doc Martens boots, so Sloane insisted I wear the slutty Catholic school girl look. The fact that I attended St. Edward's, a Catholic school, was not lost on me.

The black-and-red plaid miniskirt was paired with a black tank top I owned, Sloane's studded leather belt and black leather jacket completed the look. She'd also insisted on doing the whole smoky-eye makeup coupled with a dark red lipstick. I didn't look like myself. Which I guessed was sort of a blessing—if I saw someone I knew, they wouldn't even look twice.

"You look perfect. You'll blend in nicely," she'd said as I studied my reflection in the mirror.

I didn't look horrible, and if I were being honest, it was kind of hot. It was just weird, like wearing a costume. A punk rock vixen costume.

I sat for a second before honking my horn twice, as I'd been instructed. It was definitely weird driving to a stranger's house, not to mention picking up said stranger by way of honking. The door to the house finally opened, and what stepped out could only be described as a conundrum.

Sloane's twin brother had dark brown hair, like hers, only his was a short, spiky mess, like he'd just rolled out of bed. *Holy shit!* He was fucking hot. He was wearing flat-front khaki pants with a white button-down shirt rolled up to his elbows, exposing muscular arms covered in colorful tattoos down to his fingers. He had a tattoo of a bird on the right side of his neck.

But the real kicker was that he was wearing a sweater vest and a bow tie. He looked like Bill Nye and a hardcore biker had a love child, but it didn't detract from his wow factor. As ridiculous as it was, it maybe added to it. You had to have confidence to pull off a look like that. These thoughts had me cracking up as he slid into the front seat of my car.

"It's like Mr. Peabody decided to explore his dark side," I said to myself before my brain-to-mouth filter kicked in.

His fist clenched tight, and I noticed the tattoos on his right-hand fingers read *pain*. He looked like one of those guys that was perpetually pissed off at the world. I thought to lighten the mood with a joke.

"Seriously, did Sloane get ahold of you, too?"

His eyes widened, followed by a slow, reluctant smirk like he imagined something infinitely more amusing than my lame joke. He shook his head slowly and looked me up and down before turning to look out the passenger window without a word.

I sat motionless until he looked back at me.

"You going to put your boyfriend's car in drive, bumpkin?" There was a laugh in his tone that immediately made my face go hot with anger.

"Boyfriend? I don't have one of those—this car's mine. I rebuilt her myself." I tilted my chin up with pride as I met his eyes.

"There it is," he said with a smirk. "That slow-drawl accent, proclaiming she works on broken-down cars in her spare time. I assume you know enough about cars to drive this stick shift and move, right?"

Wow! Asshole. I put the car into gear and pulled away

from the curb. He's definitely one of those dicks that lets his looks go to his head. Such a shame.

"I'm going to ask you one more question," I said. "Then you need to answer and shut the fuck up, because I already don't like you."

"Ask away, bumpkin."

I bit back a snotty retort, choosing to ignore his goading. "How do I get to this place? Sloane didn't give me directions, because she said you'd know where it is."

"It's down by the river. Just get back on Guadalupe and take a left at Caesar Chavez. Make a right just before you get to thirty-five. You can't miss it." He pulled his thumb and forefinger across his mouth in a zipping motion, twisted at the corner of his mouth, and flicked his fingers with a cocky smirk.

I didn't think I ever actually hated someone so quickly in all my life. I just narrowed my eyes and focused on the road.

The ride was mostly silent, until it wasn't.

"This is a nice car." He raised a brow pierced with two metal loops. "Where did you come by that accent, bumpkin?"

"Thanks. My name's Laine, by the way—you can *start* calling me that anytime. And nowhere you've ever heard of if you're sitting in Austin, Texas, making fun of my accent."

"I don't know, bumpkin." One side of his mouth tilted up in a grin, revealing a dimple. "I think the name's growing on me."

I really do hate him.

"No wonder Sloane's so nice—you sucked up all the asshole in the womb," I grumbled.

He burst out laughing. "I think you're the first of Sloane's friends I like, bumpkin."

"The feeling's not mutual."

We pulled into the parking lot of the Pit. I killed the engine and bolted from the car to get away from the asshole. Unfortunately, he was faster, because he cut me off at the back of the car, looking me over from head to toe.

"That's what Sloane put you in." He closed his eyes and

shook his head slightly.

"What's wrong with it?" I asked self-consciously, looking down at myself.

"She basically doused you in blood before sending you into a shark tank," he said with a look on his face like I was stupid for even asking. "People like this don't meet people like you often, and that—" He blew out a breath and motioned to my body. "You need to stick with me, or you're going to get eaten alive."

"What the fuck's that supposed to mean? People like me? You really are too much. We're in Texas. I'm from Texas. It's really only weird to you. And you're the last person on earth I want to *stick with*. So, fuck off, whatever your name is." I dashed around him to get to the front door.

He grabbed my arm, stopping me. "My name is Law."

"Is that some sorta joke?"

"No." He looked confused for a moment. "It's short for something."

"Whatever. Get your hand off me, and don't touch me again."

"Bumpkin, please," he said, releasing my arm.

"Oh, my God!" I yelled through clenched teeth, turning back to face him. "Do you want me to slap you?"

"Laine," Sloane called. I turned to see her waving her arms in the air by the front door.

"Thank God," I grunted to myself and left, not looking back at him.

I marched right up to Sloane, who had a blinding smile on her face. She looked over my shoulder as she spoke.

"Well, this is new." She hooked her arm in the crook of my elbow and dragged me inside the noisy bar.

We weaved through the crowd until we got to a table near the stage. Max was there, nursing a drink, with a few other people I didn't know.

"Everybody, this is Laine. And… she's my new favorite person. Seriously, I might go gay for her. Sorry, Max," she said, then looked at me. "You're the first girl I brought around who didn't start drooling over my brother at first sight. And the fact that when I saw you together, you looked like you were about to stomp his ass into the ground... I knew then. You'd have my heart forever." She laughed loudly. "Anyway, this is Spaz, Monk, Tina, and Spence." She pointed to each person she named off.

I waved awkwardly.

"The guys are in the band we're here to see. Tina's Monk's girl. She's also a badass piercer if you ever want something like that done."

"Good to know," I said with a grin.

Tina pushed her black hair over her shoulder and nodded in return with a friendly smile.

Sloane pulled up another stool to the high-top table and waved me toward it.

"I'm actually gonna grab a coke first," I said, hitching a thumb over my shoulder toward the bar.

"I'll come with you," said a male voice behind me.

I turned around and glared up at Law. *What a ridiculous name.*

"I'd rather you not. In fact, if you could find a way to stay the fuck away from me for the rest of the night, then find another ride home... I sure would appreciate it." I drew the last part out in my thickest accent.

His eyes were unreadable, but the tick in his jaw muscle let me know he didn't like it.

Good. I shoved past him. *I don't care how hot you are, a dick is still a dick.* And I've a feeling that it's been a long time since someone called him out on it.

Weaving my way through the crowded venue, I was almost to the bar when a hand reached out and went straight up my skirt, grabbing my ass. I turned around and slapped the person, hard across the cheek. Shock froze since I expected it to be Asshole Law, but it was just some random dude.

He didn't look too happy as he raised his hand as if to hit me back. A hand reached out between us and caught his wrist, while another one laid a punch to his cheekbone, that had him sprawling out across the floor.

I turned to find a very pissed-off-looking Law, rubbing the knuckles of his right hand. *Pain.* He grabbed me by the wrist and pulled me after him. I struggled to get free as he dragged me behind him, pulling me into a room. He slammed the door and locked it behind us. We were in a small, poorly lit bathroom that smelled of bleach. The walls and ceiling were covered with amateur graffiti.

"I fucking told you that would happen," he said, gripping the back of his neck and pacing the small room.

I moved in front of him, cutting off his path. "Since when've I become your responsibility?"

He leaned down, looking me in the eye. "He was going to hit you."

His eyes were this gorgeous calico mix of green, blue, and gold flecks. It was distracting, but not enough to cool my anger.

"And this's your problem, how?" I leaned in, too, our noses only an inch apart. I narrowed my eyes. "I didn't ask you to play protector."

"Would you rather I let him hit you?" he sneered.

"No, but you didn't have to hit him. You could get us kicked out, or worse, you could get arrested for assault."

"Fuck," he said as he turned around and punched the bathroom stall.

Someone's got anger management issues. I walked to the sink to splash water on my face. My face felt hot, and all that makeup felt like a mask. Black mascara ran down my cheeks as I looked into the mirror and caught sight of Law. He was staring at me, his eyes running from my face back to my recently groped appendage.

"I'm going to touch you. If you don't want me to touch you, then tell me no, now," he said. His pupils were dilated to the point his eyes looked black.

As much as I didn't like him, the way he was looking at me was definitely turning me on. There was so much desire and heat in those eyes. I don't think anyone had ever looked at me like that. I didn't know what to do. I stayed silent.

He ran his hand up the back of my thigh, gripping my ass cheek and squeezing.

"Fuck, you're gorgeous. Ever since you opened that smart-ass mouth of yours, I can't help thinking about how I'd punish you for it. If you were mine." His tongue darted out, licking his full lower lip.

My stomach flipped. No one had ever talked to me like that, of that I was sure. Part of me was shocked, but I could feel the wetness pooling between my thighs. Everything about him seemed so wrong, but I couldn't deny myself the urge to find out why it felt right.

"Do it. Punish me," I found myself saying, though I'd no idea where the words came from. He just made it sound so fucking hot.

He tipped his head back and groaned. "Hold on to the sink."

He grasped my hips, pulling my lower body back until I was completely bent over. He flipped my skirt up over my waist and paused. His eyes roamed over me. The anticipation was putting me on edge. His hand pulled back and smacked my ass. It made my nerve endings sing. Chills rushed through my body as he smoothed his hand over the warmed skin. I let out a soft moan and bowed my back.

"Again," I commanded. It felt so good, and I wanted more.

He huffed air and breathed out, "Goddamn."

His other hand came down on the other cheek. My body jolted, startled, and I gasped. I could feel myself growing wet. I didn't know this was something I was into, but it was definitely working for me.

"I still fucking hate you," I said.

Law spun me around, pushing my back against the wall of the bathroom stall.

His mouth came down on mine in a brutal, punishing kiss. It was all lips and teeth and tongue, biting and caressing. He pissed me off and made me want him, which made me want to hurt him.

I pulled frantically at his shirt until it came free from his pants, ran my hands up his back, and dug my nails into his skin as I dragged them downward.

He groaned and pulled my tank top down under my breasts, popping each one out of my bra and running his thumb over my sensitive nipples. I moaned, high-pitched and breathy, at the sensation.

"Jesus, you're so fucking hot," he said into my mouth. "You're going to be the death of me."

I wrapped my leg around his waist, pulling him against me. He reached under me and grasped the lace thong I was wearing and ripped it right off. I lost my mind with want. I felt like I was burning from the inside out.

He pushed two fingers into me, and I ground against his hand. It wasn't enough. I needed more.

"I want you to fuck me. But do it hard. Make me feel it."

"One of these days, I'm going to fuck that dirty little mouth of yours. Grab on to the top of that wall behind you." He undid his pants and pulled out his cock. It was so hard, and as he stroked it I caught a flash of silver. I trembled as a thrill rushed through me. He pulled a condom out of his back pocket and rolled it on, then hoisted my lower half up, rubbed himself against me until he was lined up, and slammed his hips into mine, impaling me.

I yelped involuntarily. He was so big it stretched me, but felt so good. The piercing I only caught a glimpse of was putting pressure in just the right places.

Holy fuck. I'm having sex with someone else.

He pulled back and slammed into me again. My mind went blank. We became masses of mindless need as we moved against each other, with each other. I let go of the wall with one hand and grabbed his hair and pulled, hard.

He moaned, bit his lip, and sped up. The friction felt so good, I was almost there. Then with one hand he massaged my clit, while one of the fingers of his other hand pressed into my ass. His hot mouth enveloped my nipple.

I screamed as I fucking saw stars. I exploded into the most powerful orgasm I'd ever experienced. Every nerve in my body short-circuited as all my muscles convulsed and contracted uncontrollably, over and over. He sped up, ramming into me so hard the flimsy stall behind me was protesting the beating, thumping against its joints and groaning.

His whole body trembled violently as he met his release and slowed. His body sagged and his forehead fell into the crook of my neck. Sounds of dueling labored breath filled the room as we both came down and recovered. As we started to catch our breath, his lips and tongue ran up the side of my neck to my ear.

"You're mine. Whether you want me or not, you're mine. I'm never letting you go," he whispered and then nipped my ear lobe. I shivered in response. "Jesus Christ, bumpkin."

I started to respond, but there was a loud repetitive thump at the door.

"Yo, Law, wrap it up, man. We're all set up. We need to go on. Now."

"Shit," he said as he slowly pulled out. He steadied me on the floor and frantically put himself back together.

I stood there watching, in shock. "You're in the band?"

"Uh, yeah."

"Oh."

He came back with some wet paper towels and cleaned me up, righting my shirt and smoothing down my skirt while I stood motionless, still grasping the top of the stall.

"You all right?" he asked, stroking my jaw with his thumb and pulling my face toward him, before his lips gently caressed mine. His tongue slipped into my mouth, twisting with mine until I was breathless again. My hands fell to his shoulders, feeling numb.

When he released me, I nodded in reply.

"I've gotta go, but I'm not getting another ride home tonight." His lips tipped up in a half smile, exposing a dimple.

"You're giving me a ride."

I nodded again and wiped a smudge of the dark lipstick from his face. He turned and left the room. As the door opened, I heard another male voice speaking to Law.

"Whoa, man, that was hot. I almost got off just listening to you two. She's a hot piece—" He was cut off by a loud thud.

"You fucking speak of, or even look in her direction, you'll be waking in a fucking hospital." His voice was deadly quiet as he spoke.

"Got it. Fuck, Law. I didn't realize you were serious about her. Hey, didn't you just meet the chick?"

Their voices drifted away as the bathroom door thunked closed and they moved down the hall. It finally hit me that I was just standing in an empty bathroom.

I felt like my whole world had been turned upside down. Sex had never been like that for me before. It was messy and rough, but I felt it all the way down in parts of my soul. The fact that it was that asshole who gave it to me, left me reeling. I didn't know what to think.

I moved on shaky legs to the mirror and looked at myself. My hair was wild and disheveled; mascara streaked down my face. I set about making myself presentable again. I had to go out there and see this band play.

Almost a week later, we were sitting in their garage listening to the band practice. I didn't know what to expect of punk music. It wasn't something I was familiar with until that night at the Pit. It had an energy, a vitality like no other genre. Mix in a little rebellion and I was hooked. I loved it.

The guys had been practicing for several hours. Their band wasn't bad, but it lacked something to provide cohesion to their sound. I listened intently as I tried to pick out the problem. My fingers twitched as I thought of notes that should be there but weren't. This is what I loved to do. I wanted to live and breathe music for the rest of my life. I was addicted.

"Hey, guys, let's take a break," Law said as they finished a song.

After laying down their instruments, the guys meandered from their makeshift stage. Law grabbed my hand and pulled me from my seat, sitting in my place, then pulling me down on his lap.

Seeing his concert and the way girls threw themselves at him, I was sure he'd move on to the next girl. He didn't seem interested in them, but he was rather hands-on with me. I wasn't sure what we were. I didn't feel a need for conversations or titles. I wasn't really interested in a boyfriend after the train wreck that had been my love life to date.

I leaned into his sweaty chest. He grasped my chin and turned my head to press his lips to mine but quickly deepened it. There was a gagging noise from across the room. I smiled, even with my lips still firmly attached to Law's. I did enjoy torturing Sloane.

"You guys are gross," Sloane complained.

"Yet, you keep choosing to come here and hang out," Law spoke into my mouth with a smile.

"Maybe you should let Laine breathe. Then she could play for you."

Law's head pulled back, and he looked at me, his brows drawing together. "You play?"

I nodded.

"She's brilliant. Dude, I thought when I walked in and saw I was saddled with a guitar-playing music major this year that I was going to be relentlessly tortured with horrible playing and god-awful music. You should hear her, though. She's amazing. I love listening to her play while I study."

My breath caught in my throat. I hadn't realized that she could actually hear it since I used headphones with my amp.

"This's your practice, I don't want to intrude," I protested, waving it off. "I don't even play your kind of music anyway."

"Whaddya play?" Spencer asked, leaning forward in his chair. He propped his chin on his joined fists, his brown eyes intent on me under his green curls.

"Mostly blues and classic rock." I shrugged.

"I've gotta hear this," Spaz added. "I bet she plays circles around you, Spence. No one would ever accuse you of being *brilliant*." He twisted toward Spence. His brown mop of hair brushed his shoulders with the movement.

"Shut the fuck up, Spaz. No one would ever call your bass skills *brilliant* either." Spencer looked to me. "You can use my setup."

"I couldn't. I've never played in front of anyone other than Mr. Vaughn, my tutor, and the professors at school. I didn't even realize that Sloane could hear me."

"Undiscovered talent, I love it." Spaz clapped and rubbed his hands together with a scheming look. "Get over there and show us whatchu got, woman."

"I'll give you a beat," Monk offered with a soft smile.

Monk was an Asian kid of some descent with bleached, spiky hair and soft features. That was the first time I ever heard him talk. Dude was seriously the silent type. The only time he ever really made a sound was with his kit in front of him. It added gravity to when he did speak and made me want to do what he was asking.

"Make me proud, Bumpkin," Law said as he smacked my thigh and pushed me up and off his lap. I rolled my eyes at the stupid nickname. It still pissed me off.

I walked over, picked up Spencer's Gibson, and started tuning it. I checked the microphone as well.

"Oh shit, she's gonna serenade us too." Spaz lit a joint, and the smell of marijuana filled the garage. "I've gotta get high for this," he said, his voice strained and higher-pitched from the inhaled smoke.

I turned to Monk, who'd settled behind his drum kit. "Give me snare every four-count, and double time softly on the hi-hat. Go slow, like this." I tapped out a beat on the guitar. "You can improv when you feel it, but let's give it several bars to get a feel for playing together."

He nodded, his expression all business, and began setting out a rhythm. I started playing "Texas Flood," the famous song written by my equally famous mentor and tutor. I closed my eyes and moved my body sinuously with the seductive blues beats.

We played for a solid three minutes before I turned around and stepped up to the mic. Everyone was silently watching me, but I didn't feel the nervousness I expected. Instead, I felt electric. Like I was plugged into them and feeding off their energy.

I belted out the words, feeling their meaning in my bones. I'd played this song so many times since Jared left me, feeling every note echo my very soul's lament.

Monk set off on a solo, and I backed him up with soft, repetitive notes. We were feeding off each other. I moved to him, drawn in by the synergy, as we built the music up together.

Turning to the mic, I rasped out the end of the song, putting as much emotion into the vocals as I had my guitar playing. When we finally rounded the song to a close, I felt bereft.

Our small audience cheered and whistled, but it didn't mean as much to me as when I was feeding off the beat that Monk was laying, lost in the music. Holding the audience enraptured, that was my sweet spot. I wanted to stay there forever.

"Holy shit, anyone else wanna start playing blues music?" Spaz asked.

"Yeah, I knew she had talent," Sloane added, her voice soft as if she were in awe. "That was something else, Laine. You have presence. I feel like I just witnessed the first performance of the next legend."

"I think she should join the band," Monk said, and everyone looked to him. When he spoke, people listened, for sure.

"I don't really have time for it," I argued.

"You've been here for all our practices this week, Laine," Law rebutted. "You have time."

"I could move to rhythm, and Law could focus on vocals," Spence said, ignoring my protest.

"I'm in," Law said with zero hesitation.

"Agreed," Spaz declared. It looked like I wasn't getting much of a say. "Looks like you're in the band, chica. Welcome to *One Dollar Bet*."

Law jumped out of his seat and walked toward me. As soon as I had the guitar strap over my head, he pulled it from my hands and set it down on the ground. Before I knew it, I was upside-down, hanging over his shoulder.

"We have something we need to take care of." He adjusted himself, heading for the door. "We'll be back later."

"Ewww, Law," Sloane complained. "Do you have to be gross?"

"Put me down, Law," I protested.

He bit the side of my thigh, making me yelp. "I know you want to go gay for her, but don't be jealous, Sloane," Law called, as he hauled me outside and into the house. He didn't stop. He walked straight through the back door, up the stairs, and into the master bedroom—aka his bedroom.

I hadn't been in here before. It was clean and nicely decorated. A stark contrast from the messy boys' rooms, with pinned-up posters of half-naked chicks that Evan and Nic had. Law had actual paintings, white walls, and black bedding. The room was blanketed in darkness as he kicked the door shut.

"I wanted to slow things down with you." He slid my body down the front of his. "But every time I'm with you, you floor me."

"I bet you say that to all your girls," I joked, trying to make light of his serious tone.

He shook his head. "You're not whiny or needy like other girls. You're chill, independent, feisty," he said with a smirk.

"You don't need to woo me, Law," I said dryly.

"You're incredible, and fuck if I don't feel the need to worship you."

He leaned in, his tongue flicking along the seam of my lips looking for access. I opened for him, and his tongue moved to tangle with mine. He started trailing kisses down my neck. My head fell to the side to allow him access. He grasped my wrist at his shoulder and trailed my hand down his abs to the front of his jeans.

"This is what you do to me," he said, pressing himself into my hand.

I moaned in reply. "Are you going to shut up and use that on me, or what?"

"You have more talent in your pinky nail than each of us will ever have in years of practice," he said, ignoring my comment and shoving my hoodie off my shoulders. He smoothed his hands down my arms in the softest graze. Goose bumps formed over my skin in its wake. "Yet you sit there quietly in the background, content."

He pulled off my shirt, then my bra. Then started trailing little kisses and nibbles between my breasts, down my stomach. He slowly unzipped my pants, following the zipper with his tongue. He was melting my brain, coherent thought fleeting.

"I see you," he said looking up at me as he removed my pants, helping me step out of them. He ran his hands up the back of my legs, squeezing my ass while guiding me to his bed.

I was laid out in the center of the bed. Law leaned back, fully dressed and looking my naked form over from head to toe.

"You're so beautiful." He shook his head a little. "I need to own—" His lips crashed into mine, like the contact would say what he couldn't. I was breathless when he broke away. "Do you trust me?"

I nodded, biting my lip, although I wasn't sure why he asked.

He jumped off the bed and went into his closet. I propped

myself up on my elbows to watch him. When he reappeared, he was wearing only jeans. I'd never seen him without a shirt. He was covered in tattoos on both arms from shoulder to fingers; his torso was blank, aside from an old-fashioned revolver tattooed on his right hip near the defined V of his muscles exposed by his low-hanging pants. Holy God, was he sexy.

"His name is Law, and he always carries his six-shooter," I said, mostly to myself. I laughed and lowered my voice to do my best spaghetti western impression. *"Listen stranger, did you get the idea? We don't like to see bad boys like you in town."* I quoted *A Fistful of Dollars*, then added, "I apologize for laughing at your donkey, just keep that thing put away."

He gave me that crooked smile that showed off his dimple and I was toast. He muttered something that sounded like, "Fucking adorable." He was holding something in his right hand. The moonlight, filtering in through the sheer black curtains, glinted off shiny metal as he approached me.

"You ever used something like these before?" he asked, dangling what appeared to be leather handcuffs connected by shiny silver latches in front of my face.

I shook my head.

"Are you okay with me using these on you?"

I nodded. The thought of being helpless and bound with him both thrilled and scared me.

"Words, Laine. I need your words."

"I've never done anything like that, but if you want to—" I bit my lip, unsure of what else to say.

"You ever heard of a safe word?"

I shook my head again, but at his frustrated look, I spoke. "No."

He crawled onto the bed, leaning to sit on his knees.

"Well, we decide on a word, right now. Something random that you would never say during sex in a million years. And if you don't like something I'm doing, then you say that word. I'll stop immediately, no questions asked. Okay?"

"You mean like *barnacle* or something? I can't imagine ever saying that."

He chuckled softly. "Yes, that's perfect." His eyes turned serious as he studied me. "So, you're good with this?"

"Yes... I'm curious."

He pulled my hands out from under me, one at a time. He kissed my wrist and latched the smooth, cool leather around each one. He pulled my arms above my head and attached the cuffs to the headboard, then trailed his hands and lips down my arms.

"I don't think you know what you do to me, Bumpkin. You're perfect." He nibbled my earlobe. "And you're mine."

The anger I normally felt at that name was overshadowed by the conflicting emotions I felt about his possessive declaration. It was the second time he told me that, and I wasn't sure what to make of it.

The things he did to me after erased all thoughts of that. It was mind-blowing, but really there were no words. I didn't know that was what sex could be like. I was thoroughly impressed when over an hour and six orgasms later, I lay on my stomach, motionless. My bones felt like liquid. I couldn't move. I teetered on the edge of passing out from exhaustion.

"I think I've discovered your hidden talent as well tonight," I mumbled, my voice hoarse from screaming. I wasn't a screamer by nature, but he knew how to bring it out of me.

He chuckled as he moved to release the cuffs from my wrist. He smoothed his hands over the skin beneath as he unbound them, one after the other.

"It was my pleasure to be of service, ma'am," he said in his best Clint Eastwood imitation.

I gave a half-hearted laugh but couldn't muster the energy for any other reaction. He definitely got my spaghetti western reference.

He lay down next to me and pulled me into his arms.

"I think I need to start running with your sister in the mornings. I can't keep up with your pace."

"It would be good for you, but I've another form of exercise I was going to introduce you to."

I groaned. "No more sex."

He chuckled again. "Not what I was talking about, but there will definitely be more of that. No, I want to show you something. Do you have time this week? During the day?"

"All my classes are on Tuesdays and Thursdays, so I'm off on Monday, Wednesday, Friday. Though I've my guitar lessons every day at three."

"Tomorrow morning works, then?"

"Yeah, sure. As ever, I'm curious. I'm sure one day it'll be the death of me. Probably with you and your dick at the helm."

He laughed and kissed my temple. "That mouth of yours," he said, shaking his head slowly and smoothing his hand down my back, lightly massaging the overworked muscles.

Chapter Fourteen

Now

We gather around the long, rustic-style dining table that I had custom-made years ago. It's just over fifteen feet long and surrounded by small two-seat benches. It's not fancy but serves as a gathering place for my large extended family of friends. It could fit up to twenty people, and we're using more than half that capacity now with the twelve people present.

"…that's the first thing she said to me when we met," Nic explains. "And she was serious, too. She thought I was so stupid that I couldn't tell the difference between porn and a mainstream movie. She's a real piece of work. Thank fuck it's over." He shakes his head.

"That sucks. She's always cast as the nice girl, too. I'm not going to any more of her movies," Cat states. "Unless you're in them, of course."

"What a twatwaffle," Holly says. "You probably acted circles around her. Seriously, her shit sucks." She raises her fist for Nic. "I got you, Boo."

He pounds her fist with his, and they both make simultaneous explosion noises while spreading their fingers wide. I snort a laugh. Those two are like two peas from the same pod.

Chloe blurts out a laugh. "When have ya actually seen any of her movies, Holly? I didn't think ya were into teen rom-com."

"I'm not. That's why her shit sucks," Holly says before shoveling another bite in her mouth.

"What kind of movie is it, Nic?" Cora asks. "I can't see you doing a teen flick. Aren't you a little old?"

"It's suspense." Nic shrugs. "It's not for teenagers, but it's more mainstream than my usual stuff."

"Cool. Do we get to go to a premiere?" Chloe asks with stars in her eyes. Chloe is a film major at UT, so movie stuff is right up her alley.

Even though I'm sandwiched between Caleb and Dex, the dinner isn't as awkward as I expected it to be. Until Caleb's hand slides under the table to rest on my knee. I narrow my eyes at him, and he smirks back with a challenging lift of his chin. I scoot away from him until his hand drops and end up pressed against Dex.

Dex looks at me curiously, and my eyes dart to my lap in a silent plea. He smirks as his arm wraps around my back and pulls me into him. His lips brush my forehead before his mouth moves to my ear.

"Already planning to use me?" Dex whispers.

My gaze darts to his. I roll my eyes and give him a subtle shake of my head. Inside, I'm relieved, because if anything good is going to come out of being stuck with Dex, this would be it.

He leans back. "I don't believe we've been formally introduced," he says to Caleb. "Dexter McClellan, Audra's dad and Maddie's boyfriend." His face transforms into a toothy grin.

I turn just in time to see the uncomfortable look on Caleb's face before he reverts to a neutral expression. He reaches out and shakes Dex's offered hand.

"Nice to meet you, sir. How long have y'all been together?" Caleb asks, eyeing Dex's hand as Dex runs his fingertip down my shoulder and upper arm.

"Quite a while, actually," I respond and tilt my head back to look at Dex, leaning against his shoulder. "Isn't that right, honey?" Oh, God, I want to slap myself for saying that. *Ugh, honey?* Dex's lips land on mine in a chaste, closed-mouth kiss that startles me. My mind blanks for a moment as my focus fixates on the contact. Electricity zings from my lips down my spine, making my skin prickle with goose bumps. *Holy fuck, no.* I pinch his leg, and he jerks away.

"You met the week before—"

"Cat!" I bark, and she halts her commentary.

"It was love at first sight, too. She can't keep her hands off me," Dex adds with a meaningful look to me, like I'll pay for that pinch.

"Gross, Dad," Audra grumbles. "I'm trying to eat."

I silently laugh.

"They're adorable together," Chloe says with a sigh. Sitting across from Dex, she has her head propped up on her wrist and a dreamy look on her face. I make a mental note that we'll have to tell her the truth. Evan, who's sitting next to her and across the table from me, is shaking with silent laughter.

"That reminds me," he says on a gasp. "I was reviewing the security tapes before dinner. You do remember there are cameras in all the common areas, right?" He struggles to keep the laughter out of his voice. "But the real question is, what were you thinking about, Mads?" His eyes dart from Dex to Caleb, then back to me.

It takes my slow brain a second to run through what happened today, and when it hits me, my face turns fifty shades of red. I drop my head in my hands to hide from everyone who has now silenced their own conversations in favor of listening to us.

"What the fuck're you doing to my friend, Dex?" Holly asks. "I've never seen her blush, but around you, she turns into a human fuckin' mood ring?"

Marcus snickers.

"I don't think I have anything to do with this," Dex responds, confusion apparent in his voice.

"Probably more than she'll admit," Evan adds.

I drop my hands and cut my eyes to Evan in a glare.

"Holy shit, she *is* blushing," Nic adds.

If it's possible to get any redder, I do.

"I don't think I've seen Little Neddie blush before. I've gotta see this tape."

"Seriously, you have to spill, Ev," Holly adds. "I need some good shit to hold over her head."

Evan laughs. "Maybe later—"

He's cut off as I spring from my seat and lean across the table to grab his shirt by the collar. Glasses and dishes clatter and drinks spill, and I don't care because my mind is focused on stopping my best friend from sharing some pretty embarrassing shit.

"Don't you dare," I say through clenched teeth, my face inches from Evan's. "Delete it. Now."

Hope starts banging on the table from her booster seat and babbling excitedly.

Evan looks like he's pondering the request, not bothered at all by my anger. "I don't know. This's pretty good blackmail fodder."

"I'll kill—"

"I don't know what the big deal is. I'm—" Caleb starts.

"Caleb, go home. Now," I grind out, turning my head to the side. "This doesn't concern you."

I try to keep my calm, but this stupid, self-absorbed kid thinks this is about him and his ridiculous proposition. I can't let the girls find out about his fucking ridiculous proposal. That's on top of Evan's threat of sharing a video of me masturbating directly after. *Fuck my life.*

"Nic told me you—" Evan starts.

"Don't say another word," I warn Evan. "Seriously, Nic!"

Nic laughs. "I can take a guess as to what this is about. But who was—"

"Oh, my God, don't you start, too," I whine. I seriously want to start bashing my head into the table.

"I've gotta fuckin' know," Holly states.

"Me, too," Chloe adds.

"That's it. We're taking this outside." I stand up, glaring at Evan while my unfinished bowl of pasta unsuctions from my belly and clatters back to the table. I look down at it and the mess on my clothes and the table. "After I clean this up and go change. I'm kicking your ass for starting this and you *will* delete that video."

Then

The next morning, I woke up, every muscle in my body deliciously sore. I tried to move, but Law had an arm around my waist and his leg thrown over both of mine, pinning me to the bed. I'd no idea what time it was, but the sun was out in full force. I struggled to slip out of his hold, but he only squeezed me tighter.

"Law?" I murmured. "You have to let me go. I need to pee."

Thick lashes fluttered open, revealing hazel eyes. Law smiled wickedly, showing both dimples, and my stomach fluttered.

"Oh, really?" He moved his arm lower and squeezed. "Do you have a pressing issue?"

"Stop, I'm going to pee on you," I shrieked and squirmed to get out of his hold.

He started tickling me. I couldn't help myself as I screamed at the top of my lungs. I thrashed and kicked and slapped at him to release me.

"Oh my God, stop, I'm super ticklish, and I'm seriously going to pee on you!"

Banging ensued from the room next door. "Can you keep the volume down on your kinky shit? It's early."

I broke free and raced to the bathroom. Law lay in bed, laughing.

"That's not kinky shit. Your fucking roommate's one of those annoying morning people," I yelled back. I'm not sure if anyone heard me, but I assumed they did, since they heard my yelling to begin with. I came out of the bathroom, and Law was still in bed with an arm draped over his eyes, a smile on his face, and his shoulders shaking with laughter.

"That wasn't funny. I don't like to be tickled." I frowned at him.

He removed his arm and looked at me, his smile melting and his gaze heating up as I stood there, naked and pissed off. He cleared his throat.

"It's nine. We should get ready, so we have time to swing by your dorm, and you can change."

"I'm not the one looking at me like that."

"Ugh, don't keep me thinking about it," he said, falling back against the pillow and looking up at the ceiling. "You should get dressed. Otherwise, I won't be able to make this go away." He motioned to the tenting fabric of his bedding near his waist.

"I can take care of that for you," I said, climbing on the bed. "But you'll have to show me how. I've never really done that before."

He groaned, "You're going to be the death of me, you know? The only time you're not being sexy as fuck is when you're being adorable."

After taking care of Law's *condition*, we got ready and headed out of the house. Law had pulled jeans on over his workout shorts and a leather jacket over his white T-shirt. I was still in the clothes I had on the day before. We stepped out the door, and I headed toward my car.

"Laine," Law called.

I turned back to face him.

"I was thinking we'd take my ride." He motioned up the driveway.

I changed route and followed him. We stopped in front of a fabric-covered lump, which I could only assume was a motorcycle. He removed the cover.

"Boys where I'm from would call this a crotch rocket," I said to him, eyeing the death trap warily. It was only a ten-minute drive, but I'd never ridden a motorcycle before.

Law scoffed. "This is a Ducati, and she's my baby." He stroked the seat of the sleek black bike.

"Is that supposed to mean something to me?"

"We need to get you educated on the ways of the world, Bumpkin," he said, straddling the bike. "I can't show you what she's made of between here and the school, but someday I'll take you for a ride out of the city. Here, suit up."

He passed me a helmet. I felt like a Storm Trooper wearing the damn thing.

"Hop on," he commanded.

I sat hesitantly behind him. He reached back and grabbed me by the ass, scooting me all the way against him. He ran his hands down my thighs, patting my knees.

"Wrap your arms around me tightly, lean with me when I lean. Okay?"

"Got it," I said, but my voice just echoed loudly around the helmet, so I gave him a thumbs-up.

He started the thing up. It came to life with a purring sound as he walked it backward down the driveway. He put his helmet on, and his voice boomed in my ears.

"You ready?"

I jumped at the sound. I hadn't realized that the helmets had built-in headsets.

"When you are," I responded.

We took off, hitting breakneck speed almost instantly. Good thing I was holding on to him, because the g-force alone would've thrown me off. I tightened my hold on him, and his smooth chuckle rang in my ears. When we crossed Lady Bird Lake over the South Congress Bridge, I looked out over the water as it shimmered in the morning light. A good mix of trees and open, green spaces filled in the gaps of commercial properties that lined the waterfront. Kayaks and paddleboards dotted the surface as early risers got their day started on the water. It was breathtaking. I started to relax. He really was a good driver, fluidly changing lanes. This was actually fun. Then we were pulling up in front of my dorms.

I ripped the helmet off, smiling. "That was amazing! You

so have to take me on that ride soon," I said, hopping off the bike. He pulled me back to him with a huge smile. Full dimpled display. He grasped my chin.

"I'm glad you liked it because I've plans for you and this bike." He kissed me thoroughly.

I remembered girls were leaving the dorms then, and we were probably attracting a lot of attention, so I pulled away.

"Go get dressed, Bumpkin." He smacked my ass. "We have places to be."

I ran into the dorm and raced up to my room, still fueled by the adrenaline from the bike ride. I threw on my workout clothes and athletic shoes, grabbed Sloane's leather jacket, and was out the door in less than ten minutes.

We were back on the bike and weaving down the little two-lane roads of South Austin that were a mix of residential, commercial, and industrial lots. It was only a couple of minutes and we were pulling up in front of a string of what looked to be industrial garages. I was confused until I spied through an open garage door a wall of mirrors reflecting a boxing ring. I removed the helmet and got off more slowly this time. Sloane had said her dad was a professional boxer.

"This isn't—" I began, but he cut me off.

"It's my dad's gym," he said quickly. "I know how you like to be independent." He smiled. "I thought you could add a new skill to your collection and train here. It'll keep me from beating up a bunch of fucking losers. I teach a self-defense class on Wednesday and Saturday afternoons, but we have other options to choose from if you don't want to learn from me. It's not far from school, and he won't charge you a thing. You want to check it out?" He rubbed the back of his neck, looking down at his bike.

I tilted my head, studying him. I reached out and cupped his cheek, turning him to face me. I smiled at him.

"I think it's an excellent idea, thank you."

"Really?" He smiled.

"Yeah, but I've to warn you that I haven't done any physical activity in almost four years. I'm probably hella out of shape."

"I'll go easy on you... for now." His grin was downright wicked as he stood off the bike and gathered me into his arms. He placed a soft kiss on my lips. "Come on, let's get you all sweaty and breathless." He laced his fingers in mine and started dragging me toward the open door.

I laughed. "Is that your specialty?"

"Why, ma'am, I do believe it is."

"Are you ever going to stop making fun of the way I talk?"

"I wasn't. I'd never make fun of you, Bumpkin," he said in mock seriousness and tried to fight back laughter, but his dimples and heaving shoulders gave him away. I swatted at him, and he shrugged. "You're the one who quoted my favorite movie to me last night."

"What? A Fistful of Dollars?"

"Yeah, that's a great scene." He smiled wistfully. "I've a thing for old movies—spaghetti westerns and kung fu, mostly."

"Really?"

"Yeah, well, you saw my pistol," he said with a smirk at his double entendre. "I also have this." He pulled off his leather jacket, pointing to a tattoo on the inside of his forearm of a half-curled fist. "It's a one-inch punch. Bruce Lee and Clint Eastwood are the badasses of all badasses. And I think the way you talk is cute." He booped my nose and turned to continue into the gym.

The pungent aroma of sweat and bleach permeated the air as we entered. It was small, but an adequate size to hold all the equipment. There was a treadmill in the back and a few racks of free weights and dumbbells. Law led me through a group of about ten punching bags in all shapes and sizes, suspended from the ceiling by metal chains. Above the wall of mirrors, the words *Hold's Gym* were painted on the wall. Scattered blue and black mats covered the concrete floor.

Two people were working out when we walked in, one at the wall lined with three speed bags, and another looking at the hooks holding large groupings of jump ropes.

He walked into a back office, and I hung back, just outside the door. On the wall, there was an old framed newspaper article that read "Holden Russo Wins World Heavyweight Boxing Title."

A strange male voice asked, "What are you doing here so early? You don't train until tonight."

"I know. I brought in someone new. Off the books," Law replied. There was a pause.

"You going to explain?"

"Wasn't planning on it."

"You want to get some sparring in since you're here?"

"No, I'm just going to show her around."

"Her?" I heard a creaking noise, probably from a chair. "I gotta see this."

A huge man with sandy-brown hair filled the door frame. He made Law almost look skinny, he was so massive. They had the same nose, and the shape of their eyes was similar, but the resemblance stopped there. My guess was that Law and Sloane took after their mother. He had a huge smile on his face as he just about bowled me over when he turned into the hallway. Warm green eyes took me in, his smile decorated with dimples. Well, Law had gotten the dimples from his dad.

"Hi," I said, righting myself.

"Who's this?" he asked, looking me over. The question was directed at Law, but I beat him to answering it.

"I'm Sloane's new roommate and the bane of your son's existence. Law had to defend me last Friday night, so I think he thought bringing me here would save him from a rap sheet."

He boomed a hearty laugh. I offered my hand. He knocked it aside and swept me into a bear hug.

"Get your hands off my girl, Pops."

"Or what? You going to fight me for her?" his dad challenged.

"Please," Law scoffed. "You can't take me, old man. You're getting slow in your old age."

Holden set me down with a wink and turned to his son. "Right now, I'm about to show your girl what a real man is."

Law looked to me. "This should be quick."

"That's what I'm afraid of," I said dryly. I wasn't worried about the safety of the boxing champ, for sure.

"You'll pay for that later," Law said, his hand landing on my ass sharply, making me yelp.

"I like this girl already," Holden laughed.

They moved to the side of the ring and began putting on sparring equipment. When they were ready, they each swung their bodies through the ropes with the grace and speed of practiced professionals. My nerves ratcheted upward.

They danced around each other on the balls of their feet, gloved hands held in front of their faces. They were as graceful as ballet dancers, with the deadly air of a predator. Holden's arm popped out to swing so fast I barely saw it, but Law did. He ducked, and the flying fist only met air.

Law's fist curved up, catching his father in the ribs with an *oof*, but not so much as a flinch more in reaction. Law was fast as he dodged his father's meaty fists. With each missed hit, the pride in his father's eyes was evident. Until one of those lethal swings connected with the edge of Law's jaw. He stumbled back, shaking his head.

"Dropped your guard," Holden boomed with a steely voice. "Fists in front of your face."

"Won't happen again," Law grumbled back.

Holden came at him hard with a well-practiced combo. Law dodged the first two swings, but the third caught him on the side of his head, near his ear. His eyes unfocused and he fell to one knee. His dad ripped off his gloves with the loud sound of tearing Velcro and threw them to the ground.

"I want that combo on a bag two hundred times after you finish showing her around," Holden said. "Tonight, we'll drill block and evade two hundred more times before Keith gets here to spar with you. You're never going to make pro if you don't take this seriously." He dipped under the ropes and dropped down in front of me. "It was nice meeting you," he added with a forced smile and went back to his office.

Law still sat on one knee staring blindly at the wall to my right.

"Hey, you okay?" I asked.

He punched his fist to the ground with a frustrated grunt and fell to his ass, draping his elbows around his knees. His chin dropped to his chest.

"I didn't know you were training to go pro," I said, climbing into the ring with him.

"Yeah." He shook his head and looked back toward the office where his dad retreated. "It's not so much a choice with him. At least not for me."

He looked up and I could see the pain in his eyes, completely open to me. I knew, right then, I was in trouble. I sat down next to him and dropped my chin on his bicep. I had no words, nothing to compare it to. I had no parent to make demands of my future, but I knew my mom would've supported me no matter what I wanted out of life. So, I did the only thing I knew how. I sat there and offered silent support and would listen, if he decided to talk.

Chapter Fifteen

Now

After changing into clean clothes, I head outside to the pool house. It's a prefab, installed a few years ago in an attempt to lead normal lives without having to leave the house. Part of it is a storage closet for the pool equipment, but the majority of it is a fully functional gym.

I leave the lights off except the one near the entryway and sit on a bench against the far wall after grabbing wraps off a shelf. It's cool and dark as I proceed to tape my wrists. The hum of the window unit air conditioner is the only sound filling the space. Once I'm ready, I grab a jump rope off the wall and move to warm up my muscles. Then I start on the heavy bag and work on combos. *Thump thump.*

The door behind me opens, and I look to the wall of mirrors to find Dex.

"So, she fights, too," he says, taking in the small space. His gaze lands on me. "This is a nice setup you got here."

I release a puff of air and throw another combo. *Thumpthump thwack.* "What do you want, Dex. Why are you here?"

He shrugs. "It's my job."

"That's not what I mean." *Thumpthump thump.* "Your job requires you to wait outside the building and see if you catch someone spying. Instead, you're in here. I guess this's just how you operate. But at some point, I'm gonna hafta shower and sleep, and things are gonna get awfully awkward if you keep this shit up."

He shrugs, lips pursed, trying to hide a smile. "I can think of a few ways to make it less awkward."

Thump thwack thump. "Do you have some form of multiple personality disorder that I need to know about?"

"No, why?" His brows draw together sharply.

"I can't keep up with you. One minute you're flirting, the next minute you're rejecting me."

He took a step toward me. "I didn't—"

"Don't." *Thump thumpthump thwack.* "I don't want to talk about it. What's done is done. It's in the past, and talking about it's unnecessary. This is a professional relationship, and we should just stick to that. I think it'll make it easier since we're gonna be around each other a lot for the foreseeable future."

"You're right. I think we had a false start. Maybe we should start over. Hi, I'm Dex McClellan, an undercover cop posing as a tattoo artist. I'm here to serve and protect you. Help catch a stalker and possible murderer. And I promise not to flirt with you again. Unless we're in front of people, but only to keep up appearances." He smirks. "Deal?"

Thumpthump thump. "Deal."

He rolls his finger in circles, indicating that I should continue.

I try to fight a smile. "I'm Maddie Dobransky, aka Laine Dobransky, former rock star, and owner of Mad Lane Records. Though, apparently, that title now includes stalker bait. I'll try and be less of a bitch, but no promises. I'll also try and not be awkward when we're pretending to be boyfriend-girlfriend. But again, no promises."

He offers his hand, and I shake it. A full-dimpled smile spreads across his face.

"Now that we got the introductions out of the way… we should probably talk about the eight-hundred-pound elephant in the room."

"Dex, I told—"

"I'm talking about *that*," he says, gesturing to the weight bench near the wall.

Another flower lies across the seat, with another rolled-up piece of parchment, tied up in black satin. My stomach drops. I hadn't even seen it, though; my mind had been elsewhere. My vision starts fading. It isn't until Dex lays a hand on my shoulder that I realize that I'm holding my breath. I take in a big gulp of air, my legs giving out as I drop to the mats. *This is really happening again.*

"I can take this into the station tonight," Dex says, crouching in front of me, concern stamped on his face. "We don't have to bring anyone here. You wouldn't happen to have any gloves or Ziploc bags around, would you?"

"I think we have both in the pool closet." My voice comes out flat and emotionless. "Caleb uses the gloves working with the chemicals. And I'm pretty sure there are some Ziplocs leftover from a barbecue."

Dex looks around as if we're standing in the pool closet.

"It's accessible from outside," I answer his unasked question. "The door facing the pool."

He nods. "Okay, I'll be right back."

On his way out, he bumps into Evan, who's coming in, looking sheepish.

"You come to get your ass whoopin', Son?" I joke, but with my lack of enthusiasm, it falls flat.

Evan runs his hand over his head. "You know I was just messing with you, right? I deleted that video the moment I found it."

"Good," I say with a wan smile. "Though I'm over it, really. Doesn't seem important after *that.*" I motion to the flower.

Evan's eyes narrow as they land on the items, and his jaw ticks.

"It's really happening again, isn't it?"

"Looks like it." He shakes his head, frowning.

"I don't know if I can do this. I barely survived last time."
I release a shaky breath. "You know how bad it got."

"I know." He sits next to me and pulls me into his side.
"But you're stronger now, Mads. We'll catch this guy, and
you'll come out of this stronger than ever."

"We'll see. I know one thing for certain—I won't let this
guy drag anyone else into it this time. That's for damn sure."

"Got it," Dex says.

I turn around to see him striding through the door with a
small box in each hand. He sets the boxes down next to the
flower and takes out a pair of yellow latex gloves and gallon-
size plastic bags. He carefully places the flower and ribbon in
separate bags, then starts working on flattening the
parchment and putting it in its own bag. When he finishes, he
lifts the note to read it.

Swiftly, he pulls out his phone and hits a number. "I'm
going to need a black-and-white unit to…"

My attention to what he's saying falters as my focus on the
note increases. I stand on shaky legs and make my way to
Dex. His lips press into a flat line when I approach, but he
hands me the note, reluctantly.

The boy won't be a problem anymore

the note reads in the same crooked type.

Holy shit. Caleb. My heart thumps at erratic speeds as I turn
and head for the door. Fear infuses me. I may not like the
boy, but I don't want to see him harmed because of me. I feel
so fucking powerless, tears well in my eyes.

Evan catches me around the waist to stop me before I can
reach the door. He takes the note still clutched in my hands
and reads, cursing under his breath.

"Stay here, Maddie," Evan says and nods to Dex. "Let
them handle it. That's what they're here for."

The doorbell rings, and I roll over, facing the alarm clock. It's half past five on a Tuesday morning. *Seriously, my alarm hasn't even gone off yet.* I drag myself out of bed, thinking of all the ways I'll dismember the person who just rang the doorbell a second time. I cringe at the loud noise as I grab my robe and slip it over my nightgown.

The police detail on Caleb left last night; there should be no emergency. He was fine when they showed up. The police questioned him, and he claimed to know nothing. He said he didn't have a clue what anyone was talking about, but I think the prophetic message worked anyway, because his father told me I'd have to find a new pool boy. I haven't seen the kid since.

I make it to the foyer just as Evan is dragging himself down the stairs with a yawn.

"I'll get it," I say as I pass him.

I look out the window, and Dex is standing there, drink carrier, donut box, and a paper sack in his hands. *What in the actual fuck?* I open the door to my now-least-favorite person in the world.

"Why are you here so goddamn early?" I say without preamble.

"Just trying to be a good boyfriend," he says with a wink. His eyes trail over me.

I tug my robe closed and tie the belt.

"I brought breakfast." He lifts the stuff in his hands and pushes past me.

Audra, appearing from the darkness behind him, follows him in, looking about as happy as I am to be up this early. She mumbles something about, "Sorry... crazy dad doesn't... kids need their sleep."

"Good morning," I say and hug her. "Why don't you go crawl in bed with the girls?"

She nods and trudges up the stairs, dragging her feet.

"What's up, man?" he says to Evan, who's standing on the bottom step still looking half-asleep.

"Coffee?" Evan replies with a yawn.

"You take it black? If not, I've got the extra stuff in this bag and some breakfast tacos."

Evan perks up and follows Dex to the kitchen. "Thank God. You have no idea what it's like staying with a non-coffee-drinker."

I drag my feet after the guys. If I close my eyes right now, I'll probably go back to sleep standing here in the foyer.

"You never answered my question," I say, yawning and taking a seat next to Evan on a barstool at the kitchen counter. "I don't eat breakfast."

"I know," Dex answers. "I thought I'd feed you something besides that protein shit stick you had yesterday for breakfast."

"It's not a shit stick. It's healthy," I defend. "It's part of my training."

"Training for what?" He raises an eyebrow at me as he sets a foil-wrapped package in front of me, calling me on my bullshit. "Coffee?"

"Now *that* truly is shit. No, thank you," I answer, deciding to ignore his penetrating gaze. "Whatever, just grab me a coke."

He hands Evan a coffee and a foil package, then places the donut box between us. He comes back with a Coke and then leans on the counter, sipping his coffee. He's looking at me, so I open the foil package. The smell of eggs, bacon, potato, and sausage permeates my senses, and my mouth waters. I look back up at him as I take a bite with zero amusement on my face. He grins.

My mind runs over my schedule for the day. It's the first Tuesday of the month, so I'm heading over to the Mad House, my other business. I'll be there all day to review the books and do my monthly checks. I really don't want to take him there.

"Do you really have to go everywhere with me today?" I ask, meeting his eyes. "Can't Evan come? Or one of the security guys and leave it at that?"

He sets down his coffee and leans over, propping his

elbows on the counter. He steeples his fingers together at his chin as he watches me. I try not to squirm, but I don't feel comfortable when he gets intense like this.

"Why don't you want me to come?"

"Because it's boring, and a little weird to bring your boyfriend to work, don't you think?"

"It wasn't weird yesterday. I was even helpful. The question is—what's on the schedule today that you don't want me to know about?"

I look away. He was helpful yesterday at the office, but this is an entirely different situation. Bridget has gone to great lengths, legally speaking, to keep my name far away from it. Only a handful of people even know of my involvement.

"You're going to the House, right?" Evan asks.

"Yeah," I answer, keeping my eyes trained on the counter in front of me.

"The House?" Dex says, pressing his steepled fingertips to his lips repeatedly. "Sounds fun." He slaps his hands on the counter with a grin.

I honestly think it entertains him more when I'm bothered by his presence than if I were happily clinging to him all day. *Fucking men, I'll never understand them.*

He moves around the counter and sits next to me. I finish off my food, in a hurry to get away from him.

"You should go get ready," Dex says. "I'll get the girls up."

He brushes the hair back from my shoulder, and it's too much. I stand.

"Okay, I'm gonna hit the shower. Then we can go."

He's smirking at me as I turn to go to my room. *Fucking evil torturer.*

165

Chapter Sixteen

Then

"I've something special planned for tonight, if you're up for it," Law said as he crossed from the door to my bed in my tiny dorm.

He was wearing a black button-down shirt and dark jeans. Kind of fancy for him, since he was usually in his I'm-a-badass-nerd gear.

It'd been a year, and we were still seeing each other. Well, still fucking each other. *Seeing* implies a whole level of relationship dynamic that we weren't.

Saturdays and Sundays, I went back home, alone, to be with the twins. He never questioned what I did, or who was there, just gave me strict instructions not to orgasm without him. Though edging was encouraged. We'd never had a conversation that defined what we were to each other. We just kind of fell into a rhythm together and never got off beat.

He placed a medium-sized gift bag on the bed in front of me and sat on the edge, leaning his back against the wall.

"What could this be?" I eyed the package warily, tapping my finger on my lower lip. "It's not my birthday. You don't need to buy me things, you know?"

He grabbed me and pulled me onto the bed, rolling me underneath him in one smooth move. He pushed my hair back from my face.

"I know." He leaned down and brushed his lips over mine. "Perhaps that's why I like doing it. Because you don't expect it."

"So, if I start expecting you to buy me things, you'll stop doing it?"

"No, silly girl, I won't. I like spoiling you." He grinned, giving me dimple. "Now open it. It has a specific use for tonight, but I won't tell you about it until you open the damn thing."

He climbed off me and dropped the bag on the center of my stomach. I sat up, scooting back on the bed. The bag was a black-and-white damask pattern with black tissue peeking out the top. I pulled on the tissue and removed the first item. It was a slinky black spaghetti-strap dress.

I looked to him, frowning.

He motioned me to continue. I pulled out a pair of black leather spiked heels that looked like they were hand-picked by Sloane, not something I'd wear. I retrieved the last item—what seemed to be a thin, black scarf. It was not a scarf. I held it up. It looked like Zorro's mask.

"Is this a new role play? I'm sexy Zorro, and you're—" I couldn't think of the name of Zorro's enemy.

He laughed. "No. It's the dress code for a party. I want to take you."

"We go to masked parties now?" I asked.

The role play was more believable than that. We did that quite a bit. Like the one time Law had me tied up with ropes like a damsel in an old western stuck on the train tracks. He did have a thing for old movies. And tying me up.

"It's a club. The Black Mask Society is unofficially a part of my school. They've been extending an invitation to me for years. I've never been interested until now. You have to bring a date. It's just not like a normal party. It's a place where people experiment."

"Experiment?"

"Yeah, like… sexually. Whatever you want, it's on the

menu. There are rules, though, so if we go and you're not comfortable, we can leave, and nothing will happen."

"Rules?"

"Uh-huh, no uninvited touching. No going into occupied rooms uninvited, except the main rooms."

I nodded, absorbing this without judgment.

"And no names."

"You wanna try this?" I asked, and he nodded slowly. "What's the point? I mean, what're you expecting from it?"

"I've no expectations. I just love watching you. When you learn something new that you like, your mouth turns into this little O of amazement." He smirked. "It's—" He shook his head. "It turns me on like nothing else."

He was good at that—low-key pressure. A nudge in the right direction, the temptation of pleasing him, which always ended with my pleasure. A gentle push outside of my comfort zone, but never too far. I'd changed so much in the last year, though I had no complaints. Truly.

"Okay," I answered.

"Okay?" He looked at me to confirm he heard me right. I nodded.

"I'm serious, no expectations. You're in charge. I won't do or try anything unless you give me the green light. Okay?"

I smiled at him. "I get to be in charge? That's a first." I quirked an eyebrow and laughed.

He threw my pillow at me. "You know what I mean. You get to say go, and like always you get to say barnacle."

I laughed out loud as I lay back.

"We really should find a new word if I've to start using it in public."

"Get dressed." He pointed to the dress, his eyes darkening with lust.

I stood up and pulled off my flannel shirt. I pushed up the bottom of my tank top, exposing my stomach and enjoying the way his jaw went slack. I popped the button on my jeans and slowly pulled the zipper down. The sound echoed in the tiny, quiet room. I loved the way his eyes rounded, and he swallowed as he got a peek at my black lace Brazilian hipster underwear. Sloane was right. They accentuated all the best parts of my ass. Though she instantly regretted the recommendation, knowing her brother was the only one who'd get to enjoy them. I smiled thinking of it. I'm pretty sure she brought out my evil streak. Or Law did.

I pulled my tank top over my head and looked back at Law. He pulled his cock out and started stroking himself. I was hypnotized. My eyes tracked the up-and-down motion of his tattooed fingers. I licked my lips.

"You need to put that dress on, now. Before I have my way with you and we never make it out of this room."

I walked over to him, still entranced. I kneeled between his knees. "Perhaps I should take care of you before we go. So you won't feel any *pressure*." I whispered the last part, my eyes drifting half-shut.

"Put your hands behind your back."

I moaned, letting my head fall back, eyes shut. I knew what that tone meant, and I loved when he did this. My hands, already by my side, moved to position.

He got up from the bed, walked behind me, and grabbed the silky mask. He tied it around my wrists, not really binding me, just tight enough to remind me where to keep them.

"God, you're so beautiful," he said, stroking my hair. "So willing, so eager."

I grew impossibly wet. I loved it when Law talked to me. He had the sexiest voice and said the sexiest things.

"Please," I begged. I'd no idea how he had turned me into a wanton sex kitten, but he absolutely did.

He walked around to the front of me, his cock bumping against my lips. I leaned forward, opening the line of my throat and running my tongue along the bottom of his shaft from hilt to head, toying with his piercing to elicit a moan. I swirled my tongue around the tip and then waited for him to slide in all the way. He gripped my hair, pulling. I moaned as he began to move in and out, bumping the back of my throat with every stroke. It'd taken some training to get me to the point that it didn't make me gag.

I looked up to his face, watching him lose control. The absolute pleasure he couldn't hide made me feel powerful. He wasn't a man you got to feel powerful with often, but this was my time. I felt him pulse when I unsheathed my teeth and pushed up with my tongue. He jerked and slowed, then stopped as he spilled down my throat. I sucked and swallowed everything. He dropped to his knees in front of me, grasping the back of my head with one hand and undoing the mask off my wrists with the other.

"You absolutely undo me, Laine." He kissed me deep and passionately, moaning when he tasted himself on me. I crawled into his lap, and he stilled. "Get dressed."

I gave a frustrated sigh and rubbed myself against him.

"Do you want to leave this room?"

"Yes," I sighed and moved away to pull the dress over my head. Once finished, I looked back, and he was leaning against my dresser, all put away. He watched me silently as I moved to my desk to pull out my brush and makeup mirror. I fixed my face, but my hair still looked pretty good, falling in long, mahogany waves down my back. I looked through Sloane's things and found a black clutch and stuffed my phone, some cash, and the mask into it, then turned to face him.

"Ready," I stated.

"Let's go." He held out his hand, and I took it as I followed him out to the parking lot to his bike.

"Are you sure about this?" I asked, yanking on the sides of the dress. It rode up my thighs with him between my legs.

"Yes, it's fine. No one can see anything with me sitting here. Though I kind of wish I could see this from afar." He ran his hand down my thigh, making me shiver. "If this party is a bust, we can always go for another ride."

I smiled as I put on my helmet, remembering that day he took me out to Hill Country, speeding along stretches of back roads. When my adrenaline was nice and high, he'd pulled off the road behind a group of trees and laid me on the front of the bike, making me come twice with his mouth and fingers. Then he'd had me flip, straddling the bike with my hands gripping the handlebars as he pounded me from behind. Yeah, that was a good day.

We drove through most of downtown before stopping in front of an old, grand colonial-style house. It was huge. The kind that politicians and corporate bigwigs owned. Whoever ran this Black Mask Society had connections, or money, or both.

Law made me hop off, then jumped the curb, and parked right on the sidewalk. I wasn't sure that was legal, but I wasn't sure anyone would give a Ducati a ticket in this part of town. He shut down the bike and hopped off, taking the helmet from my hands and attaching it to the handlebars.

"You ready?" he asked, looking up at the big house and pulling his mask out of his pocket. I did the same and looked up at him. He was staring at my lips. "You look sexy as hell tonight."

"Law? What if someone recognizes me?"

"They won't. I can barely tell it's you, and I look at you more than anyone else. Besides, these are UT students. I doubt anyone from your school is here. And this whole thing exists on secrecy. People wouldn't come and participate if word were to get out about who's here. What happens here, stays here."

He pressed his lips to mine briefly, then grabbed my hand, leading me up the stairs to the front door.

The pillars that winged the door were massive. A man wearing a black suit and tie answered the door without a word. Law held up a small black card. The man nodded and held an arm out, ushering us inside. There were black curtains ahead, blocking the activity behind from view, but I could hear the murmur of voices beyond its cover.

Law led the way, and I followed, unsure about the mysterious and dangerous vibe this whole deal put out. Law held back the curtain and guided me through with a hand on my lower back.

Beyond the curtain was a massive double staircase that framed the entrance to a dimly lit room. To the right and the left were other rooms, similarly lit. I had to concentrate on not tripping in these shoes. People were everywhere. I didn't know what to expect when being invited to a sex club, but this certainly wasn't it. There were people of all shapes and sizes, in all states of dress or undress. I froze in place, shocked.

Every woman was in black, wearing the same style dress as I was. The men all had the same black button-down shirt. Well, those that were still dressed. One woman walked by wearing a cage of leather straps and metal rings fitted to her body.

"Which way do we go?" I whispered.

"Whichever way you want," Law answered. "You're in the lead here."

I looked right, at what seemed to be a dining room. A group of several men were licking and sucking on a woman who lay on the table, writhing in ecstasy. Other people sat around the table, either watching or doing things with a partner or alone. One man sat alone, sipping a drink, watching. I turned. My heart was pounding.

To the left was a sitting room with couches and chairs, all ornate and gold trimmed. A man was bound and naked on his knees while people sitting on the seating arrangement gave him commands and took turns touching him. Wow.

I was so out of my depth here. I turned to see Law watching me. Only me.

"Straight ahead, I guess?" I answered him.

He nodded and guided me in that direction. When we passed the staircase, I realized that this room had wall-to-wall windows that overlooked an atrium garden, completely encased by the house. I couldn't see what was out there because right in front of me was a sunken living room with a sectional couch surrounded by lighting equipment and several cameras. There was a TV displaying the acts taking place on said sectional. I stopped in my tracks and took it all in.

I suppose some people like to be recorded.

This whole house seemed to have a room set up to cater to every fantasy. A few people were gathered around the large flat-screen while others looked on at the live action taking place. Two men were making out with a woman.

"You like that, don't you?" Law whispered in my ear. I didn't look at or answer him, watching the scene play out before me. He pulled me back against him. I felt how hard he was against my lower back. "You're making that face, and you know what it does to me."

He reached around and pinched my nipple. I let out a breathy moan in response. He was right. I was getting turned on. I leaned my head back against his shoulder and pushed his hand down to the edge of my dress. His fingers brushed over my panties, and my back bowed. I was so sensitive.

"You have no idea how perfect you are. How sexy you look at this moment." He brushed my hair to the side, exposing my neck. I leaned my head to the side, giving him access. He trailed his lips and tongue up the side of my neck to my ear. His finger pushed aside my panties, entering me at the same time one of the men did the same to the woman I was watching. "Are you okay with this? Some people are watching you now."

I nodded.

"My dirty girl has a little exhibitionist in her. You want me to expose you?" he asked, his hand pausing at the top of my breast.

"Yes," I whispered, grinding my hips into his hand.

He pushed down my dress, exposing one breast, then the other. I was so close to coming as his hand squeezed my breast.

"Hey, Front Man," a familiar voice called to my left. "You two want to do that for the camera? Those little sounds she's making are like a mating call. She's already drawn quite the crowd."

My head snapped to the side, and my gaze met familiar green eyes. Recognition dawned in them. "Holy fuck,

Neddie?"

"Barnacle!" I yanked Law's hands off me and righted my dress. "Lucky?"

"How do you know Lucky?" Law asked.

"How do you know him?" I parroted.

"He's the one that runs this thing. He gave me the invite."

My jaw dropped, and I cut my eyes to Nic. "You're running a sex club? Using my nickname?"

Nic's mouth opened and closed, making him look rather like a fish. I was the one who was feeling out of water, though.

"I'm leaving. We're done here." I moved toward the door, but Nic grabbed my elbow.

Law's hand spread out on his chest in warning. "She didn't say you could touch her."

"Well, I can touch her," Nic growled. "I've been touching her since the day she was born."

That didn't sound right at all.

"Stop. It's okay," I said to Law, before shifting my focus back to Nic. "This is why we haven't hung out lately?"

"Do either of you mind filling me in on how the fuck you know each other?" Law asked, his eyes darting between us.

"He's family," I say, flinging my hand toward Nic.

"I'm sorry, Ned—you want to follow me?" he asked, scanning the room with his eyes. I suddenly realized we had an audience. Everyone in the room had stopped. *Fuck.* I wanted to shrivel up and fade from existence on the spot.

Nic started walking. I followed, with Law right behind me. We walked down a short hall to a locked door. Nic fished a key out of his pocket and opened it.

I held up a flat palm to Law. "Just give me a second," I said, then shut the door behind me.

"Oh, hey." Nic smirked. "Now that I've got you alone—"
He sauntered toward me across the ornate office.

"Don't start with me, Lucky." I sighed. "I just have to set a few ground rules. One, do not say anything about Jared. Two, do not say anything about the girls."

"Maddie—"

"That's number three. I go by Laine now—call me Laine."

"Fine. How 'bout I just stick with Neddie?"

"Fine. I'm not finished, though. Rule four, do *not* breathe a word of this to Evan."

He nodded. "That's your boyfriend out there?"

"No. Yes. Maybe. Not really?" My voice rose in pitch to a squeak. "Can we start with easy questions first?"

He raised both eyebrows at me. "Why are you here with him?"

"Because he invited me." I shrugged.

He stayed silent, waiting for more explanation than that.

"I maybe… I'm seeing him, sort of. We don't go on dates or anything like that. We just—" I wave my hand to indicate the world inside this house.

"How long?" A grin tipped the corner of his mouth.

"For a little over a year." I tried to distract from the discomfort I was feeling over discussing my sex life with Nic by adding, "We're in a band together."

His face scrunched in confusion. "Come again?"

"We're in a band together," I repeated. "Well, I joined them last year, but we're playing a gig next Friday. You wanna come?"

"Yeah, I do." He started pacing. "Holy shit! You're the chick with the short skirts in the band that everyone talks about? Neddie—" He pinches the bridge of his nose.

There was a light knock on the door and Law's not-so-happy face appeared in the opening. I motioned him over to me and held out my hand. He shut the door behind him and took my proffered hand, moving to stand behind me.

"Does Evan know about any of this?" Nic asked.

"Not really" I answered. "I told him that I finally made new friends and all."

He pinched the bridge of his nose again. "Neddie—"

"Why do you keep calling her that?" Law asked.

"I named us after *The Three Amigos* when we were kids," I explained. "Evan was Dusty Bottoms, he was Lucky Stars, and I was Little Neddie. We've been best friends since we were old enough to say the words. Though the names only stuck between us two. Nobody else calls us that. Except—" I looked over to Nic as a thought occurred to me. "You want to explain what you're doing running a sex club, *Lucky*?"

"To use your own words, not really."

Now

"What are you doing?" Cora asks from the back seat of the car.

"Taking y'all to school," I reply as I pull up to the light with my left blinker on.

"We always ride with the kids on first Tuesdays," Cat complains. "Audra can ride, too. She already knows most of them from school."

"Fine," I say with a sigh.

I put my right blinker on and pull out on to the road. I can see Dex studying me out of the corner of my eye, but he stays silent. The ride is quick and quiet from that point on. I think the girls are still half-asleep. The place isn't far.

We pull up to the curb in front of the Mad House just as Tina is walking out to the van full of kids. She stops and waves with a smile. The girls are out of the car before I kill the engine. Dex waits for me.

"Just don't read too much into this," I say with a sigh. "And never tell anyone that you've been here or that I've anything to do with this place."

I get out of the car and put on a smile as I approach Tina. She's smiling and shaking Audra's hand as the girls introduce her. The twins give me hurried kisses on my cheeks and say bye, then take off to the van with Audra in tow.

"You got room for one more?" I ask.

"Sure, Monk's staying here to go over stuff with you. She can take his seat." She takes a sip from her travel mug as her eyes dart over my shoulder. "Who's the hottie?"

"New boyfriend," I say with a shrug, trying to make it less

of a deal.

I feel like I need to swallow bile, that's how bitter lying to my friends tastes.

"Ew, clingy type? He doesn't look like a clinger. Though, can't say I'd complain if that's what was clinging." She tilts her head to the side, blatantly checking out Dex. She steps in front of him as he approaches. "Tina."

He shakes her offered hand, looking amused. "Dex."

She tilts his hand to the side, studying the tattoos on his arm. "Nice ink." She points to his neck. "Got a dragon back there?"

"Yeah." His face transforms into a full smile. "It's a full back piece."

"Show me." She walks around him and pulls up his shirt. "Whoa, that's nice, dude. Where'd you get it done?"

"Buddy of mine at work. I'm an artist too, but not talented enough to do my own back." He winks at me with a grin that has his dimples on full display.

I try to ignore the reason I feel the need to press my thighs together. I'm curious as to what it looks like, but the more rational part of me says I need to stay away from seeing any more of his unclothed body.

"He's the one who did your ink?" she asks, casting a glance at my wrist.

"Yeah. Tina, quit molesting him," I say in an exaggerated whisper, nodding my head in the direction of the van. "Put his shirt down. The kids are watching."

"Not molesting—yet. Just professional curiosity," Tina says to me with a wink but does as I ask. "I'm a piercer over at Tribal Designs," she says to Dex.

"You work there and here?" Dex asks.

"Nah, here's just free rent, not so much a job. Though, I do have to cook dinners and chauffeur. Monk and I enjoy the company. Anyway, I've gotta run, or these skids are gonna be late." She walks backward. "I approve, Mads. Nice meeting you."

"Nice meeting you, too," Dex replies.

He turns back to me with questions all over his face. I turn and rush to the house. He has to jog to catch up.

"You keep an interesting staff."

"Friends, not staff," I correct as I open the door and walk in.

When Tina told me that she and Monk couldn't have kids, I knew that this would be a perfect fit. Bridget and I'd already been working on bringing this project to life. When I asked, Tina was over the moon about it. Excited would be an understatement. I smile, remembering that moment.

"You want to explain what exactly this place is?" he asks as his eyes roam over the decor. He pauses in front of the logo painted in the center of a black wall to the right of the entry. The Cheshire Cat's eyes and smile peek out from behind purple, smoky letters that spell *Mad House*.

"It's basically a foster home," I say going up the stairs to the third floor, which is where the office in Tina and Monk's apartment is located. "Every kid in the state foster system has the option to apply here. They're accepted if they agree to play a musical instrument of their choice, keep up their grades, and attend our after-school music lessons."

The Mad House is larger than my house; it's an actual mansion. It's pretty cool, too. I had it decorated to look like the Mad Hatter's place from *Alice in Wonderland*, yet very modern. The kids like it, and the girls love to come hang out here. The downstairs is all general gathering rooms, like a soundproof music room, a quiet room, computer room, TV room, and game room plus the kitchen and dining room and a couple of soundproof mini rooms for the kids to practice their music.

"That's—" He pauses as if searching for the words. "You're really quite amazing."

I halt and turn to him. He's right behind me, two steps down, so it puts us at eye level with each other.

"I told you not to read into it, Dex." I fight to keep the bite out of my tone. "I've more money than I know what to do with and needed something to spend it on. That's all."

We've gone to great lengths to separate this place from my identity. Publicly, I've no ties to it. I don't want these kids being dragged out in the spotlight with me, in any way.

"Hey, I'm not reading into anything," he says in a placating tone. "Give yourself a little credit. This is a big deal. I should know."

"What the fuck does that mean?" Having him here is putting me on edge. It feels too personal and makes me feel vulnerable.

His eyes roam over the mural painted on the wall of the stairs. It's a three-dimensional depiction of the Mad Hatter's tea party that makes you feel as if you're walking sideways if you try to stare at it while going up the stairs.

"I grew up in the system, Maddie. Never in a place like this. This is like a dream."

"Oh—" I stop there because I'm struck speechless.

I look down at my hands as I twist my fingers into the rubber band at my wrist. I was never in the system like these kids, but I've heard their stories. It's what makes me feel comfortable around them. They don't judge me by my broken parts. He lifts my chin, making me look at him.

"This place is badass enough that *I* want to live here. And the fact that it's bigger and better decorated than your home says something, too. Don't bullshit a bullshitter, Mads."

I startle a bit at the name. He hasn't called me anything but Maddie since we met.

"I know what you're doing," he says softly as his fingers brush my cheek and push my hair back over my shoulder. "I've been there before."

My heart thuds erratically in my chest.

The door opens behind him. Chloe's turquoise head of hair appears downstairs.

"Hey, lady," she calls. "Sorry I'm late."

"We haven't even made it up to the office yet. No big." I shrug and turn back up the stairs, grateful for the distraction.

Chapter Seventeen

Now

Wading knee-deep into the water, I turn around to face Dex as he backs the trailer hooked to his jeep into the water.

I'm thankful that his jeep could tow the Jet Skis because we usually have to rent a truck to get them out to the lake. I signal for him to start backing up. When he's far enough, I signal for him to stop and set about unhooking the Jet Skis from the trailer with Evan.

I pull my sunglasses back down over my eyes as the lake reflects the bright sunlight into my face. The gentle waves and movement of Lake Travis lap against my knees, instilling a calmness over me that I can't find in many other places. When we have the Jet Skis pulled away from the trailer, I give Dex a thumbs-up and climb on to drive it to the beach where we're camped for the day.

Cat and Audra bounce on their toes as I approach. Cora wades out to get on the other Jet Ski with Evan.

"Y'all stay with Evan and be careful," I remind them as I climb off and let Cat take the handlebars. "Don't go too fast, and don't drive into wakes, okay?"

"Got it, Mom. This ain't my first rodeo," she says with a grin.

"Fine. Don't make me regret this, please," I beg.

This is the first time I've let either of my girls go out on one of these machines alone. Even though technically Evan'll be with them the whole time, it still makes me nervous. I hand off my life jacket to Audra, who snaps it on quickly and climbs on behind Cat.

"Later, Miss D," Audra says as I push them away from the beach.

A genuine smile blooms across me face for her. "Have fun."

Cat starts the engine and eases over to where Evan is waiting. He says something to them, the girls nod, and then they're off.

I turn and march back up the beach to our spot. Marcus and Nic are working on getting the grill set up. Those two have become fast friends. I walk over to Holly, Chloe, and Bridget, who are sitting in lawn chairs around a patch of sand where Hope plays with a variety of toys.

I dig up a beer from the ice chest and turn to take my seat, only to realize that Dex is sitting in my chair. I make a face at him, and he shrugs with a dimpled grin. I walk past him to the next chair over, when he grabs me and pulls me into his lap. His hand lands on my hip, and his mouth is at my ear before I have a chance to struggle.

"We've gotta sell it, Maddie."

He's right. We're in a public place and not at my work. We'd act like a normal couple. *It doesn't mean anything. Just relax.* I can see the logic. The lake is crowded today. I relent and lean into him, resting my head on his shoulder.

"I'm sorry. I'm not used to the physical contact. You're pretty patient with me. It's just—you just don't know—"

I'm cut off as his lips land on mine. Another chaste kiss but one that lingers long enough that my lips start to tingle from the contact.

"I know all I need to know, right now," he says, effectively cutting me off and ending the conversation.

I drink my beer as I look at him, but his attention is out on the lake, so I take a moment to study his profile. I think that if I weren't so fucked-up, I'd probably go for him. He's a very attractive guy. His square jaw lined with that short, stubbly beard. It's a good look.

"How old is she?" he asks, looking in Holly's direction.

"Two years younger than me."

He looks at me blandly. "I meant the baby."

"Oh, Hope. She's three."

"What happened to the dad?" he asks in a low voice. "Why isn't he around?"

"That's not my story to share, Dex."

He nods and looks back out to the lake. He has a cluster of little beauty marks near the corner of his left eye that I've never noticed before. I think because I'm always distracted by the scar through that eyebrow. I have to fight the urge not to touch them. He's the kind of guy that makes badass beautiful. It's kind of surprising that he's single.

"How're you still single?" I ask without thinking.

"Looking to change that?" he asks, raising one eyebrow with a smirk. I don't answer so he shrugs. "I don't know. Job's not conducive to meeting the right kinds of people. I gotta think about Audra." He nods out to the lake as the girls zoom by in a race against Evan and Cora. "I guess, I just hadn't met anyone worth pursuing."

I scrunch up my nose because I just can't see it. "So, you're celibate?"

What in the fuck happened to my brain-to-mouth filter? I can't believe I just said that out loud. My face heats up, but luckily, he doesn't look back at me.

"I never said that."

"Well, I already know you don't do one-night stands. And you just said you don't date."

"You're assuming a lot here, aren't you? I never said I don't do one-night stands."

"Oh, so it was just me?"

"You really want to have this conversation?" He looks at me again, and our faces are inches apart. "Because I'm not so sure you're ready to hear what I gotta say on the matter."

His face is serious, and I don't know what that means, but I think better of finding out.

"Maybe not," I say, turning away.

I can't take the proximity to him anymore, so I get up and walk to the edge of the water. I rest my toes over the waterline and wiggle them into the sand. I finish off my beer and crumple the can in my hand. Once upon a time, I let my body and heart control my actions, and I paid dearly for it. I promised myself never again. It was working so well until Dex came into the picture. He clouds my mind, and I can't think straight with him around. I need to get my shit together.

The girls and Evan are heading back our way. I look back over my shoulder and realize that the food is almost ready, too. I go to the picnic table and set up the tablecloth, putting out the sides and fixings for the meal.

I look back at the lake just in time to see Dex peel off his shirt as the girls beach the Jet Skis. Every inch of his back is covered by a massive dragon tattoo. I find myself wondering where it actually ends, since it obviously continues past his board shorts. I shake the thought away.

Dex dives in the water and kicks with his powerful legs. Water splashes over the girls. They shriek and dive after him.

He's laughing when he comes up several feet away. Cora makes it to him first and jumps on him, trying to take him down. He tosses her to the side with barely any effort, and she sails through the air several feet away, laughing and screaming. Cat and Audra try to work together, but he tosses them both.

"You're drooling," Evan says, walking up to me and pushing my mouth closed with a finger to the chin.

He shakes out his wet hair, and droplets splash across my face.

"Dammit, Ev." I hold up my hands in a futile attempt to block the water.

"You could do worse, you know," Evan says with a serious look on his face.

I roll my eyes.

"He's good with the girls. He's not after you for the fame or money or trying to further his career. Dex isn't a bad guy. I'm just saying you could do worse."

"I'm not ready, Ev," I insist.

"Ah, you mean you're not human. I've known you your whole life." He raises a brow at me. "You can fool yourself, but you're not fooling me."

"Do you really think he'd be okay dealing with all my baggage? My issues? You don't even know all of what happened that night. If anyone knew—" I shake my head. I have to stop talking about this. We're here to have fun, not dredge up the ghosts of the past. "Can we just forget it and have a good time?"

Evan nods but doesn't say anything else.

Shit. I'm such a fucking downer. I'm not even sure why my friends have stuck around the past few years. I sit on the bench, holding down the tablecloth from the breeze that threatens to carry it away. I put on a brave face while I wait for Nic to deliver the food, and work on getting through the rest of the day without depressing anyone else.

I feel a body sit on the bench behind me and turn back to find Evan there.

"I can hold down the tablecloth," he says. "And you've got time. Go. Have fun."

I look back out at the girls laughing and swimming and decide to join them. Evan's right about one thing—I should have fun, if not for me, then definitely for them. I pull off my shorts and shirt, tossing them onto the bench with my sunglasses, then head down to the beach. I check the straps on my black bikini as I walk to make sure everything is in place. I squint through the bright sunlight, but no one is paying attention to me. The girls and Dex are involved in their own game of take-down. I try to be as sneaky as possible as I wade out into the lake and sink below the surface of the water. I swim as fast as I can along the floor of the lake in their direction.

Soon, I catch sight of their feet. I can make out Dex from

the girls pretty easily and target him just as I'm running out of breath. I wrap my arms around his knees as the girls are clinging to him, plant my feet on the ground, and lift them up. They tip over and all go down into the water as I breach the surface. I take a big gulp of air and hear the tail end of their surprised shrieks as they splash about trying to right themselves. I grin. *Mission accomplished.*

"Ohhhh, you're gonna get it," Dex says, struggling against the force of the water to walk over to me.

I start backing up, holding my hands out as a barrier. The girls splash water in my direction and shout, "Get her!" in between giggles. I close my eyes briefly to protect myself from the splashing water, and when I open them, Dex is gone. I turn and try to run back to the shore, but I'm too late. A hand wraps around my ankle, and I lose my balance as I fall into the water. He pulls me back and slips an arm around my waist before rising to the surface.

He's cradling me to his chest with his other arm under my legs, and when I wipe the water from my eyes, I see the mischievous gleam in his. He adjusts my weight like he's preparing to throw me, and I screech, laughing as I throw my arms around his neck to stop him.

"Don't you do it," I warn.

"Or what?" he asks with a smirk. "How do you plan to stop me?"

He lifts me a little farther, and I shriek again, tightening my arms around his neck. My brain scrambles for a way to stop him from tossing me into the air, but my body reacts on instinct. His face is inches from mine, so I lean in and press my lips to his. It's the first time I've ever initiated lip contact with him, and I think it stuns him because he freezes for a moment, then his mouth opens, and his tongue slips into mine. I'm stunned, too, as the kiss deepens.

My lips tingle and goose bumps spread over my flesh. Dex drops my legs, his hand slips into my hair, his other arm pulls me tighter, and my legs drift in the water to surround his waist. His lips become more forceful, claiming me, the grip on my hair tightening with a possessive edge. I let out a soft whimper, forgetting about our surroundings as I pull him closer, seeking more.

I'm snapped back to reality when water splashes at us.

"Gross," Audra complains.

"Get a room, you two," Cat adds.

I jerk back and scramble to get away, but he doesn't let go. He just smiles at me, exposing those dimples like he knows I've a weakness for them. Like he knows they're weapons to be used against me.

He pulls me close and whispers into my ear, "I think that sold it, if anyone was watching."

My stomach twists as I'm slapped with the cold reality that this is just a job for him. He's obligated to be here and to protect me. I push hard on him until he releases me and head back to the picnic tables. *Why do I keep doing this to myself?* It's like I need a neon sign inside my eyelids that reminds me that this is not a real relationship every time I close them. He rejected me and got roped into playing this role. I need to remember that.

Then

We'd been up on stage for over an hour. The small crowd was pumped. The energy flowing throughout the room was electric. Vital.

Sweat trickled down my back despite the slits in the back of the white tank top I wore over a black lace bra. Sloane had taken to being my personal stylist for all our shows. My trademark was now plaid miniskirts in just about every color of the rainbow. Each came with a matching full-coverage panty underneath, so I didn't expose myself by being on a raised platform, but it was still provocative.

I'd be lying if I said I hadn't noticed the increased male attendance at our shows, but there was an increase in the female attendance rate, too. We were just becoming more popular.

Part of me hated the fact that I was displaying my body, but it was just the way things were. Sex sells. I didn't hear the catcalls and dumb remarks anymore. The guys in the audience wanted to be stupid. It was their problem. The guys in the band respected me as an artist, and that was all that mattered.

Spence had taken to educating me on the history and ways of punk music, and in turn, I offered suggestions to tweak their current lineup of songs. We spent a lot of time together over the past year since Spence had done most of the songwriting for the group, to begin with. We'd also written some new material and even came up with a few covers of very non-punk songs.

My personal favorite and first solo contribution to the band was a cover of "I Put a Spell on You" by Screamin' Jay Hawkins. The band, after hearing me perform it, also decided that I'd step up to the mic for that one, allowing Law a break in the middle of the set. There were only two more songs to go, and my cover would make its debut.

I put my awesome steel-toed combat boot up on one of the smaller speakers that lined the front of the stage. Some guy tried to scale the stage to get to me. His eyes were firmly fixed on the underside of my skirt. *Idiot.* I shook my head because it was never going to happen. I moved to stand in front of him and planted my boot on his forehead, giving him a shove until he toppled backward.

People laughed, but you really couldn't hear anything over the music. Some were throwing themselves against each other up front, mostly men. Others, pinwheeling their arms about, occasionally hitting others but not caring. Soon the crush of the crowd swallowed the stage climber, and I lost sight of him.

I walked over to Law, who was screaming into the microphone about revolt and *the system.* Typical punk music themes. My solo was coming soon, and we usually played off each other, gave a bit of a sexy show, which turned eyes to me for the solo. I leaned my head back on his shoulder as I launched into the guitar solo. His hand ran up the back of my thigh, squeezing my ass as he bit my neck. Not hard; it was all for show. Tina took a picture of this move once, and it made Law look like a punk rock god with his badass bitch wailing on the guitar at his side. Even though it was all part of the act, he still got to claim me offstage.

When my solo ended, I walked back near Monk's drum kit to release focus back to Law. I don't think I'd ever thought about how much choreography went into live band performances until I joined one. Every move served a purpose, and it was all about control, focusing the audience on what you wanted them to see. Another lesson from my wise punk sensei, Spence.

Finally, as the song came to an end, it was time for our midset break. I needed to use the restroom after downing nearly an entire bottle of water between each song. I made my way back to the edge of the stage where the stairs were. I was headed to the bathroom just off the greenroom when Spaz pushed me into the wall and bolted past me.

Fucker.

I chased him, knowing where he was going. I skidded to a stop in front of the bathroom door and threw my shoulder into it.

"Spaz? You can't do this to me again. I just need to pee. You can have at it after," I pleaded, losing the battle on forcing the door back open.

Spaz, on the other side of the door, trying to push it shut, said, "No can do, sweet cheeks. You know I gotta go."

The door thudded closed, and the lock slid into place.

"Son of a bitch!" I slammed my palm on the door. "Every. Fucking. Time! Spaz, just give me thirty seconds. Please? You know that bathroom won't be fit for use after you're done."

I pounded on the door relentlessly. I heard several chuckles from behind me and turned to find the other three guys watching me with amused grins. Seconds later, my nose was assaulted with a vile smell emanating from the bathroom. I gagged and moved away quickly. I was going to have to brave the crowd to make it to the ladies' room.

I started out the door and past the tables. I hadn't gone ten whole feet before the first hand grabbed my ass. *Seriously, guys are fucking stupid.* I spun around, and before he could blink, the heel of my palm was smashing up into his nose.

"Fuck! My nose," the asshole whined, holding his bleeding nose and tilting his head back like a dumbass. "You broke my nose, bitch."

"Serves you right for grabbing some random girl's ass." I spit the words at him. "Maybe next time you'll think twice before you do that shit."

"You were asking for it dressed like that." He waved his arm at me.

I caught sight of Law leaning against the doorway to the greenroom, watching me with a smirk on his face. Always vigilant, though he knew full well I could take care of myself.

"Yeah, I don't give a fuck how a woman is dressed. You should thank your lucky stars for the entertainment value alone. But permission, it's not. It's got nothing to do with *you* at all. So keep your fucking hands to yourself." I sneered at him one last time before turning back to the bathrooms. My way was blocked by three girls dressed in fishnet tights, short shorts, and some kind of athletic team T-shirts.

"Looks like we've a live one here," the brunette said and motioned the beefy guy behind her in my direction.

"I'm not looking for trouble," I said, holding my hands up in surrender. Beefy dude walked past me and grabbed busted-nose guy by the arm before dragging him through the crowd.

"Oh, we know," the lithe strawberry blonde said with a grin, highlighting the freckles across her nose.

"We've been watching you," the tall, striking blonde said.

"I was just going to the bathroom." I moved to walk past them. "Sorry."

"Good, we'll come with," the strawberry blonde said, hooking her arm around my elbow.

"Man, can you lay a path of destruction. I love it," the brunette said with a wide grin, tugging the bill of her baseball cap. "I'm Ruby. I saw you play at the Pit once. Similar shit happened."

Since we were making our way through the crowd at Ruby's, I had to ask, "Ruby? Like the bar?"

"The very one. It's my dad's place. He bought this building the same year I was born."

"Cool," I said lamely, not having any clue as to what else I could say.

"I'm Holly," said the strawberry blonde, squeezing my arm. "I'm just sayin'. Those were some kick-ass ninja moves you pulled back there. I think I might have a woman crush. So fuckin' cool."

"Bridget," the striking blonde said, waving the tips of her fingers with a wink.

Seriously, Bridget looked like a pinup model or one of those girls painted on the side of an old warplane. She had tattoos on both shoulders and several more down her arms. There were even some on her thighs that were visible through her fishnets.

"Go. Do you," Holly said pushing me toward an open bathroom stall with a smile. "We'll keep talking."

"What's with the uniforms?" I asked, sitting on the toilet. "Are you waitresses here?"

"I do bartend, but I'm off tonight." Ruby's voice rang out in the tiny bathroom. "We had a heat. The uniforms are from our team."

"That's what we wanted to talk to you about. You ever heard about roller derby?" the one named Bridget asked, I think.

"Um, no?" I answered.

"You'd be perfect on our team. You gotta be one tough bitch to hack it on the track," Holly said.

Chapter Eighteen

Now

"Have you given any more thought to recording again?" Nate asks, leaning back in his chair.

Nate's my business partner. We own the studio and record label fifty-fifty. He runs operations, and I handle the creative development side. The set-up suits us both, and we work well together. He's eighteen years my senior, but he's always respected me, and my opinions and ideas.

We're sitting in the conference room after our quarterly update meeting. Business is good—real good. He spins his pen that rests on top of his leather notebook and tracks it with his eyes before stopping it and spinning it again. I know what he's doing. He's giving me space after asking a question that he thinks I might have a negative reaction to.

"I've given it more thought. I just—I don't see how I'd have the time, between fostering the bands we've signed, scouting for new talent, and my duties at the Mad House..." The rest is implied well enough.

"It's a waste of your talent, Maddie. You have more than anyone who's walked through these doors. And, I get it. I do understand. What happened was difficult, but you've made amazing strides and you're playing again. Not just playing, but you're writing, too, right?"

193

I nod.

"I think working with those kids may be helping *you* more than them." He snorts a laugh. "It's just a shame to see it wasted. The world needs your music. You don't have to tour. Maybe we just record and you play a broadcast show for *Austin City Limits* and that's it. Just take it one step at a time."

"I agree," Dex says.

I startle at his voice and look up to find him standing in the open doorway to the conference room.

"Sorry to interrupt. You should do it. I've heard your new stuff; it's good," he says, waving his phone in the air. "We've got an emergency."

I raise my eyebrows as my body tenses.

"Not life and death," he assures. "But I'm going to need your help with this one."

"Okay?" I say, confused and curious.

He nods his head out the door. "You coming?"

"Yeah, yeah. Sure. We'll continue this conversation later, Nate. I've apparently got something to take care of right now." I look back to Nate, who has an amused grin as I gather my papers and other belongings. "I'll be back if this doesn't take too long, but I'll have Chloe call you if I don't expect to be back in the office today."

"Sounds good," Nate replies.

I dart past Dex, who is looming in the doorway, and head back to my office to gather my purse and car keys. Dex's hand lands on the small of my back, startling me. I nearly toss my papers into the air. I pause for a moment and look up at him.

"Do you want to tell me about this emergency?"

"Yeah, the school called," he says as he continues toward my office. "Audra's in the nurse's office, and I need to pick her up."

"Is she okay?"

"Yeah, she's not sick. This is—" Dex rubs the bridge of his nose. "It's a situation that could use a woman's touch."

"Oh," I say, understanding. I push through the door to my

office. "I've some stuff here to deal with that."

I bend over to rummage through the bottom drawer of my desk, where I keep a small makeup bag filled with feminine hygiene products. I keep quite a bit on hand in case any of the women here in the office are ever without. I pull a file folder out of the drawer and set it on the desk so I can see better. I'm debating on tampons or pads when I hear Dex mumble something about loving his job. I finally locate the bag and stand to pull out both and some extra, just in case.

"She's going to need all that?" he asks, scrunching up his face with a look of morbid interest.

I laugh. "Well, I'm giving her options, but yeah. It's a lifetime sentence, you know?"

"Yeah, I get that. I know how all this works. I'm just—it's different talking to her about it. I mean, it crossed my mind that it would happen one day, but..." He eats up the ground between us in a few short strides, and suddenly I'm wrapped in his arms. "Thank you. Thank you for doing this." His voice is muffled by my hair.

Inside, I'm laughing, and I'm trying my damnedest not to laugh out loud, but the way his shoulders sag in relief when I pat his back is making it hard. I disengage from his embrace and grab the bottle of Midol and toss it into my purse with all the other supplies.

"All right, I'm ready," I say, shouldering my bag, but when I do the file folder drops, scattering papers across the floor.

My heart drops, knowing what it is. I drop my purse in a scrambling attempt to put the thing away. Dex joins me to help but pauses at the first piece of paper he picks up.

"'Stateside Front Man Found Dead in Recording Studio'," he reads.

It's a printout of a blog article. The file is from when we were trying to do damage control. I haven't looked at these in years. They were hidden in that rarely used junk drawer for a reason.

I close my eyes to stop the tears that threaten. "I don't want to talk about it."

"You don't have to."

He shuffles a stack of the papers together and hands them to me. I place them in the folder. When I look up, Dex is staring out the windows. The joking mood between us is dead. I can't help but wonder when this all ends. When does it get better?

"You ready to go?" I ask, much more subdued, placing the file back in the drawer and picking up my purse.

I stop at Chloe's desk. "We have a code red. Call the girls and get them ready. I'll let you know the plan as soon as we're ready."

Chloe nods, picks up the phone, and starts dialing.

"You girls have codes for this sort of thing? What exactly do you do?" he asks with a look of surprise.

"Dex, just let me take it from here. The less you know, the better." I pat his arm and walk toward the front door.

We just about make it out when Asher comes out of the back hall that leads to the recording studio. I feel dizzy and lose the rhythm of my step, and halt in my tracks. I force a smile and look up at Asher. His eyes dart to Dex and back to me as he smiles, but the smile doesn't reach his eyes.

"Where are you running off to in the middle of the day?" Asher asks.

"Hey, Ash," I say. "You haven't met my boyfriend, Dex, have you?"

"No, I don't believe we've been introduced." He reaches out and shakes Dex's hand. "I did see him around at your birthday party, but we never crossed paths. I didn't know you guys were serious," he says to me with a raised eyebrow.

Dex is studying him, and when Ash turns to face him, they nod, like some sort of rehearsed greeting.

"It happened kind of fast," Dex supplies.

Ash's eyes dart back to mine, and he pulls me to the side. "You sure that's a good idea?"

"Yes, Ash. Dex's a good guy," I say. "You should come over for dinner with us sometime this week, get to know him."

"I would, but I'm scouting in Atlanta this week. I'm heading out in a few hours. Maybe when I get back?" He pulls out his phone. "Actually, I hafta jet. I meant to be out of here thirty minutes ago." He looks back at Dex. "Nice meeting you." He gives another dead-eyed smile and walks past us back toward the offices.

"You ready?" I ask Dex.

"When you are," he answers.

Then

"Shit, this place is cold," Sloane said, wrapping her arms around herself as we walked through the office-like hallway, following the signs leading to the warehouse space in the back.

When we pushed through the door, we were greeted by the low hum of wheels on pavement. The girls skated around the short, taped-off track on the polished concrete floor of the open space. An older woman stood in the middle, whistle around her neck. I assumed she was their coach.

We'd watched for a few minutes before Holly looked over in our direction. She tripped and toppled to the ground. I cringed, somehow feeling responsible as two more girls tripped over her.

"Pull it in. Fall small, Holly. Fall small," the woman yelled at her. "You just got a penalty for tripping a player from the other team. Do you think we're practicing skydiving here?"

Holly pulled herself up from the concrete, grimacing. She said something to the coach and then headed our way.

"Hey!" She smiled brightly as she rolled up to us. "You came."

"I brought my roommate, too. If that's okay?"

"Fuck, yeah," Holly replied.

"This's Sloane." I gestured to my roommate. "Sloane, meet Holly."

Bridget and Ruby rolled up behind her and introduced themselves.

197

"I guess we'll just hang out and watch." I smiled.

"Oh, I'm going to sit with you and explain the game," Holly said as she rolled over on to the carpet of the visitors' area, "while the team runs drills. We told Bonnie you'd be by, so she's cool with it."

She sat on a bench facing the team as Bridget and Ruby rejoined them, and they went back to practice. She patted the bench next to her, and Sloane and I sat.

"Sorry about distracting you," I offered. "That looked like a nasty fall."

"Shit, that's nothin'. I needed the practice." She smiled. "Fallin', that is. I need to practice the crash and burn. I fuckin' suck at thinkin' when I do it."

I smiled back and leaned against the wall behind us, watching the girls circle the track.

"Each team is allowed to have fourteen bitches, but we lost some girls recently, so we're down to ten," Holly explained. "When we play a *bout*, which is a full game, it's divided into *jams*. Each jam lasts two minutes, and we put five girls on the track. See Bridge has a star on her helmet?" She pointed over to Bridget.

"Yeah," I replied.

"That marks her as the *jammer*. She's the one who can score points. The offensive player. The rest of us are on defense. See Ruby's helmet has a stripe?"

I nodded.

"She's the *pivot*. The opposing team's pivot is the one the jammer has to pass to score the point. The rest are the pack, and their job is to stop the other team's jammer from passing our team's pivot. Make sense?"

"Perfect." I smiled. "What's to stop you from just grabbing a girl and throwing her off the track?"

"Rules, bitch." She laughed, shaking her head. "Rules. Normally, I'm all for breaking the rules, but this wouldn't be much of a sport without them."

"Oh, my God, we have to do this," Sloane said, gripping my forearm and almost tugging it out of socket in her excitement. "These are my people, my tribe."

I snorted a laugh. She did seem to fit right in. But then we both did because there was no one look to a derby girl outside of her team uniform. At that moment, in practice, they were all in different dress, some with tiny shorts, some with full-legged spandex. Some had loud, colorful hair and tattoos, while others looked like normal chicks. All were different shapes and sizes, but all of them looked fierce.

I listened to them chatter away, but I knew I was going to love this sport. I was so in.

Now

"Those pants you picked up are fire," Holly says to Audra, taking a lick of her ice-cream cone.

I'm still nibbling on the crust leftover from my pizza as we sit in the food court at the mall.

"I know," Audra gushes. "You guys are so awesome. Thank you for the new pants, Miss D."

I smile softly at her. "Not a problem. We do this—have done this—for all of us at least once or twice."

"Definitely," Chloe says with a smile. "Whether it's stained pants, a broken heart, or whatever ya need consoling over, these ladies are masters at making ya feel better. Ya should stick with us. We'll always have your back."

Holly winks at Audra with a smile.

"You guys are so lucky," Audra says with a sigh to Cora and Cat. "You have an awesome mom who has awesome friends."

"What about your mom?" Holly asks.

I kick at her under the table and miss. She smirks at me.

Audra fidgets with her napkin. "My mom blows. That's why I ran away and found my dad."

"You ran away?" I ask, instantly curious.

"Yeah, he's from Vegas," Audra explains, tearing her napkin into little chunks. "I didn't see him much growing up. My mom was always taking him to court to keep me away from him. And, you know, get more money and stuff. They weren't ever together, but if I had to guess, she probably had me just to try and trap him in a relationship. She wasn't ever interested in being a mother. She's always been more into *how to land a new boyfriend*." Her eyes take on a faraway look like she's getting lost in the past.

"Anyways, I stole money from a *new boyfriend's* wallet one night and snuck out to the bus station. I had to pay a guy to buy me a ticket, and then I got on a bus to Vegas. The bus made stops on the way there, and I called Dad from a gas station. Told him I was on the way, so he was there to pick me up. After I told him about what was happening, he fought for me." She smiled. "He had to transfer down here to Texas because my mom blocked him from keeping me out of state. This year I get to decide, so I don't have to go see her anymore."

"That's pretty cool of him," I say. "He seems like a good father."

"Would you marry him?" she asks, her guileless emerald eyes hopeful.

I choke on a sip of coke. My brain rushes around in circles trying to grasp at anything to give her as an answer. I gasp for breath in between coughs. Holly slaps my back with a little too much force and a devious smirk.

"I know he hasn't asked or anything." She shrugs. "You just started dating. I just think it'd be cool, you know? If you were my mom."

"Excuse me, miss?" A strange voice accompanies the tap on my shoulder.

I find a boy, about ten years old, standing next to me.

"Yes?" I ask.

"A man gave me ten dollars to give this to you." He tosses a red calla lily with a note tied to it on to the table and then turns and bolts into the crowd before I even register what happened.

I signal the Tweedles, and they get up from their post two tables away.

"One of you see if you can track down that boy," I say, pointing to the direction he ran off in. "We need to see if we can get a description. I'm calling Detective Martinez."

They nod, and one takes off in the direction of the boy, and the other stands next to our table turning a slow circle, scanning the crowded food court.

"Chloe, call Evan and tell him to come get the girls and take them home," I tell her.

"I get it now," Audra says, tilting her head. "Why Dad likes you." She shrugs, picking at her food. "Most people would be freaking out right now. I'm kinda freaking out and it's not even my stalker. But you. You're very... take-charge. It's kind of badass."

I give her my best forced smile because inside I'm just dying to tell her that she knows nothing. There are so many times I haven't handled things well, so many times I've fucked-up. But, I just keep it to myself and smile.

Then

I was home for the weekend, lying on the couch. We'd had the girls' birthday party yesterday, and I was completely drained of energy. The twin four-year-olds were playing with their new *My Little Pony* dolls and watching the cartoon of the same name. I was beat. Burning the candle at both ends was starting to take its toll.

The doorbell rang, and Cat darted from the floor to the door with almost inhuman speed. Or maybe my mind was just working at a snail's pace, so normal movement happened to appear faster.

"Got it!" Cat yelled.

"Cat! Don't you open that door without checking to see who it is first."

"It's Lord Master!" Cora squealed.

I heard the door open and a familiar male voice. "Hey, Kit Kat, Snickers. How are my minions today?"

"We playin with our birthday toys, Lord Master."

Footsteps trailed from the foyer to the kitchen behind the couch I lay on.

"Really?" Evan gasped. "Which ones are your favorite? You got a lot of toys yesterday."

"We did! We're playing ponies right now!" Cat exclaimed. "Comesee we make them do what they do on TV."

"You do? That sounds super fun!" A suction noise sounded as the refrigerator door opened. "Where's Mommy?"

"In the living room," Cora said.

The footsteps moved toward me, and Evan's face appeared over the back of the couch.

"I haven't seen you in how long? And this is how you greet me?"

"I'm fucking exhausted," I groaned, throwing my arm over my eyes. "I'm an introvert living an extrovert's life. It's draining the life from my very bones."

"Care to be a little more dramatic?"

"Why, Evan!" I fanned myself, doing my Southern belle impression. "If you don't rescue me from this undignified existence, I might just very well shrivel up and die."

"Fine, smart-ass. Keep your lazy butt on the couch."

I swatted at him, and he dodged my hand. "I don't know how much longer I can keep this up. When I'm not studying, I'm at band practice or derby practice or a heat or a gig or here with the girls. It never stops. When can I just be still, and alone?"

He walked around the couch and hit my legs so I'd make room for him to sit. I stuck my blanket-covered legs straight up in the air and settled them in his lap after he sat. Evan opened his soda and looked me over.

"I don't have any answers, Mads. You probably need to prioritize what you've committed to and let the rest go."

"I know, but in my mind, it's all important," I whined. "I feel like such a shitty mom, but I still have a semester left of school. I've no real clue of what I really want to do with my life. Plus, the girls will start school next year, so I gotta find a place and move them to Austin before then."

"You're the best mommy in the world," Cora said with a grin. Her eyes were just as beguiling as her father's.

I tucked a loose strand of black hair behind her ear and sighed. "You say that because I'm the only mommy you've got. You've got no frame of reference, little one."

"What's a frame of reference?" Cat asked.

Evan grunted, trying to stifle a laugh.

"It's just a phrase that means you have nothing to compare it to," I answered.

Her little mouth formed an O as she absorbed my answer. "Your band is playing tonight, right?"

"Yeah, you planning to come see me play?"

"Sure am." He grinned but then frowned. "Though Nic already warned me that I'm probably not going to like what I see."

"We're not that bad. I think you'll like our music."

"I don't think he was talking about that."

"Oh," I replied. "It's not that bad."

"Would you let them go?" he said, pointing at the girls.

"No," I said, scrunching my face up. "Definitely not."

"Tell me about this guy Nic calls Front Man."

I groaned and flipped over to bury my face in the pillow underneath my head. I did *not* want to talk to Evan about my kinky, casual-sex relationship. I confided in Evan more than most, but when it came to sexual stuff, Nic was my go-to guy.

"Enough about me. What've you been up to?" I mumbled through the pillow.

"Nice redirect," he said. There was a smirk on his face when I peeked up at him from my hiding spot. "We'll get to me, but you don't talk enough about what's going on with you, Mads. I've gotta get most of it from Nic."

"What do you want to know?"

"Tell me about your guy."

"He's not *my guy*. We're in a band together."

"It's more than that. Why don't you want to tell me? I assume I'm going to meet him tonight anyway."

"It's not you. It's just words. I don't want to assign words to it. Words make it mean something. Assigns value and labels. Law and I don't do that. We just have fun. Enjoy each other's company, you know?"

"Maddie, you've been with this guy how long? Nic first told me about him about a year ago."

"It'll be two years by the end of the summer."

"Is this your choice, or is he—"

"No! He's a good guy. It's not like that. He takes care of me. I'm just—I'm pretty sure *he* broke me, Ev." My eyes flicked to the girls so he gets that I'm referring to Jared. "I'm scared of calling it something because I feel like that's when he'll want to leave. I don't know how to fix it."

"Does your guy know about them?" His eyes flashed to the girls before fixing back on me, brows raised in question.

I shook my head. "They don't need to be confused any further. They already have an absentee dad, a part-time mom—" I had to stop myself because I was going to cry. They deserved better than this. "I don't want to be one of those single moms with a parade of men in my life."

"Maddie, come here." Evan opened his arms, motioning me in for a hug.

I snuggled into his side.

"I think that might be part of it, but two years, Maddie? I suppose this's sort of normal for you. You and Jared were expecting and circled each other for almost nine months before you guys even admitted to a relationship. If he's stuck around this long and he's not a total douche, you should maybe think about giving the guy some credit. One guy in two years does not constitute a parade."

I started to protest, but he placed a finger over my mouth.

"Or maybe admit to yourself that it's really over. You're not letting yourself fully move on."

Had I really been holding out hope still? That's fucking ridiculous. Four years! Four fucking years!

"I don't think it's that. Or at least that's not totally it," I defended at his bland look. "I get it—we've known each other long enough that he should know that about me. It just never seemed like the right time."

I rested my elbows on my knees and rubbed my temples.

"You know, at first it wasn't any of his business," I continued. "But later, it just seemed that by talking about it I was asking for more. I didn't know if he wanted more. Hell, I didn't even know if *I* wanted more. Now, it's starting to seem like we may *be* more, but at this point, I don't even know how to course correct. How do you tell someone you're with that you've been keeping something like that to yourself?"

"I can't tell you how to do it, Mads. I'm no expert," Evan said. "But, I think you know what you need to do."

Chapter Nineteen

Now

We're running *hitting* drills in practice tonight, so I'm paired up with Ruby as we skate at a steady pace around the track. Bridget and Holly, our jammers, round the track trying to skate between each group of paired teammates. We have to keep an eye out for when they come up behind us; then Ruby and I come together to smash the jammer and block her from passing. It takes a while for them to make it through all the pairs and round the track back to us.

You should be more careful about who you kiss.

The words from the latest note are stuck in my head. I can't think of anything else. The stalker is right. I should be more careful because I let the line get hazy at the lake, and again I got burned. Though I doubt that's the altruistic warning he meant with that message.

"I heard a certain little girl popped the question," Ruby says, keeping her eyes on the track.

It takes a moment for my brain to catch up to what she's talking about. Audra. Her innocent question about whether I'd marry her dad. This is exactly what I was worried about. Things might be clear between me and him, but not everyone is in the loop.

"Yeah, it was awkward." I try to laugh it off. "I'd no clue

what to say to her."

"I wouldn't have a clue either, but is it *that* ridiculous?" she asks, scrunching her nose. "I'd think it was already pretty serious considering we even know you're with him."

My mind spins, trying to formulate a response. *Shit.* I can't tell Ruby that it isn't real. It's not real. I'm his assignment. He's made that quite clear. Everything we do is for show. Yet, we've grown closer these last two weeks of him following me around.

After the incident at the mall, he's been glued to my side. But all everyone else sees is a caring boyfriend who wants to protect me from this threat. This whole fucking ordeal is messing with my head. I rub my temples in frustration.

I'm distracted by my thoughts and don't see Holly approach. Ruby closes the distance between us. She crashes into me, and my wheels stick to the track while my body tips off-balance, and I crash to the floor, landing on my chin. I bite my tongue. Blood swells in my mouth as I lie there in shock.

At precisely that moment, I get a tickle in the back of my throat, forcing me to cough. Blood splats on to the concrete floor.

"Oh, God, are you okay?" Ruby says as she grasps my shoulders and helps me to my hands and knees.

The coughs are still racking my body. I hold that position for a moment until they pass. Red splatters cover my arms and coat the floor. Holly skates up with a bottle of cleaner and a wad of paper towels. I look back down, and the scene transforms in front of me. I'm no longer in the practice space.

There's so much blood. It's everywhere. It's too much. There's too much blood. It coats my hands and arms, soaking the front of my torn dress. My whole body shakes violently. I can't breathe. I see the man standing there in the shadow, watching me. *He was there.* I gasp for breath, and a sob breaks free with a scream as I scramble to get away from the blood, get away from him.

Strong arms wrap around me, and I smell him first. His incredible aftershave or cologne that's been haunting me for weeks. He carries me across the room. I don't know how much time passes as I'm lost in my horrifying memories. Then I hear his voice.

"I'm here, Maddie. It's Dex. You're safe. You just fell and bit your tongue. You're going to be okay. Can you hear me?" he says in a calm, soothing voice. *How can he be so calm? I'm a messed-up freak.* "You're going to be fine. I've got you."

I nod as my breathing begins to calm and my vision starts to clear. Dex's thumbs cross my cheeks, rubbing the moisture away. *When was I crying?*

"Why do you care?" I ask between gasping breaths. "This's all fake."

His face changes from concern to confusion to something else. He hugs me close and buries his face in my neck, taking a deep breath.

"God. You kill me, Maddie," he says as his lips brush my neck.

His deep voice reverberates through my skin. Chills spread over my body, shocking my system. I find a thread to guide my focus back to reality.

"I'm sorry. I didn't mean to worry you," I say, pushing Dex away and scrambling out of his lap to my feet. "I told you, I'm a mess. I just—I need a moment." I wipe at my eyes and focus on the ground.

I turn and walk toward the bathroom attached to the visitors' area. Someone took off my skates while I was out of it. My teammates have stopped, and their eyes track me. I close the door behind me and sag against it, dropping my head into my hands as tears stream down my face. I haven't had an episode this bad in over a year.

There's a knock on the door, and I pull it open. Dex steps in.

"Hey, let me help you."

He places a gentle hand on my arm and guides me to the sink. He turns me and lifts me up to sit on the counter and grabs paper towels while turning on the water.

"I sometimes forget how hard this must be on you," he says as he wets the paper towels and starts wiping the blood off my arms. "You handle it so well from day to day. It's easy to forget."

"Handle it well?" I scoff.

He leans down, getting eye level with me. "Yeah, you do. The funny thing is, you don't see it."

"Dex, I had a complete break from reality out there."

"It's understandable after what you've been through," he argues, searching my eyes like he can see through me.

"It's been four years. And it used to be so much worse, but I'm still not past it. That much should be obvious." I look away.

He palms the side of my face, forcing me to look back at him.

"It's been less than twenty-four hours since this sicko had last contact with you. I think you're looking at this the wrong way and not giving yourself enough credit."

"You don't even know what you're talking about."

"I've read your file, so I have a pretty good idea. Plus, I went through this exact thing years ago after I made my first kill shot. I know it's not the same. It never goes away. You can learn how to cope with trauma, but we're not lucky enough to ever forget it."

I gasp, and my head starts spinning. I don't know why it never really sank in that he had access to my file—that he knows more than I've told him. I try to turn away, but he grasps the other side of my face.

"Look at me," he commands.

My eyes dart around before they come to rest on him. His eyes crinkle at the corner in concern, and his lips twist into a frown. His tongue peeks out to wet his lips, and I'm mesmerized by the movement.

"This is real for me. I'm here. I'm not going anywhere. I said I wanted to get to know you, and I have. These past few weeks you keep telling me that you're not worth it, but I'm with you every day, and I haven't seen anything to warrant that assessment. I've seen nothing that would make me want to walk away. You just keep pulling me in, Maddie. I'm hooked. Can't you see that?"

My breath freezes in my lungs. Dex searches my eyes as if expecting a response but I don't know what to say to that. My shoulders slump in defeat. Tears well in my eyes, and when I look away he lets my face go and washes off his hands.

"I can't go back on the pills. They don't make it go away. They only make it more bearable. I don't want to go back to feeling like a comfortable zombie. It's like living on a cloud watching life happen to you, not living it yourself."

He helps me down off the counter.

"No one is saying that you should. It's just increased stress that's stirring all this up. Come on, let's get you home. It's been a long day, and I don't think they're expecting you back at practice tonight."

I nod and let him lead the way out the door.

Then

It was a rare night off for both me and Law. We were curled up on his couch watching *Fearless Dragons*, one of his many beloved kung fu movies. It was the final fight scene.

"Next time you have a fight, I'm bringing a leather belt and a piece of wood. I think all fights need these sound effects."

"Are you trying to say my fights aren't entertaining enough for you?" he asked, squeezing me against his chest. His fingers inched over, directly above a known ticklish spot of mine.

"No, seeing you shirtless and sweaty, beating the crap out of some poor schmuck, is more than entertaining." I gave him a saucy leer. "It just lacks comedy."

"Comedy? You mean, I don't make you laugh enough?" And his fingers dug in.

I couldn't stop the shriek, followed by uncontrollable

cackling. I squirmed, but Law was fast and hooked his legs over mine. I was trapped.

"Stop. Please," I pleaded. "Barnacle, barnacle."

He paused long enough that the dude in blue flew to center screen and pawed bent fists in the air while neighing like a horse. I burst out laughing as the image of Law doing that in one of his fights filled my mind. I had tears leaking from my eyes.

"Oh, God, you should so use that move in your next fight. It's not technically boxing, but I doubt they'd penalize you for neighing like a horse."

He'd moved above me and was smiling down at me as my laughter died. At that point, the man in black on the TV screen made a move, hovering an open palm with bent fingers above his other fisted hand.

"The Dragon Fist. Oh no, not the Dragon fist," I taunted the movie. "Did you hear that? Only one man can survive the Dragon Fist. That's the move I'm using on you next time you try and tickle me, asshole." I laughed.

"I love you."

I turned my eyes back to Law as he hovered above me. "Do what?"

"I love you."

My breath froze in my chest.

"Don't freak out, Bumpkin. You don't have to say it back. I just can't keep it in any longer. I know you don't want to talk about it or discuss our relationship. But I fell for you. I think I've loved you since the moment you opened that smart mouth of yours." One side of his mouth tipped up into a smile, exposing one of those dimples I had a weakness for.

He leaned down, brushing his lips against mine. Once. Twice. The third time he lingered, and I kissed him back. This kiss was different from the thousands of times we'd kissed before. We both poured a flood of emotions into one single physical act.

My mind was a broken record, skipping over the same thought. I couldn't say it back unless I told him about the girls. There was just never a time where we talked about us. It never seemed like the right moment, or even necessary, because it was such a slow evolution. I couldn't let this relationship get any deeper without telling him the truth. I was pretty sure I felt the same. I loved being with him. He was kind and sweet, considerate. Well, at least to me he was. He encouraged my independence, and in return, I lent him the control he craved. It was the perfect balance for us. Except there was this wide chasm of a secret between us that only I could see. When he broke away from the kiss, I racked my brain for the best way to broach this subject.

"How do you feel about kids?" I blurted.

His eyes widened and his whole body tensed against me. "You're not pregnant, are you?"

"No," I answered, trying to figure out how to take that particular reaction. No matter how hard I tried to fight it, my mind automatically compared him to Jared at that moment. *Jared never freaked out at the mention of kids.* I fought hard to punt kick that shit from my mind.

He visibly relaxed. "Good. I'm not sure I even want kids. I don't care for them, but I've never really given it much thought. If we do have them, I want it to be years from now. Why do you ask?"

He doesn't like kids. He doesn't want them for a long time. The thoughts were running laps around my brain as I tried to think of what to say. I couldn't tell him right now. I had to think this through.

"Oh, nothing really important... I was just thinking about taking a couple of months after graduation to work with local orphans through music lessons or classes. It's not a big deal. I just figured since I had something in common with them, I'd like to give back."

"What do you mean? You have something in common?"

"Yeah, I'm an orphan. Though technically, I never went into the system. My godparents helped me get emancipated."

"Then where the fuck do you go every weekend? You've been disappearing every weekend for the past two years, turning down paying gigs and everything else. For what?" He shoved up off the couch and walked to the other side of the room. His hand went to the back of his neck. "Why didn't I know, Laine?"

"What do you mean?" I asked, genuinely confused as to why that made him upset.

"I feel like... I don't even know who you are. Why haven't you ever told me about your parents?"

My jaw dropped in shock that this would ever be an issue with him. "You never asked."

"But don't you think that's the kind of thing you tell someone you've been with for two years? Two years, Laine."

I blinked. "Yeah, well. We're usually both busy. When we're together and apart. And when we're not busy, we're fucking. When was I supposed to have confession time with you, Law?"

"You make time, Laine!"

"Don't pretend like this little arrangement hasn't worked for you. You only love me because I don't make demands of you. We don't do emotional heart-to-heart chats. We don't do labels. We don't ask questions. What I don't understand is why this's news to you?"

"Fuck!"

"What's really the issue, Law?"

He started pacing. "I've given you time. I know you have commitment issues. You've never once called me your boyfriend, despite the fact that PDA doesn't bother you in the least. You don't even look at other guys. I let it go. You've never invited me to go back home with you to meet your family. You live with my sister. You've met my parents. The only thing in my life that you don't know about is my brother. But that asshole left years ago, and nobody talks about him."

"You have a brother?"

"Yeah. How does that feel, Laine? Are you getting it yet?"

I just stared at him, silent. It was clear that telling him about the girls was going to be a big fucking deal. I just didn't know what to do.

He sighed. "I want to know everything about you."

"No, you really don't. You might think you do, thinking that you know I've got commitment issues, but that isn't even a fraction of what I've got. My dad died of cancer back when I was five. I was five, yet I can't even remember one single thing about him. I remember my first dog died, and I was three then. Two years older and I get some kind of selective amnesia that erases a whole person from my life. Looking at pictures of him is like looking at pictures of a stranger. All my life people would say they were sorry for my loss, but inside I just felt confused. Can you lose something you don't remember ever having?

"Then there's my mom. You don't even want to hear about that whole mess. But here's the highlight reel—I killed her. I screwed up by being an emotional, whiny little bitch and got my mom killed. So fucking sue me for not wanting to spill my emotions or dig up my dirty past with you. I fucking care about you enough not to drag you into that fucked-up mess. Are you happy now? Or shall we continue down this path? Because there's more, but it's not pretty. You think you love me because I'm this nice girl who plays guitar, but I'm not nice. I'm not a good person. Do you really want to see the ugly, dark side of me? Because, fuck, Law. You should probably be careful what you ask for."

His brows furrowed as he took steps to erase the distance between us, then pulled me until our bodies pressed together.

"You're a good person, Laine." He cupped my cheeks, resting his forehead against mine. His thumbs smoothed over my cheeks, gathering tears I hadn't realized had fallen. "I don't just think that I love you; I've fallen head over heels for you. I see who you are, every day, and there's no amount of guilt that you may carry that would change my mind."

I would've liked to believe that, but my story didn't just involve emotional baggage. Two living breathing humans would depend on me every day, soon enough. I wasn't positive about what his reaction would be to that sort of news. I needed to talk with someone who knew him as well as I did. I needed to tell Sloane.

Chapter Twenty

Now

We walk Chloe to her car after work. Work is probably the wrong word. There are parts of my job that just don't feel like work. Coming out of a live music venue after scouting a new band is one of them. The concert is still going on, but we got what we came for—an appointment next week with the opening act. The parking lot is full of cars but void of people.

Chloe pulls her camera bag over her head and turns to face me.

"I hope these guys work out," she says.

She'd recommended this band based on word from students at her school. Another bonus to hiring her—she keeps me plugged in to what the college kids are into these days.

"I'll only hold it against you a little if they fail to produce," I say with a shrug.

"How magnanimous of ya," Chloe says with a smirk.

"Have a good night, and be safe getting home," I add, hugging her tight. "If you see anything weird or feel like you're being watched or followed, don't hesitate to call."

I'm having trouble letting those I love out of my sight these days.

When I turn away, Dex is waiting for me at the back of

the car. I walk to him, and he puts an arm around my shoulders, kissing the side of my forehead as we stand back and watch her drive away. I'm getting better at accepting his casual touching and displays of affection.

"She's a smart kid," Dex assures me with a squeeze.

She is, but it doesn't stop me from worrying about her. Hell, I worried about her before the stalker came back into my life. She has no family from what I can tell, never leaves for home on the holidays like a normal college student, and she clams up at the mention of her family.

"Let's go get something to eat. I'm starving," Dex says as he pats his belly.

I snort. "When are you *not* hungry?"

"I'm a growing boy," he says with a dimpled smirk. "Besides, I've got something for you."

He tugs my hand, so I follow him back to my car on the other side of the parking lot. I pull my keys out of my pocket, and the sound echoes off the surrounding buildings. When we get to the back of my car, he pulls me close to him and grins down at me.

"Okay, I've been dying to ask for weeks now. But, may I?" He holds out his hand as his eyes track to my keys and back up to me in question. "I gotta special place I want to take you."

"You want to drive the Charger?"

"Hell, yeah." His dimpled grin is almost childlike with excitement.

"The only person who's ever driven this car, besides me, is Nic, and that was only out of necessity."

He gives me puppy dog eyes.

"Fine." I sigh and hand him the keys. "You damage her in any way, I'll be teaching you how to fix her."

"Sounds good to me. You have awesome taste in cars. I wouldn't mind..." He pauses with the door open, looking at me across the roof of the car, but his eyes are distant. "The image of you in those shorts you wear around the house, bent over under a hood. Let's just say that's not a scary threat." He winks and ducks into the car.

I follow and sit in the passenger seat. "What is this *special place* you're taking me to?"

"It's a surprise. Just hold tight."

He starts up the grumbling engine of my Charger and pushes the stick shift into reverse. My mind barely has time to register that action before the tires squeal, and we shoot out of the parking space and the front end of the car slides to a stop. *Holy shit.* I grab on to the door and seat, scared out of my fucking mind.

"Are you insane?" I yell at him.

"You might want to buckle up," he says with a wicked grin.

"You're going to make me regret this, aren't you?"

"Part of academy training is all these special driving courses. You get to learn all sorts of cool shit. But undercover, I rarely get behind the wheel of a car capable of driving like that. This is gonna be fun. Don't worry. I'm a trained professional."

"Nope. Absolutely not," I say, moving to open the door. "This was a—"

He stops me with a hand on my arm. I look back at him. His thumb traces over my lower lip, hypnotizing me again. I freeze.

"Relax. Just trust me, okay? I'm always going to keep you safe."

I nod, unable to speak through the hurricane of emotions that are raging inside me. I buckle my seat belt, and when it clicks, his foot hits the gas, and we peel out of the parking lot on to the empty road. A few minutes go by, and we're pulling into a dirt parking lot in front of a tiny white-brick building on the Eastside of Austin.

Across the top of the building is a huge, lighted sign that reads "Open 24 hours—Diner Grill—Play Lotto Here." Half of the lights are out, lending an even more run-down quality to the facade. Underneath the sign are plate glass windows that stretch from one side of the building to the other. I've never been here before, and the place is empty, aside from a waitress and a cook visible in the back. A lone customer sits at one of the barstools in front of the counter that runs along the length of the restaurant.

Lack of customers never bodes well, but it's too late for dinner, and most of the people at the bars are still enjoying themselves. When we walk in the door, I notice that under the windows is a line of booths covered in blue vinyl. Little tabletop jukeboxes sit on the ends, just under the windows. The smell of bacon and burgers welcomes us into greasy-food heaven.

"Grab a seat wherever you like," the waitress says in a bored, yet welcoming tone. "I'll be right over."

White subway tiles that cover the walls gleam under the harsh fluorescent lights. We walk down the path between the booths and the counter. The older gentleman looks up from his food and gives us a polite nod, his cap stating that he's a veteran. I offer a smile and choose the booth at the very back. Dex slides in across from me. He settles his leather bag next to him. I didn't even notice him grab it from the car, or that it was even in my car, but now my interest is piqued.

"What do you got for me?" I ask.

He gives me a lopsided smile. "Why don't we order first?"

"Fine. What's good here?" I ask, pulling a menu from its place next to the jukebox.

"Everything," he says simply, watching me.

"You're not going to look at the menu?"

"Nah, I already know what I want."

I study the menu. It's pretty standard diner fare. Burgers, fries, breakfast foods—but then my eyes catch something that intrigues me.

"Pimento cheese and bacon sandwich?" I say mostly to myself. My stomach growls at the thought. I've never heard of that particular combination before, but I love bacon, and I love pimento cheese. "It's on house-made Texas toast, too," I whisper.

"It's delicious," Dex says.

I meet his grinning gaze. "That's what you're having?" I ask, and he nods. "Then I gotta try it." I close the menu and startle a bit to find the waitress standing at the end of our booth.

"Did you want something to drink with that?" she asks.

"Yeah, I'll have a Coke," I answer.

"Water," Dex says.

"Fries okay?" she asks.

We both answer that it's fine, and I watch her as she returns behind the counter and places the ticket on the spinning wheel.

"We got the ordering out of the way. What's this mysterious thing you have for me?" My eyes dart to his bag.

"Patience isn't your strong suit, is it?" he asks.

"I have it in spades when I'm told to, but on my own... nah, not so much." I give a mocking frown and shake my head.

He raises an eyebrow at me as he steeples his fingers in front of his chin, elbows resting on the table. "I have trouble picturing you doing anything you're told."

"Depends on who's doing the telling." I place my chin in my open palm, elbow on the table. "And the reason, I suppose."

The waitress places our drinks in front of us with straws and then returns to her post.

"Hmm," he grunts, twisting his lips, then opens his bag. He pulls out a thick manila legal-size envelope and slides it across the table in front of me.

I look at it before I move to open it. "What's this?"

"You didn't seem to react well to the fact that I'd looked at your file. I thought I'd let you have a look at mine. It's not the same..." He drifts off as I pull the file folder out of the envelope that is clearly marked *Juvenile Records*, with a big *sealed* stamp in the middle of the cover.

"You have a juvie record?" I ask with a snort.

"I never claimed to be a good guy. People just assume that shit when you say you're a police officer."

My eyes dart around, making sure no one hears us, but Dex's eyes are still glued to me.

"Aren't you worried about people hearing you?"

"No, everyone here's on payroll. This is a drop point," he says, a dimple appearing as the corner of his mouth tips up. "They just happen to have good food here, too."

I look back around and notice that the waitress has a pretty nice hairstyle, cut and color, which you don't normally see on someone who works for minimum wage. She looks bored, but her eyes scan outside the windows every few minutes. The guy at the counter isn't eating the food in front of him anymore, but he's occasionally sipping his coffee. The waitress isn't making any move to clear his plate either. When I look closer, I notice a lump under his arm that has to be a gun. The only person that seems to be doing a real job is the cook, back in the kitchen.

This is unreal. Like being on a set of a movie and not realizing that you're being filmed. That made a thought occur to me. Sure enough, this place has some nice security cameras, for a rundown diner. Dex sits silently, watching me take it all in.

"We're gonna be leaving that here," he says, motioning to the file. "Read up. Food will be here soon."

"Before I open it, can we talk about the size of this thing? Are you kidding me? Were you some kind of child mafioso?" I'm joking, but when he doesn't laugh, it clicks who I'm talking to.

He works in organized crime. I tilt my head, seeing him, possibly for the first time. I realize that I don't really know him at all. The answers are right in front of me and I know I'm stalling as I look him over. *Do I want to know more? Yes, I can admit to myself that I'm curious.*

Opening to the first page, I find a picture of a very young Dex. I scan the sheet for an age—he's seven. He's watching me with interest when I glance up.

"Possession of stolen goods? At the age of seven?" My jaw drops open. I flip through the rest of the pages.

"Possession of a deadly weapon, assault, drug possession. Holy hell, Dex. How'd you end up here?"

"Turn to the last page," he replies.

I do, and there's Dex's picture again, but he's older. Not quite the man before me, but definitely in his teens. I scan the charges. Robbery, class A felony. The dates don't match up. His arrest wasn't made until a few years after the date of the offense. I look back up at him.

"My mom was a Vegas showgirl. Not a stripper, but a professional dancer. Until she got knocked up with me. She didn't know that my father was married. When she got fired over the pregnancy and called him for help, she found out. He didn't believe her. Thought she was blackmailing him, so he sent her money to keep quiet, and that was that." He shakes his head and looks out the window. His jaw is clenched. "That money got her by until she had me, but she was left with a ruined body and a baby. Siobhan McClellan was an immigrant, but she lost her green card when she lost that job, so she turned to the only job that she could to raise a baby on her own."

My stomach drops, and my head spins. I know where this is going, and I'm not sure I want to hear it.

"She started turning tricks," he continues, his eyes intent on me, like he's looking for the judgment he's gotten his whole life. "Let's just say it wasn't a fun, happy childhood, and we didn't live in the suburbs. I got in with the wrong crowd and did what I could to survive."

"What happened to her?"

"Her pimp got her hooked on drugs so he didn't have to pay her. She eventually OD'd."

"I'm sorry." My vision swims as I try to focus on him through the tears welling in my eyes. I reach across the table and place my hand over his.

He turns his hand into mine, squeezing it.

"I spent more time in juvie and foster homes than I did with her anyway. I knew, the first time I got busted, that telling the police where she was would get her deported." He

223

runs a hand through his hair and looks back at me. The struggle to continue is written all over his face. "That last time I was busted. The crime was committed when I was a minor, but they didn't catch me until a month before I could be tried as an adult. The arresting officer took one look at that record and decided to give me a choice. Well, some might call it blackmail." He snorts. "He said that if I agreed to enter the academy and train to be a police officer, I could work undercover for his unit. My connections with the local organized crime circuit were already established, and with that record, I'd have an easy time making contacts. Otherwise, he'd wait a few weeks and have me tried as an adult and sent to prison. It wasn't a hard choice. I knew I was a fuckup. And this was a golden opportunity. My ticket out of the slums."

I sit quietly, absorbing the information. That's a bucketload of information to dump on someone. It only leaves me with one question.

"Why're you telling me this?" I ask, my voice barely above a whisper.

"Because I want you to trust me. With you, it seems the best way to gain your trust is by trusting *you*. And there's the fact that I just want you to know me. The real me."

"Oh," I say, at a loss for more words.

Thankfully, the moment is broken by the arrival of our food. The smell of bacon and cheese and thick, fluffy toast makes my mouth water. I waste no time digging in. It's divine, and I get lost in the food before I notice Dex watching me eat with a smirk.

I swallow. "What?"

"Nothing. You've got a healthy appetite, for sure. But, do you even realize all the little moaning noises you make with each bite?" His chest is shaking with silent laughter.

"I do not."

"You do," he responds and takes a bite of his sandwich, then swallows. "It's cute, though."

Whatever, I grumble internally and return to enjoying my food. I keep thinking about what he said about trusting him.

Maybe he's onto something because I realize that I'm completely at ease with him now. And thinking back to when we first met, I wasn't comfortable at all.

Dex finishes his food before me, digs quarters out of his pocket, and starts flipping through the tabletop jukebox next to us. I'm curious as to what he'll play, so I silently watch and finish off my meal. The beginning of David Bowie's "Let's Dance" starts to play over the speakers in the ceiling. Dex looks at me, and his hand crosses the table until it's lying palm up in front of me. My eyes track up to his grinning face.

"I've wanted to do this since the first day you came into the tattoo shop."

"You like David Bowie?"

"Who doesn't?" He shrugs. "You heard the man—let's dance."

He grabs my hand and pulls me from the booth. He starts leading me, dancing around the diner. My cheeks feel hot, but I realize he's a pretty good dancer.

"Where did you learn how to dance?"

"Juvie provides all kinds of reform programs. I never thought it'd come in handy until I saw you dancing around the tattoo shop." He looks down at me. "I've been waiting for my moment."

He starts singing the words of the song. He's definitely not a singer, but the effort is sort of adorable. I find my heart melting on the spot as he spins me around the tiny strip of floor space. A group of college kids, obviously well into the drink, walks in and joins our little dance party. Dex and I break apart, and he starts doing some strange dance moves that are a combination of the robot and something else as he shakes his hips. His face is nothing but serious. I crack up laughing and completely lose my rhythm. He grins and keeps at it until the end of the song.

We move back to the booth. I notice that the waitress has cleared our plates and his file is also gone. He stands next to the end of the booth, pulling his wallet out as he grabs the check off the table.

"Let me," I say. "I can write this off since we were out for business earlier."

"No way," he responds. "This isn't a date unless it's my treat."

He tosses cash on the table and pulls me out of the booth, leading me out of the restaurant. I'm still in shock over his last words. *This was a date?*

Then

Just when I thought that I was actually getting my shit together, the evil *powers that be* who controlled my life decided to throw a monkey wrench into my plans. I never got a chance to talk to Sloane that night, because she didn't come home to the dorms.

Instead, I received a call from the General. It was strange, mostly for the reason that he'd never called me before, but also that I didn't think I'd ever seen him speak on the phone. He was one of those stoic reticent figures that led with a silent air of authority.

"Maddie, are you sitting down?"

"Uh, I can be?" I said as I fell back on to my bed. "What's up?"

"I have some news. The boys'—" He took a breath.

My stomach plummeted to my toes. I'd thought I could prepare myself for a call like that, but I really couldn't.

"Their convoy was hit by an IED. They've been flown to a hospital in Germany. Evan is stable. But Jared's condition is listed as critical. As of my last update, he was in surgery. We're flying out to Germany tonight. I thought you might want to come, too. We plan to take the girls, just in case..."

I nodded but realized he couldn't hear that. "Okay, yes. Yes, I want to go." My voice squeaked out the reply.

I wasn't going to let the girls meet their father for the first time in an overseas hospital without me.

"Maddie?"

Plus, I was sure that John and Diana would want to fully

focus on their son and not have to wrangle preschoolers.

"Yeah."

"He's going to be okay."

I couldn't speak to form a response.

"Pack your bag. I'll send Nic by to bring you to the airport. We'll meet you there. Don't forget your passport. You still know where it is, right?"

"Yeah."

I ended the call and rushed around my room, stuffing things blindly into my duffel bag. After a few minutes, I realized I had no idea what I'd packed. I upended the contents on to my bed, but I couldn't see anything through the stupid tears that had filled my eyes.

I finally had my bag packed properly when a knock sounded at the door. I opened it without looking and turned back to the search for my passport.

"I'm ready to go. I just have to find my passport. It wasn't in the shoe box where I thought I'd put the damn thing. Can you look through the desk drawers while I check under the bed?"

"Where are you going that you're packing a bag and in need of a passport?"

I whipped around to face Law. His jacket was askew and his hair even messier than usual. Dark circles shadowed his eyes.

"What're you doing here?" I asked. I turned back to the storage tote I'd drug out from under my bed.

"I couldn't sleep without you. And after what we talked about tonight, I didn't think you needed to be alone."

I spied the offending document at the bottom of the tote.

"I gotta go—"

"Goddammit, Laine," he growled as he grabbed my arm, halting my frantic movements. "Where the fuck are you going?"

I stood up and turned around to look at him. I couldn't get into this now. Nic would be here any second.

"There's been a family emergency. I *have* to go."

"I thought we covered this tonight. You don't have a family. So why don't we start with the truth? Just talk to me, Laine. Just please, please don't run away from me, from us."

"That's not what this is. It's just—it's complicated, and I don't have time to explain." I rushed around, grabbing stuff to put away, trying to reduce the mess I left for Sloane.

Nic appeared in the open doorway. His eyes darted back and forth between Law and me.

"I hate to interrupt, but we've got a flight to catch. You ready?" Nic said.

Law looked back at him and then at me. His eyes narrowed, and his jaw ticked.

"You're going away with him?" Law demanded.

"Law, you're looking in all the wrong places for an explanation," I said. "There's one, but it's not that. I just don't have time to explain it to you. I've got a flight to catch. We have to leave, right now."

"You know what? Fuck this. I can't do this anymore." Law started for the door.

"What's that supposed to mean?" I asked. "Don't say something like that and leave."

"Why? Does it not feel good to be on the receiving end of cryptic bullshit?"

"Fuck! Law, stop, I'll tell you everything. All of it. Just not now. There really is an emergency, and I have to go."

"Whatever. Too little, too late." He punched the wall before passing through the doorframe.

My body gave out, and I crumpled to the floor. He'd never walked away from me before. Not like that. I wasn't sure if he meant it to be forever.

What was I doing? Was I throwing away the man who loved me for the man who left me? My heart split in two. Weariness invaded my bones. I was too young to have to deal with all this, and the only thing I wanted, at that moment, I could never have again for as long as I lived. I needed my mom. A sob racked my body as Nic wrapped his arms around me.

Chapter Twenty-One

Now

The newcomers put on more music and are dancing again, which means we have to dance our way out of the restaurant. We stumble out of the diner, laughing. Dex catches my hand and pulls me toward the car.

I try to break away and move toward the driver's side, but he pulls me back with a spin. He backs me into the hood of the car, and I have to lean back on my hands to look up to him. My keys jingle as he pulls them out of his pocket. A smile creeps on to his face.

"I'm still driving," he says.

"I don't think I'll survive another ride in the car with you," I counter.

He leans down over me. "I'm a good driver."

"Yeah, a good driver for inducing heart attacks," I scoff.

"Not a heart attack, just your heart racing," he whispers as his hand curves around the back of my neck.

"What would give you that idea?"

"This." He pulls my head up to meet his halfway.

His lips press to mine, caressing. Then his teeth tug at my lower lip. I grip the top of his shoulders and climb his body to deepen the kiss. My tongue tangles with his, and he pulls me into him when my legs wrap around his waist.

He tastes like a fruity mint and smells like a woodsy, manly cologne. My hands curl into his hair and tighten. He moans in answer. A wave of desire sweeps through me with that sound. He starts carrying me to the passenger side of the car. I know this is a distraction, but I don't care. He can drive the car every day if he does this.

Muffled banging and yelling startles me back to reality, and I look over to the restaurant. The group of college kids inside are waving their phones around with smiles and giving us thumbs-up. I shake my head as laughter bubbles up from my stomach.

"We have an audience," I say, turning back to him. "You should probably put me down."

With my focus back on him, our faces are only an inch apart. He captures my lower lip and sucks it into his mouth, letting me slide down his body to the ground. The car door opens. Dex stands back with a grin and sweeps his arm in front of him, bowing slightly.

"After you, m'lady."

The smart-ass inside of me can't help herself. "Such a gentleman." I roll my eyes. "Who says chivalry is dead?"

I get in as he chuckles and shuts the door behind me. As he walks around the car, I'm tempted to slide across the bench seat and be in the driver's seat when he gets there. But a bigger part of me is curious about where he's taking me next, so I stay put and buckle my seat belt as he slides into the car.

"Where to next?" I ask.

"I'm going to test this theory of yours on patience now," he responds. "So be patient."

He pulls the car out of the parking lot, driving way more sedately this time. At least I'm not gripping the seat in terror.

"Patience is only extended when I know the end result is getting what I want."

"What do you want?"

"For you to fuck me," I say simply.

He chuckles. "You're not making this easy on me, you

know."

"I'm pretty sure that statement was accomplishing the opposite."

"I want to take things slow with you, Maddie," he explains. "Do this right."

"What's the point?"

He starts to talk, but I reach out and cover his mouth with my hand. "I get what you're saying, but what I'm saying is that I never understood the bases bullshit. If you're willing to suck someone's cock or their clit, why're you then unwilling to fuck? That just makes no sense. Oral is way more intimate than fucking."

He pulls my hand away from his mouth. "You're going to make me crash this car if you keep talking to me like that."

"Good. Let's keep this drive short."

I turn the radio on, and we drive. My mind wanders. I find it funny that I feel comfortable talking to him like that. I never thought I'd feel comfortable with another man like this again, but here we are. It doesn't feel awkward at all. I can only think that it has to do with him opening up to me. I feel like anyone with a story like that won't judge me for what I am.

"You don't tell that story to people often, do you?" I ask.

"You're the only one," he says. "Though Marcus knows. He's been my partner in crime for as long as I've been committing crime. He got the same offer as me."

"Wow, you've known each other that long?"

"Yeah."

"Thank you," I say.

"For what?" he asks, glancing over at me.

"For telling me. It couldn't've been easy. I know it's not easy for me to talk about my past."

"You can anytime," he says softly and then pauses. "I want to know all the parts of you, Maddie. The good and the bad. I'll never judge you for it. Just like I knew you wouldn't judge me for my past."

The words pour out of me easily as I tell him about my

parents. It actually shocks me a little. I tell him all about my dad and my mom, growing up with Evan and Nic. He drives past the entrance to my neighborhood and into the main entrance to Zilker Park. I keep talking.

"You shouldn't feel that way, you know."

"I know," I say. "Believe me, it took years of therapy to admit that I shouldn't feel guilt for my parents' deaths, but it's hard not to think of it that way still."

He pulls off the meandering road that winds through Zilker Park on to a dirt path that is blocked by a gate. The trees are so thick that once he cuts the lights and the engine, someone would need to know the path was there to see us. I read the sign next to the gate and laugh.

"Girl Scouts? How did you even know this was here? I've been out here tons of times and didn't know there was a Girl Scout camp out here."

He shrugs as he unbuckles his seat belt and moves toward me. "I've had to come out here a time or two for work. The place is vacant during the school year. Well, at night, at least."

I quickly undo mine and lean into him.

"You know we're adults and I've a house with a bed we could go to right now. Are we seriously going to do it in the car like teenagers?" I raise an eyebrow.

"Yeah," he answers. "Do you want to move this back to the house where the girls are?"

"No," I answer. I run my tongue up the side of his neck and trace it over the shell of his ear. "Enough talking, Dex," I whisper. "It's been four years for me. I want you inside me now."

His head falls back as he groans. "You're not making this easy on me."

"I'm making it more than easy." I reach out and squeeze his cock through his jeans. He's hard, and it feels big. I bite my lip to stop the moan that wants to escape my mouth. "I'm making it hard," I whisper in his ear as I move to straddle him.

He stops me with a firm grip on my hips. He kisses me,

his tongue slipping past my lips to tangle with mine. I try to move and grind against him, but he holds me still. I pull his hair, tipping his head back as my kiss becomes more aggressive. He moans and pulls me down on to him, grinding into me. My heart races and my pussy throbs, I want him so badly. I rub myself back and forth across his lap, but with my jeans on, it's not enough. His hands still my hips once more as he pulls back.

"Get in the back," he says, his voice deep and rough.

My whole body tingles at the tone of his voice. He can't be into the same stuff I'm into.

"Will you spank me if I don't?"

"I'll do anything you want me to if you get in the back of the damn car."

I rise to my feet as much as I can, hunching over him with a smirk, and make sure he gets a face full of every indecent body part I have as I climb over him. It isn't graceful at all, but effective, as I throw myself into the back seat.

His move to join me is much more graceful and fluid. I watch the rippling muscles in his arms and swallow. He kneels in the cramped space of the floorboard and leans over the seat. His eyes are heated, and his smell fills the car like he's throwing off pheromones.

I pull my shirt over my head. He grabs his by the collar and pulls it over his head the way boys do. He's got ink all over his torso, but it's too dark to make out what they are. We both sit there looking at each other, our tangled breaths the only sound in the space. He makes no move toward me, so I reach back and pop the hook on my bra and let it slide down my arms.

He still doesn't move, but I've the urge to touch him. I want to rub my body up against his and feel his bare skin touch mine, but I choose to strive for patience and wait.

I run my hands over my breasts, rolling my nipples between my fingertips, and let one trail down farther. I reach the top of my jeans, pop the button, and let the zipper pull apart as I slide my fingers into my underwear.

"If you won't touch me, I'm just gonna have to do it myself."

His eyebrows inch up. "You'd do that?"

"Of course. I like being watched. Doesn't mean I'm not going to ride your cock in a bit," I say before my brain can catch up with my mouth. I suck in a breath, waiting for him to tell me that's wrong, but it never comes.

He blinks. "I'm just trying to figure out if I'm dreaming."

"You're not dreaming," I coo, trying to suppress a smile. "Touch me."

He releases a shuddering breath, and in a blink his lips are on mine, his hand roaming over my bare flesh. I pull him until our bodies press together. He's warm and hard. My hands trace the contours of his shoulders and arms, memorizing. His lips trail down my neck, nipping and licking a path to my breasts. He sucks a nipple into his mouth. His hand follows the same path mine had traversed earlier. His teeth lightly clamp down on my nipple as his finger runs over my sensitive bundle of nerves. My back bows and I release a throaty moan.

I yelp as a loud tap on the glass sounds. I open my eyes to see a light trained on the dashboard. The windows are already fogged up, so it's not likely whoever is outside has seen anything.

Dex pulls his shirt off the ground and covers me with it. The other hand goes behind his back, and I hear a click before I see the gun in his hand. He reaches over the seat and rolls down the window. It's a slow mission since this old car is only equipped with manual windows.

"I need to see some ID," the male voice says sternly.

Dex reaches into his back pocket and pulls out his wallet and hands it to the man. The light from the flashlight bounces around as the man tucks it under his arm. With the light close enough to his body, I can now see the police uniform he's wearing. Dex sees it, too, because I hear the subtle click of the safety on his gun and he quietly tucks it in the holster behind him.

"I'm going to need you to step out of the car," the officer says.

I assume that Dex can't tell him that he's a cop because he's undercover. I want to groan, but bite it back.

"We're gonna need to get dressed first," Dex replies.

"Yeah, good idea," the officer agrees.

He holds his flashlight pointed toward the dashboard again. Dex holds his shirt up, blocking the cop's view of me as I scramble to put my bra and shirt back on and zip up my pants. Once I'm decent, Dex pulls his shirt back on and pushes the seat forward so we can get out. He holds his hands, palms up, in the view of the officer's light.

"We're ready to come out," Dex states.

The cop opens the door and takes a few steps back. Dex goes out first and then holds out a hand to help me climb out. When I stand up straight, the officer's light shines into my face.

"Good Lord, you're Laine Dobransky."

"I am," I answer.

"I'm a huge fan. My wife and I, we love your song, 'The End of What I Knew.' It helped us through some rocky times. She'd kill me if I didn't ask to get your autograph. Would you mind?"

"Ummm... I don't mind. Are we under arrest or something?" I ask.

"Shit, no—I mean, um—no, I usually just catch kids out here and talk to them, scare them straight, you know?"

"Sure. Well, you got us," I say with a half-hearted laugh. "I don't think we'll attempt to relive our youth again anytime soon."

"I get it. Mum's the word, right?" He grins. His eyes take on this far-off glassy look like he is staring at something awe-inspiring and not me.

I smile, feeling a little uncomfortable with his intensity. "You want me to sign something?"

"Oh, yeah," he says as he pulls one of those metal box-like clipboards from under his arm and shuffles through it.

He clips a piece of paper to it and walks toward me with short, quick steps. He pulls a pen out of his breast pocket and hits the clicker on it before handing that to me, too. The piece of paper is illuminated by his light, and I notice that it has a watermark on it like it's the back of a picture.

I pull it out and flip it over. It's a picture of a happy couple in their thirties or so, smiling. I look up through the harsh light and vaguely make out the same face.

"It's my wife and me, from our honeymoon earlier this year," he states.

I nod and smile, clipping it back in place. I sign: *May love keep you together always—Laine D.*

Dex is watching me with amusement.

"Here you go, Officer..." I wait for him to supply a name as I hand him back his stuff.

"Roberts. Jake Roberts," he supplies.

"There you go, Jake."

"Thank you," he says. "Oh, here." He hands Dex's wallet to him. "Y'all have a good night. And you might want to think about taking that back to the house or maybe a hotel room if it's one of those sorts of things."

"It's not," Dex says. "I'm definitely her boyfriend."

Then

It'd been three boring days sitting around in a hospital that could've been anywhere in the world, because we hadn't left the building. At all. I spent my days and nights in Evan's room, playing cards and watching crap TV shows on the Armed Forces Network. Other than the drive there, that building was the full extent of my visit to Germany. My first time out of the country was not living up to all I'd hoped it to be.

I was forced to watch the current season of *American Idol*, lying shoulder to shoulder with Evan on his hospital bed. The girls were fast asleep on the couch near the window, their little minds not adjusting well to the time shift of being on the other side of the world.

"Have you been to his room yet?"

I looked over at him. He was still watching the TV. I watched his profile for a reaction. "You trying to get rid of me?"

"No." His face squished up, and I knew he was lying.

"Really?" I drew the word out so he could hear the skepticism.

"Fine. Yes. That cute nurse comes on shift in an hour. I don't want her thinking we're a family."

"But, we *are* a family, Evan," I said in a sugary-sweet voice.

"You know what I mean." He looked over at me then to see the huge grin on my face.

"Of course I do. That's why I already introduced myself to her as your sister and told her that you were the best uncle in the world. I caught on to the way you were staring at her ass on day one." I gave him a dry look. "You're welcome."

"Speaking of staring at asses, how's your not-defined relationship going?"

"I don't know," I sighed, dropping my head back on the pillow.

"That good, huh?"

"I'm not sure."

"I think I know now, what it's like to be a dentist." He sighed and dropped his head back, too.

I looked over at him, confused. "What?"

"Because trying to get you to talk about shit's like pulling teeth."

"Fuck, Evan. Fine. He told me he loved me. We got into an argument. I ran away. And just when he shows up to talk, he finds me leaving the country. He's pissed. And I couldn't explain everything while walking out the door. You happy?"

He grinned at me. "Yeah, I kinda am. Not about what you said, but the fact that you finally said something. You've been in here looking miserable for the past three days. Sighing at the walls, and twitching like you've got somewhere to be."

"I'm not twitchy," I defended.

"What did you argue about?"

"I tried to bring up the girls. Asked him what he thought about kids. He immediately jumped to the conclusion that I was fixin' to tell him I was pregnant. He was so relieved that I wasn't. Said he didn't want kids for a long time. So, I made up some shit about volunteering with orphans. Turns out, I never told him about my parents, which to him was a big deal."

"Doesn't surprise me."

"What doesn't?"

"Any of it. The fact that you waited over a month since I last saw you to have that conversation. You, not telling him key facts about yourself. Or him, jumping to the pregnancy conclusion when you asked about kids. All guys have that moment of panic when the girl they're having sex with brings up kids."

"Jared didn't." I wanted to kick my own ass for throwing that comparison out there.

"Jared's a freak of nature, because I'd be panicking. I did panic when you told me about the girls, and they weren't even mine."

"They sort of are. You're the only father figure they've had for a while now."

"Not true."

"The General is their grandfather. And yeah, he may be around them a lot, but he still acts like a grandpa, spoiling them rotten."

"I'm not talking about the General."

"Then what are you talking about?"

"Look, I'm not supposed to say anything. I'm not getting in the middle of this."

"Fuck you. You can't say something like that and expect me just to let it go."

"Mads," he started, and I twisted his nipple. "Owww!"

"Don't feed me any more bullshit. We've been friends since the day I was born. *The Three Amigos*. We don't keep shit from each other. If I gotta hear about Nic's newfound sexuality, his aspirations to be a porn star every day, and give you painful updates every time we talk, then you have to spill shit too. This friendship isn't a one-way information street. No military *Band of Brothers* bullshit tops that. Got it?"

"Okay, fine! He's been visiting them on leave; he just avoids you and tells everyone not to mention it."

I drop my head in my hands and take a deep breath. "How long?"

"Since he got out of training and was able to take leave."

"Why? You know what? Never mind. I don't even want to know. It's good, though. The girls deserve to know their father. I thought it was going to be a little weird meeting him at a hospital in a foreign country while he's all fucked-up, but it just turns out that everyone's been lying to me. No big."

He shifted his body to turn and face me with raised brows. "I'm surprised you didn't figure it out on your own. Surely the girls have talked about him?"

"They've talked about him, sure," I replied. "Nothing specific like he's been around, but they certainly have an opinion of him. They love him. I just assumed that it all came from Diana and the General, showing them pictures or telling them stories." I shook my head in disbelief. "I just don't understand why you, of all people, would take his side."

"Mads," he sighed, reaching over and squeezing my hand. "I'm not defending him, but I didn't tell you because I understand why he's doing it. I may not agree, but I understand."

I started to ask why, but the door to the room opened and the General stepped in. He looked haggard and worn-out.

My heart went out to him and Diana. I wouldn't want to be standing around a hospital for three days waiting for one of the girls to wake up after a major trauma and surgery.

"He's awake," John said quietly. "He wants to see you before I bring the girls down, so just come back and let me know when you're done. I'll let them sleep."

"Okay." I didn't know what else to say.

Evan gave me a reassuring pat on the back as I sat up. I

gave him a wan smile, and he squeezed my hand before I turned and left the room.

I made my way through the maze of hallways, down to the ICU wing. Diana was standing outside the automatic doors. I gave her a half-hearted smile.

She also looked worn-out, but happier now that her boy was awake. "I'm going to go get some coffee. He's in room seven."

I nodded and watched her walk away before I found myself standing outside door seven. It had been four years since I'd last laid eyes on Jared. When I finally worked up the courage to push through the door, he was watching me.

He looked so much smaller lying prone on the bed, propped up slightly with pillows. But those eyes were the same as they tracked my every move. He didn't say anything, and I began to get antsy. With everything that happened with Law, and the fact that this man had been actively avoiding me for four years, I wasn't sure why I was standing in this room. I was worried about both him and Evan, worried about the girls never knowing their father. But all along I'd been played the fool. The more I thought about it, the more it pissed me off.

"You shouldn't be here," he muttered as I paced the room.

I jerked to a stop and slowly turned on my heel to face him. "Are you kidding me? I haven't seen you for four goddamn years, and that's the first thing out of your mouth."

"This is exactly why I told you not to wait for me. I didn't want you to have to go through this. All the worrying if something bad was going to happen—"

I threw back my head as a near-hysterical laugh bubbled from my throat. "You know, I used to think you were really smart, but that, I believe, is the dumbest shit I've ever heard. You're the father of my children. I won't ever stop worrying if you live or die." I started pacing the room again. "Evan told me about your secret visits, but I guess they weren't so secret. Since everyone knew. But me. Why's that?"

"I didn't want to see you. Maddie—"

The rage I'd kept locked down surged through me, setting my veins on fire. I took three steps until my face was inches away from his.

"Why? Afraid of remembering your little mistake, knocking up poor little destroyed Maddie. You know, I just don't get it. All this martyr crap about doing it for me. So I could experience the world, right? Must've been hard on you." I shook my head, unable to believe that I bought that line of crap. "You could at least try to be honest, for once in your life, and just admit that it was a mistake. You didn't want to be tied down. We were young. I get it. But to continue this farce. To continue the lie. Fucking grow up already. I did. And I've moved on, too."

I searched his face for a reaction, and when his eyes widened a bit, I felt triumph. "You want to know what I've been up to?"

My fingers were itching with the need to hurt him. With all the tubes, wires, monitors, casts, and bandages, I knew he was already in physical pain. No, I needed to dig much deeper.

"I go to school. I make good grades like a good little girl. I'll graduate in a few months with a double major and as valedictorian. I also play lead guitar for a punk band. I skate on a roller derby team. I train in MMA." A husky laugh escaped me. "And when I'm not doing that, I'm usually fucking my insanely hot boyfriend who has shown me what being with a real man is like. And who I'm totally in love with."

When I pulled back and saw the pain in his eyes, I knew I had hit my mark. Take that, Jared's ego. That little girl you thought was pining away for you wasn't so pathetic after all.

"So congratu-fuckin'-lations, you accomplished your mission, soldier. I'm no longer hung up on you—no need to play your stupid fucking hide-and-seek, mind games anymore. Just be a father to your kids and forget about me."

He started to speak, but I raised my palm to halt him. I

was mortified that tears started building up in my eyes.

"No, you don't get to say anything else. You gave up that right four years ago. But right now… right now, I'm walking out this door and away from you. And I hope it feels just as good for you as it did for me." With that, I pushed out the door and left.

Chapter Twenty-Two

Then

I was so tired when I let myself into the dorm room, I didn't even bother turning the lights on. I dropped my bag and collapsed on the bed. International flights sucked. I felt like shit, both physically and mentally. Physically, because I was crammed into a tin box with hundreds of other people for an ungodly long time. Mentally, because I'd been regretting my words to Jared.

I was mad because he never came to see me, but he did visit the girls. I should've been happy for the girls that their father gave a shit about them. He was trying to be a decent parent. Instead, I reacted like a selfish, immature brat. I shouldn't have cared what he did. I should've just let it go.

My eyes slowly drifted shut of their own accord.

When my eyes opened, they were greeted by the bright light of the sun. It took me a few moments to realize my phone ringing had woken me up. I reached into my back pocket and dug it out, because yeah, I hadn't even had the energy to change clothes or get under the covers properly last night.

"Hello?" I answered, my voice groggy with sleep.

"Maddie?" Jared's voice asked.

I grunted in the affirmative.

"Can you talk? I can call back some other time if you're busy or with someone."

"I was actually sleeping, but I'm awake now. I was so tired getting home last night, I still have my shoes on."

He laughed. We sat in silence for a few beats. My eyes started to drift shut again. I snapped them open and sat up.

"Did you have a point to calling? Other than to find out if I took my shoes off?"

"Yeah, hold on. I'm getting there. I don't want to screw this up."

"Well, while you're collecting your thoughts, I should tell you I'm sorry. I shouldn't have said what I said. I just have a lot going on, and then everything was upended going to Germany. I'm not trying to make excuses, but I was stressed. I think it's good that you've been spending time with the girls. They need you in their life. And you don't owe me a damn thing."

"Maddie, I—you don't have to apologize. I deserve your anger. I just—I don't know what I expected to happen. Fuck."

The line went quiet, and I began to wonder if he hung up. I looked at the phone, and the call was still connected, so I waited.

"I meant it when I let you go to follow your dreams. I wanted you to do good in school, to learn guitar, maybe join a band. I want you to be happy and not regret anything. I guess I just didn't think it all the way through." He sighed and went quiet again.

I'd no idea what to say, so I remained quiet, too. I lay back on the bed and fumbled with the edge of my comforter.

"You do MMA and roller derby?" he asked.

"Yeah, my boyfriend teaches a self-defense program that's a combination of Krav Maga and Brazilian jujitsu."

Crap. I was talking about Law, to Jared. *So awkward.*

"Since they're both fighting styles based on fighting larger and stronger opponents, it works well as self-defense. I've been doing it for the last two years. I pretty much help him teach the class now. I won my weight class at a city-wide jujitsu competition last summer. But I'm not really competitive with it. It's more for personal growth and fitness."

"Yeah, you looked good. Stronger, not that you lost weight or were fat before." He laughed. "I'm going to stop now before I get myself in trouble."

I laughed, too, and it felt good. It was nice to have a normal conversation with Jared again.

"Roller derby helps with that, too. I found derby because some of the girls came to one of my band's shows. It's amazing, though. I get a rush from just racing around the track during practice. The bouts are fun whether you're a blocker, pivot, or jammer. It's so much fun. And the girls on the team are awesome. I'm not kidding. I've found my place, my people."

"I'm glad to hear it, even though I only understood half of what you just said."

I laughed. "Sorry, I'm not used to talking derby with people who don't know all the lingo."

"I got the gist. It's good to hear your laugh again."

He sounded sad, and something deep inside me felt stretched thin. I couldn't do this with him. I loved Law, though I'd yet to tell him that. I didn't even know if he was going to take me back or even talk to me, but I hoped. This conversation shook up the turmoil already bouncing around in my brain.

"I should let you go, Jared. It was nice talking to you. I'm glad I got to apologize."

"Maddie, please—I didn't expect this to happen. I thought maybe you might go on a few dates with other guys, but I didn't think you would fall in love with someone else."

"Jared, this isn't a good idea. What's done, is done. It's in the past. We just need to let it go."

"I'm getting out."

"What?"

"My contract is up July of next year. I'm not going to

245

reenlist. I'm coming back home."

"That's great." I used my fake cheerful voice, but inside I was panicking. "We can talk about custody and visitation with the girls soon, then. I'm getting a place after graduation in May. I plan on moving them to Austin, here, with me."

He could ask for custody, and I wouldn't have enough money left for a lawyer after five years of college tuition.

"I'm not taking the girls away from you. I wanted us to be a family."

"That's not going to happen, Jared. It's been over four years and not a single phone call or even a letter, an email, nothing. What did you think would come of that?"

"Fuck! I know. It was stupid. I just couldn't do it. I couldn't talk to you or see you without wanting you back. I would've asked you to give everything up to be with me. And I knew—I knew that would've made you miserable. So I stayed away. But you don't know how many times I sat there with the phone in my hands, your number dialed, just staring at it. Just wanting to hear your voice. How many letters I wrote you and never sent—"

"I can't. I can't do this with you, Jared," I said as tears broke loose and rolled down my face. "It's too late. I gotta go."

I hung up the phone and set it down beside me as sobs racked my body.

When the tears dried up, I knew I had to wash the plane smell off my body. I was disgusting. I got up from the bed and took two steps toward my desk to grab my shower tote. I halted in my tracks. There on the desk was a single red calla lily. It had to have been Nic, sneaking it in here for Jared. Jared's the only person who'd ever given me red calla lilies. Nic did have my keys all week. I shook my head. I was going to have a talk with Nic about helping Jared in his misguided attempt to win me back.

Now

This is the point in my life where I realize that I've lulled myself into a false sense of security. Who could blame me, though? Four years of nothing is long enough to allow anyone to relax and start to believe that their life is normal. I should know better. My life has never been normal.

Though it takes a few minutes for the cop to put his car in gear and leave so we can back out of the little dirt driveway, the drive from the park is short. My house is close to Zilker Park, so it's only a matter of minutes before we turn into my neighborhood.

As we turn on to my street, I realize something's wrong. Cars are lined up on both sides of the road. News vans and personal vehicles are interspersed for about two-hundred feet on either side of my driveway. It's not a foreign scene to me, but not one I ever expected to happen again. At least not while I wasn't asking for it.

"What do you want to do?" Dex asks, slowing the car.

"Just keep driving," I say, pulling the gate remote off the visor. "I'll open the gate. Don't look at them. Don't respond to them. You ever been famous before?"

"No," he answers.

"Well, you're fixin' to be. Is this going to hurt your career?"

"No. If anything it helps," he says, not taking his eyes off the road. His brow is furrowed in concentration. "People are less suspicious of public personalities because they assume the media will dig up the dirt for them."

"Well, I hope, for your sake, that file you showed me doesn't end up in the wrong hands."

"That file's been easily accessible my whole life. It's part of my cover, so I don't care one way or another. You know that's not who I am now." He pauses, concentrating on navigating through the crowded street. "That's more than I've ever had before. It means more than you know that I can be real with you, that I don't have to feed you the lie, too."

I can't think of a response as we drive by the first cars on this side of my house. People are standing around mingling, but they look up and watch us pass. The second they recognize me, a shout rings out, and a flurry of activity starts.

Dex speeds up a bit but is forced to slow by people walking across the street. They hold cameras and microphones, lights and video cameras. Hands reach out and slap the car, trying to get our attention. Cameras flash and questions are shouted, both at Dex and me. I can't understand everything that they're saying, but I catch a few of the questions thrown our way.

"Laine, how do you feel about your cases being reopened?"

"Laine, is this your new boyfriend?"

"Are you worried that her stalker is back because of you?"

"Are you worried that she'll kill you next?"

I keep my head down but glance up to see when we're close enough to the gate to hit the opener. I sneak a look at Dex, but his face is blank as he looks ahead to see where he's driving. There are still people between us and the gate, but I can see it now, so I hit the button to open it. Dex remains quiet through the shouts and banging on the car.

We drive through the gate, and no one attempts to sneak in. Dex pauses, watching the gate close in the rearview. One of the Tweedles is standing near the gate, looking menacing as it shuts.

"You can go to the garage now," I say. "That one there looks like he's got it handled."

He doesn't answer as he guides the car into the garage and cuts the engine. We sit there as the garage door shuts behind us.

"That's how you live?" Dex asks.

"Well, it hasn't been like that in a long time, but yeah." I stare out the window, waiting for him to tell me that it's too much. Something is running through his head right now, and I've this feeling I'm not going to like it.

"I'm sorry," he says.

"For what?"

"That…" He tips his head in the direction we came from. "Nobody should have to live with that on their doorstep."

"It's not your doing. It's my own damn choices that got me here."

"Stop that. This isn't your fault. You have a talent, and I don't think you could hide it if you wanted to. It was going to happen one way or another. Stop blaming yourself for things that are out of your control. This is more about those cases than your music. You have to see that."

"They were around before that, Dex. When it gets like this, people decide that every aspect of your life is their fucking business. Every person you know, conversations you have, places you visit. It's all there for their entertainment. It's a domino effect. One decision leads to an outcome that leads to another. I've no one to blame but myself."

"I've seen the evidence." His knuckles turn white from his grip on the steering wheel. "You didn't kill him."

"I'm not talking about it." I throw open the car door and head toward the house, not paying attention to whether he's behind me or not.

When I open the back door, I find Holly and Evan and the other Tweedle sitting at the kitchen counter, hunched over something. They all whip their heads in my direction.

"Thank fuck, you're back," Holly says as she rushes me. "We tried calling, but you weren't answering your damn phone. The freak show out there arrived about an hour ago." She wraps me in a hug.

"I thought y'all would be asleep," I say. "I turned off my phone because we were busy."

"We figured as much and, well, we weren't worried so much about your safety, considering what set the hive to swarm," Evan says with a smirk.

"And that is…" I prompt.

"This." Evan motions me over to his side.

I stand behind Evan's shoulder as he turns to his laptop. I can feel Dex behind me before his arms come around my waist, tugging me against him. Evan clicks on his browser, and the TMZ website pops up.

My stomach drops. I feel like I'm going to throw up. I never imagined I'd be back on this website, watching a video of myself ever again.

Evan clicks the Play button. Dex and I are in a dirt parking lot, and I already know what's going to happen. Those stupid fucking college kids recognized me. They didn't say anything when we were in that diner, but they certainly took the opportunity to get their payday, and they were fast about it.

Despite the warmth of Dex's arms around me, cold blooms from within, spreading throughout my limbs. The numb, empty feeling settles into my bones. It's such a familiar feeling that I find myself shocked that I didn't realize that it had gone until this moment. *How am I going to fix this so it doesn't harm the girls? What is the fallout on the company going to look like?* So many things start racing through my brain.

I can't do this again. I push Dex's arms off me just as video-me is wrapping my legs around his waist. I turn and head to my room without a word. I can't drag someone else into this bullshit with me. I want nothing more than to curl up on my bed and wake up from this nightmare. I start to shut the door behind me, but Dex is there in the doorway.

"Talk to me," Dex says as he steps inside and closes the door behind him.

"I can't. I can't do this. I'm not—I won't drag you or anyone else into this." I pull back the blankets on my bed and rearrange the pillows. "You need to get out while you still can. There's a room upstairs you can sleep in tonight. You don't have to fight through that crap out there. Evan'll show you which one. You can tell Martinez whatever you want. It doesn't matter. But we're not doing this."

I can't do anything more for the pillows. I need something. I reach over to my wrist and realize that I hadn't put my rubber band on. I turn to the nightstand and grab it off the surface. Once it's in place, I pull it out and let it snap. Tears build in my eyes at the death of hope. I search for something else to distract me.

"You done?" he asks.

"Yeah, that's what I just said."

"No. I meant, are you done trying to tell me what to do?" His tone is harsh, and it stops me in my tracks.

I turn to face him. His fists clench at his side. I've never seen him look this angry before, but his brow sits low, shadowing his eyes, and with that scar he looks menacing. My mouth dries up, and I don't think I could speak even if I could think of words to say.

"In case it wasn't clear to you. I signed on for this. Hell, even Audra signed on for this. It's not just my choice. It's also my job. Though if I hadn't made it clear, let me make it now. This case was a means to an end. I made my choice, and that choice was you. I want you. And not just the pretty, happy parts. All of it."

His hand runs through his hair. "I'm not going to walk away. I'm here, and the only thing that's going to make me walk out that door is if you tell me that whatever you felt twenty minutes ago, in that car, is gone. But you're not going to decide you know what's best for me and push me away. That's not how this works."

"You don't even know how this works. You think you know, but you only have half the story."

"Yeah, I know. The redacted parts—"

"Sure, the redacted parts are part of it. Like I said, it's a domino effect, and if you put yourself in line, you're going to get knocked down. We all did, and the only reason I'm standing today is that I learned to pick myself back up. But not one fucking part of that was good or fun. I promise you that."

"Come here," he demands.

He's standing still as stone, the air around him seeming to vibrate with tension like it's radiating from him. His face is serious and angry, but I'm not scared of him. I don't think Dex would ever hurt me.

I walk over to stand in front of him, and he wraps me in

his arms, breathing a sigh. His body relaxes as he buries his face in my neck.

"I'm going to take the room upstairs tonight. I think you need some time to think this through. I've told you who I am and made it clear what I want. You just have to decide what you want." He pulls back and looks me in the eyes. "But don't think for a second that you can decide what's best for me. You need to decide if you feel something for me because I'm convinced that you might be my forever girl. I'm willing to walk through fire to find out."

His lips brush over mine gently. There's a pressure building in my chest. I can't explain it, but it's there. I'm stunned into silence as my mind blanks.

"Good night," he whispers, then turns and leaves the room.

Chapter Twenty-Three

Then

"Where are we going again?" Sloane asked from the passenger seat of my car. "Because it's beginning to look like we're lost."

"Shit, I think she's taking us this far from fuck all because she doesn't want anyone to find our bodies," Holly added.

"Really?" I asked. "For the last time, I'm taking you back to my hometown. It's about fifteen more minutes. And I'm dragging your asses out here because I need you to meet some people. Now, will you shut the fuck up?" I grinned at them to soften my words and turned up the radio.

This was my best idea for how to break the news to my best friends that I was a mother. I'd hidden in my dorm since returning from Germany. Waiting until Sloane returned, I then abducted her. I needed her advice before I talked to Law. Holly was a necessity. We three had grown close since joining the derby team, and I knew if I only told Sloane, Holly would be hurt.

When we finally entered the city limits, my heart rate increased. I'd no idea how they were going to react. Our friendship had been built on the fact that we were in a similar place in life, but really, I'd been hiding the fact that I wasn't like them at all. And time was running out. Soon enough, I'd be a full-time mother and a college grad, just in time for my twenty-first birthday.

"I'm warning you now that today is family day. Every Sunday we get together and barbecue, play games, and whatnot. My friend Nic and his family will be there. So will Evan's parents. It gets a little—well, you'll see."

"I'm feeling a little nervous now that this comes with a warning. Do I need protective gear?" Sloane asked.

"No. Though, you do need to watch yourself with Nic. He'll try to get in your pants. He's harmless, but he's got skills as a charmer."

"I'm sure I can resist," Sloane said dryly.

"Speaking of resisting. Have you talked to your brother?" I asked.

"Yeah," she answered, sounding sad. "He's not doing so well."

He's not doing well? "Did he tell you he broke up with me?"

"You guys were officially together at some point?" Sloane retorted.

"Shut up," I grumped, but I knew I deserved it. I felt like I was finally seeing things clearly, and I'd been deluding myself. "I'm pretty sure I was the only one that didn't think we were. Did he talk to you about what happened, though?"

"Not really. Wednesday, he asked if you'd called. Then yesterday, he asked if you were back yet. You know him, though, he doesn't talk about his shit. You either. You two are so much alike it's scary."

She didn't even know the half of it, I thought. "He told me he loved me the night I left."

"And?" Sloane drew out the word, not understanding the significance of what I was saying.

"For the first time," I clarified.

"Holy shit! You guys have been together for over two years." Sloane shook her head. "You two are like poster children for the emotionally unavailable."

My hackles rose, but I forced myself to leave it. "The point is that, yeah, it took two years to get there, but I left the country right after. I didn't have time to explain—"

"You're gonna explain now, aren't you?" Sloane interrupted.

"I'm working on it," I sighed. "That's why we're going to Diana and John's house."

Holly finally chimed in. "Who are Diana and John?"

"Shh, we'll get to that soon enough," I chided. "One step at a time."

We pulled into the driveway at the house. This was it. My stomach tied in knots. The girls always could hear the Charger coming down the road, so when they came bursting out the door to greet me, I wasn't surprised. They were at the car door as soon as I swung it open, and they crashed on to my lap before I had a chance to get up.

"Mommy," Cat said, throwing her arms around my neck. "I missed you."

I laughed. "Hey, Runt, dramatic much? It hasn't even been a full twenty-four hours since we got back from Germany."

I looked over to Cora. Her eyes were wary as she took in the strangers sitting silently in the car with me. I tracked her eyes back to Holly, whose mouth was hanging open in shock.

"Sloane, Holly, I'd like you to meet Catherine and Coraline. My daughters."

Cat climbed over me to the center of the bench seat in front of Sloane. "You're Auntie Sloane. Mommy said you'd be pretty." She reached over and twirled strands of Sloane's dark brown hair in her fingers.

Sloane grabbed her and hugged her to her chest. "Oh, my God, can I keep her?" She looked at me smiling.

"They look just like you," Holly said, awe tinging her voice.

"You're pretty, too, Auntie Holly. Mommy told us about her bestest friends."

"I wish I could say the same, Munchkin," Sloane said to Cat while giving me the side-eye. "Your mommy decided to surprise us. And I say she wins a prize for the biggest surprise ever. Don't you think?"

"Me and Cora aren't that big. We're four, but we'll be five soon."

"Oh, honey, you're a big adorable surprise," Holly said. "And you both look just like your mother. It's crazy."

"Can I tell you a secret?" Sloane asked Cat. "My real name is Elizabeth—Sloane is my middle name. Your momma said your name is Catherine. Do you like to go by that?"

Cat shook her head. "Mommy and Nana and Pop Pop call me Kit Cat, but you can call me just Cat, too."

"Kit Cat is perfect. What about you, sweetie?" Sloane looked to Cora.

Cora buried her face in my neck and remained silent.

"That's Cora. She doesn't talk to anyone, but Mommy and Nana and Pop Pop. She talk to Daddy when we went to Gernmany."

Sloane's eyes met mine, and I saw them flood with understanding.

"She talks to Lord Master and Uncle Lucky, too."

Both Sloane and Holly did a double take at that.

"Evan and Nic," I explained. "Hey, girls. Why don't you tell Nana we're here so we can get out of the car? It's starting to get hot in here."

"Okay, see ya inside," Cat said, climbing over me as Cora slid to her feet. "Race me?"

"Sure." Cora shrugged, and they both took off to the house.

I watched them until they got to the door and then turned to look at my stunned passengers. Neither of them looked angry, so that was a good sign.

"Say something," I whispered.

"I'm just trying to wrap my head around Little Miss Responsibility being a teen mom." Sloane laughed. "It fits, though, because you have two, and you're always an overachiever."

"Word, bitch," Holly agreed with a chuckle, reaching out to fist-bump Sloane.

"You're not mad?"

"Why would we be mad?" Holly asked.

I dropped my head back to the headrest and sighed. "Because I never told you about them?"

"Do you think we never noticed that you're not exactly the sharing type?" Sloane asked. "It's cool, really. It means you rock at keeping secrets, you listen, and you give great advice. That's why we love you. Everything makes more sense now, why you're always so adamant about going home every weekend."

"Fuck, I just like the way you live in the moment," Holly said. "You don't dwell on shit. And Sloane's right. You're always there for us. Why would we get bitchy about you having kids? Though now you're even more superhuman. Balancing this shit with what we know already. I might kind of hate you for that. Shit, I'm doing good to get through culinary school and make it to practice on time." She grinned. "Is this why you and Law got into a fight?"

"Sort of," I said, then gave them the rundown of last Friday night. "That's why I thought it'd be better just to bring you here so you understand. How was I supposed to tell him I've two kids and their father was in critical condition on the other side of the world, while I'm walking out the door?"

"Yeah, that would've been a pretty fucked-up way to break the news," Holly agreed.

"I just don't think I realized how serious I was about Law until he walked away from me." Tears started welling in my eyes. "I just don't know how to fix this, and I need to fix it."

"My brother does not deserve you," Sloane said, squeezing my hand. "He'll probably be crawling back to you the second he realizes you're back. I'm not sure what he'll make of the kids. He pretty much hates kids. He hated kids when we were kids."

Relief ran thick in my veins. She knew her brother better than any of us.

"He only got worse when our brother came into the picture."

"He said something about that." Curiosity got the better

of me and I asked, "I didn't know y'all had a brother?"

"We do—he's not around anymore. Him and Law—" She shakes her head. "To say they didn't get along is putting it mildly. But that's not my story to tell. You want the gory details, talk to Law."

It was just past eight when I stepped onto the porch at Law's place. I stood there for a moment, not knowing what to do. Should I knock? I'd never knocked before. It felt all sorts of weird to be standing there, on the outside of a place that was pretty much my second home. I stood there, my stomach twisting in knots. I finally gathered up the courage and knocked.

The door swung open.

"What the fuck are you doing here?" Spence asked.

My stomach plummeted. *Oh, God, they all hate me.* I began to feel dizzy and may have swayed a bit.

"Shit, I didn't mean it like that. Get in here. I just meant that Law heard you were back, and he went to your dorms to grovel. You two must've passed each other," he said as he grabbed my arm to steady me and pulled me inside.

He sat me down at the dining room table.

"You want something to drink?" he asked and walked to the kitchen, coming back with two Shiner Bocks. He set the beer in front of me and opened his, taking a swig before speaking again. "I know I'm not your boyfriend, but you want to explain to me why I got a text last week saying you had an emergency and didn't know when you'd be back? I had to cancel two gigs this past week."

"Yeah, sorry. I've a confession, and it's kind of a big one." I took a deep breath.

Holly and Sloane had taken it well, but that didn't mean everyone would. I knew this was just the beginning of the rounds I had to make in my own personal walk of shame.

"I'm all ears," he said, a smile teasing his lips.

I decided just to spit it out. "I have two kids."

"Ummm, what? How's that possible?"

"Well, you know when two people have sex—"

"I get the mechanics, Laine," he said dryly.

I laughed. "I've two girls, twins. They're four years old. It's why I refuse to do gigs on Sundays and practice on Saturdays."

"What was the emergency?" He quirked a brow. "I hope they're okay."

I smiled at his concern. "That's where it gets complicated. Their father's in the Army, and he was critically injured by an IED. He's been over in Iraq. We flew out to Germany to see him. He's in the same unit as my friend Evan—you guys met him once, remember? He was injured, too."

He nodded. "Are they okay?"

I hadn't expected him to care. I sat in shock for a moment before answering. "Yeah, Jared came out of surgery just fine. He took shrapnel to the gut, and there was a piece lodged in his armpit that was near his heart, which was why he was listed as critical. Evan took a huge piece of metal to his thigh. He's going to need physical therapy, but for the most part, he's fine. I'm sorry about the text, but I really couldn't think through all the worry and stress to explain it all. Plus, for Law, this is an explanation I owe him in person. Please don't tell him before I've a chance to talk to him about it."

He rubbed a hand over his face before pinning me with his gaze. "I won't. You're right. It's not something you tell someone over the phone or as you're running out the door. That's rough. I'm sorry to hear it. You're not still with him, are you?"

"Huh?" I asked, my mind immediately going to Law, but then I quickly caught on at his bland look. "Oh, God no. He broke up with me back when we graduated from high school. It's been four years since I last saw him. It's not like that at all."

"Good," he said with a firm nod. "I couldn't imagine you doing something like that. But I also never pictured you as a MILF. That increases your hot points, for sure."

"Shut up." I laughed out my discomfort.

"Now, this may come as a shock to you, but you're a bit of a nerd. Always so studious. Though you shed that shit for the stage, so we're cool. But finding out you're not Little Miss Perfect—I think it makes you more relatable. You get me?"

The front door slammed shut, and keys jingled as they were thrown on a table. Spence held a finger up to his mouth to keep me silent and got up to move to the doorway.

"You find her, man?" Spence asked.

"No. I think she may be avoiding me. Not that I don't deserve it. I was an ass to her before she left." Law sounded exhausted.

"You're always an ass. You don't think she's used to it by now?" Spence laughed and ducked as one of the couch pillows sailed over his head into the kitchen. "See, case in point."

"Fuck off, asshole. I'm going to my room."

"You sure you don't want to come join me for a beer?" He held up his beer to illustrate. "I got some pretty fine company that comes with it, too."

"There's no way you have a chick in here."

"You doubt my mad skills as a chick magnet?" Spence shook his head, then shrugged. "Eh, she's not here for me anyway. She came looking for you, but if you don't want her. I'll take up the cause for—"

Spence was shoved aside as Law filled the doorway. Longing filled me as I realized how much I missed him in that moment.

He crossed the room in two strides and was on his knees before me. He wrapped his big arms around my waist, pulling me toward him as he laid his head in my lap.

"I'm sorry," he murmured into my leg.

Tears filled my eyes. "You don't even know what you're sorry for. I'm the one that's sorry. I've been keeping things from you. Important things. None of this would've happened if I wasn't so screwed up."

"Sloane called me and told me that you were back and you had a damn good reason," he said, still muffled by his face on my leg. "And that I shouldn't be an asshat and screw this up."

I laughed through the tears. "She's eloquent, if nothing else."

"I'm gonna go grab something. You two have a nice night," Spence said, dumping his beer out in the sink and grabbing his keys and wallet off the counter. "I agree with your sister for once. Don't be an asshat." He left through the back door, and we were alone.

"Everybody knows but me?" He looked up at me with those hazel eyes, so beautiful with their flecks of green and amber.

"No, but he did get the scoop on the story because he was here. Your sister and Holly were the test run."

His brows rose in question. "Let's hear it."

"You might want to sit down for this," I warned.

"Okay?" He eyed me warily as he stood and took the seat Spencer had vacated.

"Remember when I asked you about kids?"

He nodded.

"I was asking because I already have two. Twin girls—they're almost five now. It wasn't something that I wanted to blast around. People aren't typically receptive to the idea of teenage mothers."

He stayed silent, so I continued. "When I graduate in May, I plan to move them here, with me. I honestly didn't expect this—" I motioned between him and me. "—to become what it has. And how do you tell someone, when they've known you that long, that you're a package deal? When you told me you loved me, all I could think was that I love you, too, but couldn't say it back until I told you. And you said you didn't want kids for a long time. Then—"

"Say it again," he said, startling me as he stood from his seat and pulling me to stand.

261

"I love you."

He pressed his lips to mine. My body melted into his as I released all the tension I was holding. He pulled back and looked over my face before resting his forehead on mine.

"Then none of the rest matters. We'll make it work."

"But they're kids, Law. Actual humans with feelings and needs."

"It doesn't matter. I love you, Laine. I felt like I couldn't breathe properly without you here. I missed you every second you were gone. Whatever it takes, we'll make it work."

He picked me up, and I wrapped my legs around his waist as he carried me back to his bedroom. We spent the rest of the night properly making up.

Chapter Twenty-Four

Now

I stand at the window of my office in the studio, watching raindrops create little circles on the surface of Barton Creek below. Something is wrong. Things are not adding up. I'm not sure where the record is damaged, but I feel the skip in my gut and know that something's not right.

When I woke up this morning, Dex was gone, I assume to go home and change, but he left no message. The rain had cleared out the paparazzi, so I convinced Evan to ride with me to work. I didn't want to wait for Dex to come back. I'm not sure what to tell him. I don't know how I feel. I just know something feels off this morning.

I lean my forehead on the cool glass, wrapping my arms around my waist. My leather jacket protests the movement. The rain outside brought with it a cold front, and today is chilly. The heat hasn't kicked on in the building yet, so it's just as chilly inside.

"Hey. Morning, Mads," Chloe greets. "Ya need me to get something?"

"No," I answer, my voice rough from lack of use.

"Ya okay?" she asks.

"Yeah. I love the rain. I was just watching it, but I should probably get to work." I force a smile as I turn to face her.

Her hair is blue today, and it brings a real smile to my face when I see the new color. She moves across the office and wraps her arms around me in a hug from the side. She rests her head on my shoulder.

"We haven't gotten to hang out much lately. I just want ya to know, I'm here for ya. Always."

I lean my head on top of hers and relax into her. "I know," I say as I pat her hands. "Thank you, Chloe. I don't know what I'd do without you."

She breaks away and heads for the door. "I sent ya the information on your appointment at three with the new band. They're all set up in the system, and Nate assigned Josh to sound tech for them. Did ya want Brian to work with them, or will ya be taking this one?"

"I'm not sure. Hold off on telling Brian," I say. "Can you find out what his schedule looks like? I may have to take them if his workload is too much. Either that or consider hiring another AR&D."

"Will do," she replies. "Ya should consider Asher for AR&D and hire a new scout. I think the travel's wearing on him. Plus, lack of creative outlet. Just a suggestion."

"A good one, though. Thanks, Chloe."

I sit at my desk and open my laptop to get started. The strange thing is, it's already on. I could've sworn I turned it off before I left yesterday. I drag my finger over the touchpad and a video starts playing. Images of Dex and me. The video from TMZ, a picture of us in the car at Zilker before the windows fogged up or clothes came off, another from our day at the lake, and the last one is the video feed of me, leaning against my front door pleasuring myself. Then the screen goes black. Words pop up on the screen like someone is typing real time.

Don't trust him. He's not who he says he is. He's not there to help you. Don't tell him anything.

The screen goes black again. My heart is racing, and my hand trembles as I reach up to see if I can replay the video. The Play bar appears at the bottom of the screen, so I should be able to. I don't want to watch it again, ever, so I don't even attempt it.

"Chloe," I shout.

"Yeah, Mads?" She sticks her head in the door.

"Call Evan. Get him back here now." My voice trembles and her expression turns to concern before she nods and leaves for her desk.

It doesn't take long for Evan to arrive, since he'd just left, so I'm not surprised when he bursts through my office door a few minutes later. I'm lying on the couch, trying to stave off a mounting headache, when he enters.

"What happened?" he asks.

"I thought you said you deleted that video?" I counter, exhausted by all this.

He looks confused for a minute, and then his face settles. "I did."

"Well, not fast enough. Look at my computer."

His fingers brush over the touch pad and his expression changes from concern to anger. There's no sound on the video, so I'm not sure if it's still playing or if he's just staring at the screen, lost in thought.

"Did you call Detective Martinez?"

"No. I'm not sure I want to. For numerous reasons."

"Maddie," he says, sounding tired and exasperated. "I'm sure this shit's embarrassing, but—"

"It's not just that, Ev," I say sitting up. "Something's been bugging me about this whole situation since last night. I'm not sure who I can trust—"

My door opens and Dex walks in. He stops, looking back and forth between me and Evan. His face says he's not happy to find me here without him, before confusion takes over. An odd pressure settles in my chest.

"Did you need something?" I ask, failing to keep the bite from my tone.

"I've been looking for you," Dex answers as he moves out of the doorway and shuts it behind him. "You were supposed to be at the house. I left to go get a change of clothes and some breakfast for us." He tosses a paper sack on to the coffee table in front of me. "When I got back, you were gone."

"I had to get to work," I answer.

Chloe steps inside my office, pressing her back to the door. Her face drained of color. "The FBI is here," she says.

Then

I pulled into the parking lot of the Barton Creek Food Truck Park just after six in the evening. I'd promised to meet Jared there to discuss the girls' living arrangements now that he was back stateside. It'd been nine months since I'd last seen him in Germany.

I didn't see him right away, so I made my way down the L-shaped line of food trucks to see what was on the menu. I was starving. I hadn't eaten all day, studying for final exams.

I finally decided on chicken in a cone. Food trucks were a quickly growing, gourmet phenomenon in Austin, fueled by the city's many music festivals and active night life. And off-beat food was their specialty.

"Your name, sweetie?" the nice, older lady in the food truck asked. She had a full sleeve of tattoos running down her left arm and gray streaks in her dark brown hair.

I froze because I didn't know how to answer. I'd been Laine for so long now. Laine was the Austinite city girl who would eat from food trucks and play in a punk band. But I was meeting Jared here, and with Jared I was Maddie.

"Maddie," I answered in a choked voice.

She smiled like I wasn't having an identity crisis and handed me my change. I turned to find a place to sit, only to see Jared standing about ten feet away. I offered him a smile and walked toward him.

"Hey, I went ahead and got some food," I said, hitching

my thumb back at the truck behind me.

"I'm glad you came. Give me a minute," Jared said and walked past me to place his order.

I sat down at a nearby picnic table and tried not to notice that he'd changed so much. Gone was the boy I once knew. He had filled out with broader shoulders, more muscles, and his jawline had a more masculine edge. I looked away.

Things had been going well with Law, and I was looking forward to introducing him to the girls soon. Though the fact that he had put it off and always had a reason not to meet them worried me.

Night had fallen, and a warm breeze sailed through the space. It was a nice night to eat outdoors.

Jared joined me at the table.

"I gotta admit," I started, "I'm a little nervous about why you asked me here to discuss the girls' living arrangements. You said you wouldn't try and take them away."

"I'm not, Maddie," he said in a reassuring tone. "I've no intention of that. I want what's best for you and the girls. I asked you here because I have something for you, but I want you to hear me out before you make a decision."

"Okay?"

He pulled his wallet out of his back pocket and dug something out of it. He slid it across the table in front of me. When his hand pulled back, I was looking at a brass key.

"I bought a house, and I want you and the girls to live there."

I started to protest, and he held up a hand to stop me.

"Hear me out. I asked you to meet me here because we can walk to it from here. If you're interested, we can head over there after we eat. The best thing about it—it has a garage apartment that I can stay in. I can be close by, but you get to have your own place. I've checked out the schools and they're really good. Highest rated in the state."

"So, you'll be living there, too?"

"In an apartment above the garage. It's detached, so we wouldn't be living together. Just neighbors. I want to get to know them, Maddie. The only thing I ask is to keep the music room in the house. I can't fit the piano in the apartment. But that'll give me a good place to spend time with them when I come to the house. I can start teaching them whatever instrument they like."

My heart ached with the thought of him teaching the girls his love of music. They'd love that.

"I want to check it out," I said.

His smile grew.

"I'm not saying yes, yet. I'm gonna need more than a few minutes to think it over, but I'm curious."

Our names were called then, and we ate in relative silence. Only music from one of the food trucks filled the space under the park's canopy. When I finished, he held out his hand for my trash, and I let him take it.

"You ready?"

"Actually, you want to split a cupcake? I love those cupcakes from the truck over there, but they're huge, and I can never finish one by myself."

"You know what you want?"

"Yep. Red velvet." My mouth watered at the thought.

"Stay," he said when I started to get up. "I can get this." He smiled and went to the cupcake truck.

I followed anyway. "You don't have to do that. This isn't a date, you know."

His eyes shadowed. "I know that, Maddie. I got a job today, and I wanted to celebrate anyway. So really, I'm just letting you eat half of my celebration cupcake." He grinned.

"You got a job?"

"Yeah, it's nothing big. I got a teaching position over at the Austin School of Music."

"That's awesome," I said, genuinely happy for him. I knew how much his music meant to him.

"I'll be working a lot of evenings and weekends, since it's mostly after-school tutoring and weekend classes. If you get a day job, then we'll hardly see each other." He smiled sadly.

"I'm not sure what I'm going to do after graduation. I

should've figured it out by now. I just haven't had time to stop and think about it."

"What kind of degree are you getting?" he asked as he took the cupcake from the food truck window. We walked leisurely as he pulled it apart and gave me half.

"I forgot, I never told you. I double majored in music theory and general Business. I thought by now I'd've had a clue about what I wanted to do. I went into it thinking that I'd just work in the music industry in some capacity. I'm still there to be quite honest, no fucking clue."

"Well, now that you've been around it some, what do you like the most?"

"Honestly, I think it's that moment when Spencer comes up with a new song. He's the other guitarist in my band. Anyway, Spencer plays it for me, and I can always hear how to make it better. Notes to add or change, tempo tweaks. I'm not that good at writing from scratch, but give me a jumping-off point and I can work my magic."

"Have you thought about producing? You could apply to a few recording studios around. See if they have an opening, maybe as an intern."

"I never thought of that." I smiled and nudged his shoulder with mine. "Hey, look at that. You're not useless after all."

He smiled back, and I had to look away.

I finally took in my surroundings and realized that we were far enough away from Barton Creek Drive that I couldn't hear the traffic any longer. We were completely surrounded by residential houses in one of Austin's older neighborhoods near Zilker Park. The houses here were spaced far apart with large green yards. It was peaceful.

Jared turned up the circle driveway of a large two-story brick house. A wide front porch flanked with white columns sat in the middle of the facade, kissing the edge of the herringbone brick-paver drive. I noticed his truck parked in front of the detached garage.

My feet halted, and my jaw dropped. Jared took a couple

of steps farther before he noticed I was no longer next to him. He turned to me.

"How in the world did you afford this?" I asked.

"I've been doing tutoring on different musical instruments since freshman year of high school, never spent any of it. Then, you know, the Army pay with dependents that never got spent. I invested it with my dad's help. I had a good amount of money saved up. Enough to buy it outright so we can afford the bills. Well, I can. I don't expect you to pay anything. Just stay here with the girls so I can be near them." He ran his hand over his short hair. "Do you not like it?"

"No. I like it. I never imagined I'd ever live in a place like this. What about school? What if you decide to go to school? You can't tie all your money up in this."

"School's paid for if I decide to go. I get the GI Bill."

"Oh, right."

"You want to come inside? Check it out?"

"Yeah, sure," I said absently.

I followed him up the driveway and looked at the neglected landscaping that made up the front yard. This house would be spectacular with a little work. We walked up the path to the front porch. There was paint peeling up on some parts of the house, but nothing too bad.

He unlocked the door, and we stepped inside the eerily silent house. I found myself standing in a marble-tiled foyer that had an inlaid design like they had in old art deco films. There was no furniture, so our footsteps echoed on the walls that surrounded the entrance and wide staircase. To the right was a room closed off by glass french doors and to the left was a room separated only by a wide archway.

"I thought that this would be the music room," he said, pointing to the room with the archway.

I nodded and followed him around as he pointed to rooms and told me his plans to tear down walls and update things.

We also looked at the kitchen, the family room, the dining room, and the master bedroom. Upstairs were five more bedrooms, most with their own bath, except two that were connected with a Jack-and-Jill bathroom. I was in shock. It seemed much bigger on the inside. It needed some repair and updating, but it was still beautiful.

"Don't you think six bedrooms is a little much?"

"I just figured since all our family was back home, you'd want enough space that they could all visit for the holidays. And—" He cut himself off and turned away.

An awkward silence filled the space between us.

"Well, I better head back to my car. I've another round of finals tomorrow."

"Here, let me drive you. It's not that far, but you won't have to walk, and I was going out anyway."

"Oh." I wondered where Jared would be going at this time of night. Then I quickly smacked that thought away as none of my fucking business. "Okay, lead the way."

We walked out of the house, making sure the lights were off and the place was locked up tight. When we got to his truck, he unlocked and held open my door for me before heading around to the driver's side.

"I was wondering if I should sell this old thing and get something more practical. Car seats won't really work in here."

It was such a harmless statement, but it threw me for a loop, reminding me that he was their father and the girls were not mine alone. It was an odd mixture of relief and panic. I made sure my face was neutral as I turned to him and tried to school my voice into nonchalance.

"They use booster seats now. You don't have to do that. They'll be just fine in here."

"You'll think about it? Living here at the house?" His voice was hopeful.

I wasn't going to lie—it helped alleviate a ton of pressure I was facing, but it still made me feel uneasy. Not unlike stepping out on a high wire to cross a chasm to the last source of water and food.

"Of course, but I do need to think about it. There are

down sides. What happens if we get in a fight and you kick me out?"

"That's not going to happen. It's your place, Maddie."

"No Jared, it's your house. You're just letting me live there."

He sighed. "*If* anything happened, and that's a big *if,* I'm not going to be a dick and just throw you out. You can move somewhere else anytime you want. There's no contracts, no requirements."

That may have been true, but it required a fair amount of trust to put faith in that scenario. And that was something he and I were fresh out of. I swallowed down the retort, though. I didn't want to drag this conversation out when I really just needed some time to myself to process everything.

"Okay, I'll keep that in mind."

Chapter Twenty-Five

Then

I thought about Jared's suggestion of the house for days. I'd struggled to keep my mind on my final exams. In the end, it all boiled down to the fact that I had limited options. Jared was also right in the fact that I'd, at best, find an internship, which meant no income. I'd a little money left to struggle through that, but not if I had to pay for a two-bedroom apartment, even in the shitty parts of town. Which would mean two jobs.

The girls deserved the best their parents could offer, and what he was offering was really good for them. I couldn't deny them a steady roof over their heads and good schools to attend. Not when all I could give them, on my own, was a crappy apartment and a mom who had to work two jobs to make ends meet.

Then there were the scary thoughts: Jared could file for custody and take them away if I put them in subpar conditions. I knew he'd said he wouldn't, but would he have sat by and let them go to low-rated schools and live in dangerous neighborhoods just to appease me?

Holly and Sloane would've been good roommate options for me, but I couldn't ask them to alter their lives for my kids. I didn't want to be put in the situation of telling my friends that they couldn't bring home guys in Holly's case, or have loud sex with their boyfriend, in Sloane's case. It would just cause problems.

With my mind pretty much set, all that was left was to discuss it with Law. I'd no idea how he'd take this, but it couldn't be that bad. I wasn't going to be living with Jared.

I went by Law's house, but he'd already left for the gym, so I drove over there. I was pulling into the parking lot when I spied him through the open garage door. He was pounding away on a heavy bag, working combos. There was no one else around as I walked into the gym. The only sounds, other than the repetitive thumps of the heavy bag, were from the radio propped on a shelf playing a local station, and the humongous shop fan that kept the place cool.

I watched Law for a minute before making my presence known. He really was beautiful to watch like this. He had talent, even if he didn't want it. He was all grace and strength pulled together in a deadly package.

I walked around to the direction he was facing, and it still took a moment for him to see me past his intense focus.

When he stopped, he gave me a huge smile and dashed around the bag to sweep me into a sweaty hug.

I laughed. "Stop. Jesus, you're gross."

"What's that, Bumpkin?" he asked, wiping his cheek across my face.

"Yum. You got some in my mouth," I said dryly, sticking my tongue out.

"Oh, admit it. That taste wasn't enough. You want to take me in the back room and lick it all off," Law said, walking me backward.

"I'm not sure it'd be about the sweat if I did that. More about what I was licking."

His eyes darkened and he picked me up, my legs wrapping around his waist like they had so many times before.

"God, I love you," he said as his lips brushed over mine before he intensified the kiss.

Next thing I knew, he had kicked the door to the storage

closet shut. It was dark, but we didn't need light to find what we knew by heart. My heart raced. I gasped for air as his mouth trailed down my neck.

"Hmm," he hummed in my ear. "You taste so sweet."

"Won't your dad think it's weird we're back here?"

"He left to go run errands. We're the only ones here right now."

He pushed me back on a table in the tiny room and started working to get my pants off. He always got worked up after a fight or during an intense workout, but we'd never been together at the gym. His tongue ran down my thighs as he pushed my knees toward my arms.

"Do you want to tell me why you're here during the middle of the day?" His mouth descended on my core, and my head hit the wall behind me with a moan.

"Now? You want me... to form coherent sentences, now?"

"Ummmhmmm," he replied, the vibrations caused tingles to race up my spine.

"Oh, God, Law. I can't think—" My mind frittered out as my words stumbled. "I came—"

"You will come," he mumbled, still working his tongue over my sensitive nub. "When I tell you to."

"I came here to tell you that I found a place to—"

He was working me to the edge as he pushed two fingers into me.

"Law, I can't."

"Do you want me to stop?" He halted his tongue and fingers.

I gripped his sweat-soaked hair, shoving his face back between my legs. "Don't you dare."

"Then talk," he commanded and resumed his work.

"I found a place to live after graduation."

"Ummmmhmmmm?"

I gripped his hair tighter, the fingers of my other hand curling over the edge of the table. *Guys should always talk to your pussy; it makes everything they say more pleasurable.*

"He—uh, he. He bought a house and wants us to live there. Oh." Pricks of light floated through my vision as my body spasmed, my release rocking through me.

Before I even came down fully, he flipped me over. Bending me over the table, he entered me roughly. My hands flailed, searching for purchase, and pressed against the wall so I could push back into him.

He gripped my hair, pulling my head back. His tongue tracing the line of my neck to the shell of my ear.

"Who's he?" he whispered.

His pace was brutal as he began to slam his hips into mine over and over.

"Don't—don't—make me—say—his—name. Not now," I responded through his punishing rhythm.

"Mine," he growled as he bit down on my neck.

My eyes rolled up in the back of my head as a violent orgasm rocked through my whole body. I jerked and convulsed before my body collapsed, unable to move. He slowed his pace, dragging in and out so slowly that every nerve ending inside me fired off in slow succession. My breath stolen.

He gently pulled my hands from the wall and folded them together behind my back, gripped in one of his hands. His other hand brushed over my sensitive clit.

A low, shaky moan erupted from me as my body involuntarily twitched from the contact.

"Why am I supposed to be okay with my girlfriend living with her ex?"

"He's not living there. Well, not in the house. There's a garage apartment. He just wants to be close to the girls." My voice sounded husky.

"And if I say I don't like it?"

"It's a—it's a good opportunity," I stuttered as he pulled out and flipped me back over, setting me back on the table and lining himself up to push in again.

He held the back of my neck, bracing my upper body with his forearm. His other hand pushed the hair out of my face as he looked at me. He entered me slowly, filling me up.

It took all my effort to keep my eyes trained on his as he pinned me with his gaze. He trailed his fingertips down my cheek and my neck, stopping just over my heart.

"This belongs to me?" He reversed and started dragging out slowly.

My answer was part moan, part shaky groan. "Yeeessssss."

His hand trailed down farther as his fingers pinched the bundle of nerves at my core.

"Come," he commanded.

And like a good little trained monkey, my body responded and did exactly as he said. He picked up the pace of his thrusts, not releasing the pressure on my clit. The waves of my climax rolled over me repeatedly with his every movement. My arms and legs jerked along with his thrusts like a marionette. He was completely in control of my body.

"This is definitely mine," he said, and his movements stuttered as he found his release.

He collapsed on top of me. My body accepted his delicious weight with glee. My heart was pounding as I fought for breath and coherent thought.

Law's breathing was labored, too, as it rushed across my cheek in the silence of the tiny room.

"I don't like it," he said, breaking the silence.

"It's what's best for the girls."

"What about what's best for us?"

"Law, I'm trying to do what's best for the girls. If it doesn't work, then I move out. It's not like I'm signing a contract to stay there for a specific length of time. It's a nice house in a good neighborhood—better than anything I can afford. And it has great schools. This is a good opportunity for them."

"No," he said simply.

"What the fuck do you mean, no?" I asked, shoving him off me and scrambling to find my clothes.

"I mean no," he said in his tone that brooked no argument, and illustrated by the stubborn set of his chin.

"You're not doing it."

I wasn't having it. "What—who the—what the fuck makes you think you even have the right to say no?"

"I think I just made my point pretty clear." He gave me that sexy, one-dimpled smirk, and his eyes darted to the table I was just on.

"Oh, I let you get away with a lot of stuff when we fuck." My voice escalated with every word. "But you don't ever get to tell me what to do outside of it. Especially, when it comes to my kids. Do you get me?" I crossed my arms over my chest and pinned him with a steely gaze.

He hesitated for a moment but then just smiled at me like I was a cute cat video on the internet.

What the fuck?

"You know what? You can wipe that stupid look off your face because this isn't going to work. I'm moving in there after graduation whether you like it or not. And if you don't like it, you can eat a dick. I'm out."

I pulled on my final piece of clothing—my shirt—and stormed out of the room, the door slamming into the wall on my way out.

"Laine? Fuck!" He grabbed my arm to halt my exit. "Stop. Don't do this. We can talk about it and find something that works better for all of us."

"You're not hearing me." I shook off his grip and continued out the door. "Because I said, this is what's best for the girls. I'm not compromising their lives for my pleasure."

He halted in his tracks. "Do you mean that?"

"Yeah, I wouldn't have said it if I didn't." My brows drew together, confused as to why he needed clarification as I turned back to him.

"So that's how this is going to be," he yelled. "I'm always going to take a back seat. Nothing I want matters."

"Of course, because that's what it means to be a parent. Why don't you fucking get that?" I screamed at him. I turned and stomped toward my car. The man was infuriating. I loved him. I loved my girls. I shouldn't have to choose one over the other, but if there was a choice, they were my responsibility and he wasn't. They'd win. Even if it ripped my soul apart in the process.

Lost in my thoughts, I almost fell over as I ran into a man entering the gym. He gripped my arm and helped me regain my balance.

"Oh, crap. Maddie?" I looked up to a familiar face I hadn't seen in ages.

"Blake? What are you doing here?"

"Oh, I just joined this gym. Coming here to work out on my lunch break. Hey, are you okay?"

"Yeah, just a disagreement. I've gotta run. Enjoy your workout."

"Yeah, see you around."

I gave a half-hearted wave as I turned and continued to my car. I pulled out of the parking lot, squealing my tires.

Now

A knock echoes around my office as Chloe scurries to my side and steps behind me, putting me between her and the door. My curiosity over her odd behavior is interrupted by the sound of knuckles on glass. We can't see who's on the other side because the shades are pulled, but nobody moves until the second knock sounds.

Dex breaks the standoff and strides across the room to pull open the door.

Two men in suits walk in, their eyes roaming over each of us, but linger on me.

"Miss Dobransky, sorry to interrupt," the taller of the two says. "I'm Agent Dobbs; this is US Marshal Sanders."

I nod at each one, at a loss as to what's going on. They couldn't possibly be elevating the murder to a federal case. Not after all these years.

"What can I help you with?" I ask.

"We're not here for you," Marshal Sanders says. "We're

here for Miss Meade."

Chloe? My eyes dart to her, and she meets my gaze with a worried plea in her eyes before she looks away.

"I never told them," she murmurs, her eyes focused on the FBI agent. "I never said a word about my past to anyone. You can't take me."

The room seems to shift as I try to adjust to the shock that our sweet, quiet Chloe apparently has one hell of a secret.

"I'm afraid the fault isn't on you, Miss Meade," Agent Dobbs says. "Your file was hacked. We have to take you in. We're not sure at this time who may have broken into your file or why they targeted you specifically. But this was a targeted security breach. You're going to have to come with us."

Dread swamps my gut. I can't help but think this is related to everything that's going on with me. But I can't say anything without sounding like a crazy person unless I'm willing to hand over that video. And I'm not. The dominoes are starting to fall once again. One by one. I feel powerless to stop it.

"I can't leave," Chloe mutters. "This is my family now. They need me. Maddie needs me here, especially, with all that's going on."

"We can't let you stay," Agent Dobbs says. "We need to keep you safe to testify."

"Hey, if you need to go to stay safe, Chloe, do it," I say, cradling her face in my hands. "We'll be here when you get back. You're part of our family, and you always will be. But I need you to be safe." I look to Evan. "Evan can go with you."

He nods in agreement.

"He'll make sure you stay safe. And make sure that you come back to us."

Her blue eyes shift from me, then to Evan. Her eyes are red rimmed with unshed tears. "You'd do that?"

"Of course he would," I assure her. "Family first."

"But what about you?" she asks.

"I'll be fine. I've plenty of people around to protect me." I smile at her and run my hand over her sleek blue hair. I gather her close, hugging her tightly, tears welling in my eyes. I'm not sure I can keep those promises, but I'm going to try. I squeeze my eyes before releasing her.

"I'm sorry, but we can't allow anyone to come with her," Marshal Sanders says, looking at me and then Evan. "We're taking her to a safe house now, but eventually she'll be relocated and receive a new identity."

"That's not gonna happen," I say, my eyes narrowing on the agents.

"I won't go, then," Chloe protests. "If he can't come with me, then I'm safer here with everyone. I'm not starting over again. I can't do that, not after finding where I belong."

"You can't stay here," Agent Dobbs says. "You agreed to testify against your captor."

"Hold on," I say, rubbing my forehead and trying for patience. My default reaction right now is to scream at everyone to stop talking. "Agent, Marshal, would you like to take a seat? I've no clue what you're talking about. I can advise Chloe to go, and Evan *will* go with her, but I think we need to know what we're up against, don't you?" I direct the last bit at Chloe, and she nods.

There's a couch and two chairs in my office that surround a coffee table. Chloe and I sit on the sofa while the agents take the chairs. Evan wheels my desk chair around and sits at the end of the coffee table. Dex leans against the wall, silently watching this drama unfold.

I nod to Chloe to start. This is her show. I can't fill in the blanks for her.

"Ya ever heard—" She stops and clears her throat, her eyes darting to the federal agent, seeking approval.

Agent Dobbs gives her a nod. "It can't hurt at this point. Just no details about the case, okay?"

Chloe's lower lip trembles as she looks back to me. "Did ya ever see the story on the news about Charlene Clancy?"

Goose bumps travel across my skin like a wave. I nod. I'd heard the story. You would've had to be hiding under a rock three years ago not to hear about it. Personally, for me, it was the story that finally pulled the spotlight from my life: a girl kidnapped when she was eight years old escaped her captors at eighteen.

The media was pretty vague about what happened to her, but she was held against her will for more than a decade. It couldn't have been a sweet fairy tale. News shows speculated what had happened to her during that time while a nationwide manhunt was conducted to find her kidnappers and bring them to justice, only that never happened. And then one day, the story just vanished. People moved on to the next thing, and that was that.

I never thought twice when this lonely eighteen-year-old girl applied to the job listing for my personal assistant. Fear and worry embed itself under my skin. I reach out and squeeze her hand in support.

"That was me. I'm the girl that escaped." Her eyes plead with me. "I'm sorry I kept it from ya."

I snort a laugh. "I'd be the last person in the world to judge you for keeping secrets."

"Ain't that the truth," Evan scoffs.

I cut him a look, and he looks away, struggling to hide a smirk.

"He shouldn't come with you," the US marshal interrupts. "But if that's the only way to get you to go with us, then so be it. We'll run his background once we get on the road. We need to get you to a safe house, now. We can deal with that issue later."

"I agree." The FBI agent smiles at Chloe and shrugs. "I really don't want to arrest you on obstruction. Taking you in could put you at risk, so we'll figure it out. But we need to leave. We don't know how fast they'll act upon receiving your location."

Chloe sucks in a breath and nods. She looks at me, fear and doubt as plain as day in her eyes.

"It'll be okay," I say. "You're getting the best of the best in my circle of trust to keep you safe. Evan'll take care of you. I bet my life on it."

I stand, and everyone else follows. My brows draw together when Evan hugs me and slips his phone into my hands.

"I don't want to have to throw it away, and I think that would be the first task on their to-do list." Evan cuts his eyes to the agents, then back to me. "I'll find a way to check in with you. I don't like leaving you in the middle of this, but I know you wouldn't ask if it wasn't important to you."

I nod in reply, scared that the sob building in my throat will unleash if I open my mouth. I'm worried about Chloe and scared about what'll happen if the person they're hiding her from finds her.

I hug Chloe one last time before she and Evan disappear through my door with the FBI agent and US marshal.

I stare at the door, willing myself to wake up. I gotta still be in my bed, dreaming. This is too unreal. Tears stream down my cheeks, falling to the carpet at my feet, silently. It isn't until arms come around me that I remember with a jolt that I'm not alone.

In the back of my mind, a thought scratches to the surface—I'm losing people I trust on a day when I'm beginning to doubt who I can trust.

Chapter Twenty-Six

Then

I weaved through the crowd, looking for my family. The commencement ceremony had ended, and everyone was scattering into the crowds to find their loved ones. I finally gave up, deciding to stay put and texted them my location. I kept my eye on the crowd for anyone familiar. Most of these people I'd seen around the small campus, but none I knew well.

"Sloane!" I yelled as I spotted her weaving her way through the crowds full of caps and gowns and hugging family members.

"Oh, my God! We did it. It's finally over!" She had a huge smile on her face.

I stood there awkwardly, trying to find something to say besides the one thing I wanted to ask her. *How is Law doing?* My heart panged again at the thought. *Shit.* This should be a happy occasion and here I was, stuck in Mopeyville, population: one.

"Come on, I know what'll cheer you up." Sloane bumped my shoulder with hers. "We're going to Salt Lick for lunch-slash-dinner. What would you call it? Dunch? Linner? That's it, we're having linner at the Salt Lick. I bet that mind of yours is now drooling to wrap your lips around a hot...

juicy... rib." She grinned, and I couldn't help the reluctant laugh that spilled out.

"The idea does have its merits," I tried to joke along with her. I just wasn't in the right head space to be funny. "But, I'm sure if your family and mine went out together that'd be boatloads of awkward."

"I don't plan on being there." Law's voice sounded over my shoulder, and I froze.

I turned slowly. I didn't know if I could handle seeing him just yet. When my eyes landed on him, I instantly regretted it. It had only been days since our fight, but he looked amazing. I felt like a moron, but I was doing what I had to do. We were never going to see eye to eye on it either. I couldn't just make decisions based on what I wanted or how I felt. I was a mother, and I had to put the girls' needs above my own. It still fucking hurt, though.

"Hey," I said lamely.

"Hey," he replied.

Awkward silence stretched between us.

"Fuck, you guys talk too much," Sloan said. "I'm gonna find Dad."

She left in the direction that Law had arrived. We stood in more awkward silence until I couldn't take it anymore.

"I miss you."

His head dropped as he stared at the ground, kneading his neck. The move, filled with familiarity, built a mounting pressure in my chest. I held my breath as tears swam to the surface.

"I miss you, too," he replied, hazel eyes peeking up at me through thick lashes.

I released my held breath with a whoosh. "Then why can't we make this work?"

"Why can't you change your mind and move in with Holly or my sister?" he followed without hesitation.

We'd gone over these options in the many conversations we had since I first brought it up, but it always ended the same. There were just too many negatives to doing that. I didn't want to risk my friendships—Holly and Sloane meant the world to me. My anger surged with the reminder of all the arguments we'd had in the past week. It was like we were a broken record, stuck skipping on a scratch.

"Fuck, we already beat this horse to death, Law."

I couldn't hear this anymore. If it was so damn important, why hadn't he offered us a place to stay with him? His dad owned the house that he and the guys lived in. Yet, not once had he offered that as a solution. To him, it was my problem to fix, and to me, this was the best way. I wasn't going to ruin friendships and burn bridges to make him more comfortable. Not with my kids at stake.

"Mommy!" A tiny shriek sounded as Cat launched herself at me, wrapping her arms around my waist, Cora following right behind her.

"Hey, guys, did you see Mommy walk across the stage?" I bent down to their eye level, a reluctant smile gracing my face.

"Yes! We heard them call your name."

"Mommy, who's dis?" Cora said, pointing to Law, who was watching us with a crease in his brow.

I couldn't believe that she was talking in front of him.

"That's Mommy's friend Law," I said to her, then looked up at Law. "Law, these are my daughters, Cora and Cat."

Cora's little mouth dropped into an *O*. She walked over to him and touched his arm. Then she turned to face me. "He has pretty colors on his arms."

I snapped my mouth shut. *She touched him.* "That he does, baby."

Cora took a good while to warm up to someone. I took a deep breath to fight off the tears that threatened. I didn't know why he put off meeting them for the last nine months; things might've gone better if it had happened before this whole house mess.

"I told you they'd find her. They've built-in Mommy radar," Nic said. He and Jared approached our little group.

"Daddy! Did you see Mommy's friend Law? He has

painted arms. I want painted arms," Cat said running over to Jared and tugging on his hand.

Every muscle in my body tensed as these two approached each other. With everything as it was between Law and me, the tension was palpable.

"Hey, Front Man," Nic greeted and did that whole man-hug, handshake, back-slapping ritual that guys do. "How's it going?"

"Good. Could be better." He cut a sideways glance at Jared.

"I'm Jared." He held out his hand for Law to shake. "Nice to finally meet you."

"Likewise," Law said through clenched teeth, shaking his hand with a white-knuckle grip.

I closed my eyes, hoping this would all go away. I opened them and was suddenly struck by the contrast between the two. Both were the same height, but one was a tattooed and pierced punk rocker while the other was a straitlaced military guy.

In that moment, I felt like a fraud. I wasn't the girl I used to be when I was with Jared, but I felt like I was never the girl I pretended to be with Law. The only people who got a genuine version of me was my girls. Other than that, I no longer knew where I fit in, in either life. I shut my eyes again to hold back the tears that wanted to break free.

"Hey, it's clearing out a bit. How about we go wait over there by the stage so you can finish your conversation?" Jared motioned to his destination and picked Cora up. Cat and Nic followed in his wake.

I sighed, watching them until they were out of earshot.

"I can't do this anymore. It fucking hurts, Law. You're trying to make me choose between you and my girls. And the girls win. They're my responsibility. It's my job to do what's best for them."

"He's trying to win you back, Laine," he said in a flat, emotionless voice, his eyes tracking Jared's retreating form. "Even I can see the way he looks at you. No guy buys a woman a house without some kind of interest in her." He turned back to me. "Why can't you see that? Or are you being naive on purpose, Bumpkin?"

"You know what? Fuck you, Law. You're reading too much into this whole situation. He hasn't even come close to showing any interest since he's been back. He's doing this for his kids. So, no, I'm not being naive. You're being an asshole. You see those little girls over there? Those are my responsibility, and I'm willing to put their happiness above my own. That should be another thing that you love about me. But clearly, it's not."

"I don't see why we can't compromise on this. This, me and you, is a relationship. Those things take work and compromise."

"Exactly! Which doesn't start with *no*. It starts with weighing the pros and cons, which you were never interested in hearing. How can you rule something out without even hearing the reasons why it's a good thing? You can't. And I'm done talking with you about this."

"Laine, wait. Please don't do this. I love you." He grabbed my arm to stop me, his other hand running over my cheek and his eyes frantically searching, pleading with me.

"I love you too, Law. But I guess, sometimes, love isn't enough." I pulled my arm from his grip and walked away from him, wiping the tears from my eyes before the girls could see them.

Three months of living in the house and I finally relented and let Jared stay for dinner. He scraped the dishes into the trash, I scrubbed them, and he'd put them in the dishwasher. We'd just put the girls down for the night after dinner and a repeat performance of the latest Disney movie.

When we finished, he grabbed two beers from the fridge

and popped the top before handing one over to me. In moments like that, the guilt crept in. My heart felt like it was being squeezed.

It was hard to keep going each day like everything was fine. So easy to tell Law it was over, but harder to live with that decision. Sometimes, I doubted myself. I was anything but fine. But I had to lie in my bed the way I made it.

The band broke up, and that was another source of sour feelings. Law didn't want to do the band anymore and had thrown himself into fighting. He was likely to go pro soon, and that made me want to cry, too. I knew how much he hated the idea. He was much more passionate about MMA, but his dad wouldn't have it. If he was fighting, he'd be boxing.

"Hey, where did you go?" Jared asked as he hooked a finger under my chin and tilted my head up to meet his eyes.

"I need to go play," I said removing my chin from his touch. "Lock up on the way out."

I didn't wait for a reply. I walked past him and went straight to the music room to grab my guitar, leaving Jared standing in the kitchen. My fingers were itching to play Ben Harper's "Walk Away." It would sound as melancholy as I felt, and the words—the words were my life at that moment.

I picked up my acoustic and sat on the piano bench, then poured my heart out. I was on the verge of tears, my voice shaky with emotions, so I didn't sing. Just whispering the words as I played softly. My chest ached as the feelings released with my whispers, and the pressure inside me decreased if only a fraction. As I finished the song, I realized that Jared was leaning against the frame of the archway, one hand in his pocket, drinking his beer and watching me.

"You're good," he murmured as he crossed the room and sat on the bench next to me.

"You should've left. Do you get some kind of pleasure from watching me wallow in misery?"

His jaw clenched as he leveled his icy-blue eyes on me.

"No, I don't. Quite the opposite. All this is my fault. None of this would've happened if I hadn't made a dumb decision. Come here," he said as he wrapped an arm around my shoulder and pulled me to his side. He kissed my forehead. "It hurts to watch you go through this. Even when you're not saying anything, I can see it written across your face. I want to do anything I can to make it better for you, but I know I can't. I just need to suffer along with you until you get to a place where it doesn't hurt so much anymore."

"None of this is your fault. Quit doing that. I'm the one who fell in love with him, and I'm the one who broke up with him. He's the one who couldn't let it go. None of that has anything to do with you. You should be out sowing your wild oats and shit. Not sitting around watching me mope."

"I don't want to do that. Here. Turn around, let me play you a song. I think we both communicate better through music." He gave me a crooked smile and nudged me to turn and face the piano.

I propped the guitar up next to the piano and settled on the seat next to him. It felt like ages since I sat with him and listened to him play. The soft, bluesy notes rang out in the quiet house. Then he started to sing in that raspy voice of his I loved to hear.

I finally recognized the song as one by Etta James, "I'll Take Care of You." I'd almost forgotten what it was like to be around someone who loved the blues as much as I did. I got lost in the song, absorbing every note. My fingers twitched as I heard the guitar come in on the second verse in my memory.

I listened, carried away by his voice and the song, but as it came to a close, a thought occurred to me.

"He was right, wasn't he?" I asked.

He stopped his playing and looked at me. "About what?"

"You're doing all this. This house—everything. All this is to try and win me back." I stood, flailing my arms to encompass the whole room.

"And what if it is, Maddie?" he asked calmly.

"If it is? Then that'd make you an asshole. And me the

biggest sucker on the face of the planet."

"Why? Why does it have to be that way between us? We had something good." He rose from the piano bench to face me.

"Had! We had it. And you threw it away. Four fucking years, Jared. We don't get to go back. We don't get to pretend that nothing ever happened."

"Why?" he asked as he stalked toward me. "What's stopping us?"

I stepped back, in time with his advances, until my back hit the wall.

"You think this hurts you? Watching me go through this? Do you have any idea—any clue what you did to me? It took me two years just to talk to someone else. To make friends. Even Nic gave up on me."

His arms came up, and he pressed his hands into the wall on either side of me as he stared me down.

"I think I can imagine. Do you think it was a cake walk for me, Maddie?"

"It was your decision," I yelled at him. "You don't have the right to be hurt over it or even pretend like you know how it felt."

But even as I said the words, I knew they weren't true. It was my decision to break up with Law. Didn't mean it hurt any less. And the fact that he could've been hurt and still do that to us pissed me off. Or maybe I was pissed at myself. A frustrated cry broke free through clenched teeth. I tried to slap him, but he caught my wrists, pinning them above my head to the wall.

"I want to kiss you right now," he said, breathing heavily, his body, his face inches from mine. "But you're not ready yet. I'm not making a move tonight; it won't be tomorrow either. Understand me, though…" His eyes grew serious, his tone quiet but firm. "I'll fight for you. I've never loved anyone. Just you. I want no one, but you."

He released me, turned, and walked out the front door.

I stood there speechless, in shock. I was full of conflicting emotions as I stormed to my room. I wanted to scratch his eyes out. Rip off his balls and feed them to him. But part of me, a shameful part of me, liked his declaration and even the way he handled me. I'd always be a sucker for him. I wanted to apologize to Law. I wanted to run away from them both. From everything. It was all too much.

I closed the door quietly behind me, careful not to wake the girls, and spied a red calla lily on my bed. Fucking Jared. I felt the impotent rage well within. I grabbed that little innocent flower and did the unspeakable things I wanted to do to Jared, himself, at the moment.

When I stopped my rage, tiny little pieces of red petal and green stem littered the floor of my room. I buried my head in a pillow and screamed at the top of my lungs.

What I wouldn't give to have never had met the man. That's not true, though, because without him my two little angels wouldn't exist.

I fell asleep into a fitful rest without dreams, my mind playing his words over and over, to torture me beyond consciousness.

Chapter Twenty-Seven

Now

I turn in Dex's arms and gaze into his turquoise eyes. From afar, his eyes appear to be a solid shade of blue-green, but up close there are little flecks of green in the blue that become denser around the pupil. It's beautiful enough to get lost in. I search those eyes for signs that confirm my suspicions, or if I'm just being paranoid.

My stalker can't be right about him.

He watches back, and I'm not sure how long we stand like that before his thumb brushes over my lower lip. I have to close my eyes as chills race down my spine. Then his lips are on mine.

His kisses are like air, and I feel like I've been trapped in space, slowly dying of asphyxiation. This need controls me beyond all rational thought. I don't hold back; I don't think I could if I wanted to. Running my hands around his waist, I tug his shirt up until I feel the heat of his skin under my fingertips.

His hands come up to cradle my face, and I moan into the kiss just before he breaks away. He rests his forehead to mine, his breathing labored.

"Maddie, we need to talk."

Nothing good ever comes out of a conversation that starts

with those four words. But he's not wrong. *The video.* Ice fills my veins as I remember, pushing away and stepping back. My mind keeps mulling over the fact that if Chloe could've kept something so big from me for years, odds are pretty good that the stalker is right about Dex. And no matter how careful I think I'm being, I'm still entirely too trusting for my own good. I feel a pressure build behind my eyes.

His face scrunches in confusion. "I think—" He's cut off as the door to my office opens, again.

Bridget stands there looking her usual combination of sultry badass professional. She's not wearing the jacket to her suit, so the tattoos on her arms are visible. Her lips are pressed in a flat line, and in combination with the crease between her brows, I know she's not happy.

"Sorry to interrupt, but I was hoping to have a few words with you," she says, leveling her gaze on me.

"Can it wait a few minutes?" I ask, raising both brows.

"No. I need to speak with you. Now."

I look back at Dex, and he nods his assent. I guess *that* talk will have to wait. I walk with Bridget toward her office, leaving Dex behind in mine. *This better be good.*

"Is this important? We were fixin' to—"

"Yes, it's important," Bridget whispers, her eyes darting back to my door. "And it has to do with him."

"With Dex?" I ask, halting in the middle of the hall.

"Shhh." She puts a finger over her mouth as she grabs my arm and drags me the rest of the ten feet into her office.

Once inside, she shuts the door behind us and pulls her blinds closed. My brows draw together as she pulls a file from her desk drawer and tosses it onto the surface.

It takes a second before I realize what I'm staring at— Dex's juvenile records, the same ones I had in my hands yesterday.

"How'd you get that?" I ask in a hushed tone, my eyes darting to the door and back to her.

Her lips purse as she studies me. "You know what that is?" she asks.

"Of course I do. He showed it to me yesterday. What I don't understand, is how in the hell is it sitting on your desk right now?"

"Maddie," she sighs. "We need to have some real talk. How much do you know about your new boyfriend?"

"Whaddyou mean?"

"What I mean is that I ran a background check on him because, you know, all the other stuff going on. I found this file on him. I went down to the station and asked my contact. Turns out he's an undercover cop. You don't want to know what I had to do to get that info either."

"I knew that," I say. "He's actually shown me that file."

"What in the ever-living fuck are you thinking, then?" she yells, her hands flailing around in the air.

I raise an eyebrow at her. "That he was assigned to follow me and try to catch my stalker. Under the guise of being my boyfriend."

"You've gotta be kidding me. Why am I just now finding out? I'm your fucking lawyer, Maddie. You don't need to be talking to the police, much less romping around with an undercover cop." She pauses and pinches the bridge of her nose. She stops and leans down to level a look at me. "What do you think he's investigating?"

"They said they think the stalking and murder cases are tied. They wanted Dex to follow me and see if he picked up on clues or somehow sees the stalker by being near me."

"What has he done to further his investigation?"

My stomach drops, because I think I know where she's going with this. It's the same niggling feeling I've had since I woke up. Confirmed, first, by my stalker, and now Bridget. *Could this get any worse?* I drop my head into my hands, burying my fingers in my hairline. *How fucking gullible am I?* I feel sick.

"He shared that file with me last night. Told me about his life growing up and why he ended up becoming a cop. He said he was telling me to earn my trust, but the thing is..." I sigh as I sit back in the chair and look at Bridget. "He told me when we got to the house and all the paparazzi were there that—that file is easily accessible and part of his cover. It didn't even strike me as odd until I woke up this morning. And last night after we left the diner where he showed me that, a cop conveniently shows up before we get down to *business* when we parked at Zilker. One that just happened to know who I am." Tears well in my eyes. "Fuck, Bridget. I screwed up."

She comes around her desk and drags the other chair next to the one I'm sitting in. She pulls me into her arms and holds me there.

"I don't have any proof of what his purpose is," she says softly. "But his eyes are always on you when you're around, and either he's bad at his job and really likes you, or he's investigating *you*, Mads. It's been four years, and as far as I know, you're the only person they ever investigated. Your DNA was all over the crime scene, and no one else's."

"But you said the security tapes—"

"Put you somewhere else at the time of death, I know, but that still doesn't rule you out completely. They can still make a case. You should've come to me, Maddie. Always let me handle the police. I know you want to trust Detective Martinez, but you need to let me handle this. And you need to get Dex out of here, now."

I nod and take a deep breath. My finger twists in the rubber band at my wrist.

"Before you go, I need to know what else you told him. Did you tell him anything else about that night? The stuff I had removed from the case file or otherwise?"

"No, we haven't talked about it at all."

"Good," she says with a half-hearted smile. "Let's see if we can clean this mess up before it gets out of hand."

I rise from my seat, and she stands with me. Inhale, summoning strength and courage to move forward. Exhale, releasing my fears and reservations. I can do this. I'll fix this.

Then

"Have you heard back from any of the places you applied to?" Jared asked.

We sat on a park bench at Zilker Park, steps away from where the girls were playing with tons of other kids on the huge playground. The sun was bright as I leaned back and looked over at him through my sunglasses.

"Yeah. I've three interviews set up for next week. All internships, but I've gotta start somewhere."

"That's awesome. I'm proud of you." He smiled but still faced the playground, keeping an eye on the girls.

"Yeah... I'm excited about the possibilities. Learning the ins and outs of recording."

"You'll do great."

This was what we had become. Harmless chitchat about trivial, day-to-day things. We hadn't spoken again about that night three months ago when he told me he was going to fight for me. He hadn't made a move or acted awkward.

I hadn't talked to Law either. He went out of town with his father, according to Sloane. He'd qualified for pro and started the fight circuit. I wanted to be happy for him—it was great news—but I knew deep down that it wasn't what he wanted. The guilt that I'd inadvertently pushed him into it surged within me every time he crossed my mind.

"What are you thinking about?" Jared asked, snapping me out of my melancholy thoughts.

"Nothing important," I said with a sigh and looked away.

"It'll get better."

"You speakin' from experience?" I asked snidely. I instantly regretted it.

"No. It never got easier for me. But that's what they say. The general consensus."

"How're you okay with this? Why isn't this driving you crazy or making you angry? If it really means that much, I'd think you'd feel something other than okay about it."

"Goddammit, Maddie." He turned to face me. "What do

you want me to say? What do I need to do? I can't hate you or get angry with you because this is my fault. I can hate the situation, and I do. There's just nothing that can be done about it. You're not ready for it."

"What if I'm never ready? What, then? Because it's always lingering in the back of my mind that what I went through with you was worse. I can't do that again. In fact, I'm thinking I may just decide to be celibate at least until the girls are out of the house. Fuck all you men—your stupid drama and mind games. Men fucking suck from where I'm sitting."

He chuckled, his clear blue eyes sparkling with mirth. It reminded me of the first night we met, back when he let me in on his apple juice secret. When we joked about cars, horror novels, and the charisma of his guitar skills. The lighthearted charm and easy conversation that drew me to him was still there.

"I'll wait," he said. "You won't feel like that forever. And believe it or not, to me, you're worth it. All of this."

My heart fluttered in my chest at his words. *Stupid fucking traitorous heart.* I crossed my arms over my chest and began to scan the park for the girls. I didn't see them.

"Do you see the girls?" I asked.

"They were right there on the swings, dammit. I only took my eyes off them for a second."

My heart raced as we both got up and walked in opposite directions on the path that circled the big jungle gym. Blood thundered in my ears, muting the laughter of children and the chatter of parents. Dread tensed up my muscles as I scanned the faces of every child and didn't recognize one. *Oh, God.*

When I turned the corner, I saw Cora and Cat barreling toward me with huge grins on their faces. I almost collapsed. They stopped right in front of me.

"Mommy, look what that man gave us. Aren't they pretty?" Cat held out her little fist, and my heart stopped.

I could feel the blood drain from my face as she and Cora showed me the single red calla lilies they each held. Searching the faces of the crowd, I didn't recognize anyone. Some played with their children; a few sat chatting on the short walls around the playground or on the nearby benches. People picnicked at nearby tables. I caught sight of a man in a green T-shirt watching me, and I held his stare until a kid came down the slide in front of him. He lifted the giggling child in the air. Nothing and no one looked out of place.

My chest squeezed, stealing my breath.

"What man?" I gripped her shoulders. "Who gave that to you?"

"I don't know." Cat shrugged. "He was nice. Said he'd been wanting to meet us for a while."

"Cat, show me who he is!" I demanded, panic overtaking rational thought.

"Mommy, why're you getting mad?" she said as her chin started to tremble and tears welled in her eyes.

"I'm not mad, baby." I tried to calm my voice. "I just want to meet the man who gave you the flowers."

"You found them," Jared said, walking up to us. One look at me and his demeanor shifted from relief to concern. "What happened?"

Tears swam in my eyes, making the world blurry. "Have you been leaving me these flowers?"

He looked down at the flowers clutched in the girls' hands, and I could see the recognition bloom in his features.

"I haven't given you those since high school."

"Oh, my God," I gasped. I felt faint.

"Why don't you sit down?" Jared pulled me up from my crouched position and forced me to a nearby bench. "Tell me what's going on."

"Mommy doesn't like the flowers the man gave us," Cat answered for me.

"I've been getting flowers like that, just single red calla lilies, since the night I got back from Germany. I thought they were from you, that you had Nic put one in my room. He had my keys. And when we had that fight months ago, there was one on my bed at the house. Cat says the man that gave her that said he's been wanting to meet them for a long time." My body started shaking uncontrollably.

"I'm calling the cops. Plus, you may need an ambulance. I think you're going into shock. I've seen the guys in the field do this." Concern laced his voice as he dialed his phone.

Was I going into shock? My fingers were starting to feel numb. *Someone had been in my room. Someone had been following me.* And that someone now had face-to-face alone time with my girls. I couldn't think straight. My vision began to blur and dim. *Why?* The question kept repeating in my head. The violation made me feel sick as it sank in, permeating my bones.

Now

The hallway seems to stretch out before me as I leave Bridget's office and walk back toward mine. Everyone is busy working, so no one pays me any mind as I pass by. When I get next to Chloe's desk outside my door, I'm reminded that she and Evan are gone. My heart pangs in my chest.

This day fucking sucks.

She lied. He lied. Hell, I've lied. Well, I haven't lied so much as omit the truth. Which isn't lying. Or perhaps it is. I don't fucking know anymore. I feel like the whole world is upside-down right now.

I look over into the office next to mine. Nate is sitting behind his desk, talking on the phone. *Shit.* I need to be working, too. There are things that need to be done. As I look back at the door to my office, it seems dark with the blinds shut. I know I'm stalling, so I take a deep breath and open the door.

The lights are off, but with two full walls of windows, the office is filled with gray light from the overcast day outside. I scan the room and find Dex, sitting in my desk chair behind my desk. My computer is in front of him, and he's staring at it. He doesn't look happy. In fact, he looks the opposite of happy.

Why the fuck didn't I think to shut down my computer

before I left?

After a moment, his eyes move to me and he pins me with his gaze. He doesn't move, but a muscle in his jaw ticks as we both freeze. An impasse.

His voice breaks the silence. "Why didn't you tell me about this?"

"Because I didn't want you to know about it. I've no intention of handing that over to the police."

"Why?" he asks.

"I'd think that answer obvious, don't you?"

"That would explain why you don't want to hand it over to Martinez, but not me. Why wouldn't you tell me?"

"I'd think that answer obvious, too." I raise a brow.

He nods and steeples his hands in front of him. His elbows rest on the arms of my desk chair. His eyes burn holes through me.

The pressure in my chest feels like it's too much. I grip the end of the rubber band and pull on it. It snaps off my wrist. I look down at it. Broken. That's how I feel at the moment. Tears well in my eyes.

"What do I gotta do to make you trust me, Maddie?"

"Well, it's definitely not feeding me your cover story, that's for sure."

"That's what you think happened last night?"

"What the fuck else was it? You said it yourself in the car. That file's easily accessible. It's part of your cover. How in the fuck is telling me any of that supposed to make me trust you?"

"Because not all of that is my cover story. I've never told anyone but you, about my parents. You and Marcus are the only ones who know. And he was around back then. You're the only one I've trusted with that story."

"Fine, then what about the rest of it? The investigation? What're you doing here with me? What's this doing to help anything? Are you any closer to identifying my stalker? Do you have any answers? Because where I'm standing, it looks like the only person you're investigating is me."

He stands and starts toward me.

A sob catches in my throat as I hold a hand up to ward him off. "I don't even know if I can hear your excuses. What am I supposed to believe? You turned me down the first time I offered you sex, and then magically, one of your buddies in blue shows up the next time we're together at the park. I know you're not a prostitute; sleeping with me is not part of the job description. Isn't it likely that it's never happened because you're not what you're pretending to be? How am I supposed to trust what's real anymore if all I've got are the words of a professional liar to rely on? Do you get that at all? Do you even understand what's at stake for me?"

I run out of air and drag in an audible gulp. Silence builds between us.

"You're right," he says somberly. "I was assigned to build a case against you. If there was one to build. But I've already told you multiple times that I don't think you did it. You're not a killer, Maddie."

"You should leave," I say, so damn sick and fucking tired of everything.

"I'm not leaving you alone to deal with this. Not after you sent Evan away."

"What the fuck do you care?" I spit the words at him. My anger gives me steady footing once more.

"What do you want me to say? You just told me you're not going to believe me. How many times do I gotta say it? I'm here for you. I want to protect you. I'm telling you now, I'm not leaving your side. Not when you're getting videos like that. Tell me what I need to say."

"I don't think there's anything you can say."

"So what? You're gonna take the word of your fucking stalker over mine?"

"That's not what this is, and you know it. Nothing here is that simple." I gesture back and forth between us.

He reaches behind his back and pulls out his gun.

I take a step back, my eyes darting for the door.

"Stop," he says. He's holding the gun, but the grip is

facing toward me. He takes two strides until he's in front of me and puts the gun in my hand. "I've looked at your file. I've seen all the evidence. I know you didn't kill him. I'm not trying to build a case against you. Believe me, if I thought you were capable of killing anyone, I wouldn't put a gun in your hands."

With the gun in my hands, my arms start to tremble and tears flood my eyes.

"I trust you with my life, with my daughter. And I never thought I'd say this to anyone, but I trust you with my heart. Because I've fallen for you, Maddie."

My knees buckle and hit the floor. I lay the gun at his feet as all the fight drains out of me.

"You shouldn't trust me," I mumble. I can't see him clearly through the wash of tears in my eyes.

He bends down so he is eye level with me.

"Because I killed the father of my children. I killed Jared."

To be continued in Pivot Line...

Back of Book Shit

Welcome to the Back of Book Shit, aka the BoBS. This is the part of the book where I tell you some of the backstories to my books.

Where to fucking begin… I'm sitting here, writing this while on a ton of drugs after massively injuring my back, so you'll have to forgive me if this just comes out as a garbled, repetitive mess.

I really can't believe I'm doing this. That I'm finally sending this book off to the formatter, so I can publish it for you guys. This has been a long road for sure.

So, you've finished reading my first book, and at this point, you either love me or hate me. I don't think there is really an in-between reaction. That cliffhanger, right? But fear not, book two is coming your way awfully fast, and it will be worth it. I promise.

The Falling Small Duet truly started out as a one book concept, but after writing the entirety of the past timeline and the first half of the present timeline, I knew this story was going to be long. At that point, it was already over 140k words. Too long for one book, but I finished writing it and started posting chapters. And with every bit of feedback, it was always—add more. More words to an already long story, which everyone who read it described as fast-paced. Currently, the combined word count is over 200k. That's longer than Gone With the Wind, a notoriously long book.

So, it had to be done. I had to break it into two. I'm sorry—but I'm not sorry because this story is so worth it. Every word had to be written, every piece of this story had to be told. I love this story with every fiber of my being. And if you loved False Start, you're absolutely going to flip for Pivot Line. Maddie's story starts with a whimper and goes out with a bang. Prepare yourselves.

All the feels—that's what I aim for. I want you to laugh, to cry, to sit on the edge of your seat, to fall in love, to get turned on, to get angry, and yes, to even want to toss my book across your room in frustration. You probably did when you read that last line. And I cannot be held responsible for damaged kindles, iPads, or other eReaders.

Though technically, False Start isn't my first book. About five years ago, I wrote a book. It was supposed to be a YA fantasy novel based on a shit ton of mythological and scientific references. I wrote it. It wasn't YA. I couldn't keep my main chick from screwing people.

It happens.

And the main love interest never had an arc. I enjoyed writing it, I still love parts of it, but I don't even know where to begin with fixing it. Nevertheless, I decided that I would try again. But in my research for how to write better, I kept hearing the same thing over and over—read.

So, I read. I read 600 books (almost 700 to date) before I decided it was time to attempt to write this book. The idea of Falling Small came to me as a mishmash of events that were happening in my life at the time.

I was living in Seoul, South Korea, on the Yongsan military base. We lived in such close quarters with so many families, it was hard not to know what was going on in everyone's life. And military life has its challenges. I couldn't work, so I bided my time skating for the Republic of Korea Derby team and learning to play the guitar.

When we left Korea, my husband was getting out of the army, and we had to move back to Texas since we are originally from Houston. But I had this story that was dying to get out, and it was about a musician and derby girl. Austin is the Live Music Capital of the World and the birthplace of modern roller derby, it just made sense to set the story there.

So, we actually moved to Austin just so I could write a book that was set here. This story is kind of a sort of twisted love letter to Austin, in a way, taking what it's famous for, mixed with all the things I've come to love about living here.

There was so much research that went into this book—the whole series in fact. I'm apparently a weirdly hands-on author that has to experience things to write about them. Well, most of the time. I've failed to find a Black Mask Society, but if anyone has leads—be sure to let me know. I did, however, train in jujitsu, boxing, and krav maga, and I somewhat learned to play the guitar. I really suck at it, but we can't win them all, right?

I sat with musicians to learn how they collaborate and write songs. I toured recording studios, live music venues, drove through neighborhoods, imagining where my characters would live, what their lives would look like... and it still took me two years before I decided that it was time to write the book. I had read enough to know what kind of stories I liked, what kind of characters spoke to my soul, and most of all, I found my voice.

And while I want to tell you about how all of this came to life—where I pulled all the inspiration, it will have to wait until the BoBS in Pivot Line—because of spoilers. But just wait for it, because there is a lot of cool stories behind these books.

This book, in particular, was an exploration of the reality of human nature. We all make mistakes, we all fuck up, and most of the time we have good intentions while doing it. No one sets out to be a villain. Even some of the most horrible people on the planet could justify their actions in one way or another. But for the rest of us, we still falter. We've kept secrets. We've tried to pretend to be someone other than ourselves. We all have tempers that flare, we've all said things that we shouldn't have, and maybe destroyed relationships along the way, learning how to cope with our own nature. I have done all of that, more times than I'd like to admit.

I really do hope you enjoyed this story and I hope you

stick around for part two. Because if False Start is a good representation of me as an author and my personality—Pivot Line is my still-beating heart ripped from my chest and put on display. It is so deeply personal that I only let two people read it before I set it on the path to publishing it. Not including my editors, proofreaders, and formatter. But you'll get more on that in the BoBs for Pivot Line.

Until then. Be you. Stay Original.

Rebel

# Acknowledgements

Now I need to thank all the people who helped me get this shit together. And many people helped me bring this particular book from the deep recesses of my mind into a reality. Even though I know most of you will start tuning me out at this moment. You really should stick around these people deserve all the attention and kudos they can get.

The biggest thank you goes to my husband, Tyler. I mean, technically we're still married, though separated. And even with all the drama relationship woes bring, he never stopped believing in me. He was always there, most of the times frustrated with my incessant need for validation, to read each scene as I wrote them. He would tell me if I had accomplished my goals and was ready to move on to the next scene, but he also remained rather reluctantly impressed by my storytelling skills. He has stayed with me, helping fund my ambitions and making sure I have the chance to see my dreams become a reality. Without him, this book would never have become a reality, nor the ones coming to you in the future. And he deserves all the thanks and admiration I can bestow upon him.

Next to thank are my kids, Rye, Skye, and Brody. You three are the best cheerleaders a burgeoning author could ask for. Always willing to give me space when I need it, your endless support and boundless faith have helped me tremendously. I love you from the deepest part of the ocean to the farthest star in the universe, and back.

My critique partners—Lori Diederich, JJ Ashton, Bryan Fagan, and Amy McKenna. Thank you so much for your early belief in my writing. Without your gracious help, your eagerness to read more, and consistent encouragement—I wouldn't have gotten this far, for sure. I really do appreciate you putting up with my whining and tantrums. Especially when I couldn't figure out how to make people see the message behind what I was writing. And for weeding through my horrible grammar and helping me relearn some long-forgotten lessons. But most of all, thank you for your time and patience in coaxing me to get it right.

To Kimberley Tremblay, thank you for taking pity on a new writer and reading my book to give me direction on what kind of editing I needed. I was truly lost, and without your guidance, I'd probably still be lost.

To all my betas, Cimone Watson, Cassie Sharp, Trisha Haberthur, Abagail Roy, Amanda Mujsce, and Tara Tyndall. Thank you so much for your time, your feedback, your kind words, and your harsh ones. Without you, this story wouldn't work. You helped me identify where I was failing to get my point across and what wasn't working, and I am eternally grateful for your help in reaching my goals and telling the story that I needed to tell.

To my editor, Traci Finlay, thank you for pushing me so hard. I know I resisted—a lot—but I do think the story is better for it. You put up with my nearly endless explanations behind every questionable action my characters had and helped me really hone in on the parts that needed to be said to get my message to readers and fully convey my story.

And Sandra Depukat, you are a godsend proofreader—your attention to detail and thoroughness puts me forever in your debt. Your responsiveness to my many questions, the time and care you put into not only correcting but educating me to help me be a better author is beyond appreciated. I have loved every moment working with you.

Lastly, I need to thank my amazing cover designer. She turned a piece of my book into a reality and captured the symbolism of the tattoo and how it relates to the story so perfectly. It only took one phone call, and she knew that going the route of having tattoo images for my covers was going to capture the essence of me and my stories. And that's the sign of a true professional. Regina, you are amazing, and I can't wait to see what else you have in store for me in the future.

About the Author

Rebel Farris is a romantic suspense author. She's also the mom of three lunatics plus two perfect pups (Spike and Snakefinder) currently residing in Austin, TX. A native Texan and former military wife, she spent three years living in Seoul, South Korea (where part of her heart will always belong) and every corner of her home state before settling down. One day she hopes to live out the dreams of her nomadic soul, by traveling the world. All while pouring out the myriad of stories that fill her not-so-normal mind. She'll just have to wait until her brats graduate and leave the house first.

When she's not busy writing her newest project, she can probably be found curling up with a good book, hiding behind a lens of one of her many cameras, or going on adventures with her kids. Champion of the anti-hero, Rebel loves to write suspenseful and unpredictable stories while making people fall in love with the bad guy and the broken souls.

Standalones
Snapshot

Falling Small Duet
False Start
Pivot Line
(Find the first four chapters at the end of this book.)

Seven Hummingbirds Series
(Coming In 2019)
Penalty Kill
Whip
Transition
Substitution
Blocker
Turn Stop
Target Zone

Social Media

I have a reader group on Facebook, so if you're into meeting like-minded readers or just want to shoot the shit with me, please join us at Rebel's Villains: http://facebook.com/groups/rebelsvillains

Stalk me on Social Media…
  facebook.com/rebelfarris
  twitter.com/Rebel_Farris
  instagram.com/rebelfarris
  www.pinterest.com/rebelfarris
  www.goodreads.com/rebelfarris
  youtube.com/AnimalLogicProd
  Website: rebelfarris.com

If you prefer to skip the social media scene altogether and want to find out all the latest happenings and get in on exclusive shit… *and* have it all delivered straight to your inbox, then be sure to sign up for my monthly newsletter at subscribe.rebelfarris.com

 *False Start's Music*

Scene Inspiration Songs
Body Moves by DNCE
If I Knew by Bruno Mars
Let's Dance by M. Ward
Lucky Boy by DJ Mehdi
Million Years Ago by Adele
My Oh My by David Gray
My Silver Lining by First Aid Kit
Reasons For Living by Duncan Sheik
River by Bishop Briggs
Unsteady by X Ambassadors
Until We Go Down by Ruelle
Us by Movement
Waiting Game by Banks
Walk Away by Ben Harper

Blues
Champagne & Reefer by Muddy Waters
I Put a Spell On You by Screamin' Jay Hawkins
Little Wing by Stevie Ray Vaughan
Mojo Hand by Lightnin' Hopkins
Texas Flood by Stevie Ray Vaughan

Classic Rock
Hotel California by Eagles
Let's Dance by David Bowie
Love Shack by The B-52's

Sweet Child O' Mine by Guns N' Roses
Wish You Were Here by Pink Floyd

Punk

Banned in D.C. by Bad Brains
Chinese Rocks by The Heartbreakers
Free Money by Patti Smith
Hybrid Moments by The Misfits
Live Fast Die Young by Circle Jerks
New Rose by The Damned
Rise Above by Black Flag
Sound System by Operation Ivy
Straight Edge by Minor Threat
Suggestion by Fugazi
Waiting Room by Fugazi

**You can find the whole playlist on
Spotify by searching for Rebel Farris.**

Pivot Line

rebel farris

THE
FALLING SMALL
DUET, PART TWO

FIRST FOUR CHAPTERS

Chapter One

Now

I killed Jared. I can't believe the words ever came out of my mouth again. How many times did they tell me talking like that would get me nowhere? Bridget would be livid if she heard those words again. My hands are shaking. The room seems to spin. I gasp for breath before a sob forces its way out.

The cab of the truck is silent except for the muted sounds of navigating the streets of Austin. I drop my phone into my lap and look at Asher. His brow is furrowed and his jaw ticks. He's angry. But there's a tinge of sadness in his eyes like he knows that this is the end of the tour. The end of our band. And I can't stop the flood of guilt—I'm the cause of that.

The fog is thick, settled over the city like a heavy blanket. It feels foreboding, but I'm sure it's just the situation. The reason we are in this truck to begin with.

He pulls the truck into the parking lot of the recording studio, and I can feel immediately that something is off. Even before I open the door— the fog swirling with the movement—and hear the piercing wail of the building's alarm, I feel it. Shutting the truck door, I take a deep breath, steeling myself for the reckoning that is about to happen. The moist air fills my lungs. It feels heavy like my heart, my stomach. How did we get to this point?

I can't see more than a couple of feet in front of my face, but the flashing red lights of the alarm color the fog between me and the building, showing the way. Asher joins me once we reach the sidewalk leading to the building, but stays silent. Step by step on shaky legs, I move closer. Closer to the love of my life. Closer to facing the consequence of my decisions. Shattered glass crunches under my borrowed shoes as I reach the front door that is nothing more than a metal frame now.

Blinking, I clear the memories. That's not a path I need to go down. Not now.

Dex is sitting next to me, holding me across his lap. He pulls back and brushes the hair away from my face before running his thumb over my cheek to chase away the tears. He believes me. I can see it in his eyes. It's not pity; it's heartbreak. His eyes say he knows I'm responsible and he doesn't want me to have to live with it. He gathers me in his arms and sighs. I'm not exactly sure what he's thinking, but his gun is still sitting on the floor in front of me, and he's not telling me that I'm under arrest. Nor is he trying to placate me with words about how I'm not at fault. That's a bit of a relief.

"What am I going to do with you?" His voice breaks through the quiet patter of raindrops on the office windows.

His brows are drawn together as I lean back to look at him. "That's it?"

His shoulders tense. "What do you want me to say?"

"I don't know. You're under arrest... or something? Isn't that what you wanted? A confession? I'm so tired of fighting this. If you're gonna arrest me, just do it." My arms hang limply at my sides as he lets me go.

His hands move to frame my face, his sea-green eyes locking onto mine. "No. That's not what I want. It never has been. I'm not lying to you, Mads. I've seen the evidence. I know you didn't do it and I'm going to prove it. I've been looking for another angle, something that Martinez hasn't considered, but I haven't even found a place to start. I'm gonna end this for you. I promise. I want you to tell me everything about that night when you're ready." His eyes close and his lips brush over mine tenderly. "But I think we should call it a day and head home right now. I'll go next door and tell Nate that we're leaving. Will the receptionist cancel your appointments?" He sighs again, leaning his forehead against mine.

I nod, speechless and a bit dazed.

"I'll go talk to her, too. Just gather your stuff to leave. When we get home, we'll deal with all of this. Together."

I reach out and skim my thumb over his bottom lip. A shiver runs throughout his body, and I feel it when it reaches his hands that still bracket my face. The corner of my mouth tugs upward slightly. I like that I seem to have the same effect on him. He half-heartedly smiles back at me and places a quick kiss on my lips before standing up. He silently picks up his gun and puts it back in the holster.

My eyes are glued to him as he walks with an athletic grace toward the door. He stops and looks back at me once more.

"Be right back," he says. There's a hint of exhaustion in his voice, like he just fought a battle.

And perhaps we did because I feel it, too.

Sitting there for a minute, I stare at the door. I don't want to get anywhere near that video again. There's a feeling creeping up my spine, like even coming close to the computer will make it start playing. Releasing a breath through my nose, I steel myself. I grab my computer case from the closet, then walk to the desk, pushing the laptop shut and disconnecting the power cord.

With that taken care of, I gather my purse and look around for anything else. The sight of Evan's phone on my coffee table sends a pang through me. I scoop it up and clutch it to my chest. That's it. I take a deep breath and turn to the door. Dex is there, waiting for me. He holds out his hand, and I take it.

Minutes later, I'm sitting in the passenger seat of my car, heading home. My mind is replaying everything that has happened today from the time I woke up, but it all comes to a screeching halt when I remember one thing he said.

"What did you mean by *we need to talk?*" I ask.

"Yeah," he says absently. "That reminds me—"

"You do understand that those words are like the international lead-in to a breakup, right?" I interrupt him.

"What?" His face scrunches as he briefly takes his eyes off the road to glance at me. "That's not what I meant. I wanted to run through possible suspects with you and get your thoughts on them."

"What do you mean?"

"It's likely the stalker's someone you know."

"It took you the last almost two months to come to that conclusion? Because Martinez was saying that years ago, but it never helped because everyone checked out, had alibis and such."

"You don't think there's a way they could get around something like that?" His lips tip down into a half frown. "I'm just thinking about all the evidence, and there seems to be a protective vibe, you know? That tells me that the motivation isn't sexual, it's caring. Twisted, but still good intentioned. And it stands to reason, with all these people surrounding you, who care for you, one of them might be the suspect."

"That's ridiculous. None of my friends are stalking me. They know what all this has done to me and that it hurts more than helps, so I don't buy that at all."

"What about Nic? He hasn't been around much, and he has access to your house—"

"I trust Nic more than most people in my life. No. He wouldn't do that."

"What about that guy Asher?" he asks.

"Asher has been in Atlanta for weeks. On a commercial flight when the stalker was at the mall."

"What about—"

"Dex, just don't. It's not a great way to start a relationship, accusing my friends of shit they wouldn't do, and making me pissed off at you in the process."

"We're in a relationship?" he asks, threading his fingers

through mine and raising my hand to his lips. He kisses the back of my hand and smiles.

"I didn't—" My mouth opens and closes as I flounder for the words.

"I get it. I had a nice long conversation with someone who knows you far better than me, so I understand. I'm in it for the long haul. I have a feeling that when you realize what this means to you, I'm gonna be a lucky man."

He kisses my hand again as we pull into the garage at my house. I take a deep breath, not knowing what to say, so I say nothing. I don't understand what I feel for him. I haven't had time to think about it. Police, paparazzi, stalkers, FBI, US Marshals, Chloe and Evan leaving... it's all too much. Last night feels like so long ago when I think of all that's happened since we left the park.

"Let's get you inside," he says, turning off the car.

Then

"I'm moving into the house," Jared said as he sat on the couch next to me.

We'd finally gotten the girls to sleep after several hours of coaxing and assuring them that everything was going to be okay. It took several hours, giving statements to the police, handing over the flowers as evidence, being treated for shock by the EMTs out of the back of an ambulance, and then finally walking home.

I started to reply, but he halted my words when he spoke again.

"I don't like that he's been in this house. Especially because he's taken an interest in the girls, but also because I'm worried about you, Maddie. I don't like that I could be thirty feet away from the house if something were to happen. I know how you feel about me right now, but this changes things. I can take one of the rooms upstairs, and if anything happens, I'm here."

"Okay," I answered quietly.

"Okay?"

"Okay, I get it." My voice rose in defense. "Frankly, I don't want to be here alone right now anyway."

"Really? You're not going to fight me on this?" he asked, looking dumbfounded.

"You act like I'm irrational. Since when have I ever defied common sense?" I stood up and started to pace. "Someone has broken into my home, has been watching me for God knows how long. I can protect myself, but I'm not stupid enough to turn down help. I don't care who it comes from." I choked back a sob that was threatening to come out. "Jared, he was with our girls. He could've taken them. I'm not going to take any chances, not with them."

"Okay. I'm also going to call a security company and have a security system installed tomorrow. You okay with that too?"

"Yeah, sounds good," I said absently.

My mind kept running through my entire life, searching for clues to who it could be. What did I do that could've invited such behavior? It had to be something around the time we went to Germany, but I was drawing a blank as to what that might be. I couldn't think of anyone suspicious hanging around.

"Hey, I'm sorry about this." Jared stopped my pacing, grasping my shoulders and blocking my path.

"It's not your fault," I sighed. "I just feel so stupid. I had to've done something to invite this, but honestly, the only thing I can think of is the band. Maybe it's a deranged fan, pissed about the band breaking up. Though, even that doesn't make much sense—we were never that popular. That's the only thing I can think of at the moment. I can't even fathom another scenario."

"Does it matter? Who knows why they're doing it? You can't always explain crazy. The only thing that matters is that we stay safe and that the police catch him." He tipped my chin up to meet his eyes.

The guilt forced me to look away, and I broke from his

hold to continue pacing. "Did Officer Martinez tell you when they expect to have the results of the testing they're doing on the flowers?"

"Yeah, he said he'd probably stop by tomorrow once the report gets processed. He told me you might need to meet with a detective. If they decide to investigate."

I stopped in my tracks. "What do you mean, *if* they decide to investigate? There's even a chance that they won't look into it?" I turned back to face him.

"Maddie, there isn't much to go on." He sighed, running a hand over his head. "Just your word that you had flowers show up in your room and a guy giving our girls a flower at the park. It isn't exactly a violent crime."

I felt the sudden urge to throw something well up in me. All the frustration, fear, and anger needing an outlet, a release. I reached for the first object within reach without thinking.

"That's bullshit! Someone broke into my dorm and now my house to leave those flowers. That's fucking creepy. Do you have any idea what that feels like?" I looked down at my hands and realized I was holding onto a clay bowl that Cora made at school. She'd be devastated if I broke it. The thought grounded me as I set it back down.

"Of course I do." He was in front of me as I straightened. "I feel that way, too. I don't like it either. Because I love you and the girls, Maddie. I care about what happens to you as if it were happening to me, too." He reaches out to touch my cheek.

"You've gotta stop fucking saying that." I slapped his hand away. "I've got enough to deal with at the moment."

"No," he said.

"What the fuck do you mean, no?"

"I mean no, I will not stop telling you that I love you. I will not stop fighting for you. I'm never going to leave your side, and if you want to keep pushing me away, that's fine. Push all you want, but I'm not going to leave you alone ever again. You wouldn't be fighting this so hard if you didn't care. Deep down, I know you feel this. This—you and me. What we have. Something like that doesn't go away."

"What if I'm fighting it because I'm still in love with him—you ever think about that?" I spat the words at him.

"Fuck it," he said and took the step to close the distance between us.

His hand dove into my hair, and he pulled my face to his. Faster than I could blink, his mouth descended on mine. It felt like we were moving in slow motion. At the first contact, tingles spread over my lips. My heart raced, and goose bumps chased a shiver that echoed throughout my whole body. I wanted to fight it, but the sensations he was causing were stunning me into inaction. I'd forgotten that indescribable magic pull he held over me. I opened for him, and his tongue drove in, twisting with mine. I lost all coherent thought as the familiar taste and smell of him filled my senses, sending my brain into overload. He pressed his body flush against mine, and I surrendered to him.

Moments later, he pulled back, resting his forehead on mine. "You feel that? People die for that feeling. They start wars and conquer impossible odds for that," he whispered between heaving breaths. "That's real, and I'm not walking away from it."

He pushed a loose strand of hair behind my ear as his eyes searched mine. I remembered the same look on his face just before he told me we were through. Coming to my senses then, I pushed him away. I wasn't doing this with him.

"You can't love two people. And I know I love him. So, you can take your little demonstrative kisses and shove them up your ass. We—we are not doing this. Ever. Again."

Turning, I ran to my room, away from him. Ashamed of my traitorous body and the stupid way he made me feel. All I could think about was how shitty it felt when he left, and I knew I never want to travel down that road again. Not with him. We had no epic romance. Fairy tales did not involve the prince up and leaving the princess for years to find herself, before they could have their happily ever after. That wasn't the way it worked. There was no such thing as true love.

What I felt for Law was proof of that. Jared could try to convince me until the day we died that we had something epic, but I'd never risk my heart with him again.

Chapter Two

Now

I open the back door, and the alarm starts its warning beeps. I toss the laptop bag, my purse, and keys on the kitchen counter and hurry over to the panel. Once the beeping stops, the quiet of the house becomes evident.

Everyone is gone. The girls are at school, Nic's at his place, and Evan left with Chloe. Nic doesn't live here full-time. He has a room here that he uses when the loneliness of his lifestyle becomes too much for him. Here, he has family and love.

I know the feeling all too well, myself. It's the quiet moments that everything becomes too much to bear. When the sound of silence is so deafening, you can't think beyond it. It echoes in your ear, forcing your darkest thoughts to repeat in your mind on a loop.

The snick of the door shutting behind me reminds me that I'm not alone. The realization settles in my mind that this is the first time Dex and I've been truly alone. Well, if you don't count our failed romp in the car.

I take a deep breath and turn to face him. "Looks like we have the place to our—"

I'm cut off as his lips descend on mine.

A shiver runs down my spine at the contact. My heart

races double time. Dex sweeps his fingertips down the side of my arms, leaving a trail of goose bumps in their wake. He curls his hand around the back of my neck while his thumb teases over the pulse point in my neck. An involuntary moan escapes me, and I gasp as I pull away.

"What do you want, Maddie?" he murmurs as he lets go of my neck to smooth his hand down my back.

"I don't know." I search his face. "I mean, I do know. I just don't know how to tell you. I've never had to do this before. I just—I don't think I'm ready."

"What if you're never ready? You willing to pass up a good thing because you're too afraid to leap?"

I close my eyes. Dex's thumb traces my lower lip. I shudder, spurred by the heightened sensation of the contact. His touch feels almost electric. I open my eyes to find him watching me, not missing a thing.

"Everything that's been happening scares me, but it all pales in comparison to the way you scare me, Dex."

"I don't know how to get you past whatever is holding you back," he says, shaking his head slowly. "I've never been so sure about something in my whole life."

I break away and walk back to my bedroom to do something other than this.

"You can't say that about someone you don't know. And you don't know me—the other half. The part that only close friends and lovers know is so different from the person I am every day. What happens to me when you see that side and decide it's not for you? I can't go through that. I can't open myself up to something like that right now."

"We all have our secrets. Everyone is hiding something. Sometimes we just have to trust that when we're ready to share the heavy stuff, love will be enough to overlook our faults. Just let it go and let me decide. I'm never gonna do anything to hurt you on purpose."

I stop in the middle of my bedroom and close my eyes, considering his words. No one can guarantee they won't hurt another person. I know that better than most.

"*Some lose all mind and become soul, insane,*" Dex quotes. "*Some lose all soul and become mind, intellectual.*"

"*Some lose both and become accepted,*" I finish for him, cocking my head to the side. "I didn't take you for a hipster." I raise an eyebrow at him for quoting Charles Bukowski to me.

He shrugs. "I'm an artist. And it's the best way to get my point across." He shifts a bit, looking uncomfortable. "We're all some mixture of mind and soul. My theory's always been that when you meet that person you're willing to work for, it's because their level matches your own. Maybe not in the same way, or for the same reasons, but enough for them to accept you as you are."

"How do you know?" I take a step toward him. "How do you know I'm at your level? You don't even know me."

"It's hard not to recognize when you're staring at a piece of yourself. I told you about my mom and my past and you didn't even bat an eyelash. Instead, what I got was just a taste. An hour of what it feels like to have your trust. I've watched you since the moment I met you. You embrace life in the little moments. You're compassionate. Hell, in the short time I've been shadowing you, I've met at least fifty people who rely on your kindness in some way. You're not just talented, but smart, and successful beyond most people our age. You're strong because most people would've buckled under this situation and run or hide. But there's also a darkness to you, and in some ways you're broken. I get that. What I don't get is, why don't you see it?"

"See what?"

"All of that. Everything that makes you, you. And all the reasons I've fallen in love with you."

I draw in a breath and hold it. I freeze because I just don't know what to say. Dex crosses the space between us in two short strides and cups my face. His eyes search mine.

"Don't. Don't freeze up. I don't expect you to say it back. I don't expect you even to know how you feel. You haven't had time to breathe yet. I just can't keep it in anymore. I love you. That's not going to change, no matter what you're hiding."

He kisses me. It starts out slow, lingering. A gentle exploration. He slides his hand to the back of my head, while his other arm wraps around my waist, pulling me to him.

"Just breathe, Maddie," he whispers.

"I can't," I say, pushing away from him. "I think we did this all wrong. If I'd met you some other way, if you knew the other stuff first, then I could believe you and this would work. But you've inserted yourself into my life. I can't just think about the fallout of my secrets in terms of myself. And that's always going to be a problem."

"You're saying that if we can't make a go of a relationship, we can't be friends?"

"No," I say. "I'm not—I don't know." I shake my head, rubbing my temples.

"I'm not saying this because I think it's necessary, but if you need reassurances, I'll still be around if things don't work out. I love your girls almost as much as I love you. And Audra loves you, too."

"I don't know." I sigh. "I don't know how to do this. Any of it."

"Just let go."

His breath caresses my shoulder one second before he presses his lips to my skin. A fine shiver courses through me, and I can't deny one thing—I want him. I don't know why. It defies all my rational thoughts. *Fuck it.* I turn and grasp his face, pulling him down to me. I kiss him. I'm not gentle or loving. I'm ravenous. Turning off every nagging thought in my head, I let go. Every doubt and worry fall away as his hands cup my thighs and he lifts me in an effortless motion. I wrap my legs around his waist.

Wetness pools between my legs at the feel of him. His strength, his size, the hardness pressing against me. It's almost too much. I don't even feel us moving, but he lets go of me, and I've a second of panic before I bounce on the bed. The shock must be written all over my face because he watches me with a smirk before leaning over me.

The bed dips down as his hands press into the mattress next to my head. "We do this, you're mine. You get me?"

I nod, running my hands up his arms, feeling his shoulders flex as he dips down.

"Are you sure?"

"Yes," I reply. "I want you."

His head tilts to the side as he regards me. "I'll take it."

"How gracious of you," I say with a smirk.

He hooks his arm under my waist and tosses me farther toward the center of the bed. "You're gonna get it."

"I certainly hope so." I laugh out the words.

His eyes darken as he pulls his gun out of his waist holster and sets it on my nightstand before kicking off his shoes. He moves with a slow, predatory-like grace. My skin prickles in anticipation of his touch. My phone rings from my purse in the kitchen. He pauses.

"Ignore it," I say, reaching over to tug him onto the bed.

He moves above me just as the phone stops. I pull at his shirt, and he leans back, pulling it over his head by the collar. My hands are already on him, smoothing over the hard planes of muscle before my mind catches up. Beautiful.

The phone starts ringing again.

"You should probably get that," he whispers.

I groan, pouting. "It's not on my list of priorities at the moment."

He leans forward and catches my puckered lower lip with his teeth. My body arches up toward him, and he takes advantage, pulling me over him as he rolls onto his back.

"The sooner you find out what they want, the sooner you can get back here," he says, slapping the side of my thigh.

Sitting back, I decide to be naughty, trailing my tongue down his chest. I caress his hard length through his jeans, keeping my eyes trained on his. I'm satisfied when his eyes roll back into his head with a groan as I nip him just before standing up. The phone stops, and before I can decide to ignore it, it starts up again. With a frustrated sigh, I leave the room. I choose to cut through the dining room, in a hurry to grab my phone from my purse before the voicemail picks up, when I halt in my tracks.

"Dex!"

I can hear the panic in my voice, so it's not too shocking when he comes running around the corner shirtless and holding his gun. He lowers his weapon and takes in the scene.

Seven dead hummingbirds are scattered across the dining room table, with a message spray painted in sloppy blue letters on the wall. The paint, still wet and dripping in streaks, spell out the words:

One by one, they all must fall.

Then

"We really ought to work on furnishing these bedrooms," Jared said as we set boxes down in the empty bedroom he'd chosen.

He picked the bedroom farthest away from the Jack and Jill-style rooms the girls occupied. More privacy for him. Due to the state of our individual finances, though, the other two rooms were still bare and unfurnished.

"That's all I have for now. Nic's coming over later to help me move the furniture." He offered me a strained smile and turned away. "Thanks for helping me."

I felt dismissed, and I didn't know what to say. I'd woken up from a restless sleep to the doorbell and found Jared on the porch next to a stack of boxes. We'd carried the boxes upstairs in silence. That was the first thing he'd said to me all morning. I walked back down to my room and went into the bathroom. Catching sight of myself, I cringed. My hair was sticking out in all directions. A huge rat's nest of tangles on one side and the makeup I forgot to wash off was running down my face.

Yuck. I wouldn't want to look at me either. I showered quickly, then dressed and went to the kitchen to grab a Coke. I halted in the doorway at the sight before me. Jared was on his hands and knees. Cat was hanging underneath him, her little arms and legs wrapped tightly around him. Cora was sitting on his back, holding on to his shoulders. Giggles echoed around the room.

"Do it again, Daddy," Cat demanded.

"Again," Cora echoed.

"You ready? Hold on tight," Jared said, and then his hands came off the ground, and he gave a growly bear-like roar.

The girls squealed with glee. I didn't want to interrupt, so I leaned on the doorframe and watched them play together. He bucked and crawled around for their amusement. I smiled. He really was good with them. The longer he was around, the more they adored him. Maybe I was too hard on him. I decided then that I'd at least stop yelling at him, but I still needed to keep my distance and set clear boundaries.

The doorbell rang again. Jared twisted and spotted me.

"I'll get it," I said, pushing off the doorframe and heading for the door.

I peered out the vertical window that framed the door and saw a van with a security company logo. There was a man in a uniform and baseball cap standing on the front porch. I opened the door.

"Hi, I'm here for the install—Maddie?"

I squinted my eyes to make out his face. The bright light of day behind him kept his face in shadow. I leaned forward a little.

"Blake?"

"Funny, I keep running into you. Small world, huh? Though, I did see Jared's name on the work order this morning. Chose this one to see what kind of place he lived in. I'd no idea you guys were still together," he said, smiling. His eyes roamed over the space, taking in the house. "Didn't you have his kid right before graduation?"

"Kids," I corrected. "Twins. A few days after graduation."

"Oh, cool. That makes sense."

I frowned, not understanding what he was saying.

"I haven't seen you back at the gym. It's pretty cool now, isn't it? All the new equipment they're getting."

REBEL FARRIS

"I wouldn't know. I don't go there anymore."

"Really? Oh." His shoulders dropped. "Well, you want me to come in and get this system set up for you?"

"Yeah. Come in."

I stepped aside, and he followed me into the foyer, putting those paper booties over his shoes.

"I'm going to start with the attic. A lot of times these old houses've had previous systems in them at one point, and there might be existing wiring. That'll save you some money if I have less wall drops to complete the install. You want to show me where the attic access is?"

"Sure. It's upstairs. This way." I led him up the stairs to the door and pulled it down from the ceiling, unfolding the built-in ladder.

Blake started climbing up to the attic.

"Do you need anything else, right now?" I asked. "A flashlight? I don't think the lightbulb up there works."

"Nope. Got one right here." The sound of ripping Velcro was loud as he opened a pocket on his uniform pants and pulled out a tiny flashlight.

"Okay, I'll be down in the kitchen if you need me. Jared's around, too."

"Okay. Thanks, Maddie," he said and disappeared into the dark space above the house.

I walked back down the stairs. Just as my bare feet touched the cool tile floor of the kitchen, the doorbell rang again.

"What is this, Grand Central Station?" I complained to no one.

I spied Jared and the girls out in the backyard, digging in the garden that ran along the concrete patio. I internally sighed as I made my way back to the door. This time when I glanced out the window, there was a squad car parked behind the security van, and Officer Martinez was standing on the porch. I opened the door and gave him a polite smile. It was a lot like trying to smile at people at a funeral. It felt awkward to do it, but manners dictated that you smile anyway.

"Miss Dobransky. You're looking much better today." He returned my awkward smile.

I assumed he was referring to the fact that I was pale, clammy, and on the verge of passing out last time I saw him. I nodded.

"Please, come in." I stepped aside and opened the door wider for him.

I led him to the living room and started to sit on the couch but remembered again that I was thirsty. He sat across from me on the chair.

"Can I get you something to drink? A coke or some bottled water?"

"Do you have Dr. Pepper?"

"Sure do. Lemme get you one."

I retrieved his drink and sat down on the sofa.

"I assume you have some news regarding my case?"

He dug into his pocket and pulled out his wallet. Flipping it open, he pulled out a small square of paper and slid it across the coffee table between us. It was a picture. A girl, probably a few years younger than me. Her hair was reddish brown like mine, and she had warm brown eyes. My face twisted in puzzlement as I looked back to the officer.

"That's—" He cleared his throat. "That's my sister. She's been missing for a little over four years now."

"I'm sorry," I said, furrowing my brow. "But does this have something to do with my case?"

"They decided not to assign your case to a detective."

"Can I ask why?" I asked. "I'm not making this up."

"I believe you. There's just not enough evidence, and even if there were, we're still very limited in how we can handle stalking cases."

"I'm not following."

"We can't just arrest people for being near you or giving your kids flowers. You can file a restraining order, once we find out who he is. But even then, we have to catch him in the vicinity or have evidence of breaking and entering before we can press charges."

I cursed internally before asking, "And your sister?" I was failing to understand the connection.

"Before she disappeared, she said that weird stuff was happening to her. Things moved in her room like someone had been in there. She swore someone was after her. No one believed her. We thought she was being dramatic, just looking for attention. Then one day, she was gone. She wouldn't have run away. She loved her family, and we loved her. There were other things, too. It never added up. That's why I became a cop. They wouldn't investigate. They wouldn't look for her. She was eighteen, an adult, so they said she probably left. There was no evidence to suggest otherwise." He sighed. "Look, I know this is probably just the consolation prize, but I believe you. The guys at the station, not so much. So I'm going to look into this for you when I can. They keep us pretty busy, but I'll make time."

"Thank you." I didn't know what else to say. "I appreciate it."

I saw movement out of the corner of my eye and found Blake standing there.

"I've gotta get some equipment from the van. I just wanted to let you know that I'll be right back. Is it okay if I let myself back in?"

"Yeah sure, that's fine," I answered and then turned back to the officer. "They didn't find any fingerprints or DNA on the flowers?"

"No. The only thing we have is your statement and the vague description your daughters gave. That's not enough to go on. But here—" He opened his wallet and slid another rectangle of paper across the coffee table. "That's my card. If you have another incident or notice anything else suspicious, give me a call. That's my cell listed."

He stood, and I followed him to the door.

"Though I'd like to not hear from you again. You know?" He smiled. "I hope nothing else happens."

"Yeah, one can hope that this is all over. Thank you again for your help. And for believing me."

"Have a good rest of your day." He smiled again and turned, then halted. "Are you installing a camera-capable system?"

"I have no clue. Jared set this all up."

"Well, if you do, remember to save the recordings after any event. Those systems self-purge after a preset length of time. We'll need all the evidence you can get."

"I'll keep that in mind. Thanks. You have a good day, too." I waved and closed the door.

Chapter Three

Now

"I need to call Diana and John," I say, racing across the dining room to the kitchen.

"Who?" Dex asks.

"Cora and Cat's grandparents," I explain. "They're retired. I'm going to send the girls with them, on vacation, somewhere far away. Out of the country or something. I can't have them around this. This is too much. In all the years of stalking, whoever this is hasn't made a threat like that before."

I make it to my purse and pull out my phone, searching the contact list. My heart is racing, and I'm struggling for breath.

"Hey," Dex says, placing his hand over the phone. "Slow down. Let's think this through."

"Think this through!" I yell and then struggle to drag in air. I brace my hands on my knees to control my breathing and calm down while I finish. "Listen, Dex. We don't know each other that well. You asked me the other day why I was training. This. This is why I've been training. I'm not going to sit around like some delicate flower, waiting to see what the bad man will do to me."

"That's not what I—"

"I know, but what you don't know is that I've plans in place. I'm not going to sit quietly by and let my life get torn apart again. I'm not going to wait and see if one of those dead birds symbolizes my girls. He made the mistake of leaving me alone for three years. I've had time to think about everything. Time to realize what I did wrong. Time to put plans in place to make sure it doesn't happen again." I don't know if it's the words or just the act of talking, but as I finish that spiel, I catch my breath, and the anxiety attack passes.

"I'm just saying that you need to calm down," Dex says. "Just talk to me, Maddie. Tell me where your head's at."

"This is worse." I start pacing the floor in front of the kitchen counter. "The last time he started escalating, it was nothing like this. And you were right in the car. Nothing he has ever said has seemed malicious, but this—that's not caring. That's…"

Dex takes a seat at one of the barstools. "It's not good."

"Yeah," I say, still pacing. My hands are shaking, my words spilling out faster than normal. "First things first. I'm getting the girls out of here, and Hope, too. Audra can go with them. If you're okay with sending her away? I mean, if you want to stay around for this. I don't blame you if this is too much. But if you are, I think you should separate her from me."

"You've gotta stop this, Maddie. I understand the impulse—believe me. Though I wish I handled things like you. You have this knack for pushing everyone else out of the way so you can face problems alone. I get it. But you need to understand that it's not always what's best for you or them. Your strength is the fact that you have all these people who love you and are willing to stand by you."

"They're just kids, Dex," I shout. "They aren't going to help in this situation, and I won't leave them in harm's way."

"I'm not asking you to," he shouts back, matching my tone. "I'm just saying that we should wait until we know what this even is. What if it's a prank? This doesn't match your stalker's MO. It could be anything. Flying off the handle and pulling the kids from their school could end up being an unnecessary disruption to their lives. So why don't we call Martinez and get the investigation started on this, and then decide what we're doing? Okay?"

Dammit. I don't like it, but Dex's right. We don't know what this is.

"Okay." I nod. "I'm calling Bridget, so she can get here before the police." I check the time on my phone. It's only one in the afternoon. "After that, I'm going to call the security guys and have them take the girls to the Mad House after school. I don't want them coming home to this and a swarm of police in their home. Then we can call Martinez. You good with that?"

"Sounds like a plan," Dex says and then tugs my elbow, standing and pulling me to him.

His arms come around me, and he kisses my forehead.

"You probably should get a shirt on," I remind him when I become all too aware that he's still shirtless.

"Yes, ma'am," he says as he grins down at me. "I love it when you get bossy with me."

I snort and shake my head. That's exactly what makes me nervous about him. My phone rings. I jump, and it falls out of my hands, tumbling to the ground. I move out of Dex's arms, reaching down to pick it up but kick it across the room instead. *What am I? One of the Three Stooges?* I cross the kitchen and finally get a grip on the phone. Bridget's face is on the screen.

"Bridget?" I answer, a little freaked out that she's calling when I just decided to call her.

"Finally," Bridget says. "I've been trying to call you. I have some news. Is Holly around?"

I walk over to the window in the kitchen that overlooks the driveway. "I don't see her car, but Marcus's Honda is parked in front of her garage door, so I assume she's there. It's only one. She doesn't leave for work for another few hours."

"Good, I'm coming over," she replies. "I'll get her and

meet over at your place."

"Okay? I was just fixin' to call you anyway because I need to call the police. There's something at my house that you gotta see."

"Shit, another flower?"

"No, this is worse. You have to see it. I'm not sure what to make of it."

"All right, I'm on my way," she says, and the line cuts off.

I turn back, but Dex is already gone. I search through my contacts. *One phone call down, two to go.*

Then

It had been three months, and there were no break-ins, no strange men lurking around the corner. Life had returned to normal. All that meant, though, was I had time. Lots of time to sit around and think about what I'd lost. Aside from derby and work, which was something. But compared to my schedule for the last few years, it felt like I was sitting still. I sighed, missing the band more and more every day. Staring at the wall, I mindlessly stirred the pan filled with pasta sauce.

"What's that about?" Jared asked over my shoulder.

I shrieked and spun around, flinging a trail of tomato sauce across the counters. "Holy crap, you scared me."

"I wasn't even quiet." He grinned. "You were just off in your own little world, staring at the wall, making little noises."

"I wasn't making noises," I grumped.

"You were, but the question is… what are you thinking about?"

"The band," I confessed and turned away to clean up the mess.

"What about them?"

"I miss it. Being onstage. Performing. Even just sitting around and writing music, rearranging covers. I don't get to spend a lot of time doing that. Don't get me wrong—I love working at the studio, and I'm learning a lot. I just spend more time filing or getting coffee than I do working on actual music."

"I see."

"Do you?" I teased.

"I do. And I think I might have something that interests you."

"I'm listening."

"I know a guy—"

"You know a guy? You know that's the way guys where I'm from tell you about some shady handyman who can fix just about anything. I'm not sure you want a handyman working on me," I said with a playfully sinister expression.

He pulled the kitchen towel from my hands slowly, the smile on his face growing. "You're going to get it for that." He held opposing corners of the towel and started swinging it so it twisted up.

I yelped and tried to dodge him, but he blocked my exit. The first snap of the towel missed completely, but that didn't stop me from yelling out and laughing. I grabbed the pot lid off the counter to use as a shield. We were apparently loud in our play because the girls dashed around the corner.

"We want to play, too," Cat said.

The pasta water started boiling over. I dashed to the stove to stop the mess, turning down the flame and stirring the noodles.

"Sorry, baby. We can't play anymore. Mommy's gotta finish dinner."

"Tell you what," Jared said. "Why don't you go pick out the movie for after dinner?"

"Cora, come on." She grabbed her sister's hand with a grin. "Daddy says we get to pick the movie." They both ran from the room, giggling.

Jared leaned against the counter next to me, crossing his arms over his chest. He leaned back a bit until he caught my eye.

"I met this guy at work. He's another instructor. Can play anything, but he prefers drums. We've been playing around on the instruments after hours a few times. He said he's interested in joining a band. I told him about you. He wants to meet you. If you're interested."

"What kind of music?" I asked.

He shrugged. "Pretty much anything."

"He any good?"

"Yeah, the best I've seen in a while. I think you should meet him. Swing by the school after my class."

"I don't know. You know, that was the thing about punk; I may have loved it, but I don't think I ever fit. Punk is born out of huge amounts of emotions that are hindered by limited technique." I sighed, remembering all the times I frustrated the hell out of Spence. "When I joined them, I had more technique than necessary. Spence and I worked on finding a middle ground because I wanted a clean sound and complexity of notes; he wanted simplicity and raw sounds. I had the emotions…"

Realizing that my anger toward him was what fueled a lot of that passion, I shifted my focus away from him. He didn't need to read that on my face. I turned off the flame underneath the pots. Tears pooled in my eyes as the enormity of what I lost sank in, but I refused to let them fall, squeezing my eyes shut.

"It wasn't about getting famous or making money. We did it because we loved the process of transforming those emotions into sound. Punk isn't just music. It's a culture. Actually, it's many cultures. Everything from the Aggro Hardcore to the Art-schooled. I've a hard time believing that I'll ever find that again."

"Then don't. Find a new journey. Create a new sound that is all you. Merge your blues and punk roots, find your current emotions, and make music that comes from where you're at right now."

I pressed my hands into the counter and bit my lip, afraid to turn and look at him. I didn't want him to see my heart breaking with the realization that I'd have to move on.

It wasn't just the music. Law hadn't called me back. I'd broken up with him, but I'd hoped that he would see reason.

That he would come by to find Jared at his apartment, me in the house, and realize that things weren't the way he imagined them. But with Jared living inside the house, due to the stalker, he might not see things that way. And maybe that was why he wasn't calling. Maybe Sloane had told him, and he'd decided to move on. Either way, it was around the thirtieth unanswered message that I decided to stop calling him.

I just needed to wake up and accept that he'd moved on. The band was over. I needed to move on, too.

"Okay," I agreed.

"Okay?" he asked skeptically.

"Yes, okay. Is there some reason why you never believe me when I say okay to you?"

"Nope," he said with an innocent look on his face. "Just making sure."

"Whatever. Drain the pasta, will ya," I said, handing him the potholders.

Now

The doorbell rings. I check the clock on my phone and realize that it's only been fifteen minutes since I hung up with Bridget—the downside to living close to work.

I round the corner into the foyer just as Dex is letting Bridget, Marcus, and Holly enter.

Bridget's eyes meet mine before she nods to her right. "We should go into your office and talk about the news I have before the police get here and we move on to the rest of it."

I nod in reply and follow them. Holly and Bridget sit in the chairs across from the desk. Dex and Marcus remain standing, and I take the seat in my office chair. Bridget looks to Holly. "Are you okay with them being in here?" She looks to Dex and Marcus. "Because I have news about Roz."

That name has both Holly and me stiffening, but Holly's eyes take on a faraway, lost look. Roz is Holly's ex-boyfriend, and to say they had a volatile relationship is putting it mildly.

She shakes her head. "No, it's okay. Just say what you've gotta say," she says, but her voice comes out rough and timid.

I can admit that hearing Holly like that puts me on edge, more than I already was.

"About thirty minutes after Chloe and Maddie left this morning, I got a call from the DA," Bridget says to Holly. "Roz's parole hearing was moved up. Due to *good behavior*, he'll meet with the parole board in December."

"How the fuck is that possible?" Holly asks, her brows drawing together as anger takes over her voice.

"I don't know," Bridget says. "But you're going to need to speak before the parole board."

I rise from my seat. Concerned for my friend, I kneel down in front of her.

"We'll do it again," I say, grasping her hands. "Together. Same way we did last time. He won't get to you, and he sure as fuck won't get to Hope. I promise."

I look at Bridget to make sure I'm not talking out my ass. I want it to be true, but I'm not confident we can pull it off. Bridget nods, but the look on her face isn't as reassuring as I hoped it would be. Holly shakes her head as tears streak down her freckled cheeks. She pulls her hands from mine and wipes her face. Standing awkwardly, I lean over to hug her. I hate seeing her like this. She's always so strong.

"I'm gonna talk to Jerry," Holly says, her voice muffled by my hair as she squeezes me back. "This is why I work for him. He promised to protect us, you know?"

I nod and lean back.

"That's bullshit, Holls," Marcus blurts. "You don't fucking need him. I told you, you don't need to be connected to that shit. Dex and I got your back."

She told him. I'm floored as I watch them curiously. Guilt seeps in that I haven't been around enough to know that they were becoming that close; Roz is a subject Holly keeps locked down.

"I already told you no," Holly snaps. "The motherfucking cops' idea of protection is a goddamn piece of paper. And that shit means nothing to him. You've gotta fight fire with fire."

I lean back against the desk as Holly stands, her face turning red with anger. That's the Holly I know. Her hands clench into fists as she faces down Marcus. They have a silent standoff as they stare at each other.

"Fuck this shit," Marcus mutters as he turns and leaves, slamming the door behind him.

"He'll get over it." Holly shrugs, waving his exit off with nonchalance. "I gotta get ready for work. The nanny got here just before we came over. I'll let you know what Jerry says."

I grab her hand and squeeze it because I know she's putting on a brave face right now. She has to be scared shitless—I am.

"Let me know if you need anything," I say. "I'll get security for Hope if it comes to that. You know I'll do anything. Money is not, and will never be, an issue."

Holly nods, but I know she's holding back. The damn stubborn woman has trouble taking help from anyone. She hugs Bridget and me, and with a nod to Dex, she leaves too.

"Well, where's this other shit?" Bridget asks after Holly closes the door. "I swear, I need a raise," she mumbles.

"Done," I say with a shrug.

She rolls her eyes at me. "I'm not serious."

"It's in the dining room," I say, moving back to my desk chair and opening my personal laptop. "Detective Martinez and the CSI unit should be here any minute. Just make sure not to touch anything."

I leave her to it as she walks out of the room, then work on pulling up the connection to the security server. I know that'll be one of the first things they ask. Dex sits across from me, steepling his fingers at his chin.

"Hey, will you go grab my purse and work computer from the kitchen counter and put them in my car?" I ask Dex. "I don't want them becoming part of the crime scene. I've an idea brewing."

"Sure. You care to enlighten me?" Dex asks.

"Later," I add, looking at my phone. "We don't have much time."

He nods and leaves the room. I pull up the security feed just as the doorbell rings. Crossing the room, I check the window next to the door just to be sure. Martinez stands there with several people behind him, his face marred by a frown. I open the door wide.

"It's in the dining room," I say without preamble. "I already pulled up the security feed server on my computer."

Detective Martinez enters and walks back to the dining room as four crime scene techs follow him in without comment. The last one halts in front of me.

"Can you point me in the direction of your computer?" she says. She's a petite woman with mousy brown hair who looks to be around my age, if not younger.

I close the door behind her and motion to her to follow me.

Chapter Four

Now

Sitting in the corner of the L-shaped sectional sofa in my living room, I'm bored out of my mind. They've been at it for hours. First pictures, then dusting everything for fingerprints. *That shit's gonna take forever to clean up.* I answered all the detective's questions, and he disappeared outside with the other cops who had arrived. Voices carry through the open front door as the media shouts questions that'll go unanswered for now.

Dex sits next to me and pulls me to his side, running his hand over my hair and kissing the top of my head.

"Are they ever gonna get done?" I ask, meeting Dex's eyes. He shrugs. "You're a cop. Don't you know about this stuff enough to say if they're getting close to finishing up?"

"Hush," he says, putting his finger over my mouth and looking around. "That's not common knowledge to everyone on the force, you know? I have very little to do with these CSI guys." He cuts his eyes to Bridget, who looks as bored as I feel with her chin propped in her hand in the chair across from me.

"Sorry," I mumble as one of the CSI guys walks by, turning his head to look at us as he passes. "But Bridge already knows." He opens his mouth to say something, and I hold up a hand to stop him. "For the record, I didn't tell her. She found out on her own." He doesn't say anything back, just looks at Bridget. "I just... we got stuff we need to do before we have to get the girls from the Mad House. We can't be at this forever."

"Soon," he says as he leans down and brushes his lips over mine.

A throat clears on the other side of Dex. I pull back and peek over his shoulder. Detective Martinez is standing there, lips pinched, eyes wandering everywhere but in our direction. Bridget raises an eyebrow at me. Dex turns to face him.

"What's up, Joe?" Dex asks.

Joe? I feel a bit ridiculous that I've known him for years and have never once asked for his first name.

"We found something on the video footage that I want you to see," Martinez says.

We all follow him back into the office where Martinez— Joe—directs the CSI tech to hit Play. The computer screen displays the view from the camera in the dining room. You can see Dex and me through the archway that leads into the kitchen, but we're far enough away that you can only see our feet, facing each other. Joe does a little hand signal to speed it up, and the tech fast-forwards. It hits me at that point that there were no birds on the table when we got home. We weren't that distracted.

A chill runs through me at the thought that he was in here while we were home.

From this view, you can see my purse and laptop sitting on the counter, and I've a sick feeling that the stalker may have foiled my plans, but soon a male, wearing a hoodie and a backpack, enters the frame. Joe signals the tech to slow the replay to normal. The intruder pauses for a moment, then squats and opens the backpack. It's clear that he knows where the camera is by the way he moves around the room, yet never turns enough to catch a glimpse of his face or even a profile.

He pulls out a can of spray paint and a plastic bag,

dumping the dead birds on the table. All of it happens over a few minutes. He paints the words on the back wall, then picks up the plastic bag and paint can, stuffing them back in his bag. He exits through the kitchen, and my mind gets stuck on the fact that he didn't pause or even look at my work laptop. I was sure he would've gone for it, and I let out a tiny breath of relief.

Martinez puts his hand on the tech's shoulder, and she pauses the recording, just as I walk into the dining room on the video. I'm relieved because I know what happens next.

"That's enough," Joe says. "If you got what you need, you can leave us, Julie."

She pulls a little thumb drive from the side of my computer and shuts the laptop. When she clears the arch, Joe speaks.

"You were in here the whole time and neither of you heard anything?"

"No," I answer.

"What were you doing?"

"We were... busy," Dex supplies.

Martinez takes a step and sits on the edge of my desk, clasping his hands together in front of him. "I have to say, I find it odd that you guys didn't hear anything. What I find more disconcerting... is that there was video footage of the incident on your security system. Up until this point, he was always careful enough to erase all evidence of his presence." Martinez's brows dip low as his lips press together. His eyes lock onto me.

"I'm not sure what you're getting at," I say.

"Come on, Joe," Dex says. "You can't be thinking that she staged this? I was here with her the whole time. I've been with her for months."

"You don't think you've been compromised? We watched the rest of that footage, and honestly, I find it hard to believe you're able to remain objective in this case."

My stomach drops as I realize what we almost did. Dex could lose his job. It was so stupid.

Dex leans against the wall, arms crossed in front of him, looking decidedly unaffected by Martinez's words.

"I'm taking this to the chief. I'm going to recommend you be removed from this case. It's clear that your interests no longer align with the department."

"And what interests are those?" I ask. "That you're trying to build a case against me?"

Martinez looks away but doesn't deny it.

"Unbelievable," I mutter as I pin the detective with my gaze. "We've known each other for years. When did you stop believing me?" The answer to that is rather obvious, so I'm not sure why I asked.

"That's enough, Maddie," Bridget intervenes, then directs a steely gaze at the detective. "I'm going to need you to leave. If you'd like to come back with a warrant, we'll cooperate at that time. But I'm advising my client to remove you from the premises, now."

I fall into the chair across from my desk while Bridget rounds everyone up and shows them to the door. Burying my face in my hands, I can't help but wonder how I got here. Every step I take turns out to be a misstep that threatens everything I've worked for. And Dex. God, Dex could lose his job.

"What are you thinking?" Dex asks, tugging my hands away from my face. He's kneeled down in front of me, so I see the concern marring his features.

I laugh without humor. "I think it's clear that once again the cops are leaving me on my own to deal with this freak." I shake my head. "I should've known that trusting them to take care of it while I try to carry on with my normal routine was a mistake."

Bridget comes back into the room. "Well, they're out of the house. What's the plan?"

"I'm thinking we take this to Dawn," I say, and Bridget pulls a skeptical face. "There's a video I didn't tell the cops about."

"When did you get a video?" she asks.

"When I came into the office this morning. Just before the FBI and US Marshal arrived."

"What? Why am I just now hearing about this?"

"Because we were distracted, discussing other things. You know?" I shifted my head to the side in Dex's direction.

"Fine," she relents. "What is it?"

"Just a collection of mine and Dex's greatest moments with a warning to look deeper into his motivations."

She raises an eyebrow at me, her gaze darting to Dex and back. Dex looks unaffected by the turn in conversation.

"Yeah, I know," I sigh. "He knows. We talked about it. He's good, I swear."

Her jaw drops. "Well, if you trust him, I will." Bridget's lips pinch together as she stares Dex down. "Just know, if you hurt her, I'll make your life a living hell and bury you in lawsuits until you can't breathe. And that's not a threat. It's a promise."

Dex shrugs. "It doesn't matter because I have no intentions of doing that. I love her. She worked her way into that number one spot next to Audra. I'm here to protect her and help her with anything she needs. You feel me?"

The corner of Bridget's mouth tips up into the hint of a smile, and she nods.

"Anyway. I'm going to take the video to Dawn and see if she can identify any digital footprint that might help figure out who this is." I sigh again. "I just need to clean up this mess first. I'm not leaving it for the girls to come home to."

"That... I can help with," Bridget says. "You'll have to pay for it"—she grins—"but I'll have a cleaning crew and painters here in no time. You don't have to worry about it or even look at it again."

I muster up a smile for her. Even if worry tinges all of my emotions at the moment, I'm still grateful to have such a great friend.

Then

It was late, and the girls had fallen asleep during the middle of the repeat performance of the latest Disney movie they'd chosen as after-dinner entertainment. Wide-awake myself, I took in their sweet little cherub faces. They were curled up on the couch between Jared and me. As my gaze traveled up, I met Jared's eyes. He smiled at me. He seemed so happy and content. My heart melted a little.

"You want to risk it and carry them upstairs?" I asked quietly.

"But I was enjoying the movie. I want to see how it ends," he deadpanned.

I smiled and rolled my eyes at him. "I'm itching to get into the music room and play right now. Plus, my foot's asleep."

"Sounds good."

He cradled Cora in his arms. She curled into his chest and sighed contentedly. Cat and I followed them up the stairs. A few moments later, we met in the hall after tucking them into their respective beds. I turned to head back down the stairs, but Jared grasped my hand, halting me.

"Thank you." His voice was near my ear, body close enough that I could feel the heat through my thin nightgown and robe, but not touching.

"For what?" I asked, turning to him. I had to drop my head back to look up at his face.

"For everything. Having the girls, living here, all of it. I'm happy, Mads. You make me a very happy man." He smiled genuinely and walked past me down the stairs.

I stood there, stunned motionless for a moment before heading down the stairs, too. When I got to the bottom, I could hear the soft strains of the piano as he plucked notes from his mind and played with abandon.

I loved when he did this. For a moment, I leaned against the frame of the archway, listening. Jared was so talented—

joining the military was truly a waste of a beautiful mind. He did it to follow in his father's footsteps, a sense of duty to make his father proud, but music owned his heart. Memories of sitting with him while he played, the day he gave me my first guitar, flitted through my mind. I'd promised to write his music for him. Crossing the room, I grabbed my journal off the shelf and dug into my bag for a pencil. I sat on the bench next to him. I'm not even sure if he was conscious of the fact that he always left a space for me. Closing my eyes, I listened to the music until I started seeing the notes in my head. I started frantically scribbling down each one as fast as I could to keep up.

When he came to a stop, I'd over ten pages of music written down.

His attention shifted to me and a tender expression overtook his face. "You wrote it down?"

I glanced away with a shrug. "I told you I would, one day."

He stared at me for a moment and then sighed, looking out the window in silence. The bright moonlight from a full moon outside was the only source of light in the room. Shadows played across his face with the movement.

"I was going to wait to do this. I've been thinking a lot about us," he said as he rose and pulled something out of his pocket. "I think the only thing keeping you from me now is fear. Fear that I'll leave you. That I would ever do something to hurt you again."

I stared at him, having no idea where he was going with this. He hadn't bothered me with talk of "us" since shortly after he moved into the house. A creaking sound broke the silence as he set an open velvet box on top of the piano in a strip of moonlight. Inside glittered a diamond ring.

"I bought this for you while I was still in training. I used to pull it out every night and think about the day I got to put it on your finger. I carried it with me every tour. Every time shit felt hopeless, I'd take out this ring and think about that perfect day I had to look forward to. It got me through a lot of rough shit. You got me through it."

Anger surged through me. "You decided to break up with me and avoid me for four years—"

"I know," Jared interrupted, his voice laced with regret. "I thought I was doing the right thing, Maddie. I thought it was the only way to give you the freedom to chase your dreams." He squeezed his eyes shut. "There's not a day that has gone by that I haven't regretted that decision. I'm so sorry... for everything."

"I get that, but why would you tell me this now?"

"I think you're afraid that I'll leave again. The only thing that's holding us back is that possibility. But you should know just how unlikely that is. I want to put this ring on your finger, right now. I'll do anything to prove to you that I'll never hurt you again. For as long as I live, you have me. You'll have me whether you say yes or no. Because you're it for me, Maddie." He pushed his hand through his hair and with his other hand pressed a key on the piano, letting the haunting sound echo around us in the quiet room. "Nobody can see into my soul the way you do. No one makes me smile or gets me as angry or can keep me on my toes like you do. No one listens to what I say when I'm not talking or is content with just being in a room with me, listening to me play the piano. Just you. Always you. Only you. Will you marry me, Madelaine Rose Dobransky?"

Tears ran down my face, falling silently into my lap. I felt like I couldn't breathe. It was surreal and very real all at the same time. He brushed the tears off my face with his thumb. It had been nine months since Law and I broke up. Law had never called, nothing, just left town. I'd gone through a whole phase of worry about what was I doing that made it so easy for the men in my life to just walk away from me without a backward glance. I realized, in that moment, that I'd just been refusing to listen to what Jared was telling me. He never walked away; he was trying to do the right thing. Misguided, but still frustratingly noble. I couldn't deny that my heart still belonged to him. He'd taken away my last good excuse.

"You going to say something, Maddie? I'm dying here." I

peered into his pleading blue eyes, so bright and familiar to me.

I nodded, incapable of voicing my response at that moment.

"Yes?"

I gasped for breath I didn't realize I was holding. "Yes, Jared. I'll marry you," I choked out.

He cupped my cheeks in his hands and pulled my face toward his. His lips brushed against mine, gentle and sweet.

"I love you," he said, relief thick in his voice.

"I love you, too, Jared."

His lips crashed into mine, and he kissed me with the same abandon he usually reserved for the piano. I stroked my tongue against his, inviting him in. Part of my mind knew that I was jumping back into treacherous waters without a life raft. He could crush me this time, and I'd never recover. But he had more than proven his intentions over the last nine months. There was no reason to doubt him anymore. That didn't make it any less scary.

He pulled me up to stand between his legs, pushing me back into the piano. The discordant notes sounded as my butt bumped into the keys. He rested his forehead on my belly, gripping my hips with both hands, trembling.

"Please tell me I'm not dreaming."

"This isn't a dream, Jared." I ran my fingers through his hair to soothe him.

He reached behind me and pulled the ring out of the box. As it slid onto my finger, a smile grew on his face. Jared stood from the bench. His body pressed into mine, his eyes growing heated as he slowly undid the belt of my robe, exposing the lace-and-satin nightgown beneath. Grasping my waist, he picked me up, placing me on top of the piano. More dissonant notes floated throughout the room as I rested my feet on the keys. He ran his hands down the outside of my thighs to hook behind my knees. With a quick tug, he pulled me to him so our bodies were pressed together and aligned perfectly. I could feel his excitement between my legs. I felt him pulse. Unable to help myself, I moaned at the hardness of him.

My surroundings faded as I wrapped an arm around his shoulders and ran my tongue up the side of his neck. I whispered, "I love you," as my tongue traced the shell of his ear.

A tremor ran through his body as he pushed me down, laying me back on the piano. He ground himself into me. He pushed the skirt of my nightgown up to my waist and ran his palm from my neck down my body to the edge of my panties, making my back arch off the hard surface. His thumb rolled over the sensitive bundle of nerves, and I gasped.

"Perfect," he exhaled. "I'm going to taste you and touch you until I've had my fill. Then I'm going to make love to you. Are you okay with that? Because once I start, we're going to be here all night."

"Yes," I hissed as he dragged my underwear down my legs.

Goose bumps broke out across my skin at the gentle tease of his grazing fingers. He sat back down on the piano bench, hooking my knees onto his shoulders and pulled me toward him until my lower body was supported only by him. He then set about fulfilling his promise.

If you're ready for the final conclusion of the Falling Small Duet, go to rebelfarris.com/books/pivot-line

34470423R00208

Made in the USA
San Bernardino, CA
02 May 2019